THE THING IN
THE ALLEY

THE THING IN THE ALLEY

Anomaly Hunters, Book 3

J. S. Volpe

Peridor Press

AH-3

THE THING IN THE ALLEY

1

Brad Vallance and Christine Ruddy strolled hand in hand down Train Avenue in Kingwood, Ohio, both of them serene and smiling and basking in the blush of young love. It was the end of what felt like a perfect evening. It had started with dinner at Kiki's, a local five-star bistro, then moved on to a performance of *I Do! I Do!* at the Blackhorse Theater, and finally wrapped up with two hours of martinis and scintillating conversation at The Speakeasy Lounge. It had been the best night of their three-month-old relationship, perhaps one of the best nights either of them had ever had, and now, as these happy, healthy young lovers strolled along, the world felt magical and at peace and theirs for the asking.

Halfway between Wheeler Road and Benton Street sat West Train Apartments where Christine lived. Much as they hated to part ways, it was quite late, well past midnight, and Brad had to be up and out the door bright and early in the morning to make the long drive to Massillon to visit his mom, who was recuperating from back surgery and needed periodic help around the house.

The couple stopped at the foot of the building's front steps and shared a long, lingering kiss.

When their lips finally parted, she smiled and said, "I love you."

"I love you, too," he said. "I'll call you tomorrow when I get back from my mom's."

She nodded. "Maybe you can find a way to talk her

into letting us use her summer cabin some weekend."

"I'll see what I can do. It won't be easy. She's really protective of that place. She's convinced that anyone who uses it is going to, I don't know, trash it, or burn it down, or call up Satan in the dining room, or something."

She adopted an expression of mock toughness. "Then we'll just have to make her an offer she can't refuse."

"No problem. I'll get to work chopping up the dead horse."

"I've got a carving knife you can borrow."

He laughed. "I really gotta go. I'll see you tomorrow."

"Bye."

"Bye."

Brad lived two blocks south on Dodge Street, and to save time coming and going from Christine's he always cut through the alley that separated West Train Apartments from the antique store next door. The alley was murky even on the best of nights, its mouth being equidistant between two streetlights, in the exact spot where the sodium-vapor lamps' glows dropped off to nearly nothing. And tonight, since only a couple of the apartment windows that overlooked the alley were lit and the moon was currently veiled behind a scrim of clouds, the alley was nearly as black as a mineshaft. As Brad entered the alley, the trio of dumpsters that stood against the apartment's wall ten feet down were merely hulking black shapes against the column of dim radiance that marked the alley's far end on Winchester Street, a spot almost as poorly lit as the Train Avenue end. Even the brightest, most colorful swatches of the graffiti that covered the alley's brick walls were dark-gray squiggles barely visible in the gloom.

Having traveled this route many times over the last three months, Brad gave barely a passing thought to his safety as he strolled along the murky corridor, not even when he heard a faint, furtive rustle from the dumpsters. It was probably just a stray cat hunting for food, or a trash bag settling. This wasn't a high-crime neighborhood. Frankly, he was far more likely to get hurt tripping over an old pizza box or slipping on spilled coffee grounds than to get mugged or murdered.

When he was about twenty feet down the alley he heard Christine call, "Brad! Wait!"

He turned. She stood silhouetted in the alley's mouth, waving for him to come back. He trotted up to her.

"What's wrong?" he said.

"I almost forgot: I promised Angie I'd have dinner with her tomorrow night, so we'll have to make plans around that."

He nodded. "Okay." He smiled and patted the oblong bulge in his pants pocket. "You could have just called."

She grinned. "Then I wouldn't have gotten to see you again."

He grinned back, then took her in his arms, and they shared the night's—and their relationship's, and Brad's—last kiss.

"See you tomorrow." She gave him a final smile and a final wave, then hurried off.

Smiling too, Brad turned around and restarted his trip down the alley.

This time he had traveled almost thirty feet down the alley and had reached its darkest part when Christine's voice called out again: "Brad! Wait!"

A trifle annoyed now—it was late, and he really wanted to wash up and get to bed—Brad fitted his smile back into place and turned.

"What is it this..." he started to ask, then paused in

confusion. The alley's mouth was empty. "...time?"

He looked around but could make out only the angular shapes of the dumpsters.

"Christine?"

No response. Had something happened to her? Was this some particularly ill-advised joke?

"Christine?" he called again, louder.

For a moment there was still no response, then: "Brad!"

Her voice was coming from the deep shadows behind the nearest dumpster. Peering at that spot, he discerned a hint of movement in the darkness. Something was alive back there. Something large. Much larger than a cat or a rat.

Thinking it must be Christine, that she had been trying to catch up with him a second time and had fallen down or gotten stuck somehow, Brad started forward to help. But then the shape emerged from behind the dumpster, and Brad stopped in his tracks.

It wasn't Christine. It was some kind of animal, something quadrupedal and surprisingly large, the top of its head nearly level with Brad's shoulders. A deer, perhaps? Brad had heard that deer sometimes strayed out of the Holly Hills Metropark southwest of here and wound up dashing up and down the city streets in a blind panic. Of course, a deer wouldn't account for the voice he'd heard, but maybe he'd misheard a yelp, or a whine, or whatever kind of noise frightened deer make.

Brad slowly backed away as the animal approached, its footfalls clocking faintly on the concrete pavement. His heart began to pound as it kept advancing. Whatever this thing was, it wasn't afraid of him. It was headed straight toward him. Shit, it might be rabid or something. He started to reach for the phone in his pocket.

Then the clouds rolled away from the moon, spilling silvery light upon the approaching figure.

Brad stopped dead, gaping dumbly.

The thing before him resembled no animal he had ever seen. Its body was wiry and sleekly muscled and covered with short tawny fur with a line of black stripes running down its back and along its sinuous cheetah-like tail. Its long, graceful legs ended in cloven hooves, like a goat's or a devil's. And its head! Good Lord, its head was a freakish monstrosity, roughly canine in shape, with a pair of pointed ears on top, a pair of faintly luminous yellow-green eyes as big around as a grown man's fist, and a long snout split by an enormous mouth that stretched from ear to ear in a demented grin like the Joker's. Instead of normal teeth, this ghastly mouth sported a plate of bone in either gum, hard and straight-edged and sharp as a guillotine.

As Brad goggled in stunned silence, the creature's mouth moved, its lips stretching around those lethal plates to form words, and in a perfect imitation of Christine's voice, it said, "See you tomorrow."

Brad still didn't move, although by now the creature was only ten feet away. He was immobilized between trusting the evidence of his senses and concluding that this was a particularly weird dream. To his cultured, 21st-century mind, the dream explanation made far more sense. It was a lot easier to believe that he had fallen asleep at the theater and that all of this was an especially bizarre night-mare brought on by some bad shrimp primavera than to admit the existence of talking monsters with cartoon bad guy smiles. Everything he had been taught about reality told him that such things simply didn't exist.

And yet the evidence of his senses was accumulating too much to be ignored: the way the creature's ears twitched and swiveled when a car horn blatted in the distance, the crusty specks of what looked like dried blood on the beast's pale ruff, the scritch and clop of its hooves on the concrete, the faint doggish odor that filled Brad's nostrils as the creature drew closer.

When it finally sank in that the thing before him was indisputably real, that this could be no mere nightmare, Brad drew in a deep, sharp breath to scream. But by then it was too late. The creature had sprung. There was a sharp clack as its guillotine teeth snapped closed, and Brad's scream remained forever unscreamed because he no longer had a throat to scream through.

2

Calvin Beckerman laid another bag of Dan-Dee Corn Twistees on one of the folding tables he had set up in the parlor of what he still couldn't help thinking of as the May house. It wasn't the May house anymore. As of today, the house, its contents, and the several acres of mostly wooded land on which the house sat were legally his. Among the house's contents was the Collection, a vast assemblage of objects related to anomalous phenomena, which the house's previous owner, Robert May, had spent his life investigating. Calvin had vowed to continue the investigations with the help of a small group of close friends. Now, with the house and the Collection officially his, they could finally get to work.

He looked around the room to make sure everything was set up for the housewarming-cum-graduation party/first official meeting of the group. Then he stifled a yawn. Great. Only seven-thirty and he was already wiped out. But that wasn't exactly surprising. He'd had an eventful day: This morning he, along with Cynthia Crow and Brandon Taylor—two of his best friends and fellow members of the nascent group—had graduated from Ames University ten miles to the north, the graduation ceremony being a grueling two hours of increasingly achy backs and asses courtesy of the granite-like seats of the Front Campus Auditorium and increasingly benumbed brains courtesy of the soporific commencement address by James Booth, president of Booth Industries, a local Fortune 500 company. After the ceremony, Calvin had driven here, his hometown of May, Ohio, where he spent nearly two hours in local lawyer Stephen Krezchek's office signing a vigintillion papers which made little sense to him but which left him one million dollars richer and the owner of the coolest piece of real estate in town. He spent the remainder of the afternoon moving his meager belongings into the house and replacing the old bedding on the antique four-poster bed in the master bedroom. Barely had he finished that than it was time to meet his mom for a celebratory dinner at the Golden Goblet, a ritzy restaurant in Kingwood. (His dad, whom his mom had divorced three years ago, had treated Calvin to a separate celebratory dinner the previous night.)

After dinner he headed back to the house to set things up for the party. It took a lot longer than it should have. The awareness of his new and improved circumstances kept intruding on his consciousness, and he would pause in the middle of unfolding a table or setting out a stack of paper plates and look around at his new home, smiling and full of dumb wonderment.

Over time, however, his gaze came to settle more and more on specific items—the coffee table, the bookshelves, the curtains—and then instead of smiling he would frown, thoughtful and a little troubled.

Though the house was now Calvin's, most of the décor was still Mr. May's. Most of the things that Calvin had retained from his apartment in Ames were currently stuck in odd corners until he could figure out where to put them, and in any case they would be barely enough to furnish a single room. Though he was excited at the prospect of redecorating this huge old house however he liked, he also worried that any significant changes to the place would be somehow disrespectful to Mr. May's memory. These had been the old man's possessions, accumulated over his long and storied life, and Calvin didn't feel quite right getting rid of any of them.

Well, okay, maybe not *any* of them. There were a few rickety wicker chairs in the basement and a hideous snot-green throw rug rolled up in a corner of a closet that were already earmarked for Goodwill. But beyond that, Calvin found himself immobilized by uncertainty, caught in the Lagrange point between his urge for self-determination and his desire to honor the memory of the man who had bequeathed him all of this.

His thoughts were interrupted by the low purr of an engine coming up the long driveway. He peeked out the curtain and was surprised to see a black Toyota Prius he had never seen before rolling to a stop behind his Honda Accord. He was even more surprised to see Cynthia Crow behind the wheel.

He hurried from the parlor and down the hall to the

front door, which he threw open to reveal Cynthia trotting up the steps to the front porch, her long red hair flapping behind her.

"Guess what I just bought!" she said.

"I saw it," said Calvin. "It's cute."

"Isn't it?" said Cynthia. "My very first car. Admittedly, it's not actually *new* new. It's used, but only about a year old. It's only got five thousand miles on it. The interior even still smells kind of new."

"Nice. But, uh, you know, I could have just walked over to look at it. As of today, we're next-door neighbors, after all."

"Screw that. I wanted to surprise you. Besides, before I came over, I took it for a cruise." She paused, a giddy grin on her face. "Hee. I can actually say, 'I took my car for a cruise.'" She started jumping up and down and shaking her fists in front of her chest as if she were playing maracas. The floorboards creaked like a bed in a porno movie. The house was well over a century old, and although Robert May had done his best to maintain it, some parts of the house, Calvin reflected, might require more than just decorative changes.

"Um, maybe we should go inside before the porch collapses."

"Sorry. But don't you want to take a closer look at the car? We could even...*go for a cruise.*"

Had he been talking to any other girl, Calvin might have inferred some kind of sexual innuendo from the way she emphasized the words and waggled her eyebrows. But Cyn was gay, however much he might wish otherwise. She was just excited about her new car.

"Later," Calvin said. "Everyone else should be arriving any minute. But I promise, you can take me for a cruise another time."

"Count on it."

They went inside to the parlor.

"Mind if I start in on the food?" she said. "Or should I wait till the others get here?"

"Help yourself."

She picked up a piece of celery from the veggie tray, which he had bought mainly with her vegetarian diet in mind, then swiped up a gob of fat-free ranch dressing on the end of it and took a bite.

"And what about you?" Cynthia asked between crunches. "Now that you've got a cool million in your pocket, have you thought about replacing that rusty bucket of bolts with something a little less fate-tempting?"

"My car works fine," Calvin said, a little defensively. She had been criticizing his admittedly rather rusty Accord for years now and seemed to think that every trip would be its last. "Besides, I was thinking about trying to fix up Mr. May's old 78 Thunderbird."

"That old thing? I figured it would have to be towed off to a junkyard. I mean, it must've been sitting under that sheet in the garage for eons."

"Not that long, actually. I was checking it out the other day, and it looks like it's in pretty good shape. The body, at any rate. It probably needs new tires, new belts, stuff like that. A new battery, too, though surprisingly enough, the battery isn't all that old. It's from 2008."

Cynthia paused in mid-bite to do the math.

"That recently? Mr. May would've been, what, about ninety-two? Judging by what we read in his files, I got the impression he gave up driving a long time before that."

"That's what I thought, but..." He shrugged. "I don't know. Just because he replaced the battery doesn't mean he actually drove the car. Maybe he just wanted to keep it maintained in case of an emergency."

Even though Calvin was still digesting the stuffed salmon and the slice of chocolate cherry cheesecake he had had at the Golden Goblet, the sight and sound of Cynthia munching away at the food compelled him to start nibbling as well.

"So, where are Donovan and Violet?" he asked as he scooped up a handful of pretzels. "I thought they would've come over with you."

Donovan was Cynthia's younger brother, who had just finished his sophomore year at Ames. After a rocky freshman year, during which he had majored in Journalism like his idol Hunter S. Thompson, he switched majors to Chemistry and appeared to have finally found his calling, earning a B-average for the first time since junior high school, a feat which compelled his family to all but break out the champagne. Violet O'Donohue was Donovan's girlfriend. In the year since graduating high school, she had gone through eighteen different minimum-wage jobs, mostly at fast food restaurants and gas stations. Whenever she got a new one, everybody bet on how long it would take before she got fired. The truth was, the only reason she got the jobs in the first place was because her dad had made gainful employment a condition of continuing to live under his roof. He never specified, however, that said employment couldn't be varied and serial and livened up by, say, taking three-hour-long Mad Dog breaks, or telling the customers what puffed-up dumbfucks they were.

"I assumed they'd come with me, too," Cynthia said. "But about an hour ago Donovan said something about some mysterious business they had to take care of, and they took off."

"Why am I suddenly worried?"

"Tell me about it."

Cynthia had never been entirely comfortable with Donovan and Violet being part of the group. Yes, Donovan was her brother and she loved him and all that, but she also knew how irresponsible he could be, especially under Violet's anarchic sway. And as for Violet herself, she was, to put it bluntly, crass, ignorant, and willfully obnoxious. Cynthia feared that sooner or later one of them would blab about the group to the wrong person, and she would wake up one morning to find the media camped on her doorstep and predacious TV producers clamoring to turn the group's doings into some vacuous reality show/cash factory. Private to a fault (just like old Robert May, really), Cynthia wanted the group to pursue their investigations quietly, without any intrusive and distracting publicity. And although Calvin had some amorphous notions about a far-flung global network of operatives like some kind of comic-book superteam, he ultimately echoed her views. But since, for good or ill, Violet and Donovan knew the truth, it was best to keep them on as short a leash as possible, which meant humoring their wish to be full-time team members.

Lights flashed through the parlor curtains. A car was coming up the driveway. Calvin and Cynthia started to head to the window to see who it was, but when they heard the cricket-like chirp of a fan belt in need of replacement and the low groan of aging brakes, they stopped and in unison said, "Brandon."

The fifth and final member of the team, Brandon Taylor was a tall, animated, bespectacled fellow with a punk fashion sense and a compulsion to recast the world around him into art. He was the only member of the group who hadn't inherited anything from Robert May. He didn't seem to mind, though. If anything, he regarded his perpetually precarious financial situation (he was currently unemployed) as a mark of his artistic integrity.

Brandon's black 1994 Ford Econoline van, whose decrepitude made Calvin's Honda Accord seem like a brand-new Rolls Royce, grumbled to a stop, then fell silent. The driver's side door slammed. And then nothing. No knock. No bell. Not even footsteps on the creaky porch.

"What's he doing?" Cynthia said.

"I'd better go see," Calvin said.

He went to the front door and opened it. Brandon stood at the foot of the porch steps, gazing up at the house's façade. In his hand he held a six-pack of Great Lakes Brewery Edmund Fitzgerald Porter.

"What are you doing?" said Calvin.

"I still can't get over how fucking awesome this house is. It kind of reminds me of the *Psycho* house."

"Yeah. Everyone says that."

Brandon stared at the house for a few moments more, then stepped up onto the porch, his black Doc Martens clumping on the boards.

"I brought beer," he said, holding up the six-pack.

"I told you before commencement this morning, I already bought plenty of beer."

"You can never have too much beer."

Calvin led him inside. As they headed down the hall to the parlor Brandon kept pausing to examine the paintings on the walls. The paintings were Mr. May's, of course. More stuff Calvin had to figure out what to do with.

"A lot of these suck, I hate to say," Brandon announced. He pointed at a painting of a white church on a daisy-covered hill. "Totally fucking banal and oppressive subject matter and a style that's duller than an egg. But some of the others are awesome." He nodded at a scene of a satyr gamboling in a clearing with some nude nymphs. "Nice." He bent forward for a closer look at the nymphs. "*Very* nice." He grinned and stuck out his tongue, looking like a satyr himself.

"Horndog. And here I thought you were interested only in aesthetics."

"Hey, man, there's nothing more aesthetically pleasing than a smokin'-hot chick with her clothes off."

"Agreed," said Cynthia from the parlor doorway. "I was wondering what you two were doing. You'd better get in here before I eat all the wasabi peas."

Brandon's jaw dropped. "You got wasabi peas? Dude!"

He brushed past Cynthia and made a beeline for the food. By the time Calvin and Cynthia caught up with him, he was already gobbling a fistful of the peas.

"Whoa," he said around a mouthful of mushy, half-chewed peas, his eyes watering. "Thethe're hot!"

The doorbell rang. Calvin and Cynthia glanced at each other.

"Must be Donovan and Violet," Cynthia said.

"This is it, then," Calvin said. "The gang's all here."

"The whole sick crew," Brandon said.

Calvin returned to the front door. When he opened it, he was surprised to find three people on the porch instead of the expected two. Standing there with Donovan and Violet was an attractive twenty-something girl Calvin didn't recognize at first. She had long, wavy dark-brown hair, skin that was creamy and flawless except for a small comma-shaped scar on her left cheekbone, and large doe-like hazel eyes that looked both friendly and anxious at the same time. She wore a thin brown cardigan over a white button shirt, a knee-length tan skirt, and black flats.

"Surprise!" said Violet.

"Uh…" Calvin said, his eyes on the mystery girl.

"Um, hi," the girl said, raising one hand in a little wave. After a brief pause, she smiled wincingly. "You don't recognize me, do you?"

He hadn't, but as soon as he heard the voice and saw her speaking, he did. It was Lauren O'Donohue, Violet's older sister, who had been in the class ahead of Calvin, Cynthia, and Brandon's in high school. Calvin had never had more than a passing acquaintanceship with her but had always found her pleasant and charmingly nerdy, especially when she started talking about history, her big passion. After graduating, she had headed off to college somewhere in Maryland. Five years away had changed her for the better; she had ditched the mousy glasses, lost about fifteen pounds, and figured out how to do something with her hair other than put it up in a ponytail. And yet, pleased as he was to see her, especially given her geek-to-chic transformation, her presence here put a major crimp in their plans.

"Lauren," he said, trying to hide his mixed feelings behind a smile. "This is a surprise."

Something in his tone or his expression must have reflected his true feelings because Lauren's smile abruptly winked out.

"Oh, crap. I'm, like, party-crashing, aren't I?" She gave her sister a light kick on the calf. "You said it would be okay, you pulchritudinous perambulator."

"Don't call me names!" Violet snapped. "Are those even real words anyway?"

"No, actually, it's okay," Calvin told Lauren. "Really.

Come on in."

He led them into the parlor. Cynthia and Brandon did a double-take when they saw their uninvited sixth, then glanced at Calvin who gave them a quick, discreet spread of his arms and a look that said, "We'll have to play the cards we're dealt."

They played.

"Lauren, hey," Cynthia said. "I didn't know you were back in town."

"Yep. Back to stay this time. I just graduated, and I've already landed an amazing job nearby. But, um..." Though Lauren hadn't seen Calvin's expression a moment ago, she hadn't been blind to Cynthia and Brandon's momentary nonplussation, nor to the smallness of the group gathered here. "Look," she said to Calvin, "if you guys have some private thing going on, I don't want to intrude. Really. I mean, if I am, just let me know and I would be more than happy to—"

"No no no," Calvin said. "Please stay. It's cool. Really. A big part of what we're doing is celebrating our own graduations from Ames this morning—me and Cyn and Brandon. So you are more than welcome to stay and celebrate yours, too."

"Um, okay," she said, not looking entirely convinced. "I can't stay too late anyway, though; I have to get up super-early for some on-the-job training tomorrow."

"So what's this amazing job?" Brandon asked.

"Actually it's at your very own alma mater. I'll be working in the Ames University Library's Special Collections."

"Cool," Cynthia said.

"Yeah. It actually puts my college education to good use, which is more than most graduates can say about their jobs these days."

"Your degree was in History, I assume?" Calvin said. "I remember that being your big interest."

Lauren bobbled her head about in a kind of semi-nod. "Partly. I actually wound up getting two degrees: History and Library Science. That's why it took me an extra year. But, yeah, a huge chunk of the Special Collections at Ames is devoted to historical texts. And not just general history, either. They've got the most extensive collection of local historical documents of anyplace in the area. They have every issue of the old *Kingwood Sentinel*, even the first few that were basically just pro-temperance screeds printed on Ebenezer Blackman's crappy basement printing press. They also have James Bard's original journals from when he was surveying this area back in 1798. Plus, they, uh..." She paused and gave a sheepish smile. "Sorry. Kinda geeking out."

"That's pretty much par for the course around here," Cynthia said. "Especially where Calvin's concerned. He has two degrees, too, you know: Physics and psychology."

Lauren grinned at Calvin. "So, what, you can psycho-analyze atoms?"

"Absolutely," he said. "I've already established that their compulsion to form covalent bonds reflects a deep-seated lack of self-esteem."

She cackled. "Oh, God. Nerd jokes. We are such nerds."

"Speak for yourself, crackwhore," said Violet.

"Pipe down, you callipygian creophage."

Violet scowled. "Stop calling me stuff I've never heard of!"

She stalked away to grab some beer from the buffet table. As soon as she was at a safe distance, Cynthia whispered to Lauren, "She really has no idea those aren't even insults?"

"Not in the slightest," Lauren said. "I call her all kinds of things, and she never looks them up. She just assumes they're derogatory. She once threw a banana at me because I called her an inveterate masticator."

Cynthia laughed. "Wow. I'm in awe of your Violet-handling skills."

"Well, I did grow up with her, after all. I know how her mind works. Or fails to, as the case may be. So what about you? You graduated today, too, right? What's your degree in?"

"Philosophy."

"Ah, yes," Brandon interjected. "The art of splitting imaginary hairs."

Cynthia rolled her eyes. "Here we go." To Lauren, she added, "I get this from him all the time."

"I think philosophy's cool," said Lauren.

"It's fine unless you're looking to actually accomplish anything worthwhile," Brandon said.

"Oh, right," said Cynthia. "Like you're gonna accomplish so much with your Studio Art degree. I'm sure you'll wind up saving the world with a wicked ceramics exhibition. I'm telling you, if you're not careful you'll be forced to swallow your indie ideals and do commercial art for some rapacious corporation."

"Oh, no. We've already determined that your sell-out date is far sooner than mine, young lady. You're the one who's already thrown in her lot with the petty bourgeoisie by taking a job at her dad's bookstore."

"For some reason I feel like I just walked in on the fifteenth episode of a serial or something," Lauren said. "I'll let you guys rocket toward episode sixteen while I grab some grub."

While Cynthia and Brandon continued to debate the relative impracticality of their respective fields, Lauren helped herself to a bottle of Bass Ale and some Cool Ranch Doritos.

After a moment Calvin appeared beside her and took a beer for himself.

"So are you going to live here in May, or in Ames?" he asked.

"I'm not sure yet. Right now I'm living at my parents' house, which is, well, far from ideal. Especially the way my dad and Violet keep inching toward mutual homicide. But I'm hoping to be out of there and in my own place after I've got a few paychecks under my belt. I guess where I live will depend on the availability of decent apartments."

She shoved a handful of Doritos into her mouth and began to chew, then was suddenly struck by an idea. Her mouth too full of half-ground corn chips to speak, she jabbed a finger at Calvin and then, grunting loudly, waved her arms about in big, broad arcs. Calvin had no idea what she was trying to convey and shook his head to express his bafflement. Lauren held up a finger, signaling him to wait, while she chewed and swallowed.

"Speaking of living arrangements," she said, "this is your house now, right? You actually own this place?"

"Yep."

"I am sick with envy. I mean, I was always fascinated by this place. The history. The architecture. Are there really secret rooms and stuff?"

"I don't think so. The twenty-eight non-secret rooms seem to be taking up all the available space."

"And you guys actually got to know Mr. May, right?"

"Yeah. We knew him for only a few days before he

died, but we all hit it off really well. By the time he died, I felt like I'd known him all my life."

"He must've felt the same way if he left you, y'know, all this. The house and everything."

"Yeah. But the weirdest part is, I found out he named me in his trust a few years before I even met him."

"And you don't know why?"

"Nope."

"What about Violet and the Crows? I know he left some money to all of them. I assumed it was because you were all searching for Emily together. But had they been mentioned in the trust for years, too?"

Emily was Cynthia and Donovan's little sister, who had been abducted and murdered five years earlier. The mention of her name caught everyone's attention.

"What are you guys talking about?" Cynthia asked, heading over to the buffet table. The rest of the group followed close behind.

"The inheritances," Calvin said. To Lauren, he said, "Yeah, according to Stephen Krezchek, the Crows had been listed for a few years, too, but in their case it kind of makes more sense, since they were Mr. May's neighbors and they had at least had some kind of contact with him over the years, minor though it was. I'm not sure when Violet was added."

"What about anyone else?" Lauren asked. "Did he leave any other surprise bequests?"

"I heard that a couple of Emily's friends also got a hundred thousand each."

"Yeah," Cynthia said. "John Coyote and Anna West. They were Emily's best friends."

"But beyond that...." Calvin shrugged. "I don't know. I never actually saw a copy of the trust documents. Stephen Krezchek was in charge of all that."

"But..." Lauren gestured at the house around them. "Didn't Mr. May keep a copy for himself somewhere?"

Calvin stared at her in silence, feeling like an absolute moron. He had never even thought to look for a copy of the trust. Though he had explored most of the house's manifold nooks and crannies, he had yet to look through Mr. May's papers, kept in file cabinets in an upstairs office. He hadn't had any reason to, and perhaps more importantly, he had always felt a bit uneasy at the thought of fingering through Mr. May's personal documents. It seemed somehow disrespectful, an invasion of privacy. And perhaps part of him feared he would uncover something unsavory or embarrassing about the old man and thus diminish him forever. Now, though, the notion that the answers to long-pondered secrets might be hidden away up there made Calvin eager to rush upstairs and start flinging open cabinet drawers.

"There might be something upstairs," he told Lauren. "I'll have to take a look around up there sometime soon."

"Gee, can I help?" she said with a big smile, eyebrows raised pleadingly.

"What?"

"I'm kidding. I really just want to see the house. I've always wanted to explore this place. Seriously, do you think you could give me a tour sometime?"

"Um..." He wanted to say yes, but there was the Collection to think of. It filled five rooms, with a sixth devoted to Mr. May's extensive files on the items and the cases they pertained to. If Calvin gave Lauren a tour, how would he explain avoiding nearly a fifth of the house? Or should they take Lauren into their confidence? It might not be a bad idea; she seemed trustworthy and likely to be sympathetic to their aims. And heck, with her knowledge of history, she might prove an invaluable asset to the team. Perhaps if she was interested she could even become a full-fledged member.

And then Lauren brought his internal debate crashing to a halt when, seeing his hesitation, she waved a hand in a placating way and said, "It's okay, you don't have to show me the Collection if you don't want to."

Calvin blinked at her in surprise. "You what?"

"Yeah, I kind of know about it already." She gave a wincing smile. "Sorry."

There was a moment of silence. Then multiple heads swiveled toward Violet.

Violet spread her hands, her face a mask of baffled innocence.

"What!"

"Hey, now, you can't entirely blame her," Lauren said. "I could tell she wasn't being entirely forthcoming about things, and, well, let's just say I know exactly what kind of leverage to use to get her to talk."

"Ooh, you'll have to share that with us," Brandon said.

"You will *not,*" Violet told her sister.

"Um, how much exactly did she tell you?" Cynthia asked Lauren.

"You mean, do I know about the anomaly investigation thing you've got going on?" Lauren asked.

"God damn it, Violet!"

"She's my sister!" Violet said.

"Yeah, well, let's just hope she inherited all the genes for dependability that seem to have bypassed you."

"Don't worry about that," Lauren said. "This little game of telephone ends with me. I haven't told anyone else and don't plan to. I think what you're doing is really cool."

"Honestly, we haven't even really done anything yet," Calvin said. "I mean, Cyn and I did have a case that sort of fell into our laps during our sophomore year of college, but other than that we've been waiting for our inheritances to kick in, which the trust stipulated would happen only once we finished college. In the meantime we read our way through all of Mr. May's four thousand files, and lately I've been researching investigative techniques. One of the things we're hoping to do tonight is discuss our M.O. You know, how we'll conduct investigations, how we'll find out about new strange happenings to investigate, stuff like that."

"Ooh, if you need strange stuff to investigate, what about the passenger pigeons? Wouldn't that qualify as a strange happening?"

Two years ago, after a spate of unconfirmed sightings, it was conclusively established that a flock of passenger pigeons, a species long believed extinct, was living here in Bard County. The government immediately sent out teams to study the pigeons and designated the birds' nesting grounds protected wildlife areas (much to the outrage of some local farmers whose lands, being part of those areas, were seized under eminent domain). When first discovered, the flock numbered barely a hundred, which researchers found worrisome, given that passenger pigeons were a highly colonial species thought to require huge populations to sustain themselves. But despite fears that the birds would sink into extinction once again, their numbers had steadily increased and recently crossed the two hundred mark.

"Um..." Calvin glanced at Cynthia, an eyebrow cocked questioningly. She understood what he was asking, and she nodded, telling him to go ahead. She, too, thought Lauren was worth taking into their confidence.

"Actually," Calvin said to Lauren, "we kind of think we already know where they've been. Or rather, where they came from."

"Oh? Do tell!"

"We think they came from the woods out back. Sort of."

"Sort of?"

"Something happened in the clearing back there around the time Emily died," Cynthia said. "You know that round clearing northeast of here?"

"Yeah," Lauren said. "That's, y'know, where they think it happened, right?"

Cynthia nodded. "Yeah, that's where he killed her. There was also a weird burned area there that no one could really explain, a circle where the grass was scorched right down to the dirt. A few days later my aunt Wendy had a seizure and died right in the same clearing. I was there when it happened, and the moment she died, this weird dome of light filled the middle of the clearing. Except I'm pretty sure it was really more of a sphere; it's just that half of it was underground."

"A sphere of light?" Lauren said. "How does that fit with the pigeons?"

"Well, when everybody finally caught up with Roger Grey, Emily's killer, he had stereotypically returned to the scene of the crime to kill a couple of Emily's friends. And all of us kind of wound up there, too."

"Except me," Brandon said.

"Except him."

"You shoulda been there, man," Violet told Brandon. "We totally kicked Grey's ass."

"That's...certainly an interpretation," Cynthia said. "The way I remember it, he headbutted you into an unaccustomed silence."

"Only for a second," Violet muttered.

"Yeah, and then he shot me," Calvin said.

"He shot you?" Lauren said, her eyes flicking up and down his body as if she expected to find blood soaking through his clothes.

"Here." He tapped an inch-long groove of scar tissue on his left temple. "The bullet just glanced off my skull, but still, it wasn't pleasant."

"Anyway, the guys from the FBI who were investigating the case were there, too," Cynthia said, "and there was a quick shootout that left Grey and one of the FBI agents dead. And then all of a sudden the clearing filled with light again, and we all saw...things in the light. Images."

"It was like a thousand movies all playing at once on the same screen," Calvin said. "Just all these overlapping images."

"And some of 'em were damn weird," Donovan said. "I remember seeing flying lady heads with bat wings where their ears should be."

"And dinosaurs," Violet said. "There were dinosaurs."

"Yeah, and I saw what looked a bit like one of those Ents from *The Lord of the Rings*," Cynthia said.

"Are you sure you didn't all get dosed with LSD or something?" Lauren asked, only half jokingly. "Or maybe you breathed in some kind of fumes that induced hallucinations?"

"Pretty sure," Calvin said seriously. It was a perfectly valid question, and one he had asked himself many times. "Besides, the stuff we saw wasn't all weird. A lot of it was more normal, realistic stuff. People and mountains and buildings and things like that."

"And then the light winked out," Cynthia said, "and all the crazy images winked out with it, and in their place there was a small flock of what looked like some kind of pigeon fluttering around the clearing. None of us really got a very good look at them before they flew off, but it wasn't more than a few weeks after that that the first sightings of the passenger pigeons started coming in."

"Okay, so…" Lauren frowned. "The pigeons were some kind of hallucination made real?"

"I don't think they were hallucinations," Calvin said. "I think something more was at work."

"Like what?"

"Magic."

"Magic?" Lauren's eyebrows nearly reached her hairline. She looked as if she were trying to decide whether everyone present was clinically insane or just pulling her leg.

"You don't believe in magic?"

"I assume you don't mean the David Copperfield kind of magic, with skinny women hidden in the stage floor."

"No."

"Well…" Lauren drew in a long, deep breath. "I'm open to the idea, at least in theory, but a claim like that needs some major-league proof."

"I don't blame you." He gave her an appraising look. "You're a history geek, right? How well do you know your local history?"

"Pretty damn good, I should say."

"Yeah," said Violet. "She really does know all that shit. She's memorized the names and favorite colors and penis sizes of every mayor dating back to, like, 1582. And the worst part is, she'll actually tell you all this stuff."

"Silence, you impavid illustrissimo."

"Fuck you."

"What about the history of the woods right here?" Calvin asked Lauren. "The Indians and the May and Crow families?"

"Of course I know that stuff," Lauren said.

"You *think* you do."

She raised an eyebrow.

"I *know* I do."

"All right, then, do you know what happened to Firebird, the chief of the Indian tribe who used to live here?"

"He killed himself on Indian Hill during a ceremony."

"And the original May house—"

"Burned down by Luther Jones in 1871 with most of the May family trapped inside."

"And Spirit Cave—"

"Was where Luther Jones hid afterward and then got killed by Turner May and Hamilton Crow." She pointed at Calvin as if she were one-upping him. "*And* that was also where Olive Crow's body was found after she drowned in the Kanseeka."

"Randolph Crow and Anna May?"

"Young lovers who met a tragic end. She died in the May house during the Spanish Flu epidemic of 1918 and he subsequently blew his brains out."

"Where?"

"Next to the Stone Pillar in the woods."

"This is like Jeopardy on speed," Donovan said.

"I'd like Fucked-Up Local History for four hundred, Alex," Brandon said.

"Okay, what about Eugene Scott?" Calvin asked Lauren.

Lauren paused, her mouth open, looking uncertain for

once. "Um, wait, that was the guy who married Wendy Crow, right? The one who died mysteriously in the Crow house?"

"Yeah. You're probably not as familiar with it because it's more recent history. The 1970s."

"But what does all of this prove? Just because a bunch of tragic events happened in the same area over the years, that doesn't mean there's some kind of connection between them."

Calvin smiled.

"Follow me," he said, heading toward the door. "I'll show you something that might change your mind."

Lauren followed, a little uncertainly. She looked behind her and saw the others following, too, the small anticipatory smiles on their faces showing that they already knew what Calvin was going to show her.

"You're gonna like this," Brandon told Lauren. "Trust me. I remember when they showed me. I was, like, 'whoa!'"

Calvin led them down the corridor to the center of the house, where a spiral staircase stood at the junction of the house's four wings. They trooped up the stairs to the second floor, then down the west wing to a door on the left, which led to the very office that not twenty minutes ago Calvin had realized he must soon hunt through in search of a copy of Mr. May's will. But that would have to wait till later. Right now his task was to show Lauren what hung on the wall behind Mr. May's desk.

It was a satellite image of the large block of land on which they now stood, a perfect square demarked on the north by Baumgartner Road, on the west by Indianview, on the east by Potts, and on the south by Oaks. The picture must have been taken in the summertime, for the woods that shrouded most of the block were lush and verdant, and everything was crisply lit by a high sun. All but the northern fifth of the block, which the city had bought long ago and transformed into Indian Hill Park, was owned by the Crows and, as of today, by Calvin. Their respective houses sat near the bottom of the map, in large round clearings connected to Oaks Road via barely discernible ribbons of driveway, Calvin's house on the west, its four wings making it look like a plus sign, the Crows' on the east, its shape more traditionally boxy. Midway between the two driveways the Kanseeka River rose up from the middle of the map's bottom edge, flowing due north. The natural and legal boundary between the two properties, the Kanseeka neatly bisected the lower third of the block before veering northeast toward Spirit Falls, a small, scenic waterfall that was visible on the map as a white knot along the green-grey thread of the river. Just beyond the falls the river curved northwest, passing the mouth of Spirit Cave in the process, the cave and the low rocky rise it penetrated showing up as tiny flecks of gray and black through the dense overhanging verdure. The river continued northwest until, shortly after crossing over into the western half of the block, it swept in a sharp curve around the base of Indian Hill, a high prominence whose composition of bare shale and clay made it a large and rather ugly dark-gray blotch on the green landscape. Coming out of the curve, the river flowed due east along the southern edge of Indian Hill Park and exited the block beneath the Potts Road Bridge.

The image was so large and clear that even the clearing where Emily and her killer had died was visible as a tiny, irregular circle that was a brighter, grassier green than the woods that surrounded it. Even the Stone Pillar—a weathered shaft of limestone of disputed origin—could be seen as a minute gray dot amid the trees. Still, visible as the Pillar and the clearing were, their small size meant that it would have taken even a trained eye a long while to locate them if their positions hadn't already been marked.

The clearing was marked by a black push pin, which Mr. May had put there in the wake of Emily's abduction. The Stone Pillar was marked in a much different manner; it was one of the five points of a perfectly formed pentagram that Calvin had drawn on the map five years ago, on the same night he and the others had witnessed the white light in the clearing and the strange visions within it. The star's other points were Indian Hill, Spirit Cave, and the May and Crow houses, the very spots where the tragedies catechized by Calvin and Lauren minutes earlier had unfolded over the last two hundred years. And the black push pin, the clearing, was situated precisely in the center of this pentacle of misery and death.

Lauren studied the map in silence for a minute. Nose inches from the glossy paper, she checked and doublechecked to make sure the image hadn't been tampered with and that the scale was regular throughout. Everything checked out, as she had been pretty sure it would. She was familiar enough with this area to know how it looked even from above. Her examination had been mainly a formality, persnickety but necessary.

"Okay, that's just weird," she said, her eyes still roving across the map. "But what does it mean? It can't be accidental." She looked at Calvin, her expression suddenly uncertain. "Can it?"

"I'm assuming not."

"But who was behind it, then? Over so many years, it'd have to be the work of some kind of intergenerational conspiracy, or else..." She trailed off, not sure she wanted to posit anything more than that at the moment.

Calvin had no such qualms. "Or someone or something extremely long-lived."

"Like what, vampires?" Lauren said with a small, nervous laugh. "Ghosts? The Highlander?"

"We don't know for sure. We have all kinds of vague and probably hare-brained theories, of course, but at the moment the important thing is the effect it all had. What happened in the clearing. The light. The birds."

"So, what, this was all just to bring a bunch of passenger pigeons back to life? That makes no sense. Most of the tragedies in question occurred long before the birds went extinct."

"I don't think the pigeons were the point. I mean, we've been debating this for a few years now, and so far the best hypothesis we've come up with is that whatever happened here in the woods, it somehow opened a gateway to..." He shrugged. "Somewhere else. Or somewhere elses."

"Somewhere elses?"

"Like other dimensions or alternate realities. That would certainly explain the diversity of the images we saw in the light. They might have been a bunch of alternate realities all being seen simultaneously."

"There are alternate realities with walking, talking trees in them? I mean, not that that wouldn't be cool and everything, but, I mean...really? No offense, but I'm not quite ready to give up on the psychotropic drugs hypothesis."

"Psychotropic drugs wouldn't explain that," Cynthia said with a nod at the pentagram on the map.

"True," Lauren conceded.

"It might not have been alternate realities per se that

they saw," Brandon said. "I always wondered if it might not have been, like, the raw stuff of imagination made manifest." He looked at Calvin and Cynthia. "Didn't you guys say that you and Mr. May had been talking about passenger pigeons a few days before they appeared?"

"Yeah," Cynthia said.

"Well, there you go. They were on your minds, and boom, there they were."

Cynthia smiled thinly. "I think Emily was on everyone's minds a lot more than some birds that got discussed for all of three seconds one day. So why didn't *she* appear?"

"Uh…"

"At any rate," Calvin said to Lauren, "the point is, yes, the clearing in the woods is where we think the pigeons came from. The precise details are still a bit fuzzy, obviously."

Lauren glanced out the window at the woods. The sun, close to setting, was obscured behind the trees, and the woods were filling with murk.

"I'd like to see this magical clearing," she said, "but I guess it's getting kind of dark for it right now."

"There isn't much to see anyway," Cynthia said. "It only does funky things when someone dies there. Otherwise it's just a clearing."

"You wanted to see the Collection, too, didn't you?" Calvin said to Lauren. "I could give you a quick tour of it right now, if you like."

"Ooh," Lauren said. "Yes, please. Thank you. But just quick. I don't want to keep you guys from your big strategy session, or whatever it is."

"It's cool," Calvin said. "There's plenty of time, and I suspect the whole strategizing thing is something that'll require more than one meeting anyway."

"Besides," Brandon said. "Calvin likes showing off the Collection. It's like his baby or something."

They spent the next hour giving Lauren a tour of the Collection, which was housed in two rooms on the second floor and three on the third. Like everyone else seeing the Collection for the first time, Lauren was agog at the array of outré items filling row after row of old wooden shelves. Naturally enough, she gravitated to items that were clearly of historic origin: a Phoenician coin (which, Calvin told her, had been unearthed in a Kansas cornfield in 1888), a Viking battleaxe (said to have fallen out of a clear sky, along with half a dozen cherry tomatoes and a number of small stones, in Darwin, Australia, in 1954), the scorched remains of an Elizabethan dress (supposedly worn by a spontaneous human combustion victim at the time of her fiery death), and so on. Lauren was particularly impressed with four cards from the so-called Ur-Tarot, the purported prototype of the Tarot's major arcana, said to have been created by a psychic monk over a thousand years ago.

"Wow," she said, studying the painted images, each safely ensconced within its own acid-free plastic bag. "You do realize these would fetch a not-so-small fortune if you ever decided to sell them, right?"

"Yeah, but they're not for sale," Calvin said. "None of it is. This is bigger than money."

"Besides, we collected that one ourselves," Cynthia said, pointing at one of the cards, which was numbered "VI" and depicted a young blond man and a young red-headed woman standing in a clearing in a forest. "It's the fruit of our only real case so far."

Lauren stared at the card a moment, then glanced at Calvin and Cynthia, then looked back at the image.

"Um, you know…" she began.

"Yes, we know. It looks kind of like us."

"That psychic monk obviously had some mad skills," Brandon said.

"That's just freaky." Lauren put the cards back on the shelf, then surveyed the vast and eclectic assortment of items that filled the room. "You guys have a lot of work ahead of you if you hope to match Mr. May's output. That man must have had quite a remarkable work ethic."

"Yeah," Calvin said with a small sigh. "We still haven't really figured out where we're going to find cases to investigate."

"I think we should try to find stuff close to home to start with," Cynthia said. "We might not find a lot of dramatic, exciting cases, but it would help us find our feet and get a sort of investigatory rhythm going."

"What about that weird murder last night?" Lauren said. "You guys could always investigate that."

"What murder?" Calvin said. He glanced at the others and found only puzzled looks that matched his own.

"In Kingwood yesterday. It's been all over the news. Haven't you heard about it?"

"No, we've been caught up with graduating and the inheritances and everything. What murder? What happened?"

"I don't remember all the details, but some guy was found dead in an alley with big chunks of him missing, and the coroner seemed kind of baffled about who or what could have caused the injuries."

Calvin checked his watch. Almost ten o'clock.

"Come on, everybody," he said, striding to the door. "If we hurry we can catch the local news."

3

Back in the parlor they all sat down, beers in hand, and Calvin turned on the TV, a twelve-year-old 24" Sony that he had earmarked for replacement as soon as possible. He had already decided that a 54" flatscreen would fit quite nicely in the old TV's space if he just scooched the nearby furniture out of the way a little bit.

The news was just starting. The top story was about a house fire in eastern Kingwood that was still being brought under control. The second was about the murder.

There was a clip of a press conference given earlier at Kingwood City Hall, during which Kingwood Police Chief Trent Dowdie and County Coroner Jagannath Chandra summarized the few known facts: A man named Bradley Vallance had been found dead shortly after dawn in an alley in Kingwood's West River neighborhood. The coroner estimated that he had been dead for about six hours, which tallied with the statement of Vallance's girlfriend, Christine Ruddy, who had last seen Vallance at around midnight the previous night in the mouth of the very alley where he was found dead. It seemed likely that he had been killed mere moments after Christine wished him good night. A resident of West Train Apartments who had a room overlooking the crime scene reported hearing "unusual noises" from the alley at around the time in question.

The condition of the corpse was grisly and perplexing. Large areas of flesh were missing, all the way down to the bone in many places, and though the damage was reminiscent of animal bites, there were no actual tooth marks anywhere.

"Whatever made the injuries came together like a set of jaws closing, but had perfectly smooth edges and left no marks of individual teeth," Coroner Chandra said. "Imagine a bear trap, only without serrations on the blades, just smooth, curved steel all the way across. I cannot say yet exactly what might have produced these injuries, or even whether it was a living creature or an implement of some kind."

Chief Dowdie then jumped in to say that in light of certain details, the nature of which he could not divulge, the police were provisionally treating this as a homicide, though an unusual animal attack could not, of course, be ruled out at this time.

"In other words, they have no fucking clue," Violet translated.

The telegenic female newscaster closed out the piece by announcing that the police were refusing to speculate whether or not Vallance's death might be connected with the mysterious disappearance of two teenage boys in the same neighborhood last Friday.

The newscaster moved on to a follow-up story about the lurid murders of two members of a kiddie porn ring in Castle Township last month. Calvin turned off the TV.

"Interesting," he muttered.

"I didn't know about the two missing teenagers," Lauren said. "I wonder if it's connected."

"Of course it's connected," Violet said. "That's as obvious as a turd on a radiator. We don't need to wait for some little egghead science lab nerds to tell us that."

"There are these things called the rules of evidence, you know," Cynthia said.

"Rules are for people who are ruled."

Calvin shook his head. "There isn't enough information for us to say whether there's a connection or not. Any time there's a sensationalistic unsolved murder, the media is quick to try to link it up with any other recent deaths or missing people in the area. And in a big, heavily populated city like Kingwood, there're always enough murders and disappearances to provide plenty of potential links. Even if there does turn out to be a link, we still don't know if this falls under our purview in the first place. An unsolved murder and some unusual injuries don't necessarily contravene any natural laws or reigning scientific paradigms."

"*Very* unusual injuries," Cynthia said. "Don't forget: Chandra's been the county coroner for nearly fifty years. He's gotten awards from the Coroner's Association of America, or whatever it's called. He's even written a couple of books. There's probably very little he hasn't seen by this point. If he's really as baffled as he seemed to be, I'd say it's at least worth checking out."

"Oh, I agree," Calvin said. "I wasn't saying we shouldn't check it out, just that maybe only a couple of us should head out there tomorrow to sniff around and try to determine if this is worth devoting more time and attention to."

"Like scouts, or something," Brandon said.

"Exactly. And in the meantime we should find out the story on these missing teens—"

"Done," said Lauren, who for the last couple of minutes had been doggedly pressing buttons on her smart phone. "I just hunted up the info on them. Charles Reed and Zenon Dovzhenko."

"Xenon?" Donovan said. "Isn't that, like, an element

or something?"

"Zenon with a Z. Says here his family's from the Ukraine. Anyhow, the two kids, both 16, went out Friday night to 'party' and never came home. The kids had no known enemies, no recent troubles with anyone…" She paused to read on, then raised her eyebrows and held up a finger. "Ah. Except the police. Turns out these two had repeated arrests for what the cops refer to as vandalism but what the kids' friends call street art."

"Ah, graffitists," Brandon said with a smile. "Fellow artistes."

"No sign of either of them since Saturday night. None of their friends or family knows anything, their cell phones go straight to voicemail, et cetera, et cetera. They basically just went out to party, or perhaps to scrawl giant illegible letters on the sides of bridges, and then dropped off the face of the Earth."

"But no bodies," Cynthia said. "I don't know. Dropping off the face of the Earth is a whole different thing from being left horribly mutilated in an alley in a busy neighborhood."

"The graffitists might have been killed somewhere they haven't been found yet," Brandon said. "I've known plenty of guys who do street art, and sometimes they do their thing in very obscure, untraveled places. You'd be surprised how many places there are like that even in the middle of a city."

"You know, this could be, like, a serial killer or something," Donovan said. "The poor graffiti guys could just be heads in refrigerators at this point."

"Maybe," Calvin said. "But if this turns out to be just some sociopath hacking up his victims with some kind of bizarre home-made choppers, then it's not worth our time.

Human psychopathology, nasty and weird as it can be, is not anomalous and isn't something we should be spending our time investigating."

He turned to Lauren. "Do you want to be part of this?" He gestured at her phone. "You're already doing our research for us."

"Um...do you mean part of the group or just this investigation?"

"Either. Both. Whatever. I mean, you're welcome to join up with us if you want. We'd be glad to have you on the team."

"Um, I don't know. I'm definitely with you for this mysterious murder. Since I'm the one who brought it to your attention, I feel a kind of proprietary interest, so I at least want to see how it shakes out. But after that...I don't know. Maybe?"

"Fair enough."

"You definitely oughta join," Violet told her sister. "You'll fit right in with all these geeks."

"What, like you?"

"Hell no! I'm just doin' this for the kicks, is all."

"So who's gonna be doing the scouting tomorrow?" Lauren asked Calvin. "I can't. Or at least not until late in the day. I've got my job training."

"Yeah, and I've got a bunch of job interviews lined up," Brandon said.

"I was thinking just me and Cyn would constitute the advance team," Calvin said. "I mean, since we read through all of Mr. May's files, I think we've developed a pretty good idea of what kinds of questions to ask and what kinds of things to look out for. Uh..." He glanced at Cynthia. "You are free tomorrow, right? I mean, I know you've been working at the bookstore a lot lately..."

"No, Donovan's the only one with bookstore duty tomorrow," Cynthia said. "So I'm good to go." She suddenly sat bolt upright in her seat with a big smile. "Ooh! And we can take my new car." She noticed how everyone was looking at her with amusement. "C'mon, I'm excited, okay? I've never had my own car before."

"Yeah, well, enjoy it while it lasts," Brandon said. "You'll be singing a different tune when you need to get the transmission fixed, and the brake lines replaced, and all the other ten billion little things that go wrong with cars and bleed your bank account dry."

"No offense, but unlike you and Calvin, I plan to take good care of my car and not let it turn into a creaky box of rust."

"Pipe dreams. Cars age and die like everything else, especially with our shitty Ohio winters and all the concomitant potholes and body-rusting road salt. As the sage said, 'This, too, shall pass.' That includes cars."

"Yes, I know. But let me keep my new-car-owner illusions a *little* while longer, okay?"

"Sorry."

"So, yeah," Calvin said, "Cyn and I will check things out tomorrow in Cyn's lovely new car, and then we can all meet back here tomorrow night, same time, same place. It looks like we'll have a ton of leftover beer, too, so we'll be able to either celebrate our first case, or drown our sorrows over the lack of one."

4

After everyone had gone home, Calvin spent a while putting the leftovers away and cleaning up. Then he went to the spiral staircase, intending to head up to the office and look for a copy of the trust and perhaps find a clue to the mystery of the inexplicable inheritances.

He began to ascend, then paused, one foot on the stairs' bottom step and one hand on the wrought-iron railing, and looked around.

From here in this central circle that flung out branches to the house's every extremity, he could see down each of the first floor's four wings to the four entrances. And the coiling black staircase beneath his hand and foot reached all the way from the basement's cold concrete floor to the wooden rafters at the top of the tower. From here he could touch and sense the entire sprawling house, all twenty-eight rooms, Turner May's mad creation engulfing him like that great biblical fish with little Jonah in its belly.

The utter silence only made the house seem vaster and Calvin tinier and more alone. Surely something in the house must be making noise, the tick of a clock, the hum of the refrigerator, the crack and pop of old boards settling, but here at the center of it all he couldn't hear a thing, and the silence freaked him out. He was used to living in a college town, where even in the dead of night something noisy was underway, whether music or traffic or drunken lovers breaking up at the tops of their lungs in the room next door. But now here he was, all alone in a huge old house, shielded from the nearest road by a couple hundred feet of woods, all of it situated in the middle of a quiet suburb where even the pizza places were shuttered and dark by ten p.m.

To make matters worse, the house was, or seemed to be, one of the main nodes on a strange magical network of misfortune. The house had been built on the ashes of a previous one and most of that previous one's occupants. Anna May had succumbed to the flu in a room upstairs; Calvin didn't know which one and wasn't sure he wanted to. Randolph Crow had no doubt raced through the very spot Calvin now occupied on his way to blow his brains out next to the Stone Pillar in the woods. And there were other incidents over the long years, so many others, all the way down to the death of Mr. May himself, who had succumbed to a stroke just down the hall next to the front door, right in front Calvin's panicked eyes.

The memory of Mr. May helped brush away Calvin's sudden and unaccustomed unease. Mr. May had chosen Calvin to be his successor, and Calvin vowed to ensure that the choice had been a good one. What kind of a paranormal investigator would he be if he let himself get spooked by a stereotypical Old Dark House? Besides, Mr. May had lived alone here for decades without any apparent trouble. If Calvin hoped to fill his mentor's shoes, he could do no less. He had to get used to silence and shadows. They came with the job.

He headed up to the office, shut the door behind him, and sat down in the high-backed office chair behind the desk. The chair creaked under his weight, and there was a faint hiss of air as the pneumatic seat settled a millimeter or two.

Before starting his search for the trust documents, he spent a moment looking around the room. The office and the master bedroom were the two rooms in the house most sharply stamped with Mr. May's personality. They were also the two rooms Calvin would have to most thoroughly restamp with his own personality, since they were where he would probably wind up spending the bulk of his time. Which meant that very soon he would have to decide what to do with everything in here.

Calvin's gaze roved over the room's contents, taking in the fifteen-year-old Hewlett-Packard on the desk; the jumble of papers and sundry office supplies that littered the desktop around the computer; the bookshelves bowed beneath the weight of hefty reference books, many of them bristling with bookmarks; the map marked with the pentagram and the black pin; and on the wall directly opposite the map, a framed poster for a 1950s movie called *The Terrible Dr. Eris,* the image showing a huge, leering face and a pair of hooked hands looming in the darkness above a brawny he-man and the buxom blonde cowering behind him. Calvin had always been baffled by the poster, an odd possession for a man who had evinced no sign of being a movie buff and hadn't owned a single DVD or videotape that wasn't in some way connected with the Collection. A couple of years ago Calvin had tracked down a copy of the movie, hoping it would provide some insight into the mind or history of Mr. May. The film turned out to be a real obscurity that had never been released on DVD, and Calvin wound up shelling out a ridiculous amount on eBay for an old, battered VHS copy released in the 80s. A substandard crime/horror thriller with a few sci-fi touches, the film concerned the efforts of a detective and the beautiful ingénue who hired him to unravel the secrets of the girl's mad scientist uncle, who, it turned out, had found a way to remotely control people's minds and was using this power to stage a coup in the United States. Calvin had scanned every credit at the end of the movie, wondering if

Mr. May himself had had a hand in its production, but he saw no names he recognized. The actors and crew had been third-raters, the sorts of folks whose profiles on Imdb sported brief filmographies and no photographs. In the end Calvin came away baffled as to why Mr. May had liked the movie enough to hang its framed poster in a spot where he would see it nearly every day. Perhaps the movie had simply held some kind of nostalgic relevance for the old man.

Calvin's gaze returned to the desktop, and he idly flipped through a few of the topmost papers. A printout about the stratigraphy of the Grand Canyon. A brief letter from somebody named Albert about the recent doings of somebody named Jack. A flier from the May Library about an "upcoming" book sale that was over five years in the past. A page of notes in Mr. May's tiny, crabbed handwriting that Calvin could only slightly decipher but that seemed to be a list of land parcels in Phoenix Township and their owners. He was going to have to sort through this stuff soon.

For that matter, he would have to replace the computer. He had turned it on once and was both appalled and amused to find that it was running Windows 98. It looked as though Mr. May had barely used the computer for anything other than online research. He hadn't even had an email account as far as Calvin could tell. Calvin's own computer was currently stashed in the game room. Once he sorted through this mess on the desk, he'd set it up in here.

But that would have to wait till later. Right now he had more important work to do.

He wheeled the chair over to the file cabinets along the east wall, where Mr. May kept his various non-

Collection documents. None of the small metal frames on the fronts of the drawers held labels to identify their contents. Calvin grabbed the handle of the nearest drawer, then paused and took a breath.

"Hope this isn't where you kept your secret porn stash," he muttered to Mr. May's shade. "If so, I apologize in advance."

He opened the drawer and found nothing more exciting than manila folders crammed with old utility bills, bank statements, and brokerage statements. A riffle through the latter two folders left Calvin feeling almost dizzy at how much money Mr. May had had. Even without a calculator he could tell that collectively the various accounts had added up to close to eight figures.

The next drawer contained care manuals and instruction manuals for various appliances, gadgets, and furniture, many of them objects that, to the best of Calvin's knowledge, Mr. May had no longer owned when he passed away. A Victrola? None of those around here anymore, unless one was hidden amid the maze of junk that filled two rooms in the basement. A 1956 Desoto Fireflite convertible? At the time of his death the only car Mr. May had owned was the Thunderbird in the detached garage out back. Why had he kept all these useless manuals? Sentiment? Nostalgia? Or maybe his globe-trotting anomaly-hunting lifestyle hadn't left him the time to clean out old folders.

Calvin moved on to the next drawer.

Bingo. Right there at the front of the drawer was a three-ring binder marked "Trust (Current)." Behind it were manila folders that contained older versions of the trust.

Calvin pulled the whole bundle of documents from

the drawer. Since he couldn't set them anywhere on the paper-heaped desk without risking an avalanche, he sat back in the chair with the folders in his lap and began to read through the trusts in chronological order.

The oldest version of the trust dated all the way back to 1960 and in it Mr. May had left half a million dollars and most of his property, including the Collection, to somebody named Chad Chapman. Lesser amounts went to various other people, including an Albert Korowicz and a Jack Fivecrows, whom Calvin surmised might be the same Albert and Jack mentioned in the letter on the desk.

A new trust was written up in the spring of 1969, this one leaving everything—every last cent and nail—to someone named Alma R. Munsen.

The next trust came only two months later, and this one was very similar to the original one, except that Chad Chapman's place was now taken by Ellen Gardner, who in the original trust had received fifty thousand dollars, while Mr. Chapman himself was demoted to receiving only ten thousand dollars and an antique Bible. There was no mention of Alma R. Munsen anywhere.

The next version dated to 1985. In it the Collection and the house were left to one Michael Hawthorne. Calvin wondered if this wasn't the same Mike whom Mr. May had once mentioned as having helped him procure some of the items in the Collection. Beyond that, various changes had been made to the various bequests, no doubt to reflect the passing of old friends and the acquisition of new ones. Ellen Gardner was no longer listed, but a Melody Gardner, who had been a beneficiary in all of the previous trusts except the Alma Munsen one, was still slated to receive fifty thousand dollars.

Another version was made in 1996, this time with only

minor amendments. Michael Hawthorne still received the Collection and the house.

Then came November 2008 and a radically new trust. A number of old names were no longer mentioned. The ones who remained received the same or lesser amounts. Michael Hawthorne received an original tin sign from the May-Crow Brewery and fifty thousand dollars.

Calvin, who had not been mentioned in any previous trust, received one hundred thousand dollars. So did the likewise previously unmentioned Anna West and John Coyote. Ditto every member of the Crow family with the exception of Emily Crow.

Emily Crow received the Collection, the house, and one million dollars.

Frowning, Calvin did the math. Emily would have just turned seven.

There was also one other recipient of a hundred thousand dollars (along with, oddly enough, a volume of *Grimm's Complete Fairy Tales*) who had not been mentioned in any previous trust. This was someone named Tiffany Fish.

Calvin had never heard of her.

The final version of the trust was the one Mr. May had made the day before he died. In it, he added Violet's comparatively small bequest, and, more importantly, switched Calvin's and Emily's bequests, so that Emily received one hundred thousand dollars, while Calvin received the house, the Collection, and one million dollars. By then Emily had been missing a few days and, although no one had been willing to say so at the time, almost certainly dead. What's more, some of Mr. May's comments and actions at the time suggested that he knew he didn't have much time left to live, which made an amendment to the trust imperative. If Mr. May died and Emily remained missing, the Collection could have been held up in legal limbo forever.

But still, why had he left it to *Calvin?* Why not one of the other Crows? Why not Melody Gardner, or Albert Korowicz, or someone else Mr. May had known all his life? Calvin liked to think it was because the old man had seen some reflection of himself in Calvin, seen a worthy successor to his life's work. But the truth was, Calvin would probably never know.

Perhaps the most important question of all was what had happened during or before November 2008 that compelled Mr. May to rearrange his legacy so dramatically. Why would he leave the Collection to a seven-year-old girl? Why would he leave even a hundred thousand dollars to Calvin when, to the best of Calvin's recollection, they had never even met? Somehow Mr. May must have known who he was. Perhaps the old man had been watching him—watching all of them—for years. But why?

Calvin looked up at the movie poster on the wall, at that huge, leering face looming above the crouched and vulnerable couple. Calvin shifted uneasily in his chair, once again acutely aware of the house's deathly silence and of his solitude.

He shook his head at himself. Letting himself get spooked out wasn't going to solve anything. He forced his mind back onto the problem at hand.

As he looked over the trust again, the year 2008 leaped out at him. Why did that seem so familiar? Someone had just mentioned that year, hadn't they?

It took him a moment to remember that it was he himself who had brought up the year when he was talking to Cynthia earlier. That had been the date on the strangely recent battery in Mr. May's Thunderbird, the car that according to evidence in the later case files, Mr. May hadn't driven in nearly a decade.

His excitement over this new connection was short-lived. Though the link was intriguing and suggestive, it didn't really tell him anything new. It merely reiterated that something significant seemed to have happened in 2008, something that had perhaps compelled Mr. May to drive somewhere. And even then, Calvin couldn't be certain that the car battery and the amended trust were indeed connected.

Given the scanty information available there seemed to be no way for Calvin to solve the riddle of the trust. Of course, it was possible that one of Mr. May's old cronies had the answer, and Calvin supposed he could crack open the Rolodex on the desk and start tracking down Albert Korowicz and Melody Gardner and all the rest of them, assuming any of them were even still alive. But he wasn't sure he was brave enough to start cold-calling strangers over something like this, and in any case he felt sure that whatever secret lay behind this, it was something Mr. May hadn't shared with anyone. Calvin remembered Mr. May's funeral and the curious, assessing looks he had gotten from some of the weird out-of-towners who had shown up. They had been as mystified by Mr. May's decision as Calvin himself had been.

But there was one person who was definitely worth tracking down, whether she knew the whys and wherefores or not: Ms. Tiffany Fish. Whoever she was, she had entered these documents at the same time as Calvin and the Crows, so presumably they all shared some larger connection. In all likelihood she, too, would be ignorant of the nature of that connection. But that didn't matter. She was linked to them somehow, and Calvin was determined to learn who she was. Seeing her name on the shortlist of major beneficiaries in the trust made Calvin feel like an amnesiac uncovering a clue to his unremembered past.

Setting the folders on the floor, he extracted Mr. May's Rolodex from the mess on the desk and flipped through it to the Fs, wondering as he did so about the identities of all the people listed therein. The Rolodex was crammed so full the lid would barely shut, and most of the names were ones Calvin didn't recognize.

Finally, between "Fiorentino, Giuseppe" (who lived in Milan, Italy) and the now-familiar "Fivecrows, Jack" (who, interestingly, had two addresses listed, one in Flagstaff, the other someplace called the Cactus Gulch Advanced Research Facility), Calvin found what he sought: "Fish, Tiffany and Andrew."

They lived at 714 Revere Place in Kingwood. Calvin plucked a Bard County map book from one of the shelves of reference books and looked up Revere Place. It was in southern Kingwood, eight blocks south of where Brad Vallance had been killed the other night. A pretty posh neighborhood, if Calvin remembered right.

It was convenient that it was so close to the crime scene. Tomorrow, after he and Cynthia had investigated Brad Vallance's death, they would zip right down to Revere Place and find out whatever there was to find out about the mysterious Ms. Fish.

5

"There it is," Calvin said. "That's the place."

It was the following afternoon. Calvin and Cynthia were heading east down Train Avenue in Kingwood, Cynthia driving her new Prius with the purse-lipped care of a ninety-year-old woman. Reluctantly swiveling her eyes from the midday traffic around them, she followed Calvin's pointing finger to a long, five-storey brick building coming up on the right. A sign above the glass front doors read "West Train Apartments." An alley separated the near side of the building from the antique store next door. Glancing down the alley as they passed, they saw only dumpsters, windows, graffiti-covered brick walls.

"Are you sure that's the right alley?" Cynthia asked.

"It must be," Calvin said. "I don't see any other alleys."

"Huh. I was expecting something more. Swarms of cops, or crowds of reporters, or at least police tape everywhere."

"Same here. Then again, it's been thirty-six hours since the murder. I guess that kind of makes it old news by now."

The parking lot on the far side of the building was barely half full. Bypassing numerous parking spaces amid the rows of cars, Cynthia drove to an area almost devoid of vehicles at the back of the lot. She pulled the Prius into an open space surrounded by other open spaces, then braked.

As Cynthia's hand moved to the gear shift, Calvin unlatched his seat belt and reached for the door handle, ready to get to work. Much to his surprise, instead of putting the car into Park, she shifted into Reverse and began to back out of the space.

"What are you doing?" he asked.

"It's crooked."

"It is?" He peered out his window at the yellow line below. "No, it's not."

"Yeah, it is. A little bit."

"So what? People park crooked all the time."

The car now fully backed out, she put it in Drive and began to inch into the space again, her gaze bouncing back and forth between the yellow lines.

"If it's crooked," she said, "there's a better chance someone might bump into it."

"Who's gonna bump into it? Who's even gonna park back here? We're fifty miles from the nearest vehicle."

She braked, then leaned forward and peered over the hood and out the side windows to make sure the car was straight.

"We're fine," Calvin said, growing annoyed. "We don't have time for this. We have work to do. The sooner we get it done, the sooner you can return your delicate little vehicle to the safety of its isolation chamber."

She smiled thinly at him.

"No need to be snarky." She put the car into Park, much to Calvin's immense relief, then said, "I mean, I apologize if I actually give a crap about my vehicle and refuse to let it deteriorate until rusty pieces are falling off of it."

"It was just that once," Calvin muttered.

"When was the last time you even ran it through a car wash?"

Calvin opened his mouth to answer. Then, realizing that the answer was last year, he changed the subject:

"Let's just get going. We have a busy afternoon ahead of us."

They got out and Calvin slung his black messenger bag over his shoulder. The bag contained his investigator's kit, a variety of items he thought might be helpful in their investigations, everything from a flashlight to a set of lock-picking tools, a compass to a pair of needle-nose pliers. He had originally envisioned keeping everything in an attaché case, mainly because he thought it would look cool, but after some experimentation he found an attaché case impractical and switched to the messenger bag, whose numerous pockets and compartments helped organize the items in the kit and saved him a lot of pointless rummaging.

Meanwhile Cynthia clipped on a white belt pack, which contained a stripped-down version of Calvin's kit, she being of the opinion that he would never use two-thirds of the junk he was lugging around. The belt pack contained only a notebook, a pen, a high-quality digital camera, a few pairs of latex gloves, a mini-Maglite, and a dozen plastic baggies for evidence.

"So what's our game plan here?" she said as they crossed the lot to the far side of the building where the alley was. "The front doors will probably be locked, you know. We'd need someone to buzz us in, and finding someone to do that probably won't be easy."

"Let's take a look at the alley before anything else. We can only cross one bridge at a time. A look at the alley might convince us not to pursue the matter any further."

She glanced at him. "You don't think that'll happen, though, do you?"

"I've got a good feeling about this."

"About what?"

"This. This case. I mean, the very day we graduate and can finally start investigating stuff, this case drops right into our laps. And at the same time it looks like we might have a new member of the team. And suddenly, after five years we have a lead on the mystery of our inheritances. It just feels like everything's coming together."

"Not for Brad Vallance."

"No," he conceded. "I suppose not."

The alley where Brad Vallance died was a tall brick corridor that received no more than an hour of direct sunlight even at the height of summer, and the moment Calvin and Cynthia stepped into its gloom their arms were studded with goose-bumps. At first glance the alley looked no different from any other alley in the city. The ground was gray concrete zigzagged with cracks. Rows of windows lined the walls above the first floors. A trio of dumpsters stood against the wall of West Train Apartments. Virtually every vertical surface within arm's reach was bright with graffiti. At the far end of the alley pedestrians and traffic moved about in the sunshine on Winchester Street; from the chilly twilight in which Calvin and Cynthia now stood, the bright vista of roadway was like a glimpse of another world.

A closer examination of the alley revealed small irregularities which hinted at recent events. There was no litter anywhere. No cigarette butts, no beer cans, no candy wrappers, nothing. And although it hadn't rained in close to a week, the pavement and the lower stretches of the brick walls were still slightly dark from having recently been wetted. Dirty puddles filled the depressions and crevices in the old, uneven concrete.

"Jesus," Cynthia muttered. "It looks like they had to hose everything down all the way to the second floor."

She glanced down the alley. "And most of the way to the back of the building."

"It must have been like an abattoir in here."

Calvin unzipped one of the compartments of his messenger bag and pulled out a pair of latex gloves. He snapped them on, then lifted the black plastic lids of the dumpsters one by one.

"They're all empty," he said. "Too empty. Even after trash day, there's usually junk clinging to the interior. These have been stripped clean."

"The cops probably took all the trash to search through it." She looked up at the building's walls, then out the mouth of the alley, then said, "Hmm."

"What?"

"No lights," she said. "No security lights on the buildings and no street lamps. It must be really dark here at night. The killer must have had pretty good night vision."

"Or pretty bad, considering the messiness."

"I don't know. To take down a grown man like that, without any screams or obvious commotion…"

"The news said one of the residents heard something."

"'Unusual noises,' wasn't it? Whatever that means. But according to the news only one resident heard anything, and whatever they heard, it wasn't alarming enough to prompt them to call the cops."

"I wonder who the resident was," Calvin said, looking up at the apartment building's windows. "I'd love to talk to him, or her." His eyes dropped to a piece of graffiti in front of him, a string of thick, angular, conjoined letters done in silver with black highlights. It took him a moment to decipher the eccentric writing: "King of Heartz." Directly below that "Tick-Talk" had been written in simple blue spray paint, the letters looking skinny and amateurish next to the chunky, stylized writing above it.

Calvin grunted, then looked down the alley at Winchester Street. "Come on, let's check out farther down."

They slowly made their way toward Winchester Street. There was a brown metal door near the back of the antique store. After glancing around to make sure no one was watching, Calvin tried the knob. It was locked. They headed on. Halfway down, a fenced-in area on the left divided West Train Apartments from a building on Winchester Street. The fence's gate was padlocked and too tall to see over, but there were gaps between some of the wooden boards, offering glimpses of a small, weedy field, which, like the alley, was conspicuously litter-free. The whole area had been picked clean by the cops. There was a similar fenced-in area across the alley but without any convenient gaps to look through. This fence's door was padlocked, too.

They continued on between Winchester Street's buildings, which were similar to those on Train Avenue: brick walls, windows, graffiti. The two brown dumpsters that sat there were as empty as those at the other end of the alley.

Stepping out into the spring warmth and sunshine on Winchester Street, they found themselves between Emperor's Gate Chinese Restaurant and Abracadabra Lock and Key Service. Each first-floor business was surmounted by a couple of floors of apartments. Through the restaurant's plate-glass windows diners sat and ate and talked and laughed as though someone hadn't recently been butchered a couple hundred feet away.

Calvin and Cynthia headed back down the alley. As they neared Train Avenue, Calvin took his digital camera from his kit.

"There isn't much left to take pictures of," Cynthia

said.

"No, but it can't hurt to have some photos of the area just to capture the layout. Plus the graffiti, too. Given that those two missing kids were graffitists..." He shrugged. "I know it's kind of a long shot, but it might be worthwhile to take note of what's on the walls."

He spent the next few minutes taking pictures of the alley from different angles, of the dumpsters, of the puddles, and finally of the graffiti.

"Not much to go on," Cynthia said as Calvin stashed his camera back in his bag.

"No." He glanced up at the apartment windows above them. "We should try to find some way inside to talk to the residents. We could say we're reporters or something."

"Is that really a good idea?"

"What else are we supposed to do? If we're going to investigate strange phenomena, we need to, you know, investigate. Which means asking questions. Interviewing."

"Yeah, but it's one thing if we're just investigating a UFO sighting, or a haunting, or an out-of-place animal, or something like that. It's different when a crime's been committed. Especially murder. The cops don't look too kindly on amateurs nosing around in their business. We learned that back in college."

"Yeah, but we made it through that okay, didn't we?"

"Barely. It was just dumb luck we didn't get hauled off to jail."

"It wasn't luck. It was quick thinking."

"It was luck that it worked out as well as it did."

Calvin gave a small, irritated gasp. "So, what, you think we should just give up on this one?"

"No. I'm just saying we should try to be more circumspect, that's all. Conniving our way into a locked apartment building and banging on strangers' doors is probably not the wisest approach."

A chirpy voice above their heads said, "You wouldn't learn very much that way anyway, you know."

They looked up, startled. An elderly woman was peering down at them from an open second-storey window. Her white hair was fine and thin. A pair of tortoise-shell granny glasses framed her crinkle-cornered green eyes. Her smiling mouth was neatly lipsticked. The faux-pearl clip-on earrings she wore complemented the faux-pearl necklace swaying from her stringy neck.

"I'm sorry?" Calvin said.

"Nobody here knows anything," the woman told them. "Except me, of course."

"You saw something?" Cynthia said.

"No."

"Oh."

"But I heard things."

"Oh!"

"I can tell you all about it, if you like. Come around to the front door. I'll buzz you in." She started to disappear inside, then stopped. "Oh." She reemerged. "Apartment 24A." She slipped inside, and a pair of daisy-print curtains fluttered back into place, hiding the interior from view.

Calvin smiled at Cynthia and gestured at the window.

"See?" he said. "It's just like I said: Everything's coming together."

"Let's just get to the front door before she changes her mind. Or forgets about the whole thing."

They hurried around to the front door. The outer door was unlocked and led to a small vestibule whose inner door was locked. Next to the door was a speaker above rows of buttons, each of which was labeled with an apartment number and a name. Calvin found the button marked "24A – Romero, B" and pressed it.

"Um, we're here," he said into the intercom. "From the alley?"

The intercom gave a brief buzz and the interior door unlocked with a quick, sharp clack.

Cynthia grabbed it and pulled it open, and they went inside. Across the lobby was a hallway that ran the length of the building. There, they turned right and headed down to 24A, the last apartment on the right. As they approached, the apartment door, which had been cracked, opened wide, revealing the old lady, who was clad in a navy-blue dress with white lace trim at the collar and cuffs, black stockings, and white orthopedic shoes. She was small and stooped and thin, no more than five feet tall and ninety pounds. But though small and old, she looked healthy and alert, and she seemed delighted to see them.

She shuffled backward, drawing the door back with her, and waved them inside.

"Come in," she said, sounding as happy as if they were her own long-lost children returning home after decades away. "Come in. Would you like anything to eat or drink? I have iced tea."

"No, thank you," Cynthia said.

She looked doubtful. "Are you sure?"

"Yes, we just ate."

"Oh." She sounded disappointed. "Well, just tell me if you change your mind."

She led them down a short hallway and into a cluttered but cozy living room that smelled of potpourri and baked beans. Floral prints dominated everything. The sofa, where Calvin and Cynthia were directed to sit, featured roses on a white background. The rocking chair that their hostess settled into sported daffodils on dark blue. The curtains in the front window matched the daisied curtains in the alley window. The walls were decorated with cross-stitch images of farms and flowers and butterflies and aphorisms like "Home Is Where the Heart Is" and "God Bless This Humble Home." Above the couch was a knickknack shelf lined with bud vases and ceramic bunnies and a few framed photos that showed a younger Ms. Romero with a balding man who had glasses and a long, thick nose.

"I'm Betty," she said once everyone was settled.

"Nice to meet you," Cynthia said. "I'm Cynthia. This is Calvin."

"Hi," Calvin said.

"You're trying to solve that poor man's death, aren't you?" Betty said, then briskly went on before either of them could reply: "Well, of course you are. I could tell from the way you were chatting back there in the alley. And pardon me for overhearing, but with you right there and my window right here and the window being open and all, I really couldn't help it, now could I? And judging by what little teensy bits of conversation I accidentally overheard you saying I'm guessing you're not regular run-of-the-mill investigators either, not like police officers or private eyes or anything like that. You investigate weird, scary things, like on that TV show, right?"

"Which show is that?" Calvin said as pleasantly as he could, hoping his annoyance at the question was tucked well out of sight. Why did everyone always compare them to a TV show? He wondered which one it would be this time: *The X-Files? Supernatural?* Or maybe it would be *Ghost Hunters*.

"Oh, what was that called?" Betty thought for a moment, her brows drawn down. Then she brightened again. "Oh, yes. *The Night Stalker.* George, my husband, loved that silly show, God rest his soul."

"Sort of like that, yeah," Calvin said. *The Night Stalker,* eh? That was a new one.

"But rest assured, you two don't remind me of that fellow on the show. What was his name? MacGuffin, or something like that. The fellow with the hat. And thank heavens you don't, either. He was such a smart-mouthed sort. Too clever by half, I say. So full of himself. Not like you two. You two seem like lovely young folks. It's such a relief to meet nice folks like you. It seems like there aren't enough people like that around anymore." She heaved a sad sigh. "Lots of bad sorts running around these days. Bad sorts and bad happenings. The world is getting mighty strange and mighty ugly. I mean, just look at what happened to that poor man in the alley. Right outside my window, too."

"You said you heard something that night?" Calvin said.

"Oh, yes. I'm the only one here who heard anything. The police officers came back to ask me questions three times. I'm the only one they were interested in talking to. Except Ms. Ruddy, of course, poor girl. She's gone to stay with her parents now. Don't know if she'll ever be back. But she didn't know anything about the attack. I was the only one, thanks to my sleep troubles. Hardly anyone's in the building on a Friday night anymore anyway. Not even Mr. Garrett. Nearly eighty now and he spends every Friday night in a bar until the small hours. Comes bumping down the hallway stinking of beer and cigarettes and waking everyone up. The most shocking part is, he used to be a schoolteacher. Eighth grade science, I think it was."

"So, um, what exactly was it that you heard in the alley

the other night?" Calvin asked. He was a little afraid she would get snappish or dejected that he had interrupted her ramble, but she veered happily down this new path without a peep of protest.

"Well, I had just gone to bed and was trying to get to sleep, and I heard a woman's voice shout, 'Brad! Wait!'"

"Christine Ruddy," Cynthia said.

"Maybe."

"Maybe?"

She held up a finger. "Listen. After that I heard some murmurs of conversation, a little too low for me to make out, even though these old windows are horribly thin. You wouldn't believe how thin they are. And single panes, too. We get ice on the insides of the windows in the dead of winter. Gets very cold. No matter how often I complain to the management, they never do anything about it. Though in a way, it's not so bad, because quite frankly I sleep much better when it's colder. I used to have such arguments with George about the thermostat."

"I can imagine," Cynthia said. "So how long did the conversation in the alley go on?"

"Oh, not long at all. Probably not even thirty seconds. Then it stopped, and there was a very faint click-clack click-clack, like dressy shoes walking on the concrete down below. It's a sound I've heard plenty of times before, of course. Everybody and his Aunt Fanny uses that alley, it seems, and always when I'm trying to get to sleep. Oh, the noise can get terrible. Especially those ladies with their heels. Clockety-clock clockety-clock. It's enough to wake the dead."

"What about those dress shoes the other night?" Calvin prompted. "What happened with them?"

"Well, after the steps had click-clacked a little ways, I

heard the same voice say the same thing I heard before: 'Brad! Wait!' And the darnedest part is, it was exactly the same. Exactly. Like an echo or something. It was very peculiar."

Calvin and Cynthia sat forward excitedly.

"An echo?" Calvin said.

"Yes," Betty said, sitting forward too, excited by their excitement. "It was exactly the same. Same voice, same rhythm, same…whatever you call it. Intonation, or whatever. Like a recording playing back. Exactly."

"What happened then?" Calvin asked.

"Then comes another weird thing. I heard a sort of clip-clop sound."

"Like the dress shoes?"

"No. Like horses."

"Horses?"

"Like hoofs. Clip-clop, clip-clop."

"Are you sure it wasn't just Brad Vallance's dress shoes, only echoing funny or something?" Cynthia asked.

Betty tutted, looking a little disappointed that Cynthia would ask such a thing. It made Cynthia squirm guiltily on the couch.

"That's exactly what the police thought," Betty said. "They thought I couldn't tell a shoe from a hoof." She shook her head at the awfulness of it. "But I know hoofs. I grew up on a farm in Freedom Township. And trust me, I know hoofs. And this was a hoof. Clip-clop, clip-clop. Not click-clack. Completely different. And it wasn't any cutting tool either. That's something else the police thought it might be. They refused to even consider the possibility that I might know what it is I'm hearing. They were making up malarkey theories that the clip-clop was actually the sound of, I don't know, a giant pair of scissors that someone was using to cut up that poor man down there. But it was hoofs, I tell you. It wasn't a tool, and it wasn't a clip-clop of just one pair of feet, either. Oh, no. It was four legs with hoofs. Like a horse. Or maybe a goat."

"Well, what happened after you heard the, uh, the hoofs," Cynthia said.

"Then I heard another voice, a woman's voice, maybe the same one I heard earlier. It was quieter than before, though, and hard to hear over the clip-clops. I think it said something about tomorrow."

"Tomorrow?" Calvin said.

"Mm-hmm. And then after that I heard a sort of thumpy noise like something falling over down there. I figured it was just a trash bag falling out of the dumpster. That happens a lot, you know. Those dumpsters fill up awful fast. It's shocking how much people throw out these days. In my day, we'd find ways to keep using things and reusing things. These days, once the shine's off something, people think it's time to throw it away. So wasteful." She shook her head. "Management really needs to add more dumpsters."

"It sure sounds like it," Calvin agreed. "Did you hear anything after the thump?"

"Oh, yes. For a while there were all sorts of, well, eating noises."

"Eating noises?"

"Chomps and slurps and such. I couldn't hear it all that well, even with the thin window, but I'm sure that's what it was. I've heard similar noises before. Sometimes we get stray dogs gobbling up the garbage back there after it's fallen out of the dumpster. Oh, I do so wish management would add another dumpster or two."

"Definitely," Cynthia said.

"Anyhow, figuring it was just some stray mutt having itself a nice gristly T-bone or something, I started drifting off to sleep again. But just when I was on the verge of falling asleep, the gobbling stopped and I heard the clip-clop, clip-clop again, only this time moving away down the alley. It got quieter and quieter, then faded away, and I fell asleep."

"Um, I don't mean to offend," Calvin said, "but are you positive you really heard what you think you heard, and that you weren't actually, say, slipping in and out of sleep and maybe only dreaming parts of it?"

Betty clucked her tongue and looked at Calvin sadly, as if she had hoped for better from such a nice lad like him. Calvin found himself squirming guiltily just as Cynthia had a minute earlier.

"That's exactly what those policemen asked me," Betty said. "And like I told them: Yes, I'm sure. I'd like to think I'm old enough to know the difference between being asleep and being awake. And trust me, I know hoofs, too."

"Understood," Calvin said. "But I had to ask just to make sure."

"Well, I suppose that's something you have to do," Betty conceded grudgingly. "That's proper scientificness, I suppose. Better than the police, at any rate. They sure weren't being very scientific. Why, they just out-and-out ignored me when I said the second voice was a perfect echo. They didn't bother asking me about it at all. They probably just thought it was someone repeating themselves in a normal way, and I was just foolish or half deaf. But I know echoes, just as sure as I know hoofs."

"When you say the voice was like an echo," Cynthia said, "did it match in *every* way? I mean, there wasn't *anything* different about it?"

Betty opened her mouth, apparently to say yes, then paused and said, "Well, come to think of it, it was a little louder. A little closer. But otherwise, yes, it was exactly the same."

"But closer. That's interesting." She looked around. "Do you mind if we take a look out the window where you heard all this?"

Betty looked doubtful. "Well, it's my bedroom. I don't normally let strangers in there." She hesitated a moment, then patted her knees. "But for you two, I think I can make an exception." She waggled a finger at them. "Just as long as you don't go peeking at things you shouldn't."

"We'll keep our minds on the job. Don't worry."

Betty led them to her bedroom, which continued the floral motif: roses on the bedspread; sunflowers on the rocking chair in the corner; a whole botanical garden's worth of flowers on a nightgown hanging on a hook on the closet door. On the walls were half a dozen more framed cross-stitch pictures, the largest, positioned above the head of the bed, showing a pasture full of fluffy white sheep with a big yellow sun above containing the words "The Lord is my shepherd."

There was only one window in the bedroom, the one with the daisy curtains, and it was still wide open. A faint stink of exhaust drifted through it into the bedroom, where it was quickly overwhelmed by the more pleasant scent of the potpourri that sat in a bowl on the dresser.

Calvin and Cynthia pushed the curtains aside and stuck their heads out. From here, ten feet up, they had a decent overview of the alley. The full breadth of the wet area was clearer. Its epicenter was directly below them.

"It must've happened right under her window," Cynthia said.

"Yeah." Calvin looked around. One of the distorted, angular pieces of graffiti on the alley's far wall, which he had been unable to read at ground level, was now fore-shortened and surprisingly legible. The huge black-outlined red words read "Nobody's Bitch!"

Calvin looked toward the alley's Train Avenue entrance. The row of dumpsters stood between Betty's window and the alley's mouth.

"Okay," he said, speaking too low for Betty to hear him, "so Brad Vallance enters the alley. Before he gets far, his girlfriend pops up to call him back."

"'Brad, wait' number one."

"Right. She leaves. He heads back down the alley, click-clack click-clack, and then..."

"'Brad, wait' redux, only louder."

"Then clip-clop, clip-clop, something about tomor-row—"

"And thump." Cynthia twisted around in the window to look back at Betty, who stood a couple of paces behind them, looking vaguely worried, as if she feared they might slip and fall out the window.

"How long did the clip-clopping noise last the first time you heard it?" she asked Betty.

"Oh, just a couple seconds."

"It wasn't traveling down the whole length of the alley like it was the second time?"

"No."

Now Calvin turned and looked back through the cur-tains at Betty.

"Just how much time did you say passed between the first and second times you heard 'Brad, wait'?"

"Not too long. Maybe ten seconds."

"And it was closer the second time, too," he muttered.

He and Cynthia turned forward to look at the alley again. "Which means it was coming from further inside the alley, rather than at its mouth."

"And that came *before* the first of the clip-clops," Cynthia said.

"Right. Which means that whoever or whatever was talking and doing all that clip-clopping was already in the alley down there."

"Maybe in a dumpster? Or behind the dumpsters?"

"Possibly." Calvin turned to look at Betty again. "Had you just gotten into bed when you heard this stuff?"

"Why, yes. Yes, I did."

"Where were you before that?"

"Well, you know..." Looking embarrassed, Betty planted a hand to her upper chest. "In the bathroom." She whispered the latter word as if it were a dirty word. "I took my bath, and, you know, other things."

"And then you came right in here and went to bed?"

"Yes."

"Can you hear sounds from the alley in the bathroom?"

"Oh, no. The bathroom's not against the alley."

"Okay." He looked out the window again.

"So?" Cynthia said.

"Just establishing that the clip-clopper could have had an opportunity to get into position without Betty hearing it." He glanced behind him to make sure Betty wasn't too near, then lowered his voice to a barely audible murmur. "Although frankly, I'm still not convinced that the police's theory is wrong. Given the weirdness of the injuries, it's entirely conceivable that they were made by some kind of bizarre, home-made cutting implement with a unique sound."

"Why don't we discuss it more once we're out of here," Cynthia whispered.

"Agreed."

They withdrew from the window and turned to Betty.

"Thank you so much, Ms. Romero," Calvin said, smiling. "You've helped us out quite a bit."

He had hoped his smile and kind words would make Betty feel proud and helpful. Instead she looked dismayed, as if their imminent departure were a deviation from the way things were meant to go.

"Oh!" she said. "Well, I…I'm glad. But…"

"Yeah, thanks for everything," Cynthia said with a kindly, grateful smile that she hoped would assuage the old woman's distress. It didn't seem to have much of an effect. Cynthia felt a twinge of guilt about abandoning Betty to her lonely, husbandless apartment again, but what choice did they have? They couldn't sit here and let her talk their ears off all day. "We need to get going now. We have a lot more to do if we hope to solve this case."

"But…"

Calvin and Cynthia strode out of the bedroom and toward the front door. Betty hurried after them, still looking dismayed.

At the door Calvin and Cynthia turned and smiled at Betty once again.

"Thanks again," Calvin said.

"But…" Betty said.

"Yeah," Cynthia agreed. "You've been a huge help."

Calvin put his hand on the knob and started to turn it.

"But don't you want to hear about how the alley's haunted?" Betty blurted out.

Calvin and Cynthia froze dead, looked at each other, then turned to look at Betty.

"What?" Calvin said.

"Oh, yes. The alley's haunted. Sort of. I think. It started after Mr. Bradley killed himself."

"Bradley?" Calvin looked at Cynthia. She just shrugged, as baffled as he was. "You mean Bradley Vallance?"

"No, Simon Bradley," Betty said. "He lived in 12E." Noting their utter befuddlement, she backed toward the living room and motioned for them to follow. "Come. Sit. I'll tell you all about it. Are you sure you wouldn't like something to nibble on? Or a nice drink? If you don't like iced tea, I have ginger ale. And milk."

"Uh, no. We're fine, thanks."

They all trooped back to the living room and sat down where they had sat before.

"So…" Cynthia frowned, trying to puzzle out what Betty had just revealed. "Some guy named Simon Bradley committed suicide in apartment 12A?"

"12E, dear. Top floor."

"Who was he? Was he a friend of yours or something?"

"Oh, no. I barely knew him. He was a young fellow, about your age. I think he was in college. I really don't know much about him."

"Except that he killed himself," Calvin said.

"That's right."

"When was this, exactly?"

Betty thought hard. "Well, let's see. It was just a year before George passed on. So that would have been…" A pause, then: "2008."

Calvin and Cynthia looked at each other, amazed. He had told her on the drive here about his discoveries in the office last night, including how Mr. May had first added them to his trust in 2008, the same year the battery had been installed in the Thunderbird.

"There were strange doings and loud voices in the alley on the night of Mr. Bradley's death, too," Betty said. "It's all a little bit hazy after so long, but I remember that George and I had been getting ready to go to bed when we heard the sounds of a scuffle and some shouts from the alley down below. I heard the word, 'No,' and then a few seconds later I heard, 'I did it.' It was a woman's voice each time, though I couldn't tell if it was the same woman or two different ones. And in between the two voices we heard a faint bang, which George immediately recognized as a gunshot. He had done a lot of hunting in his day, you know. Never caught a whole lot, as I recall. A few rabbits and pheasants here and there. I suspect he took his little hunting trips just to get away from it all for a few hours and spend some time in the great outdoors. He needed it, too. Worked a hard job. Construction. The foreman was a real ogre. A slave-driver, George always called him. Drank way too much. The foreman that is, not George. He'd show up drunk after lunch and shout at the men for no reason at all."

"That sounds pretty bad," Cynthia agreed. "So what happened after you heard the voices and the gunshot?"

"Well, not more than ten minutes later an ambulance shows up out front, and it turns out that poor Mr. Bradley shot himself."

"Had the noises in the alley stopped by then?" Calvin asked.

"Oh, yes. That only lasted a minute or two. Like I said, it happened right around the same time as the gunshot. You'd think there might be some kind of connection between the two, but the police said there was no doubt Mr.

Bradley shot himself, right in the mouth and through the brain, no mistake about it, and in any case, he was halfway down the building and five floors up from whatever was going on in the alley. Besides, like I think I told you before, we get all kinds of folks traipsing up and down the alley at all hours, making the devil's own racket."

"So, um, how exactly is the alley haunted?" Calvin asked.

"Well, admittedly, I don't know if 'haunted' is exactly the right word. I just use that because I don't know a better one. But whatever you call it, it's the oddest thing. See, a few nights later George and I were in bed again, and I heard the exact same voices repeating the exact same things, plus the gunshot between them, only they were fainter, and kind of muffled and distorted, like I was hearing them from far away, or through layers. For a second I thought I had fallen asleep for a moment and had a weird little dream about what had already happened. But then George sat up next to me and grumbled, 'Didn't we already hear that?' Turned out he heard the exact same thing I did, which was the exact same thing we heard the night Mr. Bradley shot himself."

Calvin and Cynthia looked at each other.

"Echoes," Cynthia said. "Same as last night."

"No," Betty said with a firm shake of her head. "Not really. Well, I suppose it was the same in one sense, given that it was a sound that came again, but it wasn't really the same. With the 'no' and all that, it was—it was..." She winced a little as if she hated to say what she was about to say but had to say it anyway. "It was like I was hearing it in my head after that first time, like they weren't real sounds anymore. It was more like they were the ghosts of sounds, or the memories of sounds, if that makes any sense. But last night, that was a real voice repeating itself, in the real alley, I'm sure of that." She gave an embarrassed, self-conscious smile. "Am I making any sense?"

"I think so," Calvin said.

"Yeah," Cynthia said. "I get it. It's almost like the echo a few years ago was more of a psychic event, whereas last night it was definitely physical."

"Yes," Betty said. "That's about it. Except the echo a few years ago wasn't just one echo. It kept happening every so often. The same voices saying the same things, with the gunshot between them. But each time they were fainter and fainter and more and more muffled."

"How often did these echoes recur?" Calvin said.

"The period between them grew longer and longer as time went on. Like I told you, the first time it happened was just a few days after the original incident. The next time was maybe a week after that. Then two weeks. Then about a month. And so on, until we were hearing it only every six months or so, and barely hearing it at that, since the sounds had gotten so distant and fuzzy."

"And George kept hearing them, too?" Cynthia said.

"Oh, yes. He used to joke about it, though I think deep down it kind of scared him a little. He used to say, 'That darn Mr. Bradley and his girlfriends are at it again.'"

"Do you know if anyone else heard the sounds?"

"I asked a few folks in a roundabout kind of way if they'd been hearing any weird noises, but no one ever admitted to anything."

"Are you still experiencing these echoes?" Calvin asked.

"Oh, no. Not for a couple of years now. They just kind of faded away in the end. Whatever it was all about, everything seems back to normal now." She paused, then added, "Well, except last night. I suppose what happened last night is probably another aftereffect of the earlier incident, in its own queer way."

"How so?"

"Well, because weird stuff has already happened here. Even if we're not hearing the fuzzy voices anymore, stuff like that leaves traces, you know. Prints, like an animal's. Or a bad smell that lingers. Some folks are saying it was a crazy person who killed that man last night, and others are saying it was some kind of strange deformed animal, but either way it's someone or something mighty weird. And it stands to reason something weird would be drawn to a place that's already got the stink of weirdness about it. I mean, it's common sense, isn't it? Like calls to like. Weird calls to weird. It all converges." She cocked her head as if reflecting on what she had just said. Then, pleased with her assessment, she nodded and said it again. "It all converges."

6

"So what do you think?" Calvin asked Cynthia when they were back in the Prius ten minutes later. They had questioned Betty a little longer but had learned nothing else of note except that Betty was the only remaining resident in the building who had been there at the time of Simon Bradley's suicide. Even the management had changed twice since then. Which meant there was no one else they could interview about the incident. And since no one else knew anything about Brad Vallance's murder either, there was no point in sticking around any longer. But they could always come back: Betty assured them she'd be more than happy to buzz them in should they ever need to visit West Train Apartments again.

"What do I think about what?" Cynthia said. "Betty?"

"Yeah. About what she said."

Cynthia didn't answer for a moment, being too pre-occupied with safely starting the car and pulling out of the parking space.

"I hate to say it," she finally said as she navigated through the lot toward the exit, "but she seemed kind of desperate for someone to talk to. I can't help but wonder if she might have been tailoring her narrative to suit our interests so we'd hang around longer."

"What, you think she was making it all up?"

"Not everything. Not the basics. But I'm worried she might have, I don't know, embroidered things here and there to keep us Night Stalkers interested. I don't think we should uncritically take her word for everything."

"No, but it'll be hard to verify most of what she told us."

They turned onto Train Avenue and headed west. As they passed the mouth of the alley, Cynthia slowed down a little, and they stared into the dim brick corridor.

"What was it?" Cynthia said. "'No' and 'I did it'?"

"Yeah."

"Huh. I wonder who did what." She glanced at Calvin. "Do you think it even matters? Do you think it could be connected with the death of Brad Vallance?"

"I don't know. They're both strange events, and they happened in the same location, but they happened years apart and don't have any obvious causal connection. They both involve echoes, but in very different ways. They both involve someone dying, but again in very different ways." He shrugged. "It seems like there could be something there, or it could just be a complete coincidence. It's all so vague. For now I think we should just focus on Brad Vallance's death and not cast our net too wide, at least not without a better reason. One thing at a time."

"Yeah. Besides, psychic echoes don't carve men up like that. Someone or something very real did that."

Two blocks west of the apartment building, they turned south down Benton Road, which led straight to the Elm Hill neighborhood where the Fishes lived.

While they waited at a traffic light, Calvin noticed two children, a boy and a girl about five years old, playing in a front yard. The boy had a squirt gun and kept chasing the girl round and round the trunk of a massive old oak tree, their hysterical giggles audible even with the car's windows rolled up. Calvin watched them for a moment, then turned to Cynthia.

"I was wondering," he said, "when exactly did Emily start hanging out with John Coyote and Anna West?"

"Why?"

"Mr. May added us all to the trust in 2008, which would've made Emily only seven. I was wondering if she'd even started hanging out with those two yet."

"I don't know. They were all in the same grade at school, so they at least knew each other to some degree since kindergarten. I'm not exactly sure when John and Anna first entered the picture on a more serious basis. It was probably more of a gradual thing, you know? I don't remember them visiting the house until much later—when Emily was around eight or nine—but that doesn't mean they didn't, and I just didn't notice, or that she wasn't hanging out with them at school the whole time. It's just too hard to say. It's too hard to remember details from that long ago." The light changed, and she accelerated down Benton. She glanced over at Calvin. "What are you getting at anyway? That Mr. May knew in advance who Emily's friends would be? That he was, what, psychic? Or a time-traveller from the year 2100?"

"I'm just trying to think through all the angles. But who knows? Maybe during one of his investigations he *did* learn stuff about the future."

"It couldn't have been very reliable information, seeing as how he originally left the Collection and the house to Emily. If he'd really known the future, he would've known what was going to happen to her."

They came to Revere Place and turned left. Cynthia drove slowly so they could read the house numbers.

"Wow," Cynthia said. Over the last few blocks the homes had grown larger and larger, and by now they practically qualified as mansions. "I don't think the Fishes really needed Mr. May's hundred thousand dollars very much. Every house on this street probably costs at least five times that."

"Yeah." Calvin suddenly sat forward. "There it is." He pointed at a brick neo-Colonial coming up on the left. A plaque beside its front door read "714." A dark blue Audi S5 of recent vintage sat in the driveway.

Cynthia parked next to the Audi. They got out and headed to the front door.

"Do we have a game plan here?" she asked.

"Just tell the truth, I guess. No need for guile or rehearsals."

"Do we want to admit that we investigate strange phenomena?"

"Let's wait and see where the conversation takes us.

For all we know, this guy could be some old acquaintance of Mr. May's who already knows the truth."

"Fair enough." She rang the bell.

The door was answered by a well-dressed middle-aged man with glasses, a mustache, and brown hair that was going white at the temples in a way that reminded Calvin of Mr. Fantastic from the Fantastic Four.

He quickly looked Calvin and Cynthia up and down and said, "Can I help you?" in a tone both brusque and remote, as if he suspected they were solicitors but wanted to confirm it before shutting the door in their faces.

"Yeah," said Calvin. "We're looking for Tiffany Fish."

The man stiffened, suddenly looking suspicious.

"What is it you wish to see her about?" he asked.

Calvin and Cynthia glanced at each other.

"Um, that's kind of complicated," said Calvin.

The man raised one eyebrow.

"I have time," he said, his tone conveying that he was more than willing to stand there until they gave him a full explanation.

Calvin decided to mirror the man's stiff, formal demeanor as best he could; in his experience it was easier to gain someone's sympathies if they saw a bit of themselves in you.

"It is my understanding that five years ago Ms. Fish was the recipient of one-hundred thousand dollars, left to her by a Mr. Robert May of May, Ohio."

The man's tight, wary look went slack with surprise.

"Yes," he said, his voice excited and urgent. "Do you know something about that?"

"Yes. He left money to us, as well."

"Not only that," said Cynthia. "But we actually knew him. In fact—"

Before she could say more, the man stepped aside and said, "Come in. Please."

They stepped into a long, spacious hall with a checkerboard floor and a high ceiling hung with a pair of crystal chandeliers. Doors and archways led off it to various rooms and corridors.

The man led them through a door on the left and into a large office dominated by dark woods and black leather. An executive desk faced the door, a computer humming softly upon it next to a neat stack of papers. Behind the desk hung a variety of diplomas, awards, and certifications made out to Andrew Fish, Esq. The centerpiece of the display was a diploma from Harvard Law School. The other walls bore framed prints of golfing and hunting scenes, plus several bookshelves that contained binders and folders rather than books. Two framed photos sat at the near edge of the desk, facing out for guests to see. One showed the man—much younger and without the mustache—with an attractive blonde woman, he in a tux, she in a bridal gown, their beaming faces pressed cheek to cheek. The other showed a little blonde girl about five years old, posing regally in a pink princess costume, her nose in the air, her blue eyes cool and haughty, her prim lips pressed tight.

The man gestured at a pair of black leather chairs in front of the desk.

"Please, have a seat," he said. He started to circle around the desk to the bigger black leather chair behind it, then stopped with a soft grunt and turned around, his hand extended.

"I apologize for my unforgivably lax manners," he said. "You kind of caught me by surprise here. I'm Andrew Fish."

"Calvin."

"Cynthia."

"Nice to meet you both," Fish said.

They all sat down.

"So you actually knew Robert May?" Fish said as he quickly shifted the stack of papers from the desktop to a drawer.

"Somewhat," Calvin said. "I met him only a few days before he passed away. Cynthia here knew him a bit better."

"Not by much, admittedly," Cynthia said. "I lived next to him my whole life but barely exchanged half a dozen words with him until that final week."

Fish's eyes brightened with recognition.

"Ah," he said. "I should have realized it earlier. You're Cynthia Crow, right? Your sister...I remember that incident well. I'm sorry for your loss."

"Thanks. I'm a little surprised you would recognize me, though. I wasn't really in the news that much."

"No, but, um..." Fish looked uncomfortable. "I did look into the situation fairly closely. With Robert May's death occurring so soon after your sister's, and with her abduction having occurred on his property, I couldn't help wondering if there was some connection between the two. Did you both receive a hundred thousand like Tiffany?"

"I did," Cynthia said. "And so did everyone in my family. But Calvin..."

"He left me one million plus his house," Calvin said.

Fish raised his eyebrows, impressed. "You're lucky. That's a nice house."

"You've seen it?"

He nodded. "A few months after Tiffany received the inheritance, I stopped by there one day, just out of curiosity. Nobody was home, and the house looked unoccupied—no car in the driveway, no lights on—so I just took a quick look around the outside and left." He smiled. "I assume you were probably in school at the time."

"Actually, I wasn't technically allowed to take possession until I graduated from college."

"Yes, it's the same thing with Tiffany. She won't be able to touch a cent of it for at least a few more years. She only just graduated from high school last week."

Calvin and Cynthia looked at each other, surprised. They'd been operating under the assumption that Tiffany was Andrew's wife. But no: She must be his daughter.

"Is that her there?" said Cynthia, indicating the photo of the little girl.

"Yes," he said, smiling warmly at the photo. "Although she's much bigger now, of course. That's, uh, that's an old picture." A cloud passed over his face, and his smile died. When he looked up at Calvin and Cynthia again, his expression was troubled and uncertain. "Do you have any idea why Mr. May chose to leave her that money?"

"Actually, we were hoping *you* could tell *us*," said Calvin.

Fish shook his head. "Before Tiffany's inheritance, I'd never even heard of Robert May. Neither had Tiffany. I sometimes wonder if he just picked her name out of a phone book at random."

"What about Tiffany's mother?" asked Cynthia with a glance at the wedding photo. Fish hadn't mentioned her at all, and he wasn't wearing a wedding band, which suggested that either Mrs. Fish was dead, or she and her husband had gotten divorced. "Could there be some connection on her end?"

Fish shook his head. "Not that I know of. Sarah died in childbirth. As far as I recall, she never mentioned Robert May. Or the city of May, for that matter. She wasn't even from around here. She was born and raised in California. She didn't move out here till 1997."

"I hate to say it," Calvin said, "but of all the people he left money to, your daughter seems to be the only one with no real connection to him at all."

Fish spread his hands in a display of helpless bafflement.

"You said you inherited his house," he said. "There wasn't anything in there that hinted at any possible explanation?"

"No, though I haven't gone through everything yet. It's possible there's something still tucked away in there that might explain everything. Otherwise, um..."

He glanced at Cynthia with a quick, questioning raise of his eyebrows. She intuited what he was asking and gave a small nod, albeit a bit grudgingly.

Calvin cleared his throat, then said to Fish, "Mr. May had an interest in what you might call anomalous phenomena: paranormal or just highly unusual events. Could that have something to do with it? Could you or Tiffany have come to his attention in that context?"

Fish briefly looked startled at this revelation. Then his face closed up like a cell door slamming shut.

"I don't think so," he said flatly.

It was clear he was hiding something. But given the terseness and finality of his tone, the matter seemed closed to further discussion. And yet a moment later Fish apparently reconsidered and continued to pursue the subject anyway.

"What, uh, what exactly did he do?" he asked, trying to sound casual, as if he were simply making conversation. But the hawk-like fixity with which he watched them belied his blasé tone. "Did he investigate these phenomena? Did he solve them, or explain them?"

"Sometimes," Calvin said. "He studied strange events and gathered evidence connected with them. Sometimes he was able to explain them, sometimes not. He almost seemed more interested in recording or cataloguing them than in anything else."

"I see." He gazed at them in silence for a moment, his expression distant and thoughtful. He opened his mouth to say something more, but just then a car pulled into the driveway.

Fish glanced in that direction—there was no window in the office that faced the driveway—then at Calvin and Cynthia. His mouth curled up slightly at the sides in what might have been a grimace, or a quick smile, or just a nervous tic.

"That must be Tiffany." He stood up. "I'll introduce you."

Calvin and Cynthia got up and followed him into the hall. Just as they got there the front door opened and Tiffany Fish walked in.

She was a far cry from the imperious little girl in the frilly pink princess gown. Her long blonde hair was drawn back into a ponytail with a simple black rubber band, though a number of stray wisps stuck out, forming a frizzy aureole around her head that shone goldenly in the light coming in through the front door's sidelights. She wore no makeup or jewelry, and her skin was unusually pale, as if she spent all her time indoors. She was dressed in an oversized, figure-obscuring black-and-white checked shirt which she wore unbuttoned like a jacket over a plain gray T-shirt, plus rumpled, loose-fitting blue jeans, and a pair of scruffy white New Balances with frayed laces.

When she saw the two strangers in the hall, she froze like a frightened rabbit, blinking, the plastic shopping bag she carried emitting a faint crackle as her fingers tightened around its handles.

Calvin, too, froze and blinked, but for a very different reason. Rather than anxiety or alarm, he felt something akin to déjà vu. The instant he laid eyes on Tiffany Fish he was struck to his core by a feeling of delighted recognition, as if this girl were someone special he had known long ago, or had been expecting to meet for a long time. A feeling of: *her*.

And then his college-trained rational faculties kicked in, and he mentally shook his head at himself. He had never seen this girl before in his life. He was sure of it. Perhaps she reminded him of someone he had once known and liked but didn't consciously remember—a childhood babysitter or a classmate at school. Or perhaps it really was déjà vu, only applied to a person rather than an event. (Was there a word for that, he wondered?) And surely it wasn't insignificant that the feeling (whatever it was) was inextricably bundled up with the fact that he was quite strongly attracted to her despite her frumpy, uncaring appearance.

Had he been a different sort of person he might have interpreted this remarkable and unprecedented reaction as love at first sight. But he was sure it wasn't love. How could it be? He didn't know anything about this girl, and you couldn't love someone you didn't know, except in a hippyish, all-embracing kind of way. Could you?

"Um, I'm home," Tiffany said quietly to her father,

though she was barely looking at him. Her eyes kept darting nervously back and forth between Calvin and Cynthia. She looked as if she wished she'd come home a lot later, preferably long after these two had left.

"How was the mall?" Andrew Fish asked.

For a moment she just kept staring at the strangers, her gaze now settling more and more on Calvin and flicking back to Cynthia almost as an afterthought. Then her father's question finally registered and she glanced at him and said, "It was mallish."

"Tiffany, this is Calvin and Cynthia."

"Um, hello," she mumbled.

"Hi," said Cynthia.

"Nice to meet you," Calvin said, unable to keep a big, broad smile from his face as he spoke to her for the first time. What the hell was this? Why was he feeling like this? Why couldn't he keep his eyes off her? It wasn't like him.

"You remember that money you got from that man, Robert May?" Fish said to Tiffany.

"Yes, of course."

"Calvin and Cynthia stopped by because they received similar inheritances and are hoping to learn the reasons behind it."

"Oh!" Tiffany peered closely at the duo, her shyness overridden by curiosity. "Fellow mystery giftees. I thought I was the only one."

"Nope," said Calvin. "You're one of an elite group. One of, um…" He quickly totted up the numbers in his head. "Nine."

"Nine?" Cynthia said. "Wait…"

"I'm not counting Violet. She wasn't one of the original, um, mystery giftees." He said this latter phrase with a smile and a small nod at Tiffany, as if to thank her for it.

He was disappointed to find that she hadn't even noticed. She was staring into space, her brows furrowed.

"Nine," she murmured. She bit her lip, the furrows deepening. Calvin noticed that the index finger of her left hand was twitching slightly as if she were unconsciously writing with it. "Nine…"

Andrew Fish cleared his throat loudly and said to his daughter, "They had to finish college first, too. Just like you."

"They had to too?" Tiffany muttered, still staring off into space, the comment only feeding into her strange reverie. "Had two too? Two, just like…" Tiffany looked up, all attention again. "Had to? Past tense?"

"Yeah, we just graduated yesterday," Calvin said.

"Congratulations." Her eyes drifted away again. "Congratulations," she mumbled. "Con grad you…you lay shuns? Elations? Con grad elations. Huh."

Calvin and Cynthia glanced at each other, not a little weirded out by all this. Andrew Fish looked uncomfortable, almost embarrassed by his daughter's behavior.

"Your dad told us you just graduated high school," Cynthia said to Tiffany, hoping to cut through the thicket of discomfort that had sprung up around them. "So congratulations to you, too."

Tiffany smiled politely.

"Thanks. Yes. I'm a rite of passage behind you." She looked down, her smile taking on a rueful tinge. "Whole mazes of passages, probably."

"Um, have you picked a college yet?" Calvin asked.

"I was thinking of Ames University." She said this with a wince and a small shrug as if it was an admission she found embarrassing. Perhaps it was. Ames U, while decent, seemed an unusually modest choice for the daughter of a bigwig lawyer. Either her academic history was pretty poor or she didn't want to travel far from home for some reason.

"Oh, that's where we went," said Cynthia.

Tiffany perked up, her interest piqued by this information.

"Really?" she said.

"Yep."

"Huh." She tilted her head to one side, her eyes narrowing to slits, and then in a melodramatic tone that might have been meant to be humorous but also might have been meant only to sound humorous to hide a deeper and potentially off-putting seriousness, she said, "It's *fate.*"

Something about her expression and the way she spoke those words struck some deep and joyful chord in Calvin's heart, or his soul, or his mating instinct, or whatever it was that was responding to her so powerfully, and he was barely able to keep himself from grinning in a dopey, giddy manner that was totally inappropriate in front of a girl you've just met and, more importantly, in front of said girl's father.

"Fate, huh?" he said.

Without otherwise changing her position or expression in any way, she swiveled her eyes from Cynthia's face to Calvin's, and in a decidedly non-melodramatic tone, a tone, in fact, that was plain and direct, as if she were reporting some commonplace piece of information, she said, "The world is made of secret connections."

This comment reminded Calvin of what Betty Romero had said near the end of their interview. Maintaining eye contact with Tiffany, he gave her a small nod and said, "It all converges."

Tiffany's head snapped upright, and she stared at him,

dumbstruck. Then she smiled a smile as huge and delighted as the one Calvin had been repressing. She looked as if she had finally heard the secret password she had been starting to think she would never hear.

"Yes!" she said, nodding vigorously. "That's exactly right!"

Cynthia couldn't help smiling a little herself, amused by the weird rapport Calvin and Tiffany were sharing. Clearly Calvin had found a new cute girl to obsess over. Usually these obsessions of his remained one-sided and doomed, but given how Ms. Fish was responding, this one could wind up having a very different outcome. Personally Cynthia found Tiffany's weird manner and pasty skin somewhat repellent, but if Calvin liked the girl, then good for him.

Cynthia wasn't the only one to notice Calvin and Tiffany's happy rapport. Glancing at Andrew Fish, she found that he was watching the duo with a stiff, humorless expression. Uh-oh.

Fish cleared his throat again, even more loudly than before.

"It's getting rather late," he said. "I imagine we've kept you here long enough."

Calvin and Tiffany finally broke eye contact. Calvin stared at Fish blankly for a moment, then realized what Fish had said and checked his watch.

"Oh," he said. "Yeah, I guess it is getting kind of late."

"But what about the inheritance?" Tiffany said. She looked at Calvin and Cynthia. "You haven't told me what you know about it."

"They told me all the details," said Andrew Fish. "I can fill you in later and—"

"But I want to hear it from *them*." She spoke in the

flat, demanding tone of someone ready to shut down the whole world to get her own way. This was a far cry from the bashful girl who'd come through the door five minutes earlier. Evidently the pink-clad princess wasn't entirely gone.

"Tiffany—" Fish started to say.

"I want to hear it," she said.

Father and daughter stared at each other, their expressions equally set and stubborn. Calvin and Cynthia realized they had somehow become the rope in a familial tug-of-war.

After several tense and silent seconds, Fish folded. Dropping his gaze from his daughter's, he waved his arm in a broad, sweeping gesture that said, "Go ahead; do something foolish."

In as brief and simple a manner as possible, Calvin told Tiffany what he and Cynthia had told her father earlier. Tiffany listened raptly, not interrupting once.

When he reached the end of the retelling, Calvin hesitated, unsure if he should do what his gut was telling him to do, then decided to forge ahead.

"Actually, Cynthia and I—we, uh, we're carrying on Mr. May's work," he said. He wasn't admitting this simply to impress a girl he found cute and fascinating (though that, of course, was part of it). More importantly, he thought that if he and Cynthia had any hope of getting to the bottom of the mystery of the inheritances, it was wisest to be honest and lay all the cards on the table. It was only then that any explanatory connections could emerge.

Out of the corner of his eye he saw Andrew Fish frown at this unexpected development, and he saw Cynthia's head whirl toward him in surprise. Only Tiffany took the revelation in stride, nodding calmly as if Calvin and Cynthia's being investigators of strange phenomena made perfect sense.

"Yes," she said, her eyes fixed on Calvin's. Her voice was low, almost a whisper, as if she were talking to herself as much as to him. "Connections."

She was about to say something more when her father stepped in front of her and said to Calvin and Cynthia, "It's getting late. I must insist we adjourn. I thank you for stopping by. It was...most informative."

"But Daddy—" Tiffany began, her blue eyes sparking with outrage.

"Now, now," Andrew Fish said. "It's late. It's nearly time for dinner." His tone made it clear that this time no amount of princessy insistence would sway him. Tiffany's lips pursed into an unhappy moue.

Calvin dug into his pocket and pulled out a pen and a small spiral notebook. On a blank sheet he scribbled down his name and phone number, then tore out the page and handed it to Andrew Fish, making sure as he did so to angle it so that Tiffany could read it. He was glad to see her eyes devour the info written thereon as if her life depended on it.

"Here," he told Fish. "Give me a call if you have any questions, or if any new information turns up concerning the inheritances. Likewise, I'll let you know if we learn anything more."

Andrew Fish gave a single terse nod, then took the piece of paper and slipped it into his pocket without looking at the number.

"You can call at any time," Calvin added with a quick glance at Tiffany to make it clear that the offer applied to her, as well. He was pleased to see her draw in a sudden, sharp breath, a small, nervous smile flickering on her lips.

"It was nice meeting you," she called out as her father escorted them to the door.

Before the door closed, Calvin managed to catch one last glimpse of her over Andrew Fish's shoulder. He felt glad and giddy to see that she was likewise craning over the same shoulder to catch a glimpse of him. And then the door shut hard enough for the brass handle on the knocker to flap up then drop back down with a faint *clock*.

7

"It would have been nice if we'd discussed that first," Cynthia said as they drove back to May. They were heading west on Livermore, which offered a more direct path to Route 214 than going back up to Train.

Calvin didn't need to ask to know what she was talking about.

"Sorry," he said. "There just wasn't time. I could tell by then that Fish was eager to get rid of us, and I wasn't sure if we'd ever get another chance to talk to them again, so I thought it would be best to be upfront about everything. The truth can't come out if everyone's keeping secrets. And given Fish's reaction when I told him Mr. May investigated strange phenomena, I got the distinct impression he was indeed keeping something secret, probably some kind of unusual event experienced by either himself or Tiffany. Or both."

"Or maybe even the dead wife."

"Ooh, I hadn't thought of that. But, yeah, I just

wanted to make sure they understood our real interests and intentions and that they were free to talk to us without fear of condemnation or ridicule."

She gave him a sidelong look, one eyebrow cocked, a faint smile on her lips. "'They' or 'Tiffany'?"

He shrugged, trying to look innocent. "Either one."

"Mm-hmm," she said.

"What?"

Her cocked eyebrow rose higher. He couldn't help smiling in response.

"She was…interesting," he said.

"Interesting?"

"Okay, she was cute." He looked at her. "Didn't you think she was cute?"

"She was okay," Cynthia said. Frankly her feeling of repulsion toward Tiffany had only deepened with the girl's bursts of haughtiness toward the end of the meeting, but she saw no sense admitting that to Calvin. "Not really my type, though."

"Oh." Calvin seemed disappointed.

"But attraction is totally subjective. And, hey, she was clearly attracted to you."

He grinned like a schoolboy. "You think?"

Cynthia rolled her eyes. Did he really not see it, or was he just fishing for confirmation?

"Let's just say it was clear to all present that there was major chemistry there," she said.

"Chemistry." He said it slowly, as if he had just discovered this wonderful new word and was savoring the feel of it in his mouth. He nodded, then said it again: "Chemistry."

Cynthia chuckled. "I'd say it's just a matter of time before you're writing her name in the margins of your notebooks. Tiffany Beckerman. It's got a cute ring to it, I have to admit."

"Oh, stop it." His grin was bigger than ever. Then a thought struck him and the grin faded. "I get the impression her dad might not approve."

"So what? Who cares what her dad thinks? Tiffany's eighteen. She's an adult. She can do what she likes."

"I don't think it's that simple."

"No," she conceded with a sigh. "Things rarely are."

They turned off Livermore and onto Route 214. The Prius accelerated to sixty.

"So what's our next step vis-à-vis the Fishes?" Cynthia asked. "If there is one."

"I don't know. I guess just wait and see if one of them calls. And when I have the time, I'll keep looking through Mr. May's papers and see if I can find anything else that might help explain the rationale behind the inheritances."

"Are you sure there is a rationale? How do we know he didn't pick a bunch of names just because he liked the sound of them? Maybe he picked Tiffany Fish simply because it was an animal name, like Crow and Coyote. In fact, hey, we have three major animal kingdoms covered: the mammals, the birds, and now the fish. Maybe he was just, I don't know, goofing around."

"I don't believe that. It doesn't explain why my name's on there. Or Anna West's."

"No. But I can't help but wonder: How certain are we that there is in fact a meaning to be found here?"

"Oh, come on." His tone was acerbic enough to make him pause a moment before going on in a softer, more controlled voice. "You knew him as well as I did. You read the same files I did. He might have been eccentric, but always in a very sane and organized way. He wasn't prone to reckless whims."

"Hey, I'm just playing devil's advocate here, that's all. I agree he wasn't the whimmish type. I just thought somebody should at least raise the possibility that all of this is meaningless, that we're striving to find an answer where none exists."

"No," Calvin said firmly. "I don't believe that. There's a meaning here. There has to be."

He looked out the window. They were passing a former industrial area that had fallen victim to Kingwood's—and the country's—changing economy. Large abandoned buildings sat amid empty parking lots spiderwebbed with weeds, their doors locked, their windows dark, their facades sporting dusty signs for long-defunct companies: Gecko Industries; The Kingwood Box Company; Schott Tool & Die. There was something depressing about all these barren, useless buildings, monuments to dead aspirations, concrete reflections of Cynthia's devilishly advocated meaninglessness.

But some innate instinct within Calvin recoiled at such pessimism, and like a psychological antibody, Betty Romero's comment recurred to him once again.

"It all converges," he stated, then gave a single curt nod, as if nothing more needed to be said.

8

"So how's the new job going?" Cynthia asked Lauren at that night's meeting. By general consent it was going to have to be a very short one. Thanks to various minor hindrances, nearly everyone had wound up running really late, and by the time the whole group settled down in Calvin's parlor with the remains of last night's snacks-and-beer buffet it was already nearly ten p.m.

"They're working me like a dog," Lauren said, stifling a yawn with her fist. "They had me running up and down the stacks all day long. But don't get me wrong: I love the job."

"A job you enjoy isn't really a job," Brandon said.

"I'll drink to that." Lauren clinked her Bass Ale to his Edmund Fitzgerald Porter.

"And what about you?" Calvin asked Brandon. "How did your job interviews go?"

"Eh. Most of 'em probably won't amount to anything. Which isn't so bad, because the jobs looked extremely lame. I got a good feeling about one of them, though: a local indie record company. Buck Futt Records. They specialize in punk bands."

"Oh, I know them," Donovan said. "I have some of the Razorface albums they put out."

"Yeah, they're pretty cool. The job I applied for was art director, which I thought I'd be way underqualified for. I figured it couldn't hurt to try, though. Showing up is half the battle, you know. And in this case it might actually pan out. They sounded pretty hard up for someone competent, and I think I made a good impression. I should be hearing back from them in a day or two."

"I hope it works out for you," Cynthia said.

"Thanks."

"Okay, guys," Calvin announced. "Let's get this meeting underway. We have a lot to talk about and not a whole lot of time."

"So did you guys figure out whodunit and all that?"

Violet asked.

"Not exactly."

Calvin and Cynthia took turns relating the results of their investigation that afternoon. At least in part. They didn't get around to Betty Romero's story about the ghostly echoes, much less the meeting with the Fishes, because when Calvin and Cynthia described what Betty Romero claimed to have heard in the alley on the night of Brad Vallance's murder, Lauren jerked bolt upright in her seat and waved her hand back and forth, palm out.

"Wait wait wait," she said. "Let me make sure I have this right. It sounded like someone or something was repeating exactly what this Ruddy woman had said, right?"

"Yeah," said Calvin.

"And this old lady heard a sound like hooves?"

"Yeah."

"And correct me if I'm wrong, but Coroner Chandra said that the wounds on Brad Vallance looked like they'd been made by sharp smooth plates configured like a set of jaws, correct?"

"More or less, yeah."

Lauren sat there in silence for a second, mentally running through the facts one more time just to make sure. Then she shook her head with a small, self-conscious laugh.

"That sounds like a leucrota."

Calvin frowned, trying hard to remember where he knew that word from. Then he had it: "The monster from *Dungeons & Dragons?*"

Now it was Lauren's turn to frown.

"What?" she said.

"Leucrota, right? That's a *D&D* monster."

Violet snorted. "I knew he played that shit."

"I don't know anything about that," Lauren said, ignoring her sister's comment, as did everyone else. "I never played *D&D*. The leucrota I'm familiar with is a monster from medieval bestiaries. I did a boatload of research on bestiaries for a paper I did for one of my classes. The leucrota was supposed to be this vicious man-eating quadruped. Instead of teeth it was said to have single plates of sharp bone, one in the upper gum, one in the lower, and it had cloven hooves like a goat's, and most importantly it could mimic human voices. Its favorite trick was to lie in wait near roads on dark nights and lure passing travelers to their dooms by crying for help in a woman's voice."

Calvin nodded slowly, remembering what his old *Monster Manual* had said about leucrotas. "Yeah! That's it. I should have seen the connection earlier."

"Um, no," said Lauren. "No, you shouldn't have. Because, see, leucrotas aren't real. They were actually hyenas. Kind of. They were a description of a hyena told by a bunch of ignorant, superstitious people who had never seen a hyena but had only heard fourth- or fifth-hand stories about them. The hyena's eerily laugh-like cry got distorted into the leucrota's ability to perfectly imitate the human voice. It was just a...a mistake, that's all. There's no way a leucrota could be real. I mean, they're biologically impossible. They're dog-like animals with hooves."

"Based on your description, this does sound like a leucrota, mistake or not," Cynthia said.

"But it's...it's..." Lauren shook her head. "Where did it come from, then? If leucrotas are real, where have they been hiding for the last millennium?"

"The clearing in the woods, remember?" Calvin said. "Maybe it came through there."

"Oh, yeah. The magic hole in reality. So, what, it generates not only extinct species but species that are and have always been entirely fictional?"

"Why not? We don't know exactly what's really going on with the clearing. We don't know how it works. Maybe it's funneling things from alternate realities into ours."

"I find it hard to believe that leucrotas could exist in any reality," Lauren said. "I really hate to be a pooper at your party, but there is a very clear origin to leucrotas. We know they're a garbling of accounts of hyenas with bits of a few other things mixed in. That's all they are. That's all they ever were."

"Aha," Brandon said. "That brings us back to the theory that the whatever-it-is in the woods is making the stuff of imagination into reality, like in that book."

"What book?" Cynthia said.

"I don't know. Wasn't there a novel about something like that? I never read it, but I heard something about it."

"I think we're kind of getting ahead of things here," Lauren said. "All I said was that what that old lady described sounded like it *could* be a leucrota. I'm sure there are plenty of other plausible explanations that fit the facts. Besides, I think you're overlooking one very obvious problem with your theory."

"Which is what?" Calvin asked.

"If this thing is a leucrota and it came from the clearing, then it didn't just hop a bus to downtown Kingwood. It had to travel there on foot. Or, well, on hoof."

"It hoofed it to Kingwood," Brandon said, grinning. "See what I did there?"

"Unfortunately," Cynthia said.

"The point is," Lauren said, "it would have taken this thing at least a few days to travel that far. And that's assuming this thing traveled in a straight line from here to the edge of downtown Kingwood. And bear in mind, leucrotas were supposed to be fairly large, about the size of a donkey if I remember right. A creature that big would need to eat a lot of food every day. So why haven't we heard about any attacks before this one?

"There were those two missing graffiti guys," Donovan said.

"Yeah, but that was the same neighborhood as the dead guy. That still leaves at least ten miles of ground for Mr. or Ms. Leucrota to have traveled. Ten miles of very heavily populated ground."

"It might have been sticking to woods and fields and stuff," Brandon said. "Even though it's pretty heavily populated between here and Kingwood, there're still plenty of wild and abandoned areas."

"But if it's slinking along from one secluded spot to another, it would take it that much longer to travel, and in all that time it still needs to be eating something." She shook her head. "I just don't see how a creature that large and that conspicuous could travel that far through a densely populated area without being seen and without leaving any traces."

There was silence in the room for a moment as everyone pondered this. The silence was broken by a sharp hiss as Violet twisted the cap off another bottle of beer, then the faint clatter as she tossed the cap onto the coffee table, where it joined the caps of the other four beers she had drunk since the meeting began.

"Have there been any other missing person reports lately?" Cynthia said.

"Not that I'm aware of," Calvin said. "Of course, if the creature's been feeding on transients or something, it's possible no one's noticed."

"Oh, I don't know," Lauren said. "I think even a bum getting torn up like that would attract plenty of attention."

"Not if the bum got eaten whole. Brad Vallance's remains might have been an exception. The creature might normally gobble down every last bone and belt buckle."

"And it doesn't have to have been eating only people all this time," Brandon said. "It might've been eating animals. Pets, raccoons, stray dogs, whatever."

"Or even livestock," Calvin said. "There are farms not too far north and south of this area. Plus there are wild deer. There's plenty for a carnivore to eat."

"But if that's true, why would it suddenly decide to start attacking people in the middle of a busy urban area?" Cynthia said.

"We need to do some homework," Calvin said. He looked at Lauren. "Do you think you'll have the time to dig up whatever info you can find about leucrotas between now and tomorrow night?"

"I can try," Lauren said. "There isn't really very much information to be had, and most of it's kind of silly."

"Just find out whatever you can, silly or not. In the meantime we need to start digging around and seeing if there've been any reports of mysteriously murdered or missing people, pets, or livestock in the area lately."

"Uh, who's 'we' exactly?" Brandon asked. "I mean, I'm pretty booked up with more job interviews all day tomorrow."

"Yeah, and I'll be working," Lauren said. "As it is, I'll have trouble fitting in the leucrota research."

"And, sorry, but I'm slated to help my dad at his bookstore," Cynthia said. "So's Donovan, for that matter."

Everyone looked at Violet, the only one as yet unaccounted for. She was in mid-swig of her latest beer. When she sensed their gazes upon her, she froze with her lips tightly sealed around the bottle's mouth, her eyes sweeping the faces turned her way. She plucked the bottle from her mouth with a hollow *pwok*.

"Hey, don't look at me!" she said. "I ain't doin' no fuckin' research!"

"Yeah," Cynthia said. "I mean, if we want it done right, we don't want Violet doing it."

"That's right!"

"I guess it's up to you, then," Cynthia told Calvin. "You're the only one without a life."

"Oh, thanks!" he said with half-joking umbrage.

"I didn't mean it like that. I just meant a life outside of anomaly investigating."

"Uh-huh. Sure. Anyway, can everyone make it back here tomorrow night? I know you guys all have lives and stuff"—he shot a pointed glance at Cynthia, who tutted and rolled her eyes—"but we need to get on this quickly. The leucrota—"

"*Presumed* leucrota," Lauren said. "I'm still not convinced."

"Okay, this entity that resembles a leucrota in a wide variety of ways might continue to kill people, so we ought to get on this as fast as we can."

"Maybe we should alert the cops or something," Cynthia said. "Just so they have a better idea of what they're dealing with."

"And tell them what, exactly? That they should be keeping their eyes open for a nonsensical mythical beast that's right out of the *Dungeons & Dragons Monster Manual* and can mimic voices better than Rich Little?" He shook his head. "I don't think they'll buy it. I mean, they already heard what Betty Romero had to say, and we know from their press conference that they're at least considering the possibility that some kind of deformed animal is involved. I'd say that's close enough for government work."

"What about the haunted alley and Tiffany Fish and all that?" Cynthia asked Calvin. "We never even got to that stuff. Do we want to get into that now?"

"The what and the who?" Brandon said.

Calvin checked his watch.

"Not tonight," he said. "It's already pretty late, and everyone's tired, and you guys all have to get up early for your lives tomorrow."

"You're not gonna let that go, are you?" Cynthia said.

"Not for a while. And in any case, I think the leucrota situation takes priority over the ghosts of West Train Apartments and young Ms. Fish."

"Ghosts?" Donovan asked.

"Who's Ms. Fish?" Brandon said. "Isn't that from a Psychedelic Furs song?"

"Why don't we save that discussion for another time," Calvin said. "Let's just say that the leucrota isn't the only mysterious phenomenon that's come to our attention lately."

"Are you saying we can't multi-task?"

"Not with all of you having lives, we can't."

"All right," Cynthia said with a groan. "I'm sorry I said that."

Lauren yawned loudly, then shook her head and stood up.

"Sorry, but I really need to get going, guys. I'm whipped, and I have to be up super-early tomorrow."

"Yeah," Cynthia said, likewise rising. "It's time to get this party ended."

9

After lunch the next day Calvin settled down at the still-cluttered desk in the upstairs office, got online, and started hunting through the *Kingwood Morning Star*'s archives. He thanked the gods of media that the paper kept online copies of every article they had run during the last six years. He searched first for unsolved violent deaths in Bard County but found nothing consistent with the attack on Brad Vallance. He then searched for missing persons in the area, and though he turned up over a dozen, there was no way to tell if they were connected with the leucrota attacks (or, as Lauren would have it, the *presumed* leucrota attacks). The disappearances followed no obvious patterns, being evenly distributed chronologically and more common in larger population centers, exactly as one would expect if the disappearances were random, unrelated occurrences. He checked the FBI's crime database and found that the missing person rate in Bard County matched that of the U.S. as a whole. Nothing suspicious there, then.

Next he searched for sightings of unusual animals, and here he found one possibly relevant report, nearly a year old, from Castle Township, due south of May.

On July 25th the previous year, a farmer named Ephraim Levi was awakened one night by a "hubbub" in the chicken coop behind his house. Fearing a coyote attack, of which, the article claimed, there had been a spate in western and central Castle Township in recent months, Levi grabbed his shotgun and charged outside. As he approached the coop, a large animal burst out and bolted into the nearby woods. The swift-moving animal was hard to see in the darkness, but its size and its long-legged physique suggested a deer rather than any carnivore Levi was familiar with. The farmer fired off one shot as the creature disappeared into the foliage, but managed only to blast a chunk out of a tree trunk. The interior of the coop was a slaughterhouse, over half the chickens torn to shreds and many others so badly mauled they had to be put down. The article concluded with a statement from a County Division of Wildlife officer who speculated that the animal may have been a large stray dog with Great Dane or greyhound blood.

Inspired by the reference to coyote attacks, Calvin shifted the focus of his search to attacks on and disappearances of pets and livestock. He got over thirty hits from the last two years. Some of them were clearly instances of predation by coyotes, wolves, bored dumb teens, and other non-anomalous creatures. But the rest weren't so clear-cut, and they formed a pattern that was blindingly obvious once you knew what you were looking for.

Here, from only two months ago, was a story about a pet German shepherd found half-eaten one morning in the upscale Banbury neighborhood in southwestern Kingwood. Shortly before Halloween last year there had been a brief spate of pet disappearances on the outskirts of Deermont, a quiet suburban community due south of Kingwood. One rather histrionic letter to the editor speculated that the disappearances were the work of Satanists gathering up sacrifices for their unholy rituals on All Hallows Eve. The previous summer had witnessed the string of livestock attacks in Castle Township, due west of

Deermont and due south of May. With the exception of Farmer Levi's chicken coop, everyone pinned the attacks on coyotes, whose population in Northeast Ohio had burgeoned in recent years. Despite the popular consensus, a close reading of the articles revealed that no one had actually produced any concrete evidence that coyotes were in fact responsible. There were no sightings of coyotes, no tracks, no scat. Just dead and missing animals and a lot of presumptions.

A little over a year ago a trio of cows belonging to the Pepper Family Dairy had been found dead and mutilated in a field in Riddle, a rural township west of Castle. The cows had been missing various portions of their anatomy, including their throats and faces. Calvin remembered the incident well, mainly because Riddle's alarmingly large contingent of surly right-wing kooks were convinced that the cattle mutilations had been the work of some ill-defined New World Order/UFO conspiracy, with one woman asserting that she had spotted unmarked black helicopters in the area the day before the cows were killed.

Four months earlier a horse had been "savagely butchered" in a stable in Phoenix Township west of May. The article gave few details about either the condition of the body or any suspects, largely because a police investigation was underway. If there had been any follow-up articles about the case, Calvin couldn't find them. Presumably the investigation had gone nowhere and was quietly back-burnered.

Four months before that, there was a tiny article, barely more than a blurb, about a rash of pet disappearances in western Ames, the city due north of May that was the home of Calvin, Cynthia, and Brandon's new alma mater. Since he had been a resident of Ames at the time, Calvin would have liked to say he recalled the incident, but he didn't, probably because nothing about it struck him as overtly anomalous. Everyone's favorite scapegoat, coyotes, were identified as the likeliest culprit.

Calvin was surprised that none of the later articles had mentioned this one, especially the ones about the supposed coyote attacks in Castle Township and the one about the Halloween pet disappearances in Deermont. But upon reflection he realized that the Ames story had been a minor one and had occurred two townships away and roughly a year earlier. On the other hand, the Ames article referred to an article that had run two months earlier involving a brutal attack on a pet dog on Landis Road on the far northern edge of May. Here was another close-to-home incident that Calvin felt guilty and embarrassed for not being aware of. He immediately looked the story up.

The article related how the Pritchett family had been awakened at three a.m. by the low, syrupy yowls of Bones, the family beagle, who slept in a doghouse in the backyard. At first none of the family was too concerned, figuring that a raccoon was taking a shortcut through the backyard as had happened many times before. But then came a splintering crash, and Bones's yowls twisted into a shrill yelp of pain before stopping with frightening abruptness. Flashlight and baseball bat clutched tight, Barry Pritchett raced into the backyard, where he found the doghouse torn open and splashed with blood. Inside lay Bones's corpse, the beagle's throat torn out so badly his head was almost severed. Barry frantically shone the flashlight around, but saw no sign of any animals, raccoons or otherwise. The article once again raised the specter of coyotes as a possible culprit and concluded with a plea from the local animal warden to immediately report any potentially dangerous animals and to never under any circumstances try to interact with one yourself.

And before that incident, nothing.

Calvin sat back, the office chair creaking, his gaping mouth slowly spreading into a smile.

It all formed a very clear story. Nearly two years ago something had appeared here in May, probably from the anomaly in the clearing. After killing poor Bones, the creature had headed north into Ames, gobbling down dogs and cats as it went. Then over the next twenty months it slowly traveled along a huge arc through the counties that surrounded May: from Ames southwest to Phoenix, then south to Riddle, then east through Castle and into Deermont, and finally north into Kingwood. It was all right there, incontrovertible.

Calvin barked out a joyous laugh and cried, "I've got it!" He looked up into the air as he said it, announcing his victory to the house and to Mr. May, the two of them having become somehow isomorphic in Calvin's mind. Calvin beamed with pride and accomplishment, feeling as if he had finally proven beyond all doubt that he was a worthy heir to the old man's legacy.

But then his ebullience dimmed. If the creature—like Lauren, he wasn't quite ready to label it a leucrota, but he was now certain it was not of this earth—had spent two years gladly gobbling down animals of various kinds, what had made it shift its diet to people? For that matter why had it entered the city at all? True, Kingwood was on the arc the leucrota had been following, but given the locations of the other incidents, the creature had skirted populous areas when it came to them in the past. Even the Banbury neighborhood, where the German shepherd had been killed, was situated on the edge of Holly Hills

Metropark, which originated on the border with Deermont and jutted deep into southwestern Kingwood like a giant green finger. So what had happened in the last few weeks to change the creature's pattern, to drive it out into the open and start murdering humans?

The article about Bones's death was still on the monitor, and as Calvin mulled over the problem, his gaze was drawn to the phrase "animal warden" in the last line. Something about it rang a bell. Hadn't he read something about the animal warden recently?

No, wait. It wasn't the animal warden; it was the *game* warden. The county game warden. Something about deer, wasn't it?

He looked it up in the paper's database, and yes, only three weeks ago there had been a press release by the game warden, which revealed that the deer population this last hunting season had been shockingly low, the lowest since records started being kept. For that matter, the numbers of several other wild species, including opossums, raccoons, and even coyotes appeared to have declined during the same period, at least in certain areas. Determined to learn the cause of these sudden, dramatic, and worrying declines, the warden, in collaboration with the County Park Service, planned to send several large teams into Holly Hills Metropark, one of the places where the population declines had been worst, to look for both living and dead specimens of the animals in question. The search would begin the second week of May and continue until the end of the month.

"That's it!" Calvin cried. Everything fit perfectly. The search teams must have driven the creature out of the park and into the city. In fact...

He grabbed Mr. May's old Bard County map book to

check the precise location of Holly Hills Metropark. As he had suspected, the northern tip of that thick green finger was only four blocks southwest of West Train Apartments.

He sat back in the chair again, grinning and flush with pride.

"Wow," he said.

Unfortunately, knowing how the creature had gotten there wasn't going to help them stop it from killing any more people. They had to figure out where it was holing up now. But how?

Somewhere in the depths of the house he heard a faint trill. Startled, he sat up straight, looking with wide eyes out the open office doorway and into the hall. For a moment he thought something in the Collection was acting up—a haunted mirror, perhaps, or a screaming crystal skull—but then the noise sounded again, and he realized it was the doorbell. He had heard it only a handful of times over the years, and only when he was near it on the first floor. From here, on the second floor and in a different wing, it was just a muffled phantom of the sound he had heard before. On the third floor or in the tower, it would probably be completely inaudible.

He sprang to his feet, hurried out of the office, and raced down the hall toward the stairs. That was one thing he didn't like about this house: It was too damn big. And for all his frantic effort to reach the door in time, he would probably get there only to discover the caller was a salesman or a Jehovah's Witness. He should look into installing an intercom system to spare his legs and lungs the stress.

The doorbell rang a third time as he pounded down the spiral staircase.

"Coming!" he shouted, not sure if whoever-it-was

could even hear him from here.

He leaped the last few steps, then sprinted down the long corridor that ran the length of the south wing to the front door. Through the thin white curtain that was drawn across the window in the upper half of the door, he could see a long-haired silhouette. A girl? Had Cynthia's dad let her off early? Or maybe it was Lauren. Or Donovan, sans his usual hair band.

He skidded to a halt before the door, then opened it while swiftly rearranging his red, panting face into something he hoped resembled a smile. When he saw that his visitor was Tiffany Fish, the quasi-smile froze for a moment, then blossomed into a genuine smile, huge and happy.

"Hi," he said.

"Um, hi," she said. She did one quick survey of his sweaty face and his heaving chest, then gave him a wincing smile. "This is a bad time, isn't it?" She shook her head at herself and spat out a soft, bitter laugh of self-recrimination. "I knew it," she muttered. "I should have called first. I'm so—"

"No, it's fine. It's a fine time. I was just on the other side of the house when the bell rang, that's all."

She gave him a sidelong look as if she suspected he was saying that just to be polite. "Really?"

"Really. So what brings you here?"

She didn't seem to know exactly how to answer that question. Her eyes met his, sidled away, met his again, dropped to his chest; her mouth opened, closed. Finally she gave a quick, twitchy smile and said, "I don't know, I guess I wanted to know more about...about you. And about this Robert May person and everything." She shrugged. "I figured that since he left us money and we

don't know why, we're sort of connected, entangled together in a mystery. Therefore it seemed appropriate that
we get to know each other better." She nodded at the
house. "Besides, I wanted to see this place. My father told
me a bit about it last night. It sounded architecturally interesting. Porches and towers, wings and scales."

She stepped backward off the porch and down the
steps, her eyes fixed on the facade of the house as it slowly
emerged from behind the porch roof overhead. Calvin
watched with alarm, ready to spring forward and catch her
should she stumble and fall. But she navigated her backward descent without a single misstep. She didn't even
seem aware of the possibility of having an accident.

Calvin trotted down the steps after her, facing forward
not just for safety's sake but so he could look at her while
she looked at the house. She was dressed in a white
button-front top with a white lacey collar and lacey cap
sleeves. Like yesterday, she wore blue jeans but these were
much nicer than the other pair, less worn, less baggy. Her
sneakers were also much nicer than yesterday's, though
they were the exact same brand and color: white New
Balances. In fact, as Calvin looked at the shoes he realized
they were completely unscuffed, the white whiter than
white, the laces crisp and stiff. She must have just bought
them.

For *him?* Remarkable as it seemed, it had to be true.
He felt a strange, giddy sense of lightness at the thought,
as if his body were filling with some substance more buoy-
ant than air and any second now he would float straight up
like a child's lost balloon. But at the same time, more level-
headed concerns kept him grounded. If he wanted to try
to get closer to her, as the sum totality of his being
yearned to do, he had to be careful. She seemed unworldly

and fragile. He didn't need a Psych degree to see how shy and socially awkward she was and how her odd mindset might on the one hand alienate some people and on the other make her abnormally sensitive to such reactions. And yet even as he thought this, it struck him how much courage it must have taken for her to pay him this visit, and he recalled the stubborn princess who had manifested yesterday to face down her father. Shy and fragile on the outside, but with a tough, determined core.

He joined her on the sidewalk that connected the front steps to the driveway. Her head was tilted back so she could look at the house, her right hand raised to shield her eyes from the sun. Even in the shadow of her hand the blue of her eyes shone through. Calvin couldn't keep from staring at those eyes, at the slender fingers arched across her brow, at the delicate folds of her ear, the sweeping curve of her jaw, the flutter of her pulse in the side of her bared neck. He felt an urge to lean in and press his lips to that little patch of fluttering skin and feel the warmth and rhythm of her pulse.

"This is an extraordinary house," she said.

"I take it you weren't with your dad when he came out to look at it that one time?"

The question flustered her for some reason. She glanced at him sharply, her eyes looking almost panicked for a second. Then she reined in whatever it was that had started to gallop away with her, and shook her head.

"No. I was…I didn't go."

He nodded, then resumed studying the house in silence, making no mention of her flusterment. She did likewise. After a moment she looked at the west wing on the left, then at the east wing on the right, then said, "There's another wing in the back, isn't there?"

"Yep."

"It's symmetrical. Four wings, one for each cardinal point." She frowned slightly and tilted her head to one side, then murmured, "Wings. Cardinal. Bird. Crow." The frown deepened. "Huh."

Not sure how to react to these comments—feeling, in fact, a little freaked out by them despite how much and how quickly he was growing to like their utterer—Calvin responded instead to Tiffany's initial observation about the house's symmetry.

"I've always thought of the house as being shaped like a big plus sign, myself."

She shook her head.

"It's not a plus sign. It's a wheel. The tower in the center is the axle. The wings are the spokes."

He looked at the house, trying to see it the way she did, then nodded slowly.

"You know, you might be right. I never thought of it like that. The guy who built the place, Turner May, was kind of eccentric and didn't really explain why he designed it the way he did. But if it is a wheel, it's a wheel that doesn't go anywhere."

"Sure it does. The continental plate inches along, and the Earth rotates and revolves around the sun, and they both shoot through space as the universe expands. It travels plenty."

Calvin stared at her, his huge, happy smile from yesterday returning. He loved the way this girl's mind worked, the way she effortlessly recast the world around her in fascinating and unpredictable ways. Her thoughts and comments made his own seem rather prosaic. But instead of feeling small or envious or annoyed because of this, as some people would, he felt glad she was there to share that perspective with him and thereby enrich his own.

Eyes still on the facade, she said, "Can I see inside?"

"Sure."

As he led her back up the steps, he noticed her car parked beside his in the driveway. He had been so wrapped up in Tiffany that he hadn't even seen it there till now. It was a silver Audi S5, the same as the dark-blue one he had seen in the Fishes' driveway yesterday, only several years older. Calvin guessed this one used to be her dad's car, and Tiffany had inherited it when Andrew Fish upgraded to the newer model. The sight of Tiffany's car parked next to his gave Calvin a small, warm thrill, as if it were a portent of more direct and genuine togetherness yet to come.

Calvin gave her a tour of the first floor: the parlor, the book-crammed library, the dining room with its crystal chandelier and mahogany table big enough to seat a dozen with ease, and so on and so on, through all four wings and eleven rooms. Tiffany took it all in without comment and without, it seemed, much interest, much to Calvin's disappointment. But then, what did he expect? If the Fishes' current home was anything to go by, she had grown up amid greater wealth than his and no doubt all the luxuries it could afford. Spacious rooms and pricey antiques were probably old hat to her.

But that, he soon learned, wasn't the only reason for her disinterest. When he showed her the study in the east wing, she briefly surveyed the brown leather furniture and the framed hunting prints on the wall, then said, "Most of the things in this house aren't yours, are they?"

"Uh, no. It's mostly Mr. May's furniture. I haven't gotten around to deciding what to do with a lot of it."

"You need to redecorate. You need your own things in

here. It's not right living in a house with someone else's furnishings. It's like wearing someone else's face. It's a false you. It's duplicitous."

Once again Calvin's big, broad smile returned. This time Tiffany saw it and, giving him an uneasy smile in response, said, "What!"

"I think you just helped me decide what to do with most of this stuff."

She looked alarmed. "Oh, gosh! Don't do something just because *I* said so."

"But you're right. A lot of this furniture is nice and all, but it isn't really me. I was holding onto it out of...I don't know, sentimentality, or misplaced respect, or something. It's certainly not stuff I would've bought on my own. Well, maybe some of it, like the leather couch in the parlor, and that neat old grandfather clock."

"Yes, I like the clock. The intricacy of the gold filigree on the hands is amazing. You could get lost in all those loops."

"Very lost," he agreed with a smile, looking at her meaningfully.

Her eyes went wide, and her body went stiff. For a moment she looked as if she were about to whirl around and run away and hide somewhere, maybe under that overlong dining room table. But then the sides of her mouth crept up to form a small, shy smile of her own, and the two of them just stood there smiling at each other.

"So," she said finally, shifting her gaze away from his and toward the study door, "what's next?"

He led her upstairs to the second floor. All throughout the tour he had been debating with himself whether or not to show her the Collection. She already knew that he and Cynthia investigated strange phenomena, so the existence of the Collection wouldn't exactly come as a shocking revelation. And he felt pretty sure he could trust her not to tell anyone else about it. Given what he'd learned about her so far, he suspected she didn't know a lot of people anyway. On the other hand, he remembered how unhappy Cynthia had been when he unilaterally decided to spill the beans to the Fishes yesterday. Perhaps he should discuss the matter with Cynthia and the rest of the group first.

Still, the Collection was his. He could do what he wanted with it. He could show it to whomever he liked. When he imagined showing it to Tiffany and seeing her amazed and wondering smile, his concerns about Cynthia's peevishness faded. He decided he would show it to Tiffany.

And why stop there? Maybe Tiffany could join the group, too. He had a feeling she'd fit right in.

Wanting to save the Collection for last, he started the tour of the second floor with the library in the south wing, which was twice the size of the one on the first floor and contained rarer and more unusual books, including Mr. May's extensive collection of works on the paranormal. Against the west wall sat a line of cardboard boxes that contained most of Calvin's books, which he planned to start shelving as soon as he found the time. The way things had been going, he would probably be in his nineties by then.

"Books books books," Tiffany mumbled, scanning the floor-to-ceiling shelves. "Words words words." She didn't look or sound even a fraction as enthusiastic as Calvin had expected. If anything, she sounded a little disappointed, even sad. It occurred to him that he had no concrete reason for thinking she liked books or reading. He supposed he had unthinkingly presumed that their attraction to each other meant they would share most of the same interests.

After briefly perusing the shelves, an act that Calvin got the impression was done mainly to humor him, Tiffany made a beeline for the boxes on the floor and peered through the open flaps at the topmost books.

"These are yours, yes?" she said.

"Yeah. But I'm keeping most of the others, too." He felt compelled to defend Mr. May's books for some reason. "Most of them are classics in their fields. He had impeccable taste."

"Impeccable," Tiffany murmured as she bent down to examine the books in the boxes more closely. She said it softly, absently, seemingly unaware she was saying anything, the way some people hum tunes while they work. "I'm peckable. Bird peck. Crow peck. Peck peck. Taste."

Calvin said nothing, troubled by this strange, compulsive wordplay, which could be a sign of a mild mental disorder. It didn't negate his liking for her, of course. Not even close. But it was enough to temper that liking and prevent him from seeing her as golden and perfect, her flaws fuzzed out by the misty glaucoma of young love, or at least young infatuation, something to which Calvin knew he was sadly prone. No, instead these dual feelings balanced each other, leaving him with something more cautious, more realistic. More mature, he supposed.

"You like graphic novels," she said, peering into one of the boxes. On top were the first few volumes of *The Walking Dead*.

"Yeah."

She nodded. "Words and pictures." She sounded pleased for some reason.

"Do you read stuff like that?"

She looked at him over her lace-shrouded shoulder,

her expression suddenly hesitant, nervous.

"I..." She turned and looked down at the box again, her long blonde hair, worn loose today, veiling her face from him. "I don't read much anymore."

"Oh." He wanted to ask why not, but held his tongue. He didn't want to risk upsetting her. It wasn't his business anyway.

She continued staring into the box in silence for a moment, then stood up.

"What's next?"

He decided to skip the master bedroom, afraid that showing it to her might come across the wrong way, and instead led her to the office in the west wing. He didn't expect to be in there for long. There wasn't much to see. Just the desk, the computer, the file cabinets, the shelves of reference books.

He had forgotten about the map of May on which he had drawn the pentagram, and he remembered it only after he opened the door and saw it hanging there on the far wall, facing him. By then, of course, it was too late; Tiffany had seen it, too. She stiffened at the sight of it, and Calvin heard her gasp faintly.

"A star," she said.

"Um, yeah..." Calvin's mind raced, wondering how he was going to explain its presence on a satellite map of May. He wasn't sure he wanted to tell her the truth. Not yet anyway. Informing her that his house was one of the main points of a catastrophe-riddled black-magic pentagram might scare her off permanently.

"And a black spot."

It took him a moment to realize she was referring to the black push pin that marked the clearing in the center of the pentagram.

"Yeah," he said.

She walked into the room, her gaze never leaving the map. Calvin followed, watching her closely. She walked straight forward until she came to the edge of the desk, then stopped, the front of her blue-jeaned thighs pressed against the desk's front edge. Calvin expected her to circle around the desk for a closer look at the map, but she stayed right there, staring at the map over the cluttered desktop.

Several silent seconds passed, during which Calvin desperately tried to figure out how to answer her inevitable barrage of questions.

Finally she said, "I take it those places are important somehow." Her voice was tight, clipped. For some reason the starred map bothered her.

"They might be," Calvin said. "It's, uh...sort of a local anomaly we've been looking into."

"Low cull," she muttered. "Low cal. In awe mill E." She turned to him, her face drawn, and seemed about to say something more. But then her gaze shifted to something over his right shoulder, and her eyes widened in surprise.

Calvin turned. She was looking at the movie poster, the lurid image of the sinister face and hooked fingers looming above the brave gun-toting hero and the cowering blonde damsel.

"It's a movie," Calvin said, turning back to Tiffany. Now she was simply staring at the poster with a thoughtful look. "Mr. May hung it here. I still haven't figured out why. As far as I can tell, he wasn't much of a cinephile."

"Well, it's there for a reason," she said, her gaze never leaving the poster. "Everything's there for a reason." Her eyes narrowed. "Eris. Heiress. Terrible heiress. Huh." She looked at Calvin. "Eris was a goddess, wasn't she?"

"Yeah. The Greek goddess of chaos."

She nodded, then looked back at the map.

"This is a particularly interesting room. I like it."

"I'm so glad you approve," Calvin said drily. "I rather like it myself."

She smiled.

"You're funny," she said. "I rather like *that* myself."

"I like that you like that."

"I'd like to say that I like that you like that I like that, but let's not infinitely regress."

"Good idea."

As they grinned at each other, it suddenly occurred to Calvin that he had been standing in almost the exact same position with Cynthia five years ago when he had made a misguided move on her only for her to rebuff him and awkwardly confess she was a lesbian. Calvin was fairly certain Tiffany would not rebuff him. And while he yearned to lean in and kiss those soft, pink, unadorned lips, he felt it wasn't quite the right time yet. He had met her only yesterday after all, and he had concerns about her unworldliness and her psychological soundness.

Though he held back, some trace of his desires must have shown through, for Tiffany's cheeks suddenly flushed, and she lowered her eyes with a small smile. Her gaze fell on the desktop and the items jumbled thereon. A kangaroo paperweight. A chain of paperclips. A sheet of notebook paper covered with columns of Mr. May's tiny handwriting. Her eyes finally settled on the Bard County map book, which Calvin had left lying open to the two-page spread of the West River neighborhood and the northernmost tip of Holly Hills Metropark.

Tiffany's smile slid from her face, and she looked up at

Calvin with an expression that was equal parts dread, excitement, and sorrow. Her blue eyes bored into his so intently he almost took a step away from her.

"You're investigating the death of that man in the alley, aren't you?"

He could see in her eyes there was no sense denying it. "Yeah."

"Is…" She bit her lower lip and regarded him with an uncertain sidelong look. "Is that what brought you to me and my father?"

Calvin shook his head, baffled.

"What? Why would that bring me to you two?"

"You don't know." The words were low and flat, a statement of fact rather than an accusation.

"Know what? Did you know the dead man, or something? Did you know Brad Vallance?"

"Vallance," she muttered. "Valence. Valiance. Violence. Hn." Then she shook her head and in a normal tone of voice said, "No. I never saw him before in my life."

"Then…" He shook his head again. "I'm not sure I understand."

She regarded him in silence, then heaved a deep, shaky sigh. She looked scared, though of what Calvin wasn't sure. Scared of talking about something? Scared of his reaction if she did? Calvin's heart began to quicken in expectation of whatever was about to happen.

"I know I'm weird," she said. "I talk weird. I think weird. I can't help it. I can't not be this way."

"Weird isn't necessarily bad," Calvin said gently. "Not to me."

She flashed him a small smile to acknowledge the kindly sentiment.

"The thing is, I wasn't always like this. When I was a

little girl I was a different person. I was a brat. A snobby blonde brat, as spoiled as mayonnaise left in a hot closet."

Calvin recalled the princess in the photo on her father's desk. Apparently the girl's nose-in-the-air snootiness had not been an act.

"You would have hated me," Tiffany said. "I was a spoiled little rich girl who wanted a pony and a life-size Barbie Dream House and all those other silly things that spoiled little rich girls want. And usually get. But I got something else because one night when I was nine we went to the theater."

"The theater?"

"The Blackhorse Theater, two blocks north of the alley. My dad and I went there a lot back then. He did legal work for the theater owners, and on top of his usual many-digit fees, they gave him two free tickets to every show." She cocked her head. "He's a lawyer. Did you know that?"

"Yeah. I saw all the diplomas and stuff on the wall behind the desk in his office."

"On the wall behind the desk in his office," she said with a nod at the map of May. The pentagram. The pin. "Exactly."

A chill raced down Calvin's spine, though he wasn't entirely sure why one should. Lots of people hung important items behind their desks. It was a fairly meaningless coincidence. And yet somehow, in Tiffany's presence, it felt important. Everything did. The longer he was exposed to her idiosyncratic ways of thinking, her revisionings of the world, her linguistic vivisections and homophonizings, the more everything began to feel fraught with meaning.

"I liked going to the theater," Tiffany went on, "because it made me feel smart and adult even though I didn't always understand what I was seeing or hearing, and because there was something very comforting about being there, snug in those plush velvet seats in the womby dark, passive and inert while comfortingly predictable stories were enacted on the bright stage, a whole other world brought to life before me.

"That night's free play was a romantic comedy called *Check, Mate.* Two words, with a comma between them. I seem to recall enjoying it, though I don't really remember much about it. The details got...superseded." She paused a moment, eyes distant, as if the word had set off a separate train of thought. Then she resumed the story. "We had walked to the theater. It was a long walk. Half an hour. Thirty minutes. Eighteen hundred seconds. But it was a beautiful night. The air was balmy, and the sky was starry, and the smell of flowers filled the air. Tulips and roses and Bradford pear blossoms. It was the same time of year as now. Spring. Late May." Her eyes drifted out of focus again. "Late May. The late Robert May. Huh."

Again Calvin felt a chill.

"In fact..." Tiffany looked around the room in search of something. Not finding it, she looked at Calvin. "What day is it?"

"The twenty-third."

She nodded. "The same day. It's the exact same day nine years later. And I was nine then. My whole life over again. Lived through twice now, and here we are back to that day once more. What are the odds I would be telling you about that day on the same day it happened?"

"One in three hundred and sixty-five, I should think," Calvin said in a calm, even tone that in no way reflected how spooked he was feeling. The chills were racing down his spine nearly nonstop now.

Tiffany smiled. "You have a good head for math. Anyway, the play ran late and by the time it was done, it was nearly ten. That was my usual bedtime, and with the hour so late, I was very tired. My dad was tired, too, as I recall. I think he'd been really busy with some kind of urgent lawyerly business that day, but I'm not positive (though I'm not really negative either), and I can't ask him because we never talk about that night."

Calvin almost asked why they never talked about it, but he remained silent, figuring he'd probably learn soon enough.

"So the play was over, and we headed home, leaving the theater late at night just like Batman as a boy before he loses everything that matters.

"Our path took us past the alley. The same alley, at the same time of year. We were walking past it, heading west on the opposite side of the street, our path perpendicular to the alley so that our route and it formed a giant T. T for trouble. T for me. T for..."

She gave a quick, sharp shake of her head as if trying to clear it or to jostle her thoughts back onto a more acceptable path.

"I don't think either one of us spared the alley a glance or a thought or anything else as we passed it," she went on. "But right when we were parallel to the alley's mouth, when we reached the apex of the T's stem, where the two directions intersected, a woman's voice screamed, 'No!' from somewhere in the alley. We slowed down and looked over. The alley was dark, a pillar of blackness between the buildings, and in its shadowy mouth two women were fighting, one with light hair, the other dark.

"'What are they doing?' I asked my dad.

"'I don't know,' he said.

"The light-haired one knocked down the dark-haired one, then whirled around to face us. It looked like she was pointing a small object at us. Maybe a gun. Or a camera. It was too dark to tell.

"She stopped moving for a second, then suddenly looked back over her shoulder as if she had heard a sound behind her.

"My father and I had been holding hands as we walked, and now he gave mine a tug and said, 'Come on, Tiff, we'd better—'

"And then there was a faint, muffled bang, like the report of a gun, but not from the alley. It sounded like it came from the apartment block next door, though it was hard to be sure because of the way the noise echoed off all the hard, flat planes of brick and concrete that formed the T around us. I glanced at the apartment block, saw nothing notable, and then..."

She hesitated for a moment, her eyes sad and faraway, seeing things nine years gone.

"And then I looked at the alley again, and the moment I did, the light-haired woman vanished right before my eyes, one second there, the next gone. It wasn't a trick of the light or the dark. It wasn't an illusion, optical or otherwise. I was looking right at her, and then I was looking at blackness. And out of that blackness emerged the second woman, the dark-haired one. She took a step forward and raised both arms like a runner crossing a finish line, and then she lifted her face to the stars and shouted, 'I did it!'

"And then she vanished too. And—"

She glanced at Calvin and saw the stunned look on his face.

"What?" she asked. "What's wrong?"

"I…" He shook his head. "I'll tell you in a minute. Please, just finish the story."

"There isn't much more to tell. All that's left is the bad girl's comeuppance. Everything went wrong in the wake of that night. My life. My head. Not right away, though. At first I thought the whole experience was kind of neat, like something out of a movie. But then I started having nightmares about being shot. For a long time barely a night went by when I didn't wake up screaming. I had panic attacks. I started sleepwalking and…and other things."

"What about your father? Did it affect him too?"

"I don't know. We almost never discussed that night, and the few times we did he made sure we didn't for long. He dismissed the whole thing as a non-event. I know he saw those women disappear, same as I did, but he insisted it was only a trick of the light. Maybe he even believed that. I don't know. I do know that around that time he started drinking heavily, and he grew more stressed out, more anxious, though that was probably only because of my own distress and anxiety. Being woken up nearly every night by your daughter screaming in mortal terror does nothing for your nerves, I'm sure."

"I imagine not."

"And the grim repercussions weren't limited to my dreams. I made the mistake of telling the other Barbies at school what I saw, assuming they'd be impressed that I had witnessed something so remarkable." She breathed out a bitter, rueful laugh and shook her head. "My social instincts stunk. I mean, how stupid could I be? I was one of the top dogs at school, you know. Woof woof. Bow wow. Bow down. Bitch bitch. I was pretty and blonde and my dad had money and I had all the most fashionable clothes and the snootiest, most self-centered attitude a pampered, privileged nine-year-old girl can possibly have. And then the Monday after the alley incident, when I was back in school, I met up with all my pseudo-friends, and I told them, 'Hey, guess what *I* saw,' and..."

She gave a small, sad smile. Calvin thought it had to be one of the saddest smiles he had ever seen.

"They fell on me like wolves on sheep. My former friends now dubbed me Witchy Tiff and started doing everything they could to ruin me. They even got most of the other students involved, too. I got mocked and taunted, locked in lockers, tripped and pushed, doused with Mountain Dew, pranked, slandered, and generally denigrated. Things got so bad my dad had to pull me out of the academy and have me home-schooled. It all happened so fast. One day I'm queen of the world, the next I'm toilet paper.

"Under other circumstances I might have handled things better, done some swift and brutal damage control, threatened the bitches with lawsuits, barked louder, bit harder, whatever. But my other problems—the nightmares, the anxiety—they were leaving me rattled, off-balance. And perhaps more importantly my experience on that dark and flowery May night—what I saw in that alley, or half-saw, or unsaw—it changed something in my head on a very deep and profound level. That might sound like hyperbole, but..."

She fell silent for a moment, thinking. Calvin waited patiently. Then she went on:

"Everyone thinks they understand what it would be like to experience an event that transcends the familiar rules of everyday reality because they see such things in movies all the time. Or at least fabricated representations of what the fabricators think those things would be like. But when you see it in real life it's different. It's a violation of everything your brain knows is real and possible. You're witnessing the unreal happen in the real world. It's like seeing a color that's both orange and blue at the same time. Or hearing a sound that's both loud and quiet. They're two things that can't exist together, an impossible dichotomy. And to experience them simultaneously induces a sort of existential trauma." She paused, then gave him a small, self-conscious smile. "Am I making sense? I know sometimes people think I don't. They might be right."

"I understand what you mean," said Calvin. "But there's something you need to know. You and your father weren't the only people who were affected by whatever happened that night."

Tiffany looked at him sharply, surprised. "What?"

"Do you know who Simon Bradley is?"

"No."

"Well, listen..."

He told her what Betty Romero had told him and Cynthia about Simon Bradley's suicide and the voices Betty and her husband heard.

"Now, I don't know for sure since she couldn't remember the exact date all this happened," Calvin said, "but it has to be the same thing you and your father witnessed. There was a gunshot from the apartment building, plus a commotion in the alley in which people shouted, 'No,' and 'I did it.' Plus, of course, there were puzzling psychological aftereffects, though what Betty and her husband experienced wasn't anything close to what you went through."

Tiffany stared at him with shining eyes, her breath

hitching in her chest. She was close to tears, Calvin realized. Not out of sorrow or pain, but relief. Relief that she had finally received proof her story was true. That she wasn't crazy. That she wasn't witchy. She had always known it in her heart, but until now the rest of the universe had been reluctant to back her up.

"Except…" A cloud passed over Tiffany's face. "It didn't really fade away for me. Not like it did for Mrs. Romero. In the ways that matter things only got worse. Much worse." Before Calvin could ask what she meant, she veered off in another direction. "Who was Simon Bradley? Why did he want to kill himself? It sounds like he might be the key to everything. Unless those long-locked women in the alley are the real keys."

"I don't know. Cyn and I have been too busy with the, uh…" He had been about to say "leucrota" but he was reluctant to tell Tiffany the details of the investigation until he had cleared it with the others (mainly Cynthia) first. "The investigation. We haven't had time to really look into Mrs. Romero's story." He glanced at the file cabinets. "There's also something else you should know. I don't know for sure that it ties in with everything else, but it might."

"You're full of surprising revelations today. I never guessed my visit here would be such a cornucopia of information. And here I thought I was the one who threw nothing but curveballs. So what's your latest divulgence?"

He opened the file cabinet and pulled out the penultimate trust, then sat down on the edge of the desk and cleared some space for Tiffany next to him. He really needed to put a few more chairs in here.

As she sat down, her thigh brushed his, sending a warm jolt through him. Stiffening, he glanced at her. She seemed not to have noticed anything and was eyeing the binder expectantly. Her long blonde hair smelled faintly of some kind of floral shampoo.

"Here," he said, opening the binder to the last page, where Mr. May and Stephen Krezchek had signed and dated the document. "This is the second-to-last trust Mr. May made, the one where he names us and a bunch of other people for the first time—people, so far as I can determine, he had never met. Notice the date."

"November 2008."

"Same year as the alley incident."

"You think he knew about it?"

"Possibly."

"But how? Aside from the Barbies at school and a few, um, mental health professionals my dad took me to, I never talked about it with anyone. And like I said, my dad kept mum about it, too. Besides, why make me the recipient of such a hefty sum just because I had a weird experience? It sounds like Mr. May investigated weird experiences aplenty over the years, and I can't imagine he left that much money to the numerous weirdness experiencers I'm sure he must have met along the way. Why leave some to me, then? It makes about as much sense as a gopher in a hot-air balloon."

"True." While she had been talking, Calvin had flipped to the page that listed the beneficiaries and the amounts they received, thinking that if Tiffany saw all the names together, it might jog loose some old, long-forgotten memory.

Instead, when she saw the list, she frowned and said, "I thought *you* got the house and the land, not Emily Crow."

"That's why this is the second-to-last trust. The last

one just switches me and Emily around."

"This Emily Crow person is one of Cynthia's relatives, I take it?"

"Yeah. You know: Emily Crow." Noticing her blank look, Calvin said, "Emily Crow! She got abducted and murdered here in May a few years ago?"

Tiffany shrank down, looking uncomfortable and vaguely ashamed, as if she felt she had failed to meet some basic standard of knowledge for a Bard County resident.

"I don't really watch the news. Sorry."

"No, it's...it's okay. It's just a little surprising, is all." Frankly "surprising" seemed like far too mild a word. Calvin had not yet met anyone in the area who hadn't heard about the death of Emily Crow. It was one of the most famous Bard County crimes of the last couple of decades, right up there with the Deermont child murders and the creepy triple homicide involving that FBI agent. Calvin was tempted to ask if she had heard of any of those, but he already felt bad for making her feel bad. "It's okay. It's kind of cool that you're not all wrapped up in worldly affairs."

"Thanks." She didn't sound like she believed him.

"But anyway, yeah, after she went missing, Mr. May amended the trust. I'm still not sure why he chose me to be the recipient of the Cuh..." He stopped himself before he could say "Collection." He didn't want to tell her about it yet. He wanted to surprise her. "The house and everything."

He was afraid that Tiffany had caught his clumsy reversal, but when he glanced at her he found that she was studying the trust.

"I'm the only who got a book?" she asked. She tapped the spot where it listed *Grimm's Complete Fairy Tales* as part of her bequest.

"Oh, yeah. I meant to ask you about that. Do you have any idea what that was about?"

"None at all. I was hoping you would. Your Mr. May was a very confounding and mysterious individual."

"He played it close to the vest, I'll give him that."

"I'll give him more. Whatever his reasons for bequeathing me the book, I'm very glad he did. During my...my troubles, I read it over and over. It was comforting to read all those tales of folks whose pain turned out to be meaningful and character-building and constructive." Then, as if the one thought somehow logically segued into the next, she looked up from the binder to Calvin and said, "You still have to show me the rest of your house."

"Oh." He felt a rush of excitement at the thought of showing her the Collection. If she thought he had been a cornucopia of curveballs so far, she hadn't seen anything yet.

His excitement died when Tiffany hopped off the desk and added, "But it'll have to be some other time. I need to head home. It's getting late."

"Ah," he said, disappointed. "Well, you're more than welcome to come back any time you want."

She cocked her head.

"Am I?"

"Absolutely."

She smiled. "Okay, then."

He smiled. "Okay."

They stood there smiling at each other.

Then she said, "Oooh," and poked his chest with her index finger, her touch once again sending a jolt all through him. "I'm gonna help you out. I'm gonna find out whatever's findable about Mr. Simon Bradley."

"You don't have to."

"I do. And not just for you. For both of us. I'm involved in all of this, too. Somehow. Someway. It all converges, remember?"

He smiled. "Okay, then. I look forward to hearing your report."

She went stiff as a board and clocked her feet together and gave him a snappy salute like a soldier in a slapstick comedy.

"Agent 144, on the case."

They headed downstairs and out to the driveway, where they paused beside Tiffany's car, smiling at each other once again. The high sun glinted off the corners of her Audi and his Honda Accord. Her hair shone like spun gold, almost too bright to look at directly. Calvin found himself yearning to reach out and touch that hair, to feel it hot and silky under his palm.

Tiffany's cheeks started to redden again as if she had sensed his thoughts. Or perhaps she had simply been thinking something very similar.

She looked down at her brand new shoes, then back up at him, all business and seriousness now, her smile tucked away.

"It's time for me to go," she said.

"All right."

She lingered a moment longer, just looking at him, obviously not wanting to go. But she had to. She gave him one last, crisp nod, which he returned, and then she climbed into her car.

She maneuvered her Audi around until it was facing down the driveway, then drove away. Right before the car disappeared into the tunnel of trees where the driveway passed through the woods, she waved. He waved back, and then she was gone save for the swiftly diminishing purr of the Audi's engine.

He stood there looking down the driveway until the sound of the engine was lost beneath the peep of birds and the sough of the wind in the trees, and then, still smiling, he headed back inside.

10

By the time the gang convened at Calvin's house that night, news had broken of another grisly death in Kingwood. Brad Vallance's killer had struck again. Or rather *killers*, as now seemed likely, at least in the opinion of the police and FBI. Calvin and the others gathered in the parlor and turned on the local news to catch the latest details.

Shortly before four a.m. last night, Reece Reston, a night watchman at the Red Anchor Brewery on Gater Road, heard a brief, clipped scream from the vacant lot next door to the brewery. Listening at the high wooden fence that separated the two properties he heard "horrible wet crunching sounds" and the voices of at least two people, including one man and one woman, who "kept on saying all kinds of twisted stuff about calling up Satan and chopping up the dead." Gun drawn, Mr. Reston crept to the edge of the fence and peered around it into the lot. Whoever had been there must have heard him coming, because the watchman saw only a mangled, bloody corpse in the middle of the lot and some bobbing branches amid the shrubs at the rear of the lot.

The police were called, and they eventually managed to

identify the corpse as Terrell Quinn, 48, a borderline schizophrenic who had been living on the streets for the last year. His injuries, while consistent with Brad Vallance's, were far more extensive.

"Large portions of the body were missing," Coroner Chandra said in his usual calm, understated way. "Most of the head was gone. There was no face, no teeth. In fact, there was nothing left to enable an identification except three fingerprints on one hand."

The authorities refused to speculate on what had become of the missing body parts.

Chief Dowdie summed up the opinion of the police and the FBI: "Given what Mr. Reston overheard, it seems all but certain that we are dealing with multiple individuals on some kind of bizarre crime spree, possibly with occult or ritualistic overtones."

The two missing teenage boys were still missing, and the police were still refusing to speculate if and how their disappearance might be connected with the deaths.

When the news report was over, Calvin turned off the TV and sat back in his chair, quiet and thoughtful.

"Does this change things?" Lauren asked. "I mean, it sounds like it's probably normal everyday nutjobs who are doing this."

"Not necessarily," Calvin said. "Don't forget, leucrotas are said to mimic human voices. It might have just been repeating things it heard people saying."

"Yeah, but Satan cutting up corpses, or whatever it was? That seems a bit unlikely."

Calvin nodded slowly. "It does. But if it's been prowling the streets of the city for a week or two, who knows what it might have overheard, especially at night. The West River neighborhood has a lot of bars and clubs, some of them pretty crazy places from what I've been told."

"Oh, yeah," Donovan said, smiling. "The Gemini Club is in that area. That's where all the indie heavy metal bands play when they come to town. I've been there a couple of times. It's a cool place. But, yeah, the monster could've picked up all kinds of fucked-up talk if it was hanging around on the night of a show."

Cynthia couldn't help laughing. "So, what, the monster might've just been quoting some third-rate heavy metal band's lyrics?"

"Hey, the stuff that night watchman dude said he overheard could've come from half the albums in my record collection."

Cynthia thought back to the racket she had heard blaring from Donovan's bedroom on innumerable occasions, then nodded.

"You know, he's right."

"I don't know," Lauren said dubiously. "I think I need better proof than that."

"Ask and it shall be given," Calvin said with a smile.

"What do you mean?"

He told them what he had discovered during his search of the *Morning Star*'s website earlier that day. He even brought out the Bard County map book and marked the location of each incident with a pencil on the one-page county map at the front of the book. When he was done he connected the marks as he had with the star on the map in the office five years earlier. The line he traced rose up due north from May to Ames, then curved around 240 degrees to Kingwood, forming a three-quarters circle with May in the center. The final shape somewhat resembled the power-button symbol on a computer.

"Whoa," Brandon said. "So it really did come out of that thing in the woods."

Calvin looked at Lauren, curious to see how she, the primary doubter at the moment, was greeting this new data. She was staring at the map and the glyph he had drawn on it, her brows drawn together. Finally she said, "Hm," and settled back on the couch, the green leather giving a low creak.

"Convinced?" Calvin asked her.

She opened her mouth, hesitated, glanced at the map again.

"Getting there," she said. "I'm still not ready to call it a leucrota, though. Especially not after what I found out about them yesterday."

"Ah, so I take it you managed to get the research done."

She straightened up in mock offense.

"Of course I got the research done," she said. "I am the research queen, my good man. Libraries tremble at my approach and bare their naked pages to my gaze."

"That sounds pretty kinky," Brandon said.

"You don't know the half of it," she said with a lascivious flick of her eyebrows. "Anyway..." She opened the small spiral notebook she had brought with her. "Let me preface this by saying that much of what you are about to hear is the biggest load of horseshit in existence. Bestiaries, while often fun to read, are not what any even marginally intelligent person would call scientific or coherent. I'll give you what there is, though." She started running her finger down the page, reading off each key piece of information as her finger came upon it.

"Okay, some sources claim the leucrota—aka the leucrocuta, the crotote, and a bunch of other names—is the offspring of a hyena and a lioness, others that it's the offspring of a wolf and a dog. Some say it comes from Ethiopia, others from India. All say it can perfectly imitate the human voice and, although nobody actually says so, I presume that means it can mimic other sounds, too. Its backbone is said to be so rigid that it can't turn its head around to look behind it, making it effectively blind in that direction." She looked up. "Which is, of course, completely ridiculous. I mean, how would it groom itself?" She shrugged and returned to her notebook. "Anyway, the authorities (and I use the term loosely) agree that it doesn't have individual teeth, just rigid plates of sharp bone. Beyond that, the descriptions of its body are a confusing mess. One source gives it a stag's haunches, a lion's breast and shins, a horse's head, a donkey's size, cloven hooves, and a mouth that meets its ears. Meanwhile, a different source gives it the size of an ass—"

Violet burst out laughing.

Lauren rolled her eyes. "I knew it. I knew she'd laugh at that. I knew I should've said 'donkey' instead."

Violet got herself under control long enough to say in a deep, learned voice, like the narrator of a nature show, "Another source gives it the odor of an ass," then started cackling again. Donovan joined in too, while Brandon tried to restrain his own snickers but finally admitted defeat and joined the giggle-fest. Though she kept shaking her head, Lauren couldn't help smiling, too.

"Are you sure you and Violet are actually related?" Cynthia asked Lauren.

"No," Lauren said. "I'm fairly certain that fairies swapped the real Violet for a changeling baby shortly after she was born."

"Hey!" Violet said. "I'm not a changeling baby! Whatever the hell *that* is."

Lauren cleared her throat and returned to her notes. "Anyway, as I was saying, this other source also says the leucrota has the legs and hooves of a hart and the head and face of a female badger, of all things."

"Oh, yeah," said Calvin. "A badger. That's the description they used for *Dungeons & Dragons*. I always assumed they made that up. It sounded too silly to be based on any actual source."

"Nope," said Lauren with a firm shake of her head. "It's right there in Topsell's translation of Gesner. He also repeats the bit about the mouth stretching from ear to ear, and then goes on to say, oddly enough, that this is the same creature as the mantichora, which he describes elsewhere as having a tail with porcupine-like quills, so you see what I mean about it all being mixed up and nonsensical."

"Yeah."

"Now as a final note, you might wonder why, if it's always described as being the offspring of hyenas and/or other dog-like animals, it would be as big as an"—a quick glance at Violet—"as a *donkey*. That's because, according to later authorities, Pliny, who most of the later bestiarists swiped a lot of their material from, for some reason blended the hyena with the Indian antelope, which also accounts for the hooves being another common feature."

"Wow, that *is* a big mess," said Cynthia.

"Yeah, but there are certain constants across all the bestiaries—its size, its ability to mimic human voices, its hooves, and the bony plates instead of teeth."

"Do any of the books say anything about its preferred habitat?" Calvin asked. "Forests, or deserts, or mountains, or whatever?"

"Not that I could find," Lauren said.

Calvin grunted. "All we have on that score, then, is the *Monster Manual*. If I remember right, it just says they inhabit lonely places."

"Well, duh," said Brandon. "Monsters always inhabit lonely places. You never see them shambling down Main Street at high noon."

"Unless it's Godzilla."

"It's different with giant monsters. When you're capable of wreaking huge swaths of indiscriminate destruction, it doesn't matter what time it is or where you are. But most monsters—the smaller ones especially, the ones who aren't gigantic engines of death and chaos—they have to be slyer and keep a lower profile."

Amused, Cynthia said, "Gee, I didn't know you could become an expert on the ecology of monsters just by watching lots of late-night movies."

"Sure. It's like research, only fun."

"Research is fun," protested Lauren.

"Getting back on track here," Calvin said, "we need to try to figure out where the leucrota—"

"Presumed leucrota."

"Presumed leucrota. We need to figure out where it's bedding down. Given that this latest attack was in the same neighborhood as the first one, it seems safe to assume that the monster is lying low not too far from Holly Hills Metropark, maybe waiting until the Park Service search is over before slinking back to its old haunts."

"How smart are these things supposed to be?" Donovan asked. "Would it really understand stuff like that?"

"I'm assuming it's pretty smart. If it knows what to say to lure weary travelers to their dooms, it must have a decent level of intelligence. It would have to understand human language, at least a little bit."

"Like a dog," Cynthia said. "Dogs can understand a limited number of words. And they're pretty smart."

"Yeah, only this dog can talk."

"Like Scooby-Doo," Violet said with a chuckle. "We're looking for Scooby-Doo."

"Scooby-Doo's evil twin, maybe," Donovan said.

"Scooby-*Doom,*" Brandon said.

"Given that the leucrota spent the last two years avoiding heavily populated areas," Calvin said, "and that it was only the Park Service search teams that drove it into the city, I think we can safely say the leucrota prefers wilder areas. That being the case, it would probably try to seek out places like that in the West River neighborhood."

"Parks!" Cynthia said. "Aren't there some small parks near the area where the murder occurred?"

Calvin picked up the map book and flipped to the pages that showed the West River neighborhood. Everyone else got up and crowded around him to look at the map.

"Okay, here's where Brad Vallance died," Calvin said, pointing to the approximate spot on Train Avenue where the alley was located. The alley itself wasn't shown. In fact, as Calvin scanned the pages, he found the book's lack of detail quite frustrating.

"And here's where those two missing graffitists were from," Brandon said, tapping an area in the northwest corner of the page.

"And here's where the latest body was found," Cynthia said, planting her index finger on a part of Gater Road that was almost exactly between Calvin's and Brandon's fingers.

"Okay," Calvin said. "We'll use the site of this new

murder as the center of our target area. And let's project outward a few blocks past the other two sites to form the area's perimeter. Say, to Castle Road on the east, Axelrod on the south, Pentz Lane on the west, and Miller on the north. What have we got within these parameters that might be monster friendly?"

"Like I said: parks." Cynthia tapped several irregularly shaped shaded areas on the map. "It looks like at least four or five, and that's not even counting Holly Hills."

"They're kind of on the small side."

"True, but they might be wooded. That might provide enough cover."

"There're a couple of cemeteries, too," Lauren said. "Depending on how they're landscaped, they might qualify."

"And look here," Brandon said, tracing a sinuous waterway with his finger. "There're creeks running through the area. If they're in deep, wooded ravines, they'd be good, too."

"Maybe," Calvin said. He shook his head. "We need to look at this area in person. I mean, I can see churches on here that take up half a city block, but the map doesn't tell us what the grounds are like. Is it open space? Is it wooded? Is it just a big parking lot? There's no way to know unless we actually go there and take a look." He sat back and looked at the others. "So who's available for a field trip tomorrow?"

"Are you gonna buy us lunch, like they do on real field trips?" asked Violet.

"Um, I guess that can be arranged."

"Cool! Then I'm free."

"I thought you had to work," Donovan said.

"I'm *scheduled* to work. Doesn't mean I have to."

Lauren tutted. "You've already been fired three times in the last two months!"

"Uh-uh! I only got fired twice. I quit the Dairy Queen job."

"Dad's gonna have a fit."

Violet waved a hand dismissively. "I know how to handle him."

"So who else is free tomorrow?" Calvin asked.

"I'm free," Donovan said.

"Uh, what kind of time-frame are we talking about here?" asked Brandon. "I've got a couple of job interviews early in the day, but I'll be free after one o'clock."

"I was hoping to start as early as possible," said Calvin. "There's a lot of ground to cover."

"I can't make it until after noon myself," Cynthia said. "I promised my dad I'd help him at the bookstore tomorrow morning."

"What about you?" Calvin asked Lauren. "Can you make it?"

"I get off at two tomorrow. If I head straight to Kingwood from Ames I could probably be there by two-thirty. Do you think you guys can wait that long?"

"Do you really think you can make it there that fast?" said Cynthia.

"If I really speed, sure."

"Huh. Maybe you're related to Violet after all."

"Hey!"

"We could do two-thirty," Calvin said, nodding. "It'll mean a late dinner, but I think we can pull it off."

"Awesome," said Brandon. "The whole gang together on its first adventure."

"I hate to tell you this, but we won't actually be together most of the time."

"Huh?"

"In order to do a block-by-block foot search of all this territory the way we need to, we'll have to split up."

"All alone?" Lauren said, twisting her mouth into a mock pout. "That's no fun."

"Actually, I was thinking groups of two. It would be faster singly, of course, but I figure it'd be better to buddy up just in case any of us actually run into the thing we're looking for."

"Ooh, I get to go with Donovan!" said Violet.

"No," said Cynthia.

Violet blinked at her, eyebrows raised. "Ex*cuse* me?"

"If you and Donovan go together, you'll never get anything done. You'll just end up goofing off or getting drunk or something."

"Hey!" Donovan said. "I can be responsible when I have to be."

"Not when you're with her."

"I can so!"

"If you really want to be responsible, you should go with someone else."

Donovan looked down at his shoes and murmured, "I guess..."

"Now hold on just a fucking minute," Violet snapped. Scowling, she planted her fists on her hips and thrust her face into Cynthia's, or at least into Cynthia's throat, given that Cynthia was over half a foot taller than she was. "This is a fucking democracy, isn't it? Who the hell are you to tell us who we can and can't walk around a city with? What are you, our fucking mom?"

Cynthia lifted an eyebrow. "You'd better thank every star in the sky I'm *not* your mother!"

"Actually," Lauren said, "surprised as I am to hear myself say this, Violet's right."

"What?" Cynthia said, taken aback. "What do you mean?"

"You're coming on a little strong here," said Lauren. "I mean, it's not like we're employees or something. We're doing this because we want to."

Cynthia held her hands up, palms out, in a gesture of conciliation. "Okay, I'm sorry if I'm coming across like that, but I know damn well that if we put those two together they'll just fuck around. I know what those two are like together. You know it too."

Lauren glanced at Violet and Donovan, then bobbled her head in a kind of grudging nod. "Yeah. Those two together are like, I don't know, Cheech and Chong, or something. But still..."

"Yeah," Brandon agreed. "I mean, I don't want to do this if we're just gonna get ordered around like employees, you know? I get enough of that shit outside of here."

Violet thrust her fist in the air. "Testify!"

Cynthia shot her an icy look, then sighed and spread her arms. "Okay. What does everyone want to do, then?"

Brandon and Lauren looked at Violet and Donovan, who were looking at each other, all of them with somewhat startled expressions.

"Um..." Brandon shrugged. "Actually, the plan as it is sounds okay to me. I was just objecting to your knee-jerk objections to those two pairing up."

Cynthia nodded. "Okay, I guess I was a little knee-jerk. I apologize." She turned to Donovan and Violet. "And you two insist on pairing up together, I take it?"

"I guess we don't have to," Donovan said.

Violet stepped between him and his sister and crossed her arms over her breasts.

"Yes," she said. "We *do* insist on pairing up together."

She smiled smugly. Cynthia resisted an urge to throttle the bitch. At this point Violet was doing this solely to piss her off and wasn't about to back down. But neither was she, God damn it. It was a matter of principle.

The two of them faced each other in icy silence, their glares clashing like duelists' swords.

"I have an idea that should make everybody happy," Calvin said in a soft, pleasant voice that was way too soft and way too pleasant to be anything other than a flimsy veil over a Vesuvius-like caldera of ill humor.

Everyone immediately fell silent and looked at him with apprehension.

Cynthia felt particularly apprehensive, only just now realizing how much this whole dick-fight must have pissed him off. Yes, it was a democracy and they were all equals and blah blah blah, but in the end, this was largely Calvin's show. It was his house and his Collection. By bequeathing it to him, Mr. May had clearly designated him as his successor. And as Cynthia herself had pointed out yesterday, Calvin was the only one who had no notable life outside of this. Investigating weird shit *was* his life, and woe to anyone, even a friend, who had a problem with that or got in the way of that. While Calvin was generally an extremely easygoing, understanding kind of guy, he had his limits.

"What idea is that?" Cynthia asked, dreading the answer.

"We'll just split into two groups of three, that's all. It'll take us a little longer to cover all the territory we have to cover, but it'll solve everyone's problems. This way, Donovan and Violet can stay together, and you"—he nodded at Cynthia—"can go with them to make sure they don't goof off. Meanwhile, Lauren and Brandon and I can form our own little group." He smiled pleasantly.

It was a good plan, eminently logical. And it managed to satisfy Cynthia's and Violet's complaints while making both of them feel as if they were being cruelly punished.

Violet stared at Calvin in horror for a moment, then at Cynthia. Then her shoulders sagged and she flumped down into her seat.

"Shit," she muttered. "Sometimes I should just keep my fuckin' mouth shut."

"That is true," Lauren said quietly. "And yet you never do."

"Sounds, um…sounds good," Cynthia told Calvin with a smile that didn't extend beneath her face. She felt as if she had been consigned to sit at the kids' table. She couldn't really blame Calvin for being pissed, though; a man-eating monster was prowling the streets of Kingwood while she and Violet stood here sniping at each other over trivialities.

"There's one more order of business on tonight's agenda," Calvin said, his tone normal again as if the last couple of minutes hadn't happened. His laid-back nature ensured that his bad moods passed quickly, like summer squalls. "It's something Cyn and I meant to bring up last time, but we kind of got sidetracked."

"Oh, yeah," Brandon said. "Something about ghosts and fish, right?"

"Something like that."

Calvin and Cynthia related what Betty Romero had told them about Simon Bradley's death and the strange echoes she and her husband had heard afterward. Then they described their visit to the Fishes' house.

"And there's more," Calvin said. "A lot more. Tiffany Fish visited me this afternoon."

"Oh, did she now?" Cynthia said, a grin spreading across her face.

Calvin flushed. "She was…it was just a visit."

"Wait a minute," Brandon said, peering at Calvin's spanking-red cheeks with a grin of his own. "Is there something going on here?"

"There's chemistry," Cynthia explained.

"Oh, my," Lauren said.

"Dude!" Brandon said.

Calvin rolled his eyes. "All right, guys. Let me just tell you what happened."

"Should we, like, turn on some bow-chicka-bow music for this?" Violet asked.

Calvin's face now looked as if it were about to spontaneously combust.

"All right, already. Come on, now. This is actually kind of important. Turns out she's connected to the alley, too. She was there the night Simon Bradley died."

"Wait, what?" Cynthia said.

Calvin retold the story Tiffany had told him a few hours earlier.

"She said she's going to look into this Simon Bradley fellow, then get back to me soon," he concluded.

"Aha," Brandon said, "do we have a new member of the gang?"

"I don't know yet. I think she'd be a welcome addition. But she's kind of shy."

"Except around you, clearly," Cynthia said, smiling.

"Um…" Calvin's cheeks began to flare redly again.

She looked at the others. "Like I said: chemistry."

"Dude, we totally have to meet her now," Brandon said.

"I'll talk to her about it. If she's up for it, I could invite her to the next meeting."

"Please do," Lauren said. "I want to see this legendary chemistry in action."

"Bow-chicka-bow!" Donovan sang. "Bow-chicka-bow!"

"All right," Calvin said. "I think it's time we call it a night."

11

Calvin's "In the Hall of the Mountain King" ringtone woke him up at eight a.m. With a grunt he snatched his phone from the bedside table.

"H'lo," he said, his voice and mind still thick with sleep.

A pause, then: "Um, is this Calvin?"

Tiffany Fish. Calvin found himself wide awake faster than he ever would have thought possible. He sat up and swung his legs over the side of the bed.

"Tiffany, hi," he said, his voice now amazingly clear. "What's up?"

"Um, I woke you up, didn't I?"

"Yeah, but I don't mind. You're worth getting woken up for."

There was a long silence on the other side. Calvin felt certain she was smiling and blushing. The thought made him grin.

"So, to what do I owe this pleasant little wake-up call?" he asked, hoping to coax her out of her silence.

"Oh, um, I thought I'd let you know: My mission has

been successfully accomplished. I found out about Simon Bradley, the man who shot himself."

"Wow, that was quick work."

"Actually, a trip to the Kingwood Public Library was all it took. One old newspaper clipping and two back issues of *The Clarion,* and I was done."

"What's *The Clarion?*"

"That's Kingwood University's student newspaper. Simon Bradley was a grad student there. Are you free today? I can give you all the details, and you can finish giving me the tour of your house."

"Well, I'm booked solid this afternoon, but I've got the whole morning free."

"Oh. Okay." She sounded a little disappointed. "Um, you probably need time to wash and dress and eat and excrete and stuff, so—"

"Not much time. If you can be here in half an hour, that'd be perfect."

"Thirty minutes, zero problem." She sounded positively chipper now. "See you then."

Calvin managed to shower, dress, wolf down a bowl of Cap'n Crunch, and brush his teeth in twenty minutes. For the next ten minutes he paced the parlor, pausing every thirty seconds to peek out the window in hopes of seeing Tiffany's silver Audi coming up the driveway. The minutes oozed past at a sludge-like pace.

Finally he heard the Audi's engine, and after racing to the bathroom to check himself in the mirror and make sure his appearance hadn't gone to hell in the last ten minutes, he hurried to the front door and opened it to reveal Tiffany ascending the front steps.

She lit up when she saw him, a big, radiant smile spreading across her face. She was totally devoid of the hesitancy and nervousness she had shown when she first showed up here yesterday. He could tell she felt comfortable around him now, as if they had known each other a lot longer than two days. The feeling was mutual.

"Come on in," he said, holding the door open for her. "So, tour now, or would you prefer to tell me the fruits of your research first?"

"I should share my fruits first. They're more important. Though not very pleasant. Bad apples from the tree of knowledge."

"That's okay. I'm an adventurous eater."

They sat down in the parlor, Tiffany on the green leather couch, Calvin on a matching chair that sat at a right angle to it.

"So how did you even know where to look for info about him?" Calvin asked. "I mean, I can't imagine 'Bradley, Simon' was in the library's card catalogue."

"Easy. I just searched the *Kingwood Morning Star*'s obituary section in the days following the alley incident. And bam, two days later, there he was. He was twenty-three years old. He was a Libra. He was born and raised in Kingwood. He attended Kingwood University, where he was working on a PhD in physics."

"Physics?" Calvin said, surprised. "That's interesting. One of my degrees is in physics."

Tiffany only nodded, this news not surprising her in the slightest.

"That was it for the obit," she said, "so I checked to see if the library had any copies of the university paper. Turns out they had a complete collection dating back to the paper's founding in 1935. I wound up spending a few hours poring over every issue between 2003, the year Mr. Bradley started there as a freshman, and 2008, when he died."

"You didn't have to go to all that trouble."

"This concerns me, too. I needed to know."

Calvin nodded. "So what did you learn from *The Clarion?*"

"He was in a 2007 issue, one of three students profiled as rising stars in the Physics department. It had a photo of him. He..." She gave a rueful grimace. "He deviated quite widely from common standards of attractiveness. He was short and stooped and had a wide, froggish face, with big, cavy nostrils and thick glasses that trebled the size of his eyes, and even at twenty-three his hairline was badly receding. But the way the article described him, his brains more than squared any physical deficiencies. The word 'genius' was used more than once. He was said to have had some brilliant theories about the behavior of certain subatomic particles."

"Did it say which ones?"

She shook her head. "The article didn't go into any detail about his work. It would've been over the heads of most of the readers. It wasn't a physics journal, after all; it was just a lowly student newspaper. It didn't even include any direct quotes from Mr. Bradley. Apparently he was too busy with his research to talk to reporters, which sounded like the usual state of affairs with him. The writers did, however, talk to a few professors from his department, all of whom praised his intelligence. The most interesting quote came from, uh..." She consulted a small spiral notebook she had brought with her, much as Lauren had the night before. "Professor Amos Huxley, who said that he believed Mr. Bradley 'was on the verge of startling breakthroughs in particle physics,' and that he—Huxley that is—'would bet money that future generations will mention Simon Bradley in the same breath as Einstein.'"

"Wow. That's high praise."

"Yeah. That was the December 11, 2007, issue of the paper. A little over six months later Bradley blew his super-brilliant brains all over his apartment. Professor Huxley lost his bet.

"But that brings us to the second *Clarion* article, a commemorative piece they ran right after he died. It repeated a lot of what the earlier article said. Again, they relied on his professors for quotes."

"Doesn't sound like he had many friends."

"No. His work was his life."

"What about family?"

"That was part of the problem. His father died when he was a child, he had no siblings, and his mother had been fighting brain cancer for the last year. Bradley wasn't coping with her decline very well. One of his professors—not Huxley; this was a man named Cartwright—said that during the last few months of his life Bradley's schoolwork had grown increasingly 'incoherent.' The faculty recommended he take some time off, see a psychiatrist, things like that. Bradley refused, insisting his work was flawless; the professors were just too dumb to understand it. (That's not what the article actually said. I'm reading between the lines here.) His worsening scholastic performance in turn worsened his already bleak mental state, and when his mother died at the end of April, that was the proverbial last straw. Three weeks later he decided to join her."

"Geez. So here we have an isolated, friendless geek who lost the one person he was close to and who had started out as a sort of wunderkind only to wind up spouting seeming incoherencies that alienated him from his professors. That's pretty depressing."

"Tell me about it," Tiffany muttered, staring down at her notebook.

Calvin had been only giving lip-service to the depressingness of the case—it was hard to feel too depressed about the decade-old death of a man you didn't know—but Tiffany sounded genuinely sad for Simon Bradley.

Then he remembered that her mother was dead, she lived with her father and no siblings, and she had been ostracized by her friends in school, all of whom thought she'd gone bonkers. And perhaps she had, at least to some extent, given the anxiety and nightmares she experienced. He wondered what her life had been like the last nine years. She hadn't mentioned any friends, or lovers, or jobs.

He looked at her sitting there, sad and pale and quiet in her still radiantly white shoes, her head down and her loose blonde hair hiding her face, and his heart ached with sorrow for her—and even a little for poor Simon Bradley now, too, whose pains echoed hers. Calvin wanted to do whatever he could to ease her troubled soul. She was too wonderful a person to feel that way. He wanted to make her feel happy the way she made him feel happy.

"Is that it, then?" he said.

"Yep," she said, still looking down at her notebook. "That is it. Doesn't tell us much, does it?"

"We can worry about it later. Why don't I show you the rest of the house right now, if you're up for it."

She looked up, her face bright and eager now, her somberness gone.

"Yes! I am up. I am definitely very up."

He led her straight to the Collection room in the east wing.

"I think you'll be pretty interested in this," he said, and opened the door.

She stepped inside and spent a moment surveying the diverse array of objects that crowded the shelves. Then she looked at Calvin and said: "What strange repository have I stumbled into here?"

"This," he said, waving his arm with a showman-like flourish, the way Mr. May had done for him and Cynthia five years earlier, "is the Collection. These are artifacts from Mr. May's investigations into anomalous phenomena."

"Huh." She peered at a few of the items on a shelf near the door—a black glass ashtray, a dead cicada, a music box shaped like a miniature gramophone. "Are the objects themselves anomalous in some way?"

"Some of them. Others are objects that were affected by the phenomena or connected with it in some other fashion. A lot of the actual phenomena were frustratingly intangible."

She nodded. "Like ghosts. Or words."

"Right. This isn't the only room, either. There are four more, plus one room devoted to files on the anomalies."

"Files?" She scanned the shelves again. A numbered sticker was affixed to the shelf in front of each item. She tapped the music box's sticker, which read "2314." "Let me guess: These are the file numbers, right?"

"That's right."

She nodded and looked around the room. "There are a lot of numbers in here..."

For the next hour Calvin gave her a grand tour of the Collection, pointing out some of the more notable items as they made their way first through the rooms on the second floor, then the ones on the third. Tiffany was clearly interested and intrigued, though not brimming with pop-eyed wonder as Calvin had been when he first saw the Collection. Her reaction was quieter, more thoughtful. At times she seemed almost wary, as if she were passing through rooms full of unexploded ordnance. At other times she seemed more interested in the stickers than in the objects themselves, and she scanned them closely as if watching for specific numbers.

"It must have taken Mr. May a long time to investigate so many cases," she said. They were in the west room on the third floor, a room Calvin had always thought of as the freezer room, since it contained a Frigidaire that housed the Collection's perishable items.

Calvin nodded. "Nearly seventy years. Most of his life."

She looked around the room, then back at him, her expression suddenly apprehensive.

"Am I here somewhere?" she said.

"What?"

"Have you read all the files? Every one?"

"Yes." Then he realized what she was getting at. "Tiffany, you're not mentioned in any of the files, and neither is the alley, or Simon Bradley, or any of that stuff."

"He must have known, though. If he knew of me, if he left things to me, he must have known what happened."

"Not necessarily. He left things to the rest of us, and at that point none of us had experienced any paranormal phenomena at all, at least not as far as we can recall. There aren't files about any of us. Not anywhere."

"He could have investigated things without making files."

"True. But I doubt he had time for very many investigations beyond the ones he made files on. His dance card was pretty full."

"Then why did he choose us?"

"I...I don't know. I wish I did."

She wandered down one of the aisles, watching the varied items go past, her expression closed and distant. Her eyes settled on a shelf that contained nothing but human skulls and bones, and she stopped with a faint, indrawn breath.

"Memento mori," she muttered. "Moment of death. Memento of death. More E." Pause. "Hh."

"What?"

She turned to him.

"Will you investigate the alley? You suggested you might."

"Uh, probably. Unless you would prefer we don't."

"You should be careful," she said. "Exploring the unknown might make things known to you that you would prefer you didn't know."

"I understand that."

"Do you?"

"I..." Did he? "I think I do."

"Maybe." She didn't sound convinced. "What I saw that night in the alley, it had repercussions. Echoes. It's still having them."

"I don't think all unusual events are like that," Calvin said. "I saw some birds materialize out of thin air not far from here. So did Cynthia and some other people. And Mr. May witnessed hundreds of strange events. But none of us experienced any effects like what you experienced."

"Birds, huh?" One side of her mouth curled up in a small, humorless smile. "They weren't crows, were they?"

"Um, no."

She cocked her head. "So are you saying the problem was with me, then, and not with the event itself?"

"Not necessarily. The Romeros experienced strange aftereffects, too, remember."

"Not with anywhere near the same severity. They just heard some fuzzy echoes. They didn't have nightmares, mood disorders, psychotic episodes. Their lives weren't destroyed. Not like mine. And it can't be a matter of their having only heard the incident rather than seeing it, because my dad saw it too, and he didn't experience the same shattering consequences I did. Therefore the problem must be with me, right?"

Her words suggested a swift and worrying descent into bitterness and self-pity. Her tone, however, was calm and rational, and her expression thoughtful. Still, he felt compelled to reassure her that he didn't think there was anything wrong with her. Not at all. Just the opposite; he thought she was resoundingly right in every way.

"Tiffany—" he began.

Before he could say another word, she fixed a level gaze upon him and in the same flatly demanding regal tone she had used to silence her father the other day, she said, "I want to join your group."

"You do?" Calvin felt lost but had the idea he shouldn't be. He got the impression that this was one apparent non-sequitur that really wasn't and that he was just a little slow catching up with her swiftly moving train of thought.

The look she gave him—her head sticking out, eyebrows raised, as if to say, "Haven't you been listening to a word I said?"—underscored that.

"Well, yes," she said. "The only way to determine if that hypothesis is correct is for me to expose myself to further anomalous phenomena. If I can't deal with them, then the problem is with me. If I can, then the problem was clearly with the incident in the alley itself (or perhaps with the specific combination of me and the incident). We have to know."

She said "we." What did that mean? Given her princessy tone a moment ago, it made him think of the royal we, the way a queen would speak for all her subjects. But he didn't think it was that. It was more likely either a "we" in the sense of "you and I," or a "we" as in "the group."

"Please," she added. There was nothing regal about her now. Her eyes were desperate, beseeching.

"Actually, just last night the others and I discussed the possibility of your joining," he said. "Everyone seems amenable to the idea, but of course they'd like to meet you first."

"Oh." She looked intimidated at the idea of meeting a group of strangers.

"I'll be seeing them later today. We're going to be looking for areas where the thing that killed Brad Vallance might be hiding out. You, uh, you could come if you like."

"I...I can't. I have plans. Um..."

"We'll probably be meeting up again tomorrow. Would you be free then?"

"Maybe. Probably."

"I'll give you a call once we've settled on a time."

"Okay." She flashed him a grateful smile. "Thank you." Then the smile faded, and she tilted her head to one side. "You sound certain that Brad Vallance's killer is a thing. The police think it's people, a duo or a gang."

"Yeah, uh..." Time to tell her the truth. "We think it's a leucrota. What's more, we think it came out of a, uh, an anomaly in the woods." He nodded at the north wall. "Out there."

She looked at the wall, then back at him. One blonde eyebrow rose. "I think you have a story to tell me."

"I think I do. But not here. You still have to see the tower. There are chairs up there. We can sit and talk."

He led her back to the spiral staircase, then up to the small room at the top of the tower. A card table and four chairs comprised the room's only future. On every side a window offered a view of the world below.

Tiffany pressed her face against the east window and looked out. Directly below, the roof of the east wing stretched away like a dark pier, its sides covered with fishscale singles, its edges bordered with black iron cresting shaped like alternating circles and vertical spikes. Beyond the house, the lawn extended flat and green toward the dark wall of the woods.

Mr. May had installed very thick, almost soundproof windows, so none of the traffic noises from Oaks and Potts Roads reached in here. Calvin and Tiffany might have been the only people in the world. It was so silent up here that Calvin could hear Tiffany breathing, the sound still a little ragged from her ascent of the stairs, the soft rustle of her jeans as she shifted her weight from one foot to the other, the faint wet click as she swallowed.

"It's scenic up here," she said, face still pressed to the window. Her breath had left an oval of fog on the glass, and she pulled back a little to look at it, then drew a 12 in the fog with her index finger. She started to write something next to it, but then gave a small jerk like someone startled awake from a doze. She glanced back at Calvin with a sheepish look, as if she'd just been caught doing something wrong, then wiped away the writing with her palm, her skin squeaking on the glass.

"Sorry," she said. "I probably got prints on your window."

"It's fine. I don't clean much anyway." He gestured at the table and chairs. "Have a seat."

They sat.

"So what's a leucrota?" Tiffany asked. "Does it have something to do with whiteness?"

"Whiteness?"

"From the combining form 'leuko,' like in 'leukemia.'"

"Oh. Actually, I don't know. I'm not sure of the origin of the word."

"Okay. And, um…" She looked sheepish again. "Sorry if I seem kind of obsessive about words sometimes. I'm just trying to get at the reality behind language. After all, where did language come from?"

He shrugged. "We made it, right?"

"Not wholly consciously. And in any case, if our brains made language, what made our brains? What established the patterns and thought-structures within them that guided language's form?"

"Evolution?"

"And what made the rules of evolution?"

"This is become another infinite regress, isn't it?" he said with a smile.

She smiled back. "We keep having problems with those, don't we?"

"Infinite problems."

She groaned and rolled her eyes.

"Why don't you tell me about your leucrota and why you think it came out of your scenic woods. But, um…" She checked her watch. "Bear in mind I have to leave in half an hour."

"Okay, Cliff Notes version, then." He took a deep breath. "It all started a few years ago when Cynthia's sister Emily got abducted…"

He sketched out the events surrounding Emily's murder and what happened in the clearing the night her killer died there. He then recounted their recent investigation into the murders in Kingwood. Despite his attempt at succinctness, by the time he had finished telling her the whole tale, the thirty minutes was up.

Tiffany pushed her chair back from the table and stood up. "Thank you for the enlightening story. It's given me a lot to think about."

He rose, too.

"I hope it hasn't scared you away," he said, only half joking.

She cocked her head. "Why would it?"

"You know, the house being situated on a sort of magical network of tragedy."

"No," she said. She looked out the window at the woods. The treetops were stirring in an unheard wind, their branches bobbing, their leaves flashing their paler undersides. She watched the restless foliage for a moment, then quietly said. "It probably isn't what you think it is anyway. Things rarely are."

He led her downstairs and out to her car. They turned to face each other next to the Audi.

"Call me once you've got a time set up," she said.

"Will do."

"And good luck with your monster hunt."

"Thanks."

They looked at each other in silence, neither of them making any move to part. Calvin felt an almost overpowering urge to kiss her. But like before, he hesitated, still afraid it was too soon and Tiffany too fragile.

When their eye contact carried on a beat longer than propriety recommended, a rosy flush tinged Tiffany's cheeks and a smile flickered at her lips. Calvin smiled, too, but more broadly.

Her blush deepening until it seemed as if she were wearing liberally applied rouge, she looked down at the ground, cleared her throat, and swiped a stray lock of hair from her cheek.

"Yeah," she said. "I, uh…I should go."

"Right."

She went. As before, he watched her drive away until the car was out of sight, and then, still smiling the same smile he had been smiling for the last three minutes, he went back inside.

He was about to turn on the TV to see if there had been any new developments with the Kingwood murder investigation when his stomach rumbled, reminding him that he hadn't eaten anything today except a bowl of Cap'n Crunch. He went to the kitchen and threw together a ham and cheese sandwich with a heap of potato chips on the side. He had eaten only three chips and one bite of the sandwich when the doorbell rang.

Figuring it was Tiffany, that maybe she had left something behind or forgotten to tell him something—or better yet had decided to hurl herself into his arms and pepper his face with kisses and demand to be made love to immediately—he hurried to the front door and threw it open. His expectant smile died on his lips.

It was Andrew Fish.

"We need to talk," Fish said.

"Uh…" What the hell was this about? Did Fish know his daughter had stopped by? He must. "Come on in."

Fish looked over Calvin's shoulder at the long hallway lined with paintings, then shook his head.

"Why don't we talk out here?" He gestured at the porch.

"Uh, sure."

Calvin stepped outside, no longer hungry, feeling instead a greasy, heavy sensation in the pit of his stomach, the sort of feeling you get before taking a test, or having a job interview, or some other undertaking your whole future might hinge on.

They sat down on the top step, facing the woods to the south of the house. Beyond the woods in that direction was Oaks Road, and every now and then the muffled whoosh of a passing car came to them.

"So," said Calvin, needing to fill the silence between them with something, anything, no matter how banal. "How are you?"

Andrew Fish nodded without looking at Calvin. "As well as I can be, I suppose." He stared at the woods a moment longer and then, still without looking at Calvin, said, "I know Tiffany's been coming here."

Calvin had suspected as much, but now that the words had been spoken and the truth laid bare, he felt angry, outraged.

"You've been following her? You're spying on your own daughter?"

Fish turned to him, his lips pressed together in some odd combination of guilt and self-righteousness.

"I'm making sure she's all right."

"Forgive me for saying so, but that sounds grotesquely overprotective."

Fish nodded. "It does sound that way, doesn't it? I suppose it'll sound even worse when I tell you that I did some checking up on *you*, too."

Calvin's mouth opened, but he was too flabbergasted to speak for a moment. Before he could find the words to give vent to his swiftly mounting outrage, Fish went on.

"Nothing serious. Just making sure you were who you said you were, checking your grades, things like that. Nothing that isn't publicly available. For what it's worth, I'm impressed: A double major in physics and psychology in only four years? Not everyone can pull that off."

Calvin's mouth closed. He wasn't sure what to think now. If Fish was trying to mollify him with flattery...well, he was doing a pretty good job of it.

"When I first learned that Tiffany had visited you the other day," Fish said, "I debated long and hard whether or not I should come out here to have a talk with you. It was learning of your background in psychology that convinced me to do it. I guess I'm hoping it will help you understand Tiffany's...unique history."

That heavy, greasy feeling returned, worse than before.

"Tell me," Calvin said.

Fish sighed and leaned forward a little, his elbows on his knees, his hands clasped, his eyes fixed on the ground. He suddenly looked very tired and much older than he was.

"Tiffany is...special."

Calvin frowned. "That's what they say about retarded people."

"No, that's what they say about people who are different from most." He gave Calvin a sidelong look. "When she was nine, something happened..."

"The women in the alley. She told me about that."

Fish straightened up, staring at him in surprise. "She did?"

Calvin nodded. "The two of you were walking home from a play one night in Kingwood and you saw two women vanish in an alley."

The corner of Fish's mouth twitched. "That's what *she* says. I don't think they disappeared. It was dark and at a distance."

"She said you saw it too."

"I saw what *appeared* to be two women disappear in an alley. The eyes play tricks, especially late at night when it's dark and you're tired. Did she tell you what happened in the wake of the incident?"

"She said she didn't handle it too well. She said she had some nightmares."

"Is that all?"

"Also some anxiety attacks and sleepwalking."

But that wasn't all, was it? She had said something else, too. *I started sleepwalking and...and other things.* She hadn't specified what those other things were, and he hadn't felt comfortable asking. Now, however, he had a feeling he was about to find out.

"Did she tell you about the incident with the mirror?"

"No." Calvin's stomach was a sack full of grease now, heavy and bloated and ready to burst.

Fish stared at the distant trees in silence for a few seconds, then said, "She had nightmares nearly every night for two years. She would wake up screaming in pure, primal terror from nightmares in which people were shooting her in the head. It was horrifying. I had never really understood the expression 'blood-curdling scream' until then. Nearly every night for two years I sat with her for hours, trying to calm her down, to get her to stop crying and trembling like some beaten and traumatized animal. It got to the point where she was afraid to go to bed. She would have panic attacks. I took her to a child psychologist, who wound up prescribing an anti-anxiety medication when regular psychotherapy failed to have any effect at all. It helped with the panic attacks, but not with the nightmares."

"She also told me she got ostracized at school."

Fish nodded. "There was that, too. She made the mistake of telling the other kids about the disappearing women in the alley, and, well, I'm sure you know how kids can be. That, of course, didn't help things. Not only had her dreams turned against her but her so-called friends had, too. Things got so bad I wound up having her home-schooled. It seemed easiest for everyone that way."

Fish fell silent again and looked out at the trees. He toyed nervously with a large onyx ring on the ring finger of his right hand, pulling it up to the knob of the second joint, then shunting it back down to the knuckle.

"About three months after the alley incident, she started sleepwalking. It didn't happen often, and when it did it was usually very minor. She'd wake up out of a sound sleep to find herself standing by her bedroom door or on the landing of the second-floor stairs. At first it scared her, of course, and she would come to my bedroom and shake me awake. But after it had happened a few times, she started getting used to it. She no longer felt compelled to wake me up and instead quietly went back to bed on her own.

"And then one night I was startled awake by a string of deafening bangs and quick bright flashes that lit my bedroom in stark black and white. Immediately recognizing them as gunshots, I leaped out of bed, convinced that the house was under attack and I was about to be murdered. By the time I got my bearings, the shots had stopped. In the moonlight shining in through the windows, I saw Tiffany standing near the far corner of the room, her back half-turned to me and a smoking gun in her hand. My gun. It was the Smith and Wesson I kept locked in a safe under my bed. The safe now sat in the middle of the floor, open and empty, the key, which I kept on my keychain, jutting from the lock.

"I hurried over to Tiffany. She was standing in front of the wreckage of a Victorian cheval mirror that had belonged to Sarah, my wife. The glass was shattered and lay in sharp, glittering heaps on the carpet, and the mirror's wooden backing was riddled with bullet holes.

"Tiffany appeared to be in shock; she just stood there staring at the ruins of the mirror like she couldn't figure out what it was or what was happening. But when I knelt down beside her and pulled the still-smoking gun from her hand, she whirled toward me, startled and screaming, her face a mask of stark terror. When she saw it was me, she flung her arms around me and clung to me, sobbing hysterically.

"It took a while to get her to talk, and even longer until she started making sense. She claimed she had no idea what had happened. The last thing she remembered she had been in bed, falling asleep, and the next thing she knew she was in my bedroom watching her own reflection get blown to pieces by a gun she had never even been shown how to shoot. She couldn't—or wouldn't—tell me anything else.

"Oddly, this incident, terrifying though it was to both of us, signaled the beginning of the end of her problems. Over the next few months the nightmares steadily grew rarer, and her anxiety faded to the point where she no longer needed medication. She was doing well enough that she started attending school again, though I managed to get her enrolled in a different school system where she wouldn't have to face the same kids. And for a couple of years things went well. Very well. Almost back to normal. But then when she was thirteen..." He paused again and looked down at the onyx ring, which he was now twisting round and round his finger like a millstone rotating on its axle.

There's more? Calvin thought, his heart sinking. The worst part was, something in Fish's manner suggested that everything he'd related so far was little more than a prologue to the real story.

"One morning I woke up and was heading downstairs to make coffee," Fish said. "As I passed Tiffany's room, I heard a faint squeaking sound through the closed door. I didn't think much of it. I figured she had woken up early and was just...I don't know, doing something innocuous. So I went downstairs, made the coffee, made breakfast, and called Tiffany down to eat. She didn't answer. I called again. Still no answer. I went upstairs to see what was going on. When I came to her door, I could still hear those faint squeaks. I knocked. She didn't answer. There was only that incessant squeak-squeak-squeak. So I opened the door.

"Sometime during the night she had moved all of her furniture into the center of the room—how she did it without waking me up, I have no idea—and she had covered half of one wall with...well, it looked like complete gibberish to me. The squeaking was the sound of the black magic marker on the wall's light-blue paint as she wrote.

"I couldn't see Tiffany from where I stood—she was hidden from view behind her dresser and the bean bag chair she had draped atop it—but I could hear the marker working and I could see where the line of…of graffiti, or whatever you want to call it—I could see where it stopped.

"I called her name. I think she might have made a faint noise, like an 'mm,' or I might have imagined it. Either way the squeak of the marker never even paused.

"I stepped into the room and around the dresser, and there she was. She sat cross-legged on the floor, still wearing her pajamas. Her face was close to the wall, her nose almost touching it, and she was rocking back and forth as she scribbled away.

"I asked her what she was doing three times in increasingly urgent tones. She didn't make a sound. She just kept rocking and scribbling with a pinched, intent look like a monk copying scripture.

"Finally I reached down and snatched the marker from her hand. I didn't know what else to do. I didn't know how else to make her stop and listen.

"Her reaction was…" He closed his eyes, sighed, opened them again. "She leaped up at me, screaming incoherently and grabbing at the marker. Holding it out of her reach, I tried to talk to her calmly and rationally, to ask her what she was doing and why it was so important, but she didn't even seem to hear me. She grabbed hold of the arm I was holding the marker with and started clawing at my flesh to make me let go. Within moments my forearm was covered in blood. She was savage, feral. There was nothing rational in her eyes. I'd never seen her like that. I'd never seen *anyone* like that.

"I…I slapped her. Right across the face. I had never raised a hand to her before in my life, but I didn't know what else to do. I was startled and scared and in pain, and I just…just reacted."

He glanced at Calvin as if he expected Calvin to voice

some protest. Calvin didn't. He didn't trust himself to speak. The thought of Andrew Fish striking thirteen-year-old Tiffany, even in those singular circumstances and in what could certainly be seen as self-defense, made him sick with indignation. Then again he wondered what he might have done differently had he been in the same situation. He didn't know.

Fish must have read some of this on Calvin's face because he nodded slightly as if in agreement, one side of his mouth rising in a rueful, humorless smile.

"But you know what?" he said, looking out at the trees again, his eyes old and tired and sad. "She was so far gone she didn't even notice that I'd slapped her."

He sighed again, then looked down at the wooden step between his shoes and went on:

"I finally just gave her the marker back. I didn't see any other options. I held it out to her, and she snatched it from my hand, then dropped to the floor and resumed writing on the wall as if nothing had happened."

"What exactly was she writing?" Calvin asked. "Do you remember?"

Fish gestured vaguely, as if it were a matter not worth pursuing.

"Like I said, it was gibberish. I honestly don't remember much of it. I don't *want* to remember much of it. There were some regular words but usually they were strung together in ways that didn't make much sense. Most of what she wrote wasn't even words, though. It was like...equations made of symbols instead of numbers. Strange pictographic equations, using things like skulls and spirals and squares and eyes. The symbols for Venus and Mars came up a lot, too—the same symbols used for male and female, like on the old *Ben Casey* show. You know what I mean?"

"Yeah."

"And there were numbers, too, here and there. Especially twelves. Lots of twelves. I seem to recall quite a few fours and eights, as well. Some parts of her graffiti were just lists of those weird symbols, or of cryptic abbreviations. Other parts almost looked like flowcharts, with arrows pointing to sequences of equations. There were elaborate sigils whose shapes kind of reminded me of the designs on an old Navajo rug my parents used to own. There were circles within circles, and stars inside of stars..."

Stars? Calvin remembered Tiffany's weird reaction to the star he had drawn on the map in his office. No doubt it had reminded her of her own strange wall-borne writings.

"Anyway," Fish went on, "for the next hour, I tried to talk to her, reason with her, plead with her, but she just kept writing away on the wall, oblivious to me and every single thing I said.

"I called the psychologist she had been seeing before—their sessions had ended over a year earlier, the psychologist having concluded that her problems were mostly solved—and taking his advice, I had Tiffany institutionalized.

"When the police came to take her to the hospital she fought like a wildcat. She screamed and clawed and bit as if the world would end if she didn't keep writing on the walls of her room. The policemen were finally forced to handcuff her. They wrangled her into the squad car and drove her to the hospital. I followed in my own car. I could see her in the police car ahead of me thrashing about and kicking at the metal screen that divided the front and back seats. She barely seemed human..."

His voice had grown wobbly with emotion, and now he paused and stared at his shoes for a long time. When he resumed his tale, his voice was calm and even once again.

"Her psychologist had set everything up at the psychiatric hospital by the time we got there, and Tiffany was admitted, uncuffed, and locked in a private room for observation.

"I was at the front desk with the head psychiatrist, filling out paperwork, when one of the nurses came running up and told the psychiatrist that he'd better see what was happening in Room 1001. That was Tiffany's room.

"We all ran down there and peered in through the square window set into the door. It had chicken wire in the middle, set between two panes of glass. I found that particularly depressing for some reason.

"The room was small and sparsely furnished, with only a bed, a table, a chair, and a small closet. She had dragged all the furniture into the center of the room to expose the walls, just like in her bedroom at home. The walls were a soft yellow color that reminded me of sand, and Tiffany was kneeling in front of one of them, writing. She'd already covered a swath of the wall above her with her bizarre equations. I wondered for a moment where she'd gotten hold of a marker, but then I realized the writing was dark red and she was writing with her index finger, whose tip was covered in blood. They later determined she'd simply bitten her finger till it started bleeding enough to write with."

Fish glanced at Calvin to check his reaction. Calvin simply stared out at the trees across the lawn, not sure what to think of any of this. He had difficulty reconciling the shy, pretty girl he had spent the morning talking to with the obsessive, blood-spattered creature Andrew Fish was describing.

"They rushed in to stop her," Fish went on, "but the moment they pulled her away from the wall, she started snarling and hitting and kicking just like before. Someone was about to rush off to get a straitjacket, but I pulled out the marker she had been using in her bedroom that morning. She had dropped it when the police were cuffing her, and I had absently picked it up and put it in my pocket. I shouted, 'Just give her this!' They did, and everyone was shocked when she immediately calmed down and resumed writing, this time with the marker instead of her finger. With only a little bit of trouble they managed to get her to write with her left hand, her unfavored hand, while they cleaned and treated the wound on her other hand. She didn't seem to care which hand she wrote with as long as she could keep writing. Hell, once she started writing again, she didn't even seem to be aware anyone was in the room with her anymore.

"The doctors soon determined that she would let them do pretty much anything they wanted as long as it didn't interfere with her writing. She let them change her clothes, give her sponge baths, anything, as long as they always left her one hand free to write with."

"Some things she would even do by herself. By the end of that first day they discovered that if they set a tray of food beside her, she would eventually eat it on her own, robotically spooning the food into her mouth while she continued writing. She wound up with food stains all over her clothes, but I doubt she even noticed.

"When she grew too tired to continue, she slept right there on the floor in the spot where she had stopped writing, her marker clutched to her chest like a favorite stuffed animal, ready to uncap it and start writing again the moment she awoke. And as the days went by, the writing spread farther and farther across the walls. The head psychiatrist allowed it. He thought that whatever she was writing was a key to understanding her mind, and that the act of writing might even be helping her to work out whatever was wrong with her. And maybe he was right.

"After about a week, the amount of writing she did decreased, and for long periods she would just sit there staring at what she'd written, as if she'd reached a point where she had to think through the rest of it. Every now and then she would lean forward and add a few more words, or another weird equation, or a diagram, or a shape.

"And you want to know something? After the first couple of days, I compared what she'd written in the hospital with what she'd written in her bedroom, *and they matched*. At least up to a point. In the hospital, of course, she was allowed to get much further than she had at home, but those early parts were exactly the same, word for word, symbol for symbol. Exactly."

"It meant something," Calvin said. "It wasn't gibberish. At least not to her."

"It was gibberish to everyone except her."

"I don't suppose you have a copy of what she wrote, do you?"

"I did for a while. I pored over it every now and then, hoping I might be able to understand what it meant to her. But I never discerned any real meaning in any of it, and eventually I threw it out. The doctors might have kept a record of it. I seem to recall someone taking Polaroids of the walls at one point. Whatever the case, it didn't help; the doctors didn't understand the writing any more than I did, although they spent hours discussing it. They seemed to have a weird professional interest in the situation, as if it were something they hadn't seen before. Maybe they hadn't. I don't know.

"They tentatively diagnosed her as a schizophrenic, but when they tried the various drugs normally used to treat schizophrenics, none of them had any effect at all. Nor did several other drugs they tried. Not even any side effects. Nothing. As you might guess, this only heightened the doctors' interest in her case that much more.

"I visited her every day, spending every free minute I had at the hospital. I would sit with her for hours at a time, talking to her as she stared at the wall or wrote on it. I might as well have been talking to the wall.

"But then one evening about three weeks after her admission I was sitting there with her in her room, telling her about how I'd taken on some new clients—just idle chitchat so there would be something to hear other than the squeak of her marker and the moans and cries of the other patients—and then suddenly she turned and looked at me—I mean, really *looked* at me, seeing me, focusing on me—and in this tiny, raspy voice, a voice that was rusty from disuse, she said, 'It's all so much older than we think, you know. And a lot younger, too.' Then she smiled a strange, sly smile, and went right back to staring at the wall.

"I was actually weeping with joy. It was the first articulate thing she had said in nearly a month.

"Over the following days, she started having more and more of these moments of lucidity, while writing less and less on the wall. At first her statements were bizarre non-sequiturs that I assume related to her writing. I don't recall many of them. They didn't make a lot of sense. I do remember that at one point she said something that made me think she was talking about archeology. Something about artifacts and ages.

"After a few days she started making more normal conversation. 'How are you?' and 'How was your day?' and all that. It became clear that she knew who she was, and who I was, and where she was, and on some level she probably had all along. But the writing had been more important than anything else. One day I asked her about it directly. I gestured at the wall and said, 'Why are you doing this? What does it mean?' She stared at the writing a moment, then said, 'It's everything. I have to get it all down before I forget. I think I've already forgotten parts of it.' And then she turned to me and smiled—it was so normal, that smile, just like her old smile, a smile I hadn't seen in months—and she said, 'I think I've done almost as much as I can.'

"And she was right, I guess, because she only made a few more additions to the writing after that. She started talking more and more normally, too. But she wasn't completely the same. There was an odd, haunted look in her eyes that had never been there before, a look you sometimes see in the eyes of elderly people who've lived hard, brutal lives; and she still spent long hours staring at the wall and resisted any suggestion that the writing be removed or painted over. And more importantly, the way she thought and perceived things had changed. She no longer saw the same world she used to, the world as most people see it.

"About five months after she had first been institutionalized, the head psychiatrist called me in for a meeting. He told me he was amazed at Tiffany's improvement and was going to release her, though he strongly recommended regular outpatient visits so the doctors could monitor her status. He said he believed that the writing, whatever it had been about, had indeed had a cathartic effect on whatever had been troubling her, and that I should remain vigilant for future bouts of similar behavior.

"When the time came for her to return home, everyone was concerned about how she would react at being separated from her bizarre writings, even though by that point she hadn't written anything on the wall for nearly two months. But she didn't seem to care one bit. As Tiffany was packing her bags, one of the nurses asked her if she wasn't sad to leave behind all the work she had done. Tiffany just shrugged and said, 'I don't need it anymore. You can have it now. You should probably hold onto it if you want to understand things.'

"And so I took her home, and she stayed well. Or at least as well as she was going to get. There was no more crazy writing, no nightmares, no undue anxiety or hostile behavior. Whatever had bedeviled her was over, it seemed. But whatever it was all about, it had changed her in deep and permanent ways."

Fish fell silent. Calvin figured the story was over and started casting about for something to say that would adequately convey the roiling mix of shock, horror, and compassion he felt.

Then Fish glanced at Calvin and said, "There's one other aspect to all this that I feel I should tell you. Frankly, I'm a little reluctant to do so, since I'm concerned you'll take it the wrong way."

Calvin stiffened, suddenly feeling horribly certain that despite the whole litany of madness and weirdness he'd already heard, what Fish was about to tell him was the biggest revelation of all.

"What?" Calvin said in a low voice, not sure he wanted

to hear it.

"The date."

"The date?" Calvin thought Fish meant today's date, like some weird replay of his conversation with Tiffany in the office yesterday, when she pointed out that she was telling him about the incident in the alley on the very same day it had happened nine years earlier.

"The night she had her breakdown," Fish said. "I don't know the exact time it started, of course, but it was sometime in the small hours of the morning of October 19, 2012."

Calvin sat speechless, chills chasing each other down his spine. That was the date and the approximate time Emily Crow had been murdered in the clearing.

Fish saw Calvin's expression and grimaced.

"I don't believe that there is any kind of meaningful connection between those events."

"You don't?" Calvin asked, incredulous.

"No, but I understand that some people might, including Robert May. After Tiffany received that peculiar inheritance, I tried to find out anything I could about Mr. May in hopes of learning why he had named her in his will, but I was unable to turn up very much about him at all. When I learned that Emily Crow had been abducted and murdered on his property, I naturally wondered if he had had a hand in her death and had perhaps been driven by guilt to balance the scales by helping another unfortunate young girl. I soon found out that Emily's killer was indisputably that Roger Grey fellow, and that Mr. May couldn't possibly have had anything to do with it. Once again I was left with a mystery I seemed unable to solve. Until you and Ms. Crow visited the other day. What you told me helped me to understand, I think."

"How so?"

"You told me that Mr. May investigated paranormal phenomena. As you might have guessed, I myself do not believe in such things. I believe in law and free markets and a good glass of port after dinner. The world I live in is too solid and well-understood to have any room for bogeymen or angels or UFOs. But I know that some people do believe in those things, and Mr. May was clearly one of them. I don't presume to understand exactly what went on in his mind, but it's not unlikely that he posited some supernatural connection between Emily Crow's death and Tiffany's problems. And given that one of the events in question occurred on his property, he no doubt imagined some further connection between those events and himself. And so he chose to aid someone to whom he believed himself linked in some supernatural nonlocal manner."

Calvin drew in a breath to vehemently protest what he perceived as an appallingly one-sided take on events, but Fish held up a hand, palm out in a stop gesture.

"Now now," he said. "I'm not here for a philosophical debate."

"It's not a matter of philosophy," Calvin said. "Tiffany was listed in Mr. May's trust in 2008, four years before her breakdown and Emily's death."

Fish stared at him in surprise. Then his eyes narrowed.

"Was this before or after the incident in the alley?"

"After. About six months after."

"Well then, he must have found out about the incident somehow and left her the money out of sympathy. Perhaps it was a case he investigated."

"And, what, the same girl just happened to have a psychological meltdown the very same night another girl is murdered on his property? Are you just going to chalk that up to coincidence?"

Fish raised an eyebrow, his expression calm and cool.

"Why not? The world is full of coincidences every minute of every day. They happen all around us. There are so many things going on in the world at any given moment that it's inevitable that many of those events will echo each other. It's simply a matter of statistics. Most of these coincidences are things we think nothing of. We barely even notice them because they hold no particular meaning for us, like when someone is talking about blue cars, and a blue car passes by outside. You might take note of it in a vague and amused way, but then you forget about it because it had no larger significance. It was just a quirk of chance. But statistics dictate that every once in a while coincidences that seem more meaningful will occur, and inevitably certain, ah, less critical-minded people will attach undue importance to those coincidences."

Calvin wanted to object, but in his mind he heard himself telling Tiffany how the odds of her telling him about the alley incident on the very same day it occurred were one in three hundred and sixty-five. Was Fish's argument any different in the end? It was only a difference of degree, not of kind.

Still, Fish didn't have all the facts. Fish didn't know about the anomalous events connected with the clearing where Emily died. Nor did he know that Calvin and Cynthia and the others were currently investigating a strange death that occurred in the very same alley in which Fish and his daughter had seen two women disappear (or appear to disappear, as Fish would no doubt reframe it). Nor did Fish know of the eerie echoes heard by Betty Romero and her husband.

Calvin chose not to mention any of this. He knew Fish would craft perfectly reasonable explanations to dismiss the incidents, one and all. And however implausibly huge the mountain of coincidences grew, Fish would minimize it as still being well within the realm of statistical possibility.

"We'll have to agree to disagree," Fish said, sounding a little smug and amused. Perhaps he had noticed the frustration on Calvin's face and believed it to be due to Calvin's inability to counter his arguments. In truth it was actually due to Calvin's growing awareness of the futility of arguing with someone who would employ his lawyerly wits to explain away anything not to his liking.

"I suppose we will," Calvin agreed.

Fish nodded. Then the faint smile on his lips faded.

"As far as I am aware, Tiffany doesn't know about the connection between her breakdown and Emily Crow's death. I'm sure she'll learn of it sooner or later, and when she does I would prefer the matter be handled without reference to any supposed supernatural aspects."

"So, what, is this the part where you warn me off seeing her anymore?"

Fish looked at him in surprise.

"No! Just the opposite. I want you to understand her and her unique situation. She's eighteen now. I can't shelter her forever. She needs friends. She needs people to interact with, people she has things in common with, not a stuffy old lawyer like me. It's not healthy for her. I'm happy she's meeting new people. I won't deny that I have serious reservations about this paranormal investigation nonsense, but you and your friend seem like nice people, relatively intelligent and well-adjusted, even if you believe in some things that I think are childish fantasies. No, I'm not trying to warn you off. I'm trying to lay all the cards on the table. Because you need to know."

He fixed a stern and ominous gaze on Calvin. "If associating with you and your friends starts to affect her in a negative way, if this paranormal stuff seems to be fueling her abnormalities and making her worse, I want you to cut ties with her, is that clear? I will give this a chance—she needs a chance like this—but at the first sign she's not handling it well, I want it stopped. Do you understand?"

Calvin nodded. "I understand perfectly. I don't want to see her hurt any more than you do."

"Good," he said. He stood up. Calvin did too. "I should go. I know this has been awkward, but it was necessary, as I think you see now."

"Yeah."

"And I would appreciate it if you didn't tell her I was here. Which means, as well, don't let on that you know about her breakdown. She almost never talks about it anymore. The last time I mentioned it, I later heard her crying up in her bedroom."

"What if she brings it up on her own?"

"She won't." Seeing that this wasn't good enough for Calvin, he added, "If by some unlikely chance she does, just let her tell you as much as she wants. Don't force anything. And don't talk about anything she hasn't already told you."

"Understood."

Fish stuck out his hand. Calvin took it.

"It was nice talking to you," Fish said, giving Calvin's hand a firm shake.

"Same here," Calvin said. Although, of course, it really hadn't been very nice at all.

The shake ended. Fish kept hold of Calvin's hand.

"Remember," he said, "my daughter is the only thing of any genuine importance in my life. She likes you and your friend, and I can accept that. I might think you're a kid with a head full of silly pseudoscience, but I'm willing to let that slide, because you seem to make her happy, and that's what's important. But if you should hurt her any more than she's already been hurt, well...don't forget I'm a lawyer. A very good one. I can have this house and your whole inheritance in my pocket before you can say 'bread-line.'"

Calvin said nothing.

Fish gave him a pleasant smile and a nod.

"Good day."

He trotted down the steps, got into his car, and drove away.

The moment the car was out of sight, Calvin let out a long breath and slumped against one of the porch's wooden pillars. Then he shook his head with a small laugh.

"I sure know how to pick 'em, don't I?" he said.

12

"Tiffany and Emily?" Frowning with bafflement, Cynthia settled back onto the couch in Calvin's parlor. "What's the connection?"

"I don't know," Calvin said.

He had just finished telling her about his conversations with Tiffany and Andrew Fish. It was half an hour before the others were scheduled to show up for their trip to Kingwood. Calvin had called Cynthia over early to fill her in on his eventful afternoon and discuss these new surprise twists with her.

He had debated long and hard whether or not to tell her at all. Though Andrew Fish had told Calvin only to refrain from telling Tiffany about their conversation, Calvin got the impression there was supposed to be a tacit understanding that the whole matter was confidential. Then again, although Fish didn't know of the existence of most of the group, he knew about Cynthia, and it wasn't a stretch to assume that Fish understood that Calvin would feel compelled to apprise his investigatory partner of the situation. In any case Calvin decided he couldn't *not* tell her. It involved her murdered sister, after all. Nevertheless Calvin had been concerned that Cynthia might feel similarly compelled to tell Donovan, who would likely reveal it to Violet, who would likely megaphone it to the rush-hour crowds on Main Street, his ultimate fear being that word of it would reach Tiffany's ears and make her pissed at him for sharing private information. With this in mind, Calvin had extracted a promise of the strictest confidentiality from Cynthia before he told her a word. He knew she was conscientious enough to keep it.

"Could Tiffany be psychic like my Aunt Wendy?" Cynthia said. "That might explain her reaction to both the alley and what happened in the clearing that night. Maybe she has an abnormal sensitivity to paranormal events."

"Yeah, but the night Emily was murdered, Tiffany was seven or eight miles away. Given such a distance, psychic sensitivity in and of itself seems a bit of a stretch."

"What else is there, though?"

"Much as I hate to suggest it," Calvin said, "could there be a more direct connection?"

"Are you suggesting what I think you're suggesting?"

"I'm just trying to look at all the possibilities. There are plenty of reports of long-distance psychic transmissions between family members, especially during traumatic events. Is there any chance at all Tiffany could be related to you guys? I mean, could your dad have—"

"No." Cynthia held up a hand. "Don't even go there. My dad might not be, you know, Gandhi or something, but he wouldn't cheat on my mom. He's not that kind of person. Besides, Tiffany looks scarily like her mother, except for her nose, which clearly resembles her father's: straight narrow bridge, with that kind of teardrop-shaped tip."

"It doesn't have to be your dad. There could be a link a generation or two behind that. Maybe your grandpa, or something."

"Wouldn't the gene pool be getting a little too shallow at that point for some kind of psychic link? The only psychic links between relatives that I've ever heard about were between primary relatives: parents and children, brothers and sisters, twins, stuff like that."

Calvin sighed. "There has to be something, though; some kind of link between Emily and Tiffany."

"But why? If Emily's death created or strengthened or activated the anomaly in the clearing, then why couldn't that be the main factor? Maybe Tiffany was responding solely to the anomaly. Maybe there was even some kind of obscure link between the anomaly and whatever happened in that alley in 2008."

"And Simon Bradley. He's connected with all of this, too, somehow."

"Are you sure his suicide wasn't just a coincidence? I mean, the strange effects that Tiffany and the Romeros experienced were connected more with whatever happened in the alley that night, not with Bradley's suicide."

"No. What Andrew Fish told me convinced me that Simon Bradley's suicide is part of it, too."

"What? Why?"

"Think about the night Tiffany woke up her dad with the gunshots, the night that seemed to resolve whatever was gnawing at her mind in the wake of the alley incident, only think about it kind of...obliquely, I guess. What happened there in the Fish house that night?"

"Sleepwalking? Gunfire?"

"But what did Tiffany shoot?"

"A mirror? Her reflection?" She stiffened with realization. "Herself! She shot herself in the mirror. Just like Simon Bradley, except..." She shrugged. "Well, obliquely, like you said."

"Yeah. It's hardly a scientific proof, but it's certainly suggestive, isn't it?"

"Echoes. Echoes and more echoes. But what does it mean? That Simon Bradley's death was psychically affecting Tiffany somehow? Or that they were both being affected by some other incident, maybe what went on in the alley?"

"I don't know. I don't think we know enough to know."

He fell silent and stared off into space, his elbow on the arm of his chair and his chin cupped in his hand.

"To me, the biggest question is, why did Mr. May include Tiffany in the trust in 2008? That's the thing I keep coming back to. It can't be only because she experienced a strange phenomenon, because by then Mr. May must have known thousands of people who had experienced such things, and he didn't leave anything to any of them. Just

Tiffany. Why? And why include me? I had no connection to anyone or anything. And for that matter, why leave the Collection and all the land to Emily, a seven-year-old girl?"

"Mr. May knew something."

"Yeah." Calvin shook his head, for the first time feeling a stab of bitterness and hostility toward the old man he had considered a mentor and father figure. "Something he decided to take with him to the damn grave."

13

Packed into Brandon's van, the whole gang sans Lauren parked in a parking lot half a block up Gater Road from the Red Anchor Brewery and the latest crime scene. Lauren showed up a few minutes later in her pea-green Honda Fit, and the whole gang headed to the vacant lot where Terrell Quinn's body had been found the previous day. Like the alley a few days earlier, they showed up too late to witness any police or media activity. A length of yellow police tape was tangled in the branches of a bush at the west end of the lot, its ragged plastic ends fluttering gently in the breeze.

A large square of mostly bare dirt in the center of the lot indicated that a house had stood there until fairly recently, one that had no doubt matched the two-storey homes that lined most of the rest of the block. The board fence that separated the lot from the Red Anchor Brewery to the east was thick with graffiti, and a few boards had holes kicked in them. The house directly to the west had a For Sale sign on the lawn, and its windows were covered with plywood.

Aside from the square of dirt in the center, the lot was overgrown with shin-high grass, ragweed, Queen Anne's lace, and a variety of small shrubs. An old oak tree stood in the middle of what had once been the back yard. A pair of rotten ropes with frayed ends hung from a low, thick branch, attesting to where a swing once hung.

"This is it, huh?" said Donovan, scanning the weedy field. "It's weird thinking someone died here."

"It's a crowded world with a long history," Lauren said. "Someone's probably died just about everywhere by now."

They roamed through the field, the grass and weeds whispering against their pants legs.

"So are we looking for anything in particular?" Donovan said.

"I don't know," Calvin said. "I just thought it would be a good idea to check out this spot before we started our foot search."

On the other side of the graffiti-covered fence, they heard a side door of the brewery open, letting out a blast of muffled rock music and the drone of many voices.

"Hey," Brandon said. "If we want to have dinner somewhere afterward, the Red Anchor'd be the perfect place. They've got a restaurant attached, and they serve some awesome bison burgers. The beer's good, too. The Davey Jones' Lager is particularly tasty."

"Let's get the job done before we worry about our bellies," Calvin said.

They soon found the spot where Terrell Quinn's body had likely lain: a swath of matted-down weeds and grass a few paces south of the square of dirt. Many of the plants in the center of the swath were stained rusty red.

"Whoa," Donovan said, staring at the blood. The whites of his wide, round eyes were dimly visible behind the dark lenses of his sunglasses.

"Hey, check this out," Violet said. She had strolled a little ways away onto the square of dirt to examine a piece of paper she had thought might be money (it wasn't), but had found something potentially more interesting. She pointed at the dirt at her feet. "You were just talking about hooves last night, weren'tcha?"

"What?" Calvin hurried over to join her, the others close behind. They looked down at where Violet was pointing.

There in the soil was the clear, perfectly formed print of a cloven hoof.

"Jackpot!" Brandon said.

Calvin looked at Lauren.

"So," he said. "Convinced yet?"

"Um…" Lauren eyed the hoof print a moment longer, then glanced back at the patch of flattened grass where the body had lain. "Your chain of evidence is linking up nicely."

"Isn't it, though?"

Calvin dug into his messenger bag and pulled out his digital camera to take a few pictures of the hoof print.

While he did that, the others scanned the dirt for similar prints. The dirt had been heavily tracked up by police and reporters and morbid curiosity seekers, but Cynthia soon found two-thirds of another hoof print six feet north of the first one, the remaining third having been printed over by the wide, deep tread of a size 12 Red Wing boot.

"It looks like it was heading toward the back of the lot," she said.

They found two more partial prints near the north end

of the square of dirt, both of them likewise pointing north toward the line of trees and bushes that edged the back of the lot. They spent a few minutes looking for more prints or other evidence amid the brush back there, but found nothing. The dirt there was too hard and too covered over with mats of old, dry leaves to retain prints.

They returned to the sidewalk in front of the lot.

"All right," said Calvin. "Let's go through it once more."

Everyone groaned. They'd been through it twice already.

"Brandon, Lauren, and I will take everything from here to Pentz Road in the west. Cynthia, Donovan, and Violet will cover everything from here east to Castle Road. The north and south boundaries of the search area are Miller and Axelrod, respectively. Remember: We're looking for areas where a creature used to living in the wild would feel at home—woods, parks, ravines, maybe large cemeteries. And bear in mind, this thing is supposed to be about the size of a donkey, so the location would have to be somewhere a creature that large could lurk unseen.

"If you do happen to run across this thing, do not under any circumstances approach it. Just call the others and then try to keep the creature under observation until we can all meet up and figure out a plan of action. Any questions?"

No one had any questions.

"All right, then. Let's aim to meet back here in about three hours. Good luck, you guys."

Cynthia, looking like a condemned prisoner, led Donovan and Violet across Gater, then north up the road. The others headed south.

"Dude," Brandon said as they walked along, scanning

both sides of the street for likely leucrota habitats, "that was pretty badass."

"What was?" Calvin said.

"You! You were sounding all leaderish and shit. Like a general mustering the troops. Patton Beckerman. I didn't think you had it in you."

Calvin shrugged, feeling both embarrassed and pleased. "Well, you know…just doing what I had to."

"Did you know Patton was actually really foul-mouthed?" said Lauren. "He thought obscenity was an integral part of being a soldier, and he reveled in it. I was just reading about that."

"I thought you were mostly into older history," said Calvin. "You know, ancient and medieval stuff."

"Oh, no. I love it all. I'll quite happily go from, say, some musty tome on Assyrian culture to a biography of Nixon. It's all good to me."

"A true history geek," Brandon said.

"Yep! But I have to say, there is indeed something particularly fascinating about reading about really old events, knowing that all the participants have been literally dust for centuries."

"It's something about time, right?" Calvin said.

"Yes! It really makes you understand how we're all just brief blips on a historical continuum. Everybody likes to think they're living in the apotheosis of civilization, but trust me, it'll go on and on long after we're gone, and we can't even imagine what the world will evolve into."

They came to Axelrod Road and turned right. As they walked along, Calvin's gaze was drawn south across Axelrod's four busy lanes. The road was like a boundary dividing one world from another; the houses on the far side of Axelrod were larger and more opulent than the working-class homes over here, forming an enviable panorama of trellised rose gardens, vivid green lawns, shiny BMWs and Lexuses parked in the shade of stately old elms, and picture windows that looked big enough to fit a sailboat through. This was the northern edge of the Elm Hill neighborhood, where the Fishes lived. Their house was only four blocks southwest of here. Calvin couldn't help watching the passing cars in hopes of spying Tiffany's Audi.

"Hey, check it out," Brandon said, pausing to look over the side of a short stone bridge they were crossing. He leaned over the parapet, his chest and his hands on the stone blocks.

Calvin and Lauren joined him. Twenty feet down was a narrow creek, its sides fringed with trash. The banks were overgrown with bushes, brambles, young trees. Fences lined the tops of the banks. The creek meandered generally northward, though after a hundred yards its convolutions and the unkempt verdure that in many places overhung the water hid its further course from view.

"That might be a decent leucrota hangout spot, no?" Brandon said.

"Definitely." Calvin unsnapped one of the side pockets of his messenger bag and got out his Kingwood street atlas to mark the location with a pencil. Using his finger to trace the thin black line that represented the creek on the map, he said, "It looks like it heads pretty much straight north to join the Kanseeka near King Street. And farther south it skirts the western edge of Holly Hills."

"Ooh, this might be it," Lauren said.

"Maybe. But we should still keep looking. This might be the course the leucrota followed north when it was driven out of the park, but it might have taken up a different residence by now."

"Are we gonna go down there?" Brandon asked.

"Not right now. Right now we're just noting likely locations. Later on we can merge our list with whatever the others turn up and pick the likeliest areas to start a real search."

"Then the fun really begins," Lauren said. "And by 'fun' I mean risking getting our faces chomped off."

"It beats what's on TV these days," Brandon said.

They soon came to Jackson, another working-class residential street, which they followed north. Here and there they caught glimpses of the creek ravine behind the homes on their right. Two blocks up, near the intersection of Jackson and Train Avenue, was a small park whose edges were sufficiently overgrown with trees and bushes for Calvin to make a note of it in his map book. He also noted an elementary school half a block farther on, which was abutted on one side by a strip of woods.

As they neared Miller, the northern boundary of their search area, the residential neighborhood increasingly gave way to businesses and large apartment buildings. Miller was a main artery that connected downtown Kingwood half a mile northeast with the I-60 Outer Belt a mile west. Pausing on the corner of Miller and Jackson, the trio could see a few of downtown's taller buildings above the rooflines and treetops to the northeast. The traffic speeding along Miller's six lanes sent pulses of warm, smoggy air washing over them.

"I'm betting even a creepy monster would be leery of crossing Miller," Lauren said.

"That's partly why I picked this as the northern terminus of our search area," Calvin said. "Even in the middle of the night this can be a pretty busy road."

"Yeah," said Brandon. He slapped a palm on the metal pole that was crowned with the crosswalk signal, producing a *clung* that resonated up and down the pole. "And mythical medieval beasties probably don't have a very good grasp of traffic signals."

"Why, I'll bet those little hooves can't even reach the Walk buttons," Lauren said with mock sorrow.

"Very sad."

"A real tragedy," Calvin agreed.

For the next hour they slowly made their way west, traveling up and down the blocks. Calvin noted several more locations in his map book, including another ravine, a small park, and a wooded lot behind Saint Raphael's Catholic Church.

On Hyde Road, nearly the entire block between Weber and Hays was occupied by the Verger Brothers Junkyard. Calvin, Brandon, and Lauren stopped beside the padlocked main gate and looked through the chain-link fence at the rusting hulks of old cars stretching away in uneven lines. Clusters of weeds sprouted here and there in the hard-packed dirt. A metal sign on the front gate read, "Closed Until Further Notice."

"This is a possibility," Calvin said, opening the pocket of his messenger bag for his map book and pen.

"Dude," Brandon said, "this *has* to be the place. It's a junkyard. Monsters love places like junkyards."

"They do?" Lauren said. "How do you know?"

"Cuz they just do. They love mazy places full of junk."

"They do?"

"Sure! Think of the Minotaur. Or...or..." He trailed off, unable to think of any other examples. "They just do!"

"Okay, then. I'll assume this is more sage knowledge derived from Channel 23's Saturday night Fright Fest."

"Hey, research wears many faces."

Brandon hooked his fingers through the holes in the fence, making the chain links jingle, and peered inside.

"You know, even if the monster isn't here, we gotta come back. Or at least I do. I gotta get some of these car parts for my work. I had an idea for, like, robot dinosaurs made of old car parts, and they'd be all wired up with motion detectors so that whenever someone passes by, their headlight eyes would flash and they'd make growly engine noises. I figured I could call 'em stuff like Tyranno*carus* Rex and Stega*carus*. Wouldn't that be cool?"

"Yeah," Calvin said, grinning.

Lauren chuckled. "And you call *me* a geek."

"I'll have to make a midnight raid," Brandon said.

"Are you sure it's safe?" Lauren rapped her knuckles against the sign. "It's probably closed for a reason, you know. There's probably oil and battery acid and toxic slime all over the place. Not to mention rats."

Brandon straightened his back and raised his chin with mock bravado.

"No hazard is too great in the pursuit of Art."

A pit bull bounded from one of the aisles of junked cars and barreled toward the fence, its paws thudding on the dirt, saliva arcing from its maw, a tag on its collar clinking.

Calvin, Brandon, and Lauren leaped away from the fence a moment before the dog crashed into it, making it bow outward. The dog caromed off the fence and thumped to the dirt, but if it was hurt by the collision, it didn't show it; it sprang right back up and heaved a volley of barks at the gawping humans on the far side of the fence.

"Um, okay, maybe some hazards are a little too great,"

Brandon said.

"I think we can probably cross the junkyard off our list of places to search," Calvin said. "If the leucrota tried to get in here, either it or the dog would wind up dead."

A man in a Blackjack Security uniform appeared from the same aisle the pit bull had exploded from. He was stubble-cheeked and pot-bellied and had a cigar butt in his mouth.

"Place is closed!" he hollered over the pit bull's barks. "No loitering! Move along!" He waved a grimy, pudgy hand at them. "Move along!"

"We're moving, we're moving," Calvin muttered as the trio strode away.

The remainder of Hyde Road yielded another small park and the partly wooded grounds of the Holyoak Assisted Living Facility. By the time the trio reached Axelrod and turned right toward Ferntree Avenue, the sun was halfway down the western sky and was out of sight for long periods behind the trees and rooftops. There was only an hour left till their scheduled rendezvous with the others, and they still had a third of their search area to cover plus the long plod back to the brewery. They stepped up their pace accordingly.

They had traveled nearly half the length of Ferntree when Lauren suddenly stopped with a gasp, her eyes on an old stone church a hundred yards ahead. The church was set back from the road in a narrow lot between a White Castle and a small cinderblock building whose sign read "New World Services." From here, only the church's façade and the belfry were visible beyond the cinderblock building.

"Holy shit!" Lauren said, grinning, her eyes alight like those of a treasure hunter who has just unearthed a pirates' chest. "That's the Western Reserve Congregational Church! I forgot that was in this area!" She started walking faster and faster until she was practically running toward the church.

"The what?" said Calvin as he and Brandon hurried to catch up.

"It was one of the first churches in Bard County, built in 1828. I've always wanted to visit it, but I never had the time to do more than drive past it. Wow!"

"So, is it a big deal just because it's old?" asked Brandon. "Or is there some other reason it's so cream-in-your-jeans cool?"

She slowed her pace enough to shoot him an amused glance over her shoulder.

"I don't cream in my jeans, thank you very much. But, yeah, there's another reason, which you guys should love. After all, you're into weird mysteries and stuff, right?"

"Yeah," said Calvin, perking up. "What's the mystery here? I've never heard of this place."

She tutted. "Someone has been woefully lax in their local anomaly research, then."

They stopped on the sidewalk in front of the church and gazed at the structure in silence. Its gray sandstone blocks were weather-streaked and splotched with moss and lichens. Over half the roof's slate shingles were missing or broken. The glassless windows were boarded up with stained and mildewed plywood, the only exceptions being the arched windows in the belfry, which were devoid of both glass and wood, granting a view of only darkness and emptiness within, as if the tower had been completely hollowed out by rot. The lawn was so weedy and overgrown it looked like a meadow. The decayed remains of two posts that had once borne a sign were visible amid the high grass in the middle of the yard. The heavy oak front door was listing slightly on its rusted hinges, baring wedges of darkness at the corners. Across the door someone had scrawled "Ripent!" with black spray-paint. A few other bits of graffiti were visible here and there on the grimy stone façade, though considering the church's decrepitude it was surprising there weren't more. Or perhaps it wasn't so surprising; the building had a sinister, brooding aura, and even sitting here in broad daylight it looked somehow twilit, its features dim and gray. Perhaps few vandals were bold enough to approach the place.

"This is like something from an H. P. Lovecraft story," Calvin said, both awed and spooked at the sight of the place.

"I wonder if our missing graffitists were responsible for any of these barely literate effusions," Brandon said. He glanced at Calvin. "Do you think the leucrota might be squatting here? If anyplace we've seen screams 'monster abode,' it's this place."

"I don't know," Calvin said. "I just assumed it would stick to outdoor areas. Given how big leucrotas are said to be, I figured it wouldn't be able to move around comfortably inside an abandoned house or someplace like that. But I'm hardly an expert on monster behavior. Why don't we take a look around?"

"In plain sight like this?" Lauren said, casting nervous glances up and down the street. Two little girls were playing hopscotch on the sidewalk across the street, and a freshly parked station wagon was disgorging a family of five in the White Castle parking lot barely fifty feet away.

Calvin shrugged. "There're no 'No Trespassing' signs, and it's clear no one's living here, so we're not violating anyone's privacy. Besides, it's not like we're gonna be here long; we'll just take a quick walk around the place. If anyone stops us we can just say we're students of local history on a field trip. You can bombard them with geeky info as proof."

"Gee, thanks. Leave it up to me."

After looking around to make sure no one was watching, Calvin strode down the crumbled remains of the stone walkway that led to the church's front steps. Brandon and Lauren followed close behind.

"So what's the story behind this place?" Calvin asked as they examined the front of the building. He tried the front door. It was locked and, though crooked and decaying, fixed firmly in place.

"Okay," Lauren said. "Back in 1828 when Kingwood was still a dinky little settlement named King's Mill, a group of settlers built the Congregational Church, worshipped there normally for a while, yadda yadda yadda, nothing too weird. But then in 1831 they got a new minister, this dashingly handsome young fellow named Gideon Squash."

"You are so making this up," said Brandon.

"I'm not! He really was named Gideon Squash, unless several dozen local history books were written by chronic liars. Anyway, he started preaching here, and then one day a few months later, a woman and her two six-year-old girls—twins, actually—disappeared from their home. The townsfolk searched high and low, and nobody could find a trace of them. Inevitably, suspicion fell on the new preacher because he was the only stranger around."

"Wouldn't they have suspected the Indians?" said Brandon.

Calvin groaned. "The Indians were pretty much long gone by then. Even *I* know that."

"All right, all right, history was never my forte."

The inspection of the front of the church done, Calvin led them across the weedy lawn toward the side, bits of shingles occasionally snapping and crunching underfoot.

"So anyway," Lauren went on, "the vanished woman's husband broke into the preacher's house one night when the preacher was away, hoping to find his family inside, or at least some clue to their fate."

"Did the preacher live by the church?" Calvin asked as he scanned the side of the church. It presented the same decrepit and foreboding appearance as the front, and like the front there were no openings for anything larger than a rat to get inside, at least not without scaling the sheer stone walls to the belfry windows. The trio set off for the back of the building.

"No," Lauren said. "Squash lived in a regular house on—get this—Train Avenue. Except it wasn't called Train Avenue at that point. It was just a nameless dirt trail that connected a few places on the outskirts of the town."

"Let me guess," Brandon said: "His house was where the alley of death is now located."

"Not even close. It's in the other direction. Or it was. The house is long gone now. It stood just west of where Train intersects Pentz. It was where the Mad Hatter Novelty Company's warehouse now stands. A pretty appropriate name, all thing considered."

"Actually, isn't it more like an ex-warehouse at this point?" Brandon said. "Didn't the company go bankrupt a couple years back?"

"I think so, yeah."

They had reached the back of the church. A yard as weedy and overgrown as the one in front stretched from the church's rear wall to a rickety wooden fence that marked the end of the lot. Again, there was no way inside the church. As if to underscore this, someone had written "No Entree" in gold spray paint across the locked back door. The trio continued their circuit of the building.

"So what happened with the guy who broke into Squash's house?" Calvin asked Lauren.

"That's part of the mystery. See, a couple of other local guys had gone with him, but they wound up waiting for him outside. I guess none of them were brave enough—or maybe bereaved enough—to break into a preacher's house. So these guys just hunkered down and waited for their buddy to come out. It turned out to be a really long wait. When he finally emerged two hours later, he was like a totally different guy. He was all weirdly happy, almost serene. He told them Reverend Squash couldn't have had anything to do with his family's disappearance because the preacher was a great man of God, and they've committed a horrible mistake in even suspecting him. The guy's friends were understandably baffled, and they kept asking him what happened to make him change his tune. But he wouldn't explain; he just kept telling them to trust him, Reverend Squash wasn't responsible, he was a man of God, blah blah blah.

"So they all went home, and sometime that night the guy who broke into Squash's house put a gun in his mouth and blew his brains all over his kitchen."

"Dude," Brandon said in a long, low whisper.

"Oh, I haven't even gotten to the good part yet," Lauren said with a huge smile, clearly enjoying her role as spooky storyteller.

They emerged onto the front lawn again, having discovered no place for a leucrota, much less a person, to have entered the building. The church, though decaying, was secure. They gathered in a cluster on the sidewalk in front of the church to listen to the rest of Lauren's tale.

"Nobody quite knew what to make of the guy's suicide," Lauren said. "Was he just despondent over his family's disappearance and perhaps also riddled with guilt over breaking into the house of a man of God, or was something more sinister afoot? As you might expect, all kinds of rumors began to spread like wildfire. The locals ultimately fell into two camps, one saying that Reverend Squash was innocent, the other saying he was a black magician who had sacrificed the woman and the kids to the devil and then put a spell on the husband. Soon those who blamed Squash started saying that those who defended him were also under the preacher's enchantment, while those who defended Squash claimed that those who believed he was guilty were being addled by either Satan or their own stupidity and that they were unjustly maligning a just man.

"And what did Reverend Squash say? Why, he just kept delivering his sermons, same as always, and otherwise maintaining a low profile, which his defenders saw as a sign of his maturity and wisdom but which his detractors saw as proof of his guilt.

"For a while it appeared as if things might blow over. But then, instead, things got worse. A lot worse. Three months after the woman and her kids disappeared, two young boys, both twelve, vanished while they were out fishing in the Kanseeka. No trace of them was found. Their parents, who had been firmly in the anti-Squash camp, now became its leaders and demanded that the preacher allow a search of both the church and his home. Well, the pro-Squash camp saw that as insulting and probably blasphemous, and they urged Squash to ignore the demands. And then...

"I don't know how much you guys know about local history, but have you ever heard of the Halloween Riot?"

"Uh..." Calvin cast back through his memory. "It rings a bell. I couldn't tell you anything about it, though."

"And I've never heard of it at all," said Brandon. "Enlighten us, please."

"Oh, I will. On Halloween night, the anti-Squash camp held a meeting in the town hall to figure out their next move. The pro-Squash folks decided to hold their own rally in the town square, basically right outside the hall. Well, the people in the square got so loud with their ranting and speechifying that the people in the hall could barely hear their own ranting and speechifying, so they stormed outside to tell them to scram. And, well, you know how these things go: Tempers flared, heated words were exchanged, and then somebody—no one knows who—threw a rock. It hit a woman in the pro-Squash camp right in the head. It didn't hurt her very badly, but it was enough to set off a full-blown riot right there in the center of town. Fists flew. Knives and guns were drawn. The whole thing lasted only about half an hour, but by the end five people were dead, nearly two dozen were injured, pretty much every window facing the square had been shattered, and somehow the dry goods store next to the town hall caught fire and burned down."

"Whoa," said Brandon. "I never dreamed this boring two-bit burg had such a colorful backstory."

"Ha," Lauren said. "If you think this is colorful, remind me to tell you about the King family sometime, the folks the city was named after. Or the so-called Bridge of Blood incident in 1891. Or the whole grave-tampering scandal in the 1920s."

"Grave-tampering?" Calvin said.

"Oh, that's a great story, but we don't have time for that right now. Anyway, getting back to our smoky, bloody, riot-ravaged town square, it eventually dawned on a lot of people that the very focus of the riot, Reverend Squash, was pretty much the only man in town who hadn't been there. He had told his congregation he would stop by their anti-anti-Squash rally at some point, but he never showed up, and some of his followers started to worry that maybe while everyone had been occupied with the melee, some of the anti-Squash folks had taken the opportunity to slip away and put an end to the supposedly evil reverend once and for all.

"A group of townsmen went to Squash's house and knocked. No answer. They called his name. No answer. The house was dark and silent. Figuring that maybe he had gone to the church, they went there next. Same thing: dark, silent, no answer.

"By now they were sure that something was wrong, so they headed back to his house, where they forced a window and climbed inside. Nothing seemed amiss...until they checked the basement.

"Now, the basement was a pretty rudimentary affair, with stone walls and a dirt floor. Most people back then used their basements to store vegetables and stuff like that, but Squash's was completely empty. Or at least almost completely empty. When the searchers reached the bottom of the wooden stairs and raised their lanterns they found a human skull lying in the middle of the floor. It was small—a child's skull—and it was badly discolored as if it had been buried for a long time."

"Oh, crap!" said Brandon. "He *did* kill the kids! He..." He trailed off, seeing that Lauren was shaking her head with a devilish grin.

"Uh-uh," she said. "That's what everyone else assumed at first. But a few days later the town constable, whose job it was to check these things out since Bard County didn't have a coroner in those days, determined that the skull was too small to belong to any of the missing children. The missing boys had both been twelve, and the missing twin girls had been nine. This, however, was the skull of a toddler. And based on the skull's discoloration, it was estimated to have been in the ground at least a year, and probably a lot longer.

"By then, the searchers had made another interesting discovery in the basement. Someone noticed that sections of the stone wall appeared to have been disturbed recently; some of the stone blocks weren't aligned quite right, and there was loose dirt on the floor below them. When the search party removed these stones from the walls they discovered tunnels behind them, nearly a dozen in all, leading in all different directions. The tunnels were roughly six feet high, and their walls and ceilings had been crudely but effectively shored up with stones and wooden beams. Most of the tunnels extended about thirty or forty feet, but a few ran on for over a hundred."

"Where did they lead?" asked Calvin.

"Nowhere. That's the really weird part. Most of the time when someone makes tunnels in their basement, you think they're making a secret passage to someplace else. But none of these tunnels headed toward anything of any importance. One of them ran underneath a neighboring cow pasture and then dead-ended in a stone wall. Another led to the edge of a nondescript grove of trees."

"The skull might have been something he unearthed when he was digging," Calvin said. "It might have been the skull of some Native American kid from decades or centuries earlier."

Lauren nodded. "That's what a lot of the local historians have concluded, though a few think the skull might have been planted there by anti-Squash folk to frame him."

"So what happened to Squash?" Brandon asked.

"No one knows. No one ever saw him again. Some historians theorize that someone from the anti-Squash camp murdered him and hid the body, others that when Squash learned of the riot he decided to skip town, either to save his own skin or to spare the town further strife."

"Was any of Squash's stuff missing?" asked Calvin.

"Nope. Even his personal copy of the Bible was still sitting on his bedside table."

"That argues in favor of the theory that someone killed him."

"Maybe. If someone killed him, they hid the body really well. And the same applies to the four missing kids and the missing mom: No trace of any of them ever turned up."

"And that's it?" Calvin asked.

"Yep. You want mysteries, there's a whole bundle of 'em right there: Missing people, mysterious tunnels, an inexplicable suicide, rumors of black magic, and a skull of unknown origin."

"Damn," Brandon said. He looked at the church looming before them. "I can totally see why this place is abandoned."

"Actually, believe it or not, after the Squash incident the congregation got themselves another preacher and went right on using the church for decades. Eventually the congregation grew too large for the church, and in the early 1900s they built a bigger, better church about a mile north of here. After that, this one sank into disrepair. Reverend Squash's house, on the other hand, was reputed to be cursed and wound up burning down in a mysterious fire that was almost certainly arson in the 1860s."

"And a warehouse full of kitsch and gewgaws took its place," Brandon said. "Score another triumph for the forces of capitalism and banality."

They resumed their search, walking more quickly now to make up for lost time. Calvin noted a few more places that might be worth investigating, including a wooded area behind a putt-putt course and another ravine. On Pentz Road, the last leg of their search, they paused briefly to regard the Mad Hatter Novelty Company's Kingwood Distribution Center in the industrial park across the street, the former site of Reverend Squash's house of mystery. The warehouse's vast parking lot was empty, and atop the façade, the big, unlit neon sign which showed the company's cartoonish logo, a Cheshire Cat-like grin springing out of a black top hat, sported holes and cracks from rocks hurled by vandals.

"And now the warehouse itself has been closed down," Lauren said. She gave a small, sad smile. "Time rolls on."

14

"This would've been a lot easier if we'd driven," Donovan said as he, Cynthia, and Violet plodded north up Wheeler Road.

"We already talked about this," Cynthia said. "In a car we'd pass things too quickly. We wouldn't get a good enough look at the terrain to spot all the potential hidey-holes."

"There's nothing you can see from your feet that you can't see from a car."

"Maybe not. But on foot you can see *more*. Traveling by car you're compelled to go above a certain speed, and you don't have as much time to see everything unless you go up and down each road multiple times, and then it just winds up eating up as much time as doing it on foot and wasting lots of gas and gas money in the process."

"I guess."

"Besides, at this point we're more than halfway through. It'll only be another hour or so."

"Dude, it's better this way," Violet told Donovan. "Trust me. I keep telling you: Cars're for suckers. They're just giant fucking money pits, like houses and babies and stuff. It's just another tool the world uses to keep you running for dollars in your little rat wheel and never realize what a sucker you are."

Cynthia, who had just bought a new car, couldn't help feeling that this was yet another of Violet's little jibes at her. She was debating whether or not to respond when they came upon a park on the corner of Wheeler and Weber Roads. The park wasn't very big, and considering that its only man-made features were a swing-set, a jungle gym, a teeter-totter, and a very short drinking fountain, it appeared to have been built mainly for the use of neighborhood children. Narrow bands of woods separated the park from the houses on Wheeler and Weber. The woods couldn't be more than twenty feet thick, but that was probably enough to hide and house a leucrota.

She got her pen out of her white belt pack, then opened up the Kingwood street atlas she carried, ready to note the location of the park. During their travels so far, she had already noted another small park, a ravine, and a large cemetery bordered with trees and heavy brush.

When she tried to circle the corner where the park was located the pen made only an inkless groove in the paper.

"Crap." She shook the pen and tried again. This time the pen produced a watery gray line that faded out after half an inch.

She licked the pen tip and tried once more. She was back to just a groove again.

"Do either of you have a pen?" she asked. "Mine just died."

"A pen?" said Donovan. He blew a sharp, quick blast of air between his lips as if to say "kid stuff" and started digging in the right front pocket of his black trench coat. His breezy, cocksure smile gave way to a frown as his digging went on and on.

"I know I have one somewhere," he said. "I just have too much shit in my pockets."

"Here we go," Violet said with a groan. Already looking bored, she sat down on a wooden bench next to the sidewalk on the west side of the park. "You always have too much shit in your pockets."

"No, I know I have one…" He sat down next to her and started pulling items from his pocket and piling them in his lap. Out came a packet of Kleenex, a tin of Altoids, a few slips of paper with phone numbers scribbled on them, two one-dollar bills, eighty-four cents in assorted change, a movie ticket stub, a Jack Chick comic about Hell, two safety pins, a key to a pair of handcuffs, and a tiny screwdriver.

"Maybe it's the other pocket," he muttered, and started digging through the trench coat's left front pocket.

Getting the sense that this might take a while, Cynthia sat down on Donovan's other side.

Violet leaned around him and scowled at Cynthia. "You just had to start him off, didn't you?" She flumped against the backrest, making the whole bench shudder. "Guh! We're gonna be here all fuckin' day now." She pulled out a Marlboro and lit it, then sat back with a sigh and watched two little girls playing on the teeter-totter on the other side of the park. The squall of the old metal teeter-totter carried to them across the grass. *Creeeeek.* Pause. *Creeeeek.* Pause.

By now, Donovan had pulled from his pocket his own pack of Marlboros, a disposable lighter, two books of matches, an American flag lapel pin, a Swiss army knife, a rubber band, a pair of earmuffs, a handkerchief, a pack of Wrigley's chewing gum, and a nearly used-up tube of KY jelly.

"Aw, geez." Cynthia quickly wrenched her eyes away, wishing she hadn't seen the tube or the dreamy, reminiscing smile that had spread across Violet's face at the sight of it.

"Um, sorry," Donovan mumbled, thrusting the jelly back into his pocket. He moved on to a pocket on the inner lower left-hand side of his coat. "Just hold on a second. I know there's a pen in here somewhere…"

"How many pockets do you have in that coat?"

"I dunno. Five? No, six, I think." He grinned. "Coats with lots of pockets are cool."

"Yeah," Violet said. "He's probably got more stuff in there than Calvin has in that dorky messenger bag of his. It's like an investigator's kit that actually looks cool."

"Yeah, except he doesn't have anything even remotely related to investigating in there," Cynthia said as she watched the latest batch of miscellany emerge from his pocket: a Yoda action figure, a ping-pong ball, a pair of black leather gloves, a broken cigarette (which he regarded with a grimace, then tossed onto the sidewalk), a chain of paperclips, and a snack-size Milky Way bar (which, judging by its rather lumpy shape, must have melted and resolidified numerous times).

He moved on to a pocket on the inner right side of his coat. This time he produced a battered address book with cartoon kung-fu monkeys on the cover, a compass, three black hair bands, a packet of aspirin, a small red squirt gun, and a purple bandanna with white paisley designs.

"Hey," said Cynthia, snatching this last item out of Donovan's hand. "That's *mine!*"

"I was wondering where that came from."

"I've been looking for that for, like, three months now. What are you doing with it?"

"Beats me. It's been in my pocket for a long time. I don't know how it got there."

"I think his pockets are like a black hole for stuff, you know?" Violet said. "They just suck things in somehow. It's like, you know how you lose a sock in the dryer every now and then? Well, those socks wind up in Donovan's pockets."

Donovan moved on to an inner breast pocket on the left side. He pulled out a sunglasses case, a small bottle of hand sanitizer, a pack of rolling paper, and a Baggie full of pot.

"Oh, fuck," he said, stuffing the Baggie back into his pocket while whipping his head about to make sure there weren't any cops around. "I forgot that was in there."

"I do not fucking believe this." Cynthia jabbed a finger at her brother. "You'd better not get me in trouble. If you get stopped and searched or something, I'm gonna claim I don't know you."

"Fuck," said Violet, rolling her eyes. "Paranoid much? We're not gonna get stopped and searched. I can guarantee it."

"And how can you guarantee that?"

"'Cause if we see any cops heading our way, we're just gonna run like hell in the other direction. They can't search you if they can't catch you."

Cynthia opened her mouth to respond, then realized the utter pointlessness of having a debate about something as idiotic as this with someone like Violet.

"So," she said, turning to Donovan. "That pen."

"Oh, right. Um…" He looked at his coat. "I think I tried all the pockets."

"Nuh-uh," said Violet. "You forgot the one on the outside over your right tit. And the secret one."

"Oh!" Donovan stuffed his hand into a small pocket on the right front breast of the coat. He fished around, found something, and pulled out a string of condoms. His face reddening, he quickly stuffed them back inside. "Um…"

Once again Cynthia averted her eyes, pretending she hadn't seen the condoms. She pretended especially hard that she hadn't noticed they were Magnums.

Violet was smiling dreamily again.

"Sorry," Donovan said as he felt around on the inner lining of his coat halfway down on the right. "Anyway, there's a secret pocket here. Um, it's, y'know, secret, so just forget you heard about it."

"Not a problem," said Cynthia. "I'm trying to forget

just about everything I've seen and heard the last ten minutes."

"Good, good." He groped around some more, frowning with concentration, the tip of his tongue protruding from between his lips. "I know it's here somewhere..." Then his face lit up and there was the zip of a zipper unzipping. "There we go."

From his not-so-secret pocket, he pulled a small rubber airplane, a piece of paper with a locker combination on it, another piece of paper with a few names and phone numbers of it, a wad of ten- and twenty-dollar bills, and a black Papermate ballpoint pen.

"Bingo!" he said, handing the pen to Cynthia.

She didn't take it right away, her attention focused instead on the wad of bills he was tucking back into his coat.

"Um, I know I'm gonna regret asking this, but where the hell did you get so much money? There has to be at least four or five hundred dollars there."

"Um..." Donovan glanced at Violet, whose attention had become suddenly and unswervingly fixed on the girls on the teeter-totter. Then he looked down at his coat as if he hoped it would disappear, cash and all, and obviate the need for the question. Then, reluctantly, he looked back up at Cynthia.

"It's just, uh, money I sort of, y'know, accumulated over the last while from, uh...various things."

Cynthia's jaw dropped.

"You've been selling drugs, haven't you?" Almost as an afterthought she snatched the pen from his hand.

Donovan straightened up with mock indignance, ready to deny the accusation, then realized he wouldn't be able to pull off a bluff. Not with Cynthia.

"Just some pot," he said.

Cynthia shook her head. She started to say something, stopped, started to say something else, stopped, then turned and watched the girls on the teeter-totter until her wits had cooled enough to permit coherent thought.

Creeeek. Pause. *Creeeek.* One of the little girls squealed with laughter as she ascended high upon the oar-like teeter-totter seat.

"Out of Mom and Dad's?" Cynthia exclaimed, turning to look at Donovan so swiftly her hair fanned out around her. "If you get busted, they could get in trouble. Hell, with all those bullshit forfeiture laws, they could lose the house."

"I'm careful, Cyn," Donovan said. "I don't keep it at the house. Or, well, at least not much of it. I keep it somewhere else. Somewhere safe. And I only sell it to people I know. Friends."

"And where do you *get* it? It doesn't grow on…" Her words trailed off as she noticed Donovan looking guiltier and more uncomfortable than ever. Her jaw dropped again. "You've been growing it in the woods out back, haven't you? You idiot!"

"Hey!" said Violet. "Leave him alone. Just cuz you're a big fucking chickenshit who craps her pants the minute she sees a cop, it doesn't mean we all are. Some of us are, you know, braver than that."

"Excuse me? Don't confuse bravery with an inability to think beyond the next beer."

"What the fuck is that supposed to mean?"

"It means you lack the imagination to think about the consequences of your actions."

"Yeah, well, you have too much imagination. You imagine shit that'll probably never happen and then act as if it already has. You're a coward."

Cynthia glared at her, her cheeks flaming the same color as her hair.

"Did you just use the words 'I think'?" she said. "You? Are you telling me you actually use that beer-sodden lump of tissue between your ears?"

"Fuck you, Little Miss High-and-Mighty. We might not have totally useless philosophy degrees like you, but we've got smarts that're more practical. Street smarts."

"'Street smarts'? That's what people say to justify having the I.Q. of a turnip."

"You are such a—"

"Will both of you shut the fuck up?" Donovan snapped. "We should be, like, looking for monster hiding places. You can bitch at each other later if you really want to, okay? God!" He stood up and stormed off down the sidewalk, his trench coat flapping behind him.

Cynthia and Violet just stared at him, too shocked by his outburst to do anything else for a moment. Cynthia felt her face burning redder than ever. She wasn't used to being reprimanded by her younger and generally much more irresponsible brother. But he was right; they were wasting valuable time.

She glanced at Violet and was strangely touched to see that Violet looked similarly abashed. Then Violet noticed Cynthia looking at her, and she sneered and flashed Cynthia the finger. Cynthia rolled her eyes, more disdainful than angry. Why had she even been arguing with this child in the first place?

With Donovan's pen she circled the park in her map book. Then she capped the pen, clipped it to the map book's cover, and stood up. She looked down at Violet, who still sat on the bench, her arms folded across her ample breasts.

"Come on," Cynthia said. "Let's just get this over with."

"Finally something outta your mouth that makes sense," Violet grumbled, then sprang to her feet and stomped off after Donovan.

With a weary sigh, Cynthia followed.

Behind them the two little girls kept playing on the teeter-totter.

Creeeek!

15

"Looks like we've got a lot of places to search," Calvin said through a mouthful of buffalo wings. He scanned the freshly compiled list of locations the two groups had come up with, then swiped a smudge of Blackbeard's Whiskers Hot Sauce off the paper.

The reunited group sat at a large, round table near the back of the Red Anchor Brewery's restaurant. Most of them were eating the brewery's award-winning wings, with dipping sauces to suit their individual tastes. A pitcher of Davey Jones' Lager sat in the middle of the table, already half empty. Cynthia had eschewed the meat and beer in favor of a deluxe garden salad and a glass of water. Lauren was partaking quite heartily of the lager but had ordered the beer brats and pierogies rather than wings. Calvin was treating.

"I think the cemetery's the best bet," Brandon said. He paused to suck a gob of hot sauce off his thumb, then went on: "That's totally a monster's kind of place, you know? It's like what that old lady told you: Like calls to like."

"That's what you said about the junk yard," Lauren said.

"Yeah, but there was a dog there, guarding the place. And a big jackass with a stogie. The cemetery, on the other hand, is untenanted, at least by anything living."

"I don't know," Cynthia said. "I'm inclined to go with the less dramatic but more logical choice: the ravines. They not only provide shelter and water but they run for blocks and blocks. They're like secret corridors for the creature to travel down. And at least some of them connect up with Holly Hills."

Calvin pondered the options, sipping his beer and looking over the list of locations again.

"The cemetery's woods are smaller than any of the ravines," he said, "so I say we tackle that first. We should be able to do that pretty quickly. Then, if we don't turn anything up, we move on to the ravines."

"That could get kind of dodgy," Lauren said. "I mean, who owns all that land down there? The city? The homeowners? If it's owned by the homeowners and someone sees us traipsing around on their property…"

"Then we book it," Violet said.

"I hate to say it," Calvin said, "but I think Violet's probably right. We don't have a lot of options here. We need to look in the places where the leucrota is likeliest to be, and if that involves some trespassing, then it does, unfortunately. We can't afford to waste time sussing out property rights and hunting up absentee landlords to ask permission."

"Are we gonna split up like we did today?" Donovan said with a glance at Cynthia. He wasn't too keen on winding up grouped with his sister again, since she'd no doubt seize the opportunity to royally bitch him out about the weed. As it was, he was going to have a hard enough time avoiding her when they got home tonight.

"We should probably do this as a group," Calvin said, "maybe with three of us in the search area and the others off on either side to watch for the leucrota in case it tries to slip away."

"Wouldn't that leave one person working solo?" Cynthia asked. "If there are three in the search group, that leaves only three to divide between the two sides."

"I'm hoping we'll have one more person with us. I talked to Tiffany Fish earlier, and although she couldn't make it to today's meeting, she does want to join the group." He told them the salient details about his meeting with her earlier that day. He didn't mention the subsequent chat with her dad. Cynthia was the only person he had told about his meeting with Andrew Fish and about Tiffany's breakdown, and the only person he planned to tell.

"So she wants to join as a sort of experiment?" asked Lauren. "To find out whether she's screwy or the alley is?"

Calvin squirmed, the word "screwy" hitting a little too close to home.

"In a way," he said. "But that's not the only reason. She really is interested in all of this." The moment he said it, he realized he wasn't entirely sure it was true. She hadn't actually said that, had she? Perhaps he only wanted it to be true.

"I can't wait to meet her," Brandon said. "She sounds interesting."

"Just remember, she's...shy," Calvin said. "She, uh, she doesn't get out a lot, and I don't think she has a lot of experience with people."

Violet frowned over her latest glass of beer. "What, is she some kind of weird hermit like Robert May?"

"Not exactly."

"She's just led a rather sheltered life till recently," Cynthia said diplomatically.

"She wasn't raised in a convent, was she?" Lauren said.

"No, nothing like that," Calvin said. "She's just very shy. I'll talk to her later tonight and tell her we're good to go tomorrow." He gulped down some beer, wiped a blob of foam off his lips, then nodded and added, "I think she'll be a great addition to the team. She's very good at, uh, lateral thinking."

That's a mild way of putting it, Cynthia thought. But she held her peace and just took another bite of salad.

16

The minute Calvin got home he called Tiffany's cell phone. She answered on the second ring.

"Hello?" she said. Tinny voices were audible in the background. She must be watching TV.

"Hi, Tiffany? It's me. Calvin."

"Oh. Yeah." She sounded oddly cool and casual. He thought she'd be more pleased to hear from him.

Then he heard her emit a soft grunt of exertion, and the sound of the TV slowly dwindled to nothing. There was a faint thump like a door closing.

"How are you?" she asked, her voice now excited, intimate. He guessed she had been in the living room with her father and had moved to a more private location. "How was your, um, walking tour?"

"It went well. We found a few locations we want to check out in more depth tomorrow. Can you still make it tomorrow?"

"Yes. I made sure I can make it." She gave a small, shaky laugh. "Panic-inducing though I'm sure it will be for me."

"It'll be cool," he said gently. "Really. They're good people. Well, except maybe Violet, but we usually just ignore her. Everything'll be fine. Really."

She heaved a nervous sigh, the exhalation sounding like a quick blast of static through the phone.

"I know," she said. She didn't sound like she knew, though.

"Hey, you met me and Cynthia all right, didn't you?"

"Yeah, it's just, meeting new people is always awkward. It's like discovering new iterations of yourself."

"Huh?"

"Everybody has their own subjective view of reality, which means everyone you meet will have their own subjective view of you. And not all of them will be favorable. It's..." She sighed again. "I don't know."

"Everything will be fine," he repeated. "They're nice people. You'll fit right in."

There was a pause on her end, one that went on long enough for him to start thinking he'd lost the connection. But then she said, "Sorry I'm such a basket case, or a head case, or maybe just a crank case. I'm just not used to this kind of thing. People and meetings. Dialogues. Trialogues. For a long time now my social circle has been more or less a dot."

"Then consider this the first step toward an enlarged

and more rewarding social life."

"Rewarding?" she murmured, her voice almost inaudible over the phone. "Rewarting. Rewording. So shall life. Hn." Then in a more conversational tone, she said, "What time should I be there?"

"We're scheduled to meet at five. Does that work for you?"

"It works. It plays. It does all kinds of things."

"Um, you could stop by even earlier, if you like. I don't have any plans for most of the afternoon. We could, you know, hang out and get to know each other better."

There was silence on the other end, and Calvin wondered if the offer had been a touch too forward for shy, sheltered Tiffany.

But then she said, "Hm. I don't have plans either. Getting to know each other better sounds like a fine way to pass the time."

Something about the way she said it made him wonder if she meant "know" in more ways than one. He couldn't be sure if that was her intent, or if his own subjective view of reality was coloring things.

"I'll be there early, then," she said in a decisive, businesslike tone that reminded Calvin of her father. "I can't say exactly how early, though. I have a few things I need to do tomorrow afternoon, and I'm not sure how long it'll take to get the doings done."

"I hope you get them done in record time," he said.

"Don't worry. I'll do my darnedest to beat the clock into a horrible, mangled jumble of dials, springs, and numbers."

"I couldn't ask for more."

17

The phone woke Calvin at ten to eight the next morning, wrenching him from an odd little dream in which a zombified Siamese cat had been leading him down a secret corridor that he had discovered behind the east wall of the wine cellar in the basement, a dream no doubt influenced, at least in part, by Lauren's spooky history story yesterday.

He cracked his eyes just enough to see the phone jangling and vibrating on the bedside table, then shut them again with an unhappy grunt. What was it with people calling him so damn early the last few days? He'd been so keyed up over the impending leucrota hunt and Tiffany's visit that he hadn't gotten to sleep until well after two. If he had known he might get another unscheduled wake-up call, he would've turned off his phone.

Then it dawned on him that the caller might be Tiffany, and he shot upright and snapped up the phone a moment before it would have gone to voicemail.

"Hello?" he said.

"Calvin, hi. It's me."

It wasn't Tiffany. For a moment he wasn't sure who it was, despite the voice's maddening familiarity. Then he realized the problem: It was indeed a voice he knew well, but not one he had ever heard over the phone before.

"Lauren?" he said.

"Yeah. I know I probably woke you up, but you'd better check the news."

He realized he could hear a radio on in the background of wherever she was calling from, and then, briefly, the roar of an engine accelerating. She must be on her way to work. For her to call him at this hour and under those circumstances meant it must be something serious. He got out of bed and stood there in his Chewbacca boxers, all vestiges of sleep now gone from his mind.

"What happened?" he said.

"There's been another murder. I think it's gonna change our plans. I'd tell you more, but I'm just pulling into the library's parking lot, and I'm already running late. Just watch the news, or listen to it, or whatever, and we can all discuss it at the meeting later."

After she hung up, Calvin hurried downstairs to the parlor, switched on the radio, and tuned it to WODE, which was currently airing *Good Morning Kingwood*, a morning drive-time talk/news show.

Good Morning Kingwood was hosted by William Kingsley, Jr., a local radio personality whose shtick and slogan was "Truth with a Capital T!" His idea of truth was always very contentious and ultra-conservative. His co-host, who handled the news, weather, and traffic reports, was Lisa Quimby, whose high, perky voice provided a perfect counterpoint to Kingsley's growl. Calvin considered Kingsley a bombastic buffoon of the highest order but had always liked Quimby, and not just because she was the younger sister of his high school chemistry teacher, in whose class he and Cynthia had begun to forge their friendship all those years ago. As DJ Lisa Q, Quimby had hosted WODEs *Totally 80s* show, which Calvin had listened to a lot when he was in high school, and her irrepressibly chipper attitude had always managed to cheer him up no matter how cruddy his day. Two years ago she had been assigned to join Kingsley on *Good Morning Kingwood* after his former co-host quit in disgust over one of Kingsley's liberal-baiting stunts. Calvin still wasn't sure whether Quimby's reassignment counted as a promotion or a demotion.

When Calvin turned it on, Kingsley was in mid-rant: "—ivory-towered liberals, trying to rewrite the English language just because someone's precious little feelings might get hurt. I can't even call my waitress a waitress anymore. She's a server now, which I thought had something to do with computers, but whatever."

"They're all communists, pure and simple, Will," said the current caller, a man with a nasal voice who phoned the show nearly every day. "They're trying to undermine America by destroying our God-given language."

"I'm not even sure what I'm supposed to call a midget nowadays," Kingsley said, not really addressing the caller's comment. Probably wisely, since the comment had been complete and utter nonsense. "A little person? A dwarf? Vertically challenged? An individual of lower altitude? I have no idea, and I don't think anyone else does either.

"The truth is, the liberal whiners want to strip our language of the very words we the people chose to use and retain over the course of centuries. Good words. Traditional words. And they're replacing them with a bunch of Orwellian bureaucraspeak devoid of any heritage, poetry, or intelligence.

"Is there anything else you need to say before we do the news? I've got ten seconds."

"Nosiree. You said it all, Will. Bye now."

"Goodbye."

The station's call music started up low in the background.

"That was kind of harsh," Lisa Quimby said.

"I might sound harsh," Kingsley said with a sort of

rhythmic incantatory intonation. He repeated some vari-
ation of this spiel every day. "I might sound like a bad
person. But I'm only speaking the truth with a capital T."

Calvin rolled his eyes.

"Come on, come on," he said. "Just do the news already."

As if in response to Calvin's demand, the station music
swelled and the national news started. This was not read
by Lisa Quimby. It was instead a pre-recorded segment
read by a guy named Jim Ziffle who spoke in deep urgent
tones as if he were auditioning to replace Wolf Blitzer.

Fidgeting with impatience, Calvin waited through the
seemingly endless string of Middle Eastern bombings,
presidential and congressional blather, celebrity idiocies,
supposed human-interest pieces (none of which were of
interest to Calvin or any other human beings he knew),
and over a dozen commercials for products and services
he never used and couldn't care less about.

Finally, seven-and-a-half minutes after the news began,
Lisa Quimby took over with the local report.

"A badly mutilated body was found early this morning
in a parking lot on Gramercy Road in Kingwood. The
body has not yet been identified, but police have confirmed that it appears to be the work of the same person
or persons responsible for the deaths of two other Kingwood residents in the last week. Chief of Police Dowdie
has scheduled a press conference for noon, and we will
bring you full coverage of that event, as well as any further
details of the case as they emerge. Meanwhile, in other
news, a fire gutted the Towner Street Tavern overnight..."

Calvin switched off the radio with a troubled frown.
He wasn't entirely sure where Gramercy Road was, but if
it was where he thought it was...

"That can't be right," he muttered. He snatched up the Kingwood street atlas from the coffee table where he had tossed it after getting home last night, and looked up Gramercy in the index. Page 23, section B3.

"Shit!"

Yes, Gramercy Road was exactly where he had thought it was—namely, six blocks west of Pentz Road, half a mile outside the parameters of yesterday's foot search. The area was a continuation of the sprawling industrial zone whose eastern edge was where the Mad Hatter warehouse stood.

He scanned the map more closely. There didn't appear to be a single park or cemetery or ravine in the area; Gramercy Road and the entire industrial zone of which it was a part was a place of factories, warehouses, and parking lots. In other words, acres and acres of concrete, with no green spaces in which an outdoorsy monster might build a cozy little nest.

Could Calvin have been wrong to assume the leucrota would settle down in one spot? Could the leucrota be roaming, with no fixed abode? Perhaps. Brad Vallance's death had occurred toward the eastern edge of yesterday's search area and Terrell Quinn's had occurred in the center. The two missing spray-painters had been last seen in the northwest corner of the search area, but given that nobody knew where they had gone after that, they could have been killed anywhere. For that matter, their disappearance might be unrelated to the leucrota attacks.

Which meant the only definite attacks occurred in a rough east-to-west line. First Vallance, then Quinn, now this unidentified victim.

If the leucrota was constantly on the move their chances of finding it shrank to nearly nil, especially if it kept heading west: Given its current approximate location, it could easily reach the western edge of Kingwood within another day or two. Beyond the city limits, it would be back in suburbia where it had started two years ago, free to feed on family pets once more and further unjustly blacken the reputation of those rangy, mangy coyotes.

Calvin slapped the map book shut and tossed it carelessly onto the coffee table, where it knocked against a plastic coaster and sent it shooting to the carpet like a hockey puck. He left the coaster on the floor and flung himself onto the leather couch.

"Shit," he said again.

18

For the rest of the day Calvin checked the news every hour on the hour. There was no new information until the noon press conference, at which Chief Dowdie repeated what had already been revealed and then added that the latest victim was a middle-aged woman who had now been identified but whose identity was being withheld until her family could be tracked down and notified of her death. The body, which had suffered severe mutilation consistent with the other victims, had been discovered by a patrolman shortly before dawn. Coroner Chandra estimated the time of death to have been between midnight and three a.m. As far as was known, there were no witnesses, visual or aural, to the death.

Dowdie then revealed that another person had gone missing in the West River neighborhood, a fourteen-year-old girl named Maisie Dayton, who had snuck out of her parents' house the night before last to meet her boyfriend and had not been seen since. The boyfriend, a seventeen-year-old with a history of petty theft and assault, had been considered the prime suspect in the girl's disappearance—and hence the disappearance had been considered unconnected with the string of murders—until last night when his alibi had been confirmed beyond doubt. Now, the police feared she may have met the same fate as the other murder victims and, possibly, the two missing graffitists. Chief Dowdie urged anyone with information to come forward. He reiterated that the police believed the murders to have been committed by at least two individuals armed with some kind of odd, large cutting implement.

The conference ended with a flurry of questions from reporters, none of which yielded any further useful information from Dowdie.

Calvin switched off the TV, then consulted the map book. The Daytons' home was on a stretch of Jackson Road that Calvin's team had traversed during yesterday's search. Calvin didn't remember seeing the house. Then again, he and the others had been focusing on heavily foliated areas, not on houses. The house was a few blocks southwest of where Terrell Quinn's body was found, which was consistent with the hypothesis that the leucrota was traveling west. On the other hand, the Dayton home was simply where the girl had last been seen, not where she died. Calvin wasn't even sure which direction she went after leaving home; Chief Dowdie hadn't said where Maisie Dayton planned to meet her boyfriend.

Calvin continued tuning in to the news every hour, but subsequent reports only repeated what was already known. Apparently the police weren't having much luck tracking down the latest victim's relatives.

He spent the rest of his time surfing the internet for information about the nesting habits of hyenas, wolves, and other animals that leucrotas resembled or were reputed to have been based on, hoping that the parallelisms extended beyond the merely physical to include the behavioral as well.

Tiffany arrived at ten to four, early as planned. The first thing she asked when he met her at the door was, "Have you heard about the new murder?"

"Yeah. It kind of makes hash of our search yesterday."

"Why?"

"Come on. I'll show you."

He led her into the parlor, and they sat down on the couch, Calvin careful to keep a body-length of space between them. Given what her father had told him, he was more reluctant than ever to be too bold, move too fast, press too hard, afraid he might reopen old wounds in her psyche. He figured—or perhaps only desperately hoped—that she would give him some kind of a signal when it was time for him to make a move. He looked at her as she settled into her seat, and found it hard to reconcile her pretty face and mild demeanor with the feral fighting thing her father had described. He tried to imagine her scrawling incomprehensible symbols on a madhouse wall with her own blood, but he just couldn't see it.

And then he stopped thinking about it altogether, distracted by her nearness. He couldn't help but be aware of her warm and solid body within arms' reach of his, so close he could smell some kind of peach-scented product she had used earlier—shampoo, perhaps, or body wash. And the couch's springs and cushions connected them, too, transmitting the vibrations of their restless bodies' shifts and squirms to each other. Her every movement made him move too, and vice versa.

Calvin picked up the map book, which lay open to the two-page spread showing the West River neighborhood, and held it between himself and Tiffany.

"See, look here..." he said.

As she leaned toward him for a better look, her forearm brushed his. She was wearing a cap-sleeved shirt similar to the one she had worn the other day, and the feel of her bare skin grazing his made him stiffen, his heart jumping. He glanced up at her only to find that she had chosen the exact same moment to glance up at him. Their eyes met.

"Um..." He cleared his throat and looked down at the map book. What the hell had he been saying? Oh, right. "See, the area where we, uh, where we searched yesterday, it was, uh...it, uh..." His index finger made aimless circles over the splayed pages. He couldn't think. Tiffany's arm was still touching his—only lightly, but he could no more ignore it than he could a stripper giving him a lap dance. Out of the corner of his eye he saw that Tiffany hadn't moved. She was still looking at him. He glanced at her again.

She hadn't heard a word he said. She was intently studying his face, her eyes roving over his nose and lips and cheeks, her pupils big as those of a cat about to pounce, her nostrils dilating rhythmically as if she were savoring his scent. Her eyes rose to meet his. They were fierce with desire.

Fragile, my ass, he thought. This was all the signal he needed.

He leaned toward her, slowly at first to give her time to back away or protest on the off chance he had misread her. But he hadn't misread anything. The language of her face had been unmistakable. Instead of backpedaling, she thrust her face forward to meet his.

They kissed. What Calvin had meant to be a delicate lip-touch, again playing it safe with this potentially frangible girl, swiftly got hijacked by Tiffany, whose mouth muscled at his with savage abandon, her lips pushing and sucking at his in a sloppy, confused way. After a few seconds, apparently realizing her efforts weren't achieving the desired results, she abandoned her enthusiastic if inchoate technique and instead started mimicking what Calvin's lips were doing, only with ten times the vigor.

It was clear she had never kissed anyone before, which almost certainly meant she was still a virgin. Calvin suddenly felt a little guilty, as if he were taking advantage of her somehow. In his head he heard her father warning him not to harm her.

Then her tongue thrust through his lips and dove deep into his mouth, and any notion that *he* was taking advantage of *her* dissipated in an instant.

He met her passion with equal force. At least for a moment. She upped the ante almost immediately, shoving her body against his, her hands clutching his chest, her hungry advance taking him by surprise and pushing him backward. The map book slid from his fingers and thwacked onto the carpet. Calvin sank back onto the seat of the couch with Tiffany atop him, her lips smacking wetly and hungrily on his, her tongue driving into him, her hands now pushing up his T-shirt and touching and stroking his bare belly. All the while she made soft, quick grunts, like a ravenous dog devouring a long-overdue meal.

Then she drew back, her lips separating from his with a quick wet *smeck,* and looked him dead in the eye. The blaze in her eyes had blossomed into a Hindenburg-like inferno. Her lips were curved into an impudent smile. The little princess was back and intent on getting exactly what she desired. And what, pray tell, did her majesty desire?

"I want to have sex with you," she said. "Right now. On this couch."

"Um, okay." He glanced at the clock in the corner. "Are you sure, though? We don't have a lot of time. The others'll be here in about half an hour. Cynthia might show up even earlier."

"I don't care," she said flatly. Her fingers found his nipples and pinched them hard enough to make his already half-erect cock jump in his jeans.

She felt the warm length of him press against her thigh. Grinning wickedly, her mouth a white crescent of teeth, she maneuvered about until her jeans-sheathed crotch settled over his bulge. Then she wiggled her hips back and forth, grinding herself against him.

He stiffened with a gasp, then rocked his hips to match her movements. He cupped her full, round breasts and squeezed, feeling the padded shape of her bra cups under her shirt, and, under the bra, faint but distinct, the hard little stones of her nipples. She growled and flung herself flat against him again, her lips mashing into his so hard his upper lip got pinched against his front teeth. There was a quick sting of pain and the coppery tang of blood. He was so aroused by now he couldn't care less. In a weird way, the savagery added to the eroticism.

Her hips lifted off him, and for a moment he thought she was about to dismount for some reason. Then her right hand slid down his body and settled on the straining hump in his pants. Her eager fingers explored its denim-draped contours.

"It feels so hot," she breathed into his mouth. "It's like a fever."

His hands gave her breasts a final squeeze, then moved to the column of pearly buttons running down the front of her shirt. He undid the top one, and her shirt slipped open a little, exposing a triangle of smooth skin below her throat.

When she realized what he was doing, she broke off their kiss and drew away from him, giving him easier access to her chest and belly. Her hand kept stroking the rigid length of him. Her hips kept rotating, grinding her crotch against his thigh. Her teeth were clenched, her nostril flaring wide with her hot, quick breaths.

He undid the buttons one by one until her shirt fell fully open, baring her smooth, creamy belly and the two pale globes quivering in the cotton cups of her plain white bra. He seized her breasts, his fingers sinking into the plump, soft flesh. He found her nipples through the fabric and pinched them between his thumbs and forefingers. Tiffany grunted, and increased the tempo of her hip-thrusts and her lascivious caresses. Calvin's cock felt close to bursting.

"I have condoms," she said.

"What?"

She shrugged, looking a little sheepish. "I...I've had them a long time. I've never actually used any of them, but I carry them around just in case. You never know."

"How long have you had them? What's the expiration date?"

"They have an expiration date?"

"Um, yeah."

"Oh." She nodded slightly and muttered, "That makes sense. Everything expires."

She sat up and dug a hand into the right front pocket of her jeans. After a few seconds of digging and groping, she wriggled out a three-pack of Trojan condoms. The box was old and crumpled, its corners dented and frayed, its gloss long since faded.

She studied the box for a few seconds, turning it this way and that until she found the expiration date stamped on the bottom. Given the crinkled, battered condition of the box, she had to tilt it back and forth in the light for a few seconds before she could make out the date.

"It expires next month," she announced with a happy smile. "We're just in time."

"Okay," Calvin said, smiling just as happily.

"Okay," she echoed. She stared at him a moment, the box of condoms still in her hands. Her eyes surveyed his bared chest, his slim waist, his small red nipples made hard by her tweaks and tugs. "Take off your clothes," she demanded. "I want to see you naked."

In the midst of his surprise, he couldn't help feeling a little amused. The domineering little princess popped out at the oddest moments. Or maybe not so odd. Maybe it popped out only when there was something she really, really wanted.

"Tell you what," he said. "Why don't we take turns?"

She raised an eyebrow. "Quid pro quo?" Then she nodded. "Good idea. Tit for tat."

"I don't have any tats," he said.

"Get that darn shirt off already." She plucked at the rucked-up T-shirt under his chin.

He lifted his head and shoulders off the couch, tugged the shirt the rest of the way off, and dropped it onto the floor beside the couch.

"That barely counts," she said with mock poutiness. "It was practically off anyway."

"So's this." He tugged at the panels of her shirt. "So get it off. I want to see you naked, too, don't forget."

Smiling, eyes on his, she slipped off the shirt and tossed it atop his on the carpet.

He slid his hands over the smooth domes of her shoulders and down her upper arms, savoring the warmth and softness of her skin. Then his hands swerved inward, his fingertips grazing the sides of her breasts. He slipped his fingers under the bra straps and pulled at them, stretching them. The tops of the bra cups pulled away from her skin, exposing more and more of the creamy globes behind them.

She batted his hands away.

"You can get that later," she said. "It's your turn to disrobe."

"You should have gone first. You're wearing more clothes than I am."

She flashed a big, triumphant grin. "I know. That was why I agreed to your terms in the first place. I've got more quids than you've got quos."

"You vixen." He sat up and reached around her to get to his shoes. This put them face-to-face, and as he started to unlace his sneakers, he kissed her. She snuggled closer, wrapping her arms around his back, her tongue darting into his mouth, her breasts flattening against his bare chest. Her hips, which had fallen mostly quiescent over the last couple of minutes, now began to grind with a vengeance, her crotch sliding up and down along the length of his cock.

The doorbell rang.

They stared at each other, completely frozen, not even breathing. Calvin saw a flash of anxiety in Tiffany's eyes as if she'd been caught doing something wrong. Shit, could it be her dad at the door? Had he been following Tiffany again? Or was it simply Cynthia arriving earlier than expected? He glanced at the clock and saw it wasn't quite as early as he had thought: It was already 4:15.

The bell rang again.

Tiffany jumped off him, snatched her shirt off the floor, and began to put it back on, her fingers fluttering at each button like the wings of panicked birds.

Calvin likewise sprang off the couch and pulled his shirt on, glad he didn't have to monkey with buttons like she did. He was fully clothed before she had even gotten the first button buttoned.

"You keep buttoning up while I get the door," he told her.

She nodded.

"Oh, and put these back in your pocket." He snatched the box of condoms from the seat of the couch and handed them to her.

"Thanks," she said with a small, nervous laugh.

He strode down the hall to the door, reaching it just as the bell began to chime a third time.

The bell-ringer turned out to be Cynthia after all.

"Did you hear the news?" she asked as she stepped inside and he shut the front door behind her.

"The new murder? Yeah." Hoping to give Tiffany a bit of extra time to make herself presentable, he lingered at the door, twisting the knob back and forth as if there were something wrong with it.

"Yeah, I only just found out," Cynthia said. "I figured I'd head over early and we could brainstorm about it." She looked down the hall at the open parlor door. "I take it Tiffany Fish is here? I saw her car."

"Uh, yeah. She came by early, too." He gave the doorknob a little shake, then nodded as if satisfied and gestured at the parlor door. "Let's go."

"Is the door okay?" she said, twisting around to look at it as they headed down the hall.

"It is now."

When they entered the parlor Tiffany was sitting calmly on the couch studying the two-page spread in the Kingwood street atlas that Calvin had started to show her earlier.

She looked up and smiled at them, the picture of perfect innocence.

"Hi," she said to Cynthia. "Nice to see you again."

"Hi," Cynthia said, looking first at Tiffany, then around the room as if she sensed something amiss but couldn't quite put her finger on what. She sat down on the couch near Tiffany, then nodded at the street atlas. "So, what, were the two of you discussing the case?"

"A little," Calvin said. "I was hoping to bring her up to speed on things, but we kind of got to talking about other stuff."

Calvin sat down in the antique claw-and-ball chair, which, it was tacitly understood by one and all, was his and his alone. Calvin preferred it because it had been Mr. May's favorite and because its ornate carvings and gold upholstery lent it a throne-like air that flattered his ego and felt in keeping with his position as de facto head of the group. But now he wished he could sit on the couch next to Tiffany. Well, he *could*, of course. It was his house and he could sit anywhere he liked. But there were only just enough seats in here for seven people, which meant that if he commandeered a spot on the couch, someone else would have to use his chair, and that wouldn't do at all. He'd have to see about adding another chair or two.

He looked longingly at Tiffany across the coffee table, wishing he could be sitting where Cynthia was. Tiffany clearly felt the same way. While Cynthia pointed out the location of the new murder in the map book, Tiffany looked up at Calvin from beneath her lowered blonde brows, her eyes smoldering with longing, a trace of a naughty smile playing on her lips.

"The unidentified woman's body was about...here," Cynthia said, tapping a spot in the map book, oblivious to all this. "And our search grid yesterday..." She reached out and flipped a page. "It was here." She traced the rectangle of streets with her index finger.

"Ah," Tiffany said, glancing down at the map. "That's unfortunately far away." Her eyes rose to meet Calvin's as she said this to make sure he caught the double entendre. He did. He gave a rueful grimace and nodded.

"Yeah," Cynthia said with a sigh, still studying the map book. "Looks like we'll have to rethink our approach."

She drew back from Tiffany a little to contemplate the overall street plan, while Tiffany lowered the map book slightly, both of which actions revealed a swath of Tiffany's torso that had been hitherto hidden from Calvin's view. One of her shirt's buttons was unbuttoned right below her breasts, and her shirt bowed open there, exposing a roughly circular patch of pale skin at the top of which a glimpse of her white bra was visible.

Tiffany, still watching Calvin with that small lusty smile, noticed his sudden look of surprise and alarm, and she cocked her head with a puzzled frown.

Calvin jerked his head downward while raising his

eyebrows, trying to communicate to her that she should look down.

She did, but both the swell of her breasts and an extruding fold of her shirt hid the revealing gap from her sight. Concluding he must mean the map book instead, she examined its open pages. Finding nothing amiss, she looked back up at Calvin and gave a small, baffled shrug.

He did the head-jerk/eyebrow-raise again, more vehemently this time. He was about to raise his hand to pluck at the front of his shirt when the doorbell rang.

Cynthia glanced toward the front door, then looked at Calvin.

"That's probably Donovan and Violet," she said. "When I talked to them earlier, it sounded like they were going to try to show up early for a change." When Calvin just sat there, looking uncertainly from her to Tiffany to the corridor outside the open parlor doorway, she added, "You gonna get that?"

"Um, yeah." He stood up, then looked at Tiffany, who was still watching him in bafflement. Cynthia was staring at him, too, no doubt wondering why he was acting so weird, which meant he couldn't pluck at his shirt to alert Tiffany without Cynthia's noticing. Maybe when he came back he could head straight to Tiffany under the pretense of getting the map book from her, and in the process whisper to her to button up. That might work. He hoped. "I, uh, I'll be right back."

He hurried out of the room.

Cynthia began to study the map book again. After a moment, without looking up from the book, she quietly said, "You might want to check your shirt."

"What?" Tiffany looked down, flattening the bulging fold with one hand while leaning forward a little to see the entirety of the front of her shirt. When she saw the gaping hole, she flushed, then quickly wrangled the button through its hole.

She glanced at Cynthia. Cynthia had a faint smile on her face. Tiffany's face was now the color of a boiler a few degrees away from exploding.

"Um, thanks," she mumbled.

"No problem," Cynthia said, her eyes never leaving the map book.

Calvin returned with the rest of the group in tow. Not just Donovan and Violet, but Brandon and Lauren as well. They had arrived at the same time, all of them having decided to show up early to get a jump on things. They had heard about the new murder and comprehended the increased gravity it lent their task: The longer the leucrota (even Lauren was no longer qualifying it with "presumed" anymore) remained at large, the more deaths would occur.

Tiffany stood up as they entered, nervously rubbing her hands up and down her thighs.

Calvin immediately started to head toward her to implement his plan, but then saw that her shirt was fully buttoned now. She must have finally translated his signals correctly.

"Everyone," he said, "I'd like you to meet Tiffany Fish, the newest member of our little group."

Calvin introduced the others to Tiffany one by one. She greeted them calmly, smiling, not looking a fraction as panicky as Calvin had feared she would. He suspected their soft-core interlude earlier had something to do with that. It had deepened her bond with Calvin and confirmed she had someone on her side, come what may, and it had left her a little more experienced, a little worldlier, than she had been when she showed up half an hour earlier.

"Thank God I'm not the newbiest person around here anymore," Lauren said.

"You haven't even confirmed whether or not you want to officially join," Calvin said.

"Not yet, no. I'll let you know."

"Damn," Donovan said to Calvin, grinning. "The chicks totally outnumber us now. Not that I'm complaining. They're all hotties."

And then he said, "Ow!" as Violet's foot connected hard with his leg.

"As far as you're concerned, *I'm* the only hottie here," she growled. "Got it?"

"That included you, too," Donovan said, rubbing his leg. "I did say you're *all* hotties." He noticed Cynthia staring at him with a look of appalled disbelief. "Well, except you, of course," he told her. She scowled. "I think. Wait..." He realized he had just talked himself into a very uncomfortable corner.

Cynthia raised one hand in a stop gesture. "I refuse to take any part in this ridiculous conversation."

"Look," Violet told Donovan, "the point is, you're only supposed to notice *me*. In return, you will get laid. That's how relationships work."

Donovan stared at her, his mouth gaping, as the truth sank in. "Oh, man. I'm totally sorry. Really."

Brandon made a noise like a whip cracking followed a cat's meow.

Donovan shook a finger at him. "Hey, you just wait till you get a steady girlfriend. This is how it is, man."

Brandon gave him a smug grin. "Not if you just hire escorts."

Cynthia buried her face in her hands and muttered, "I don't believe this."

"You hire escorts?" Donovan asked in an awed voice.

Brandon looked shocked. "On *my* income? Fuck, no. But once I start making more money, well, I tell you, there's no fucking way I'm putting up with all that crazy chick shit. I'm just gonna pay for a little nooky once in a while and that's that."

Violet noticed the thoughtful look on Donovan's face.

"You can't afford it," she said in a low, menacing tone. "And I don't mean financially."

Donovan looked at her, saw how things stood, and let out a long, sad sigh.

"Can we please skip to the non-flesh-crawling part of the meeting?" Cynthia said.

"I don't think there is one," Lauren said.

While all this had been going on, Tiffany sidled over to where Calvin stood and whispered, "So evidently I'm a hottie?"

"Oh, absolutely," Calvin said.

"Why was I never informed of this before?"

"I guess you need better informants."

"Clearly."

As soon as everyone was seated, Calvin called the meeting to order.

"Okay, so we all know about the new murder and the new missing person, right?" he said.

"Yeah, and it kind of makes all that walking around we did yesterday totally irrelevant," Brandon said.

"Not necessarily," Calvin said. "I thought the same thing at first, but now I'm not so sure. The leucrota could still be nesting within the search area. It might simply have traveled a little farther afield last night."

"Or it's not nesting at all and is constantly on the move," Lauren said.

"Ah! I did some research into the nesting habits of hyenas and various canids. It turns out that hyenas prefer to sleep in underground dens, usually the burrows of other animals."

"Underground?" Donovan said. "Should we be checking sewers and basements and stuff?"

"Maybe. The thing is, though, hyena dens are communal places. The creature we're looking for is just a solitary individual."

"Yeah," Lauren said, "not to mention the fact that it's not technically a hyena either."

"That is correct. That's why I widened my research to include other dog-like mammals. Generally speaking, they prefer to make their lairs in sheltered areas. Wolves, for instance, sleep out in the open, but usually in an area with a lot of cover."

"That's kind of what we were looking for yesterday, wasn't it?" Brandon said. "Areas with cover?"

"Yeah. I guess the main point is, all of these animals will seek out the areas where they're least likely to be disturbed and they'll stay there. That's the one thing that holds true for all of them."

"Least likely to be disturbed..." Tiffany muttered. She picked up the map book and opened it to the pages showing the West River neighborhood.

"What about urban coyotes?" Brandon said. "Did you look them up? That's probably the only animal I can think of that would be analogous. You know, a wild creature prowling a city. I mean, you're not likely to find any hyenas or wolves in cities very often. But I know there're coyotes in Kingwood."

"I did look those up," Calvin said. "Urban coyotes, like everything else, stick to areas with a lot of cover. They also have a tendency to roam a lot more than some of the other things I looked up. However, bear in mind that what we're looking for is supposed to be considerably larger than a coyote, which would make it harder to stay hidden if it's traveling."

"So you think it's holing up somewhere after all?" Lauren said.

"I don't know for sure, but I think it would want somewhere it would feel secure. It would want cover. And given its size and its appearance, I can't help but think it would be spotted if it was spending most of its time roaming around. It's a big, busy city."

"So, what, should we do another foot search, just including this new area?" Brandon said.

"What would be the new epicenter of the search area if we take this new death into account?" asked Lauren.

"Ah, that's an interesting point," Calvin said. "I was looking at that earlier, and it turns out the epicenter would shift west to somewhere around the intersection of Ferntree and Sycamore, where the Congregational Church sits."

Lauren sat bolt upright, her big, doe-like eyes blinking.

"Whoa!" she said. Then she frowned. "But we checked there. There's no way anything could've gotten in."

"The junkyard was near there, too, don't forget," Brandon said. "I'm tellin' ya, monsters like big mazy places like that. It's tradition."

"What's this church you're talking about?" Tiffany asked.

"Oh, she needs the Reverend Squash story!" Lauren exclaimed, gleeful at another opportunity to tell the story.

"Try to abridge it a bit," Calvin said.

Lauren quickly filled Tiffany in on the strange story of Reverend Squash.

"Wouldn't the reverend's house be a more likely location for a monster?" Tiffany said. "It sounds like the house was the locus of the weird activity, and if we posit that like attracts like and that monsters are drawn to liminal places like the alley then the house would be a monster lodestone. If it's still there, that is."

"It's not," Lauren said. "It's long gone. That location is now the home of the Mad Hatter warehouse."

Tiffany gasped.

"Mad had her! Where house? Right there! That's it!"

Everyone looked at her, then at each other, then at her again.

"What?" Calvin said.

"I know the Mad Hatter very, very well. My dad did a lot of work for them over the years. The Mad Hatter Novelty Company used to be one of the biggest employers in Kingwood. Then about three years ago they filed for bankruptcy, but for a lot of arcane legal reasons, their Kingwood Distribution Center, the place we're talking about, got sealed up, all its contents still there on the shelves, and it's stayed that way ever since. It's just a huge darkened building full of gimcrack novelties, like plastic dog doo and reverse-color playing cards and tiny beans containing twelve tiny elephants."

Calvin felt a chill, remembering one of Andrew Fish's comments when he was telling Calvin about his daughter's crazy graffiti: *And there were numbers, too, here and there. Especially twelves. Lots of twelves.*

"All of it's just sitting there in the dark, gathering dust," Tiffany said. "At least until the legalities can be sorted out, which, at the rate legalities tend to get sorted out, will be sometime around the year three thousand. It fits all the criteria. It's abandoned, more or less, while still remaining the sort of dark, mazy place monsters prefer, as Brandon here pointed out. It's located on a spot where strange things happened, like the alley and the clearing in your woods out back. And its corporate logo—why, that's just a big neon giveaway."

"What, a grin popping out of a top hat?" Lauren said.

"A grin. Which is what you said the leucrota's ear-to-ear mouth is most often likened to. Which means the hat must represent the anomaly in the clearing out back; like a magician's hat it's a sort of magical space from which various unexpected things can be pulled or apported. It all fits together perfectly, don't you see?"

(And at this point Donovan leaned toward Violet and whispered: "Is she, like, *on* something?"

Violet regarded Tiffany a moment, eyes narrow and thoughtful, then whispered back: "I don't know. But if we could extract her brain chemicals right now, I bet we'd make a fortune on the stoner market.")

"It fits," Tiffany repeated. "The pieces all fit. It all converges."

Calvin nodded. "It does."

"Whoa whoa whoa," Cynthia said, waving a hand back and forth. "What is this? How exactly does all of it fit?"

"The world is made of secret connections," Calvin said. "Look, I know the evidence is largely circumstantial—"

"Largely? I'd say completely."

"Okay, granted. But the Mad Hatter warehouse does fit on a number of levels. It's sheltered and unused by people, which fits with the canid info I looked up. It's dark and mazy, which fits with Brandon's ideas. It was on the site of Reverend Squash's house, so it may well have the stink of weirdness about it, just like the alley, which might be to the liking of a monster. And you have to admit its corporate logo is eerily apt."

"Wouldn't there be people there, at least once in a while?" Lauren asked. "Security guards or something?"

Everyone looked at Tiffany expectantly.

"I don't know," she said, squirming under the sudden attention. "My dad only did legal work for them. They didn't apprise him of their distribution facilities' security setup."

"Maybe they don't have a night watchman," Calvin said. "Maybe the powers-that-be think the place is secure enough without one. Or maybe they can't afford one."

"Or maybe the leucrota ate him," Violet said.

"Listen," Cynthia said. "All I'm saying is, we don't have any actual evidence. It's all circumstantial. There are probably a number of different places in that area that are closed down and mazy and would provide decent shelter for a monster."

"Yeah," Calvin said, "but they didn't conspicuously come up in conversation the day before—a conversation that occurred on the spot that is now the brand-new centerpoint of the area encompassed by the multiple deaths—and they didn't have links to our newest member of the group, and they don't have a logo that resembles the most prominent feature of the beast we're looking for."

"It's just a lot of...of hocus-pocus," Cynthia exclaimed, her voice rising. "It's not proof. If I'm going to do something, I want it to be for a real reason, not magical thinking." Out of the corner of her eye she saw Tiffany flinch. She felt both guilty and glad at the same time.

Then Tiffany rallied.

"But magic is afoot," she said, gesturing at the north wall, the direction of the woods, the clearing. "You've seen it yourself."

"Yeah, and you haven't."

Tiffany shrank down in her seat a little.

"Look, I don't mean to be mean or anything," Cynthia hastened to add. "But this is different. I don't like the idea of rushing into action based on nothing more than a few spurious coincidences."

"I don't think they're spurious," Calvin said.

"They're not *proof.*"

"No," he conceded. "They're not. Not in a legal or scientific sense. But remember what Betty Romero said: Everything's connected. We're just following the connections."

"You're turning an off-hand remark by some possibly dotty old lady into a standard of evidence."

"Look, just go with it. Maybe we're wrong. I admit that. But the only way we're going to find out is if we check it out ourselves. And don't forget: During investigations of weird phenomena, weirdness will abound. Remember that one case Mr. May investigated, the one in New York City with that department store? The only reason he figured out what was going on was because he remembered the song that little girl had been singing and he made the leap that it might be connected to the murders."

"Yeah, I remember."

"And that time he escaped the explosion in Poland because he had that weird dream?"

"Okay, yeah. I get it. It's a big, weird world."

Cynthia admitted defeat. She realized now that part of her problem was her odd, instinctive repulsion toward

Tiffany Fish, a feeling which, she now reflected, was just as seemingly arbitrary as Tiffany's proofs. The other part of her problem was that she was afraid of what it would mean if Tiffany were right. If a bundle of vague coincidences constituted valid proof, it meant reality didn't always follow the sane, linear rules she was used to. It meant there were hidden patterns underlying the world, patterns no one really understood. And that was something she found frightening on a very deep and existential level.

"All right," she sighed. "Let's try it."

Calvin nodded and gave her a smile, pleased she had bent to his new girlfriend. Cynthia managed to smile in return.

Calvin looked at the others. "What about the rest of you? Everyone else on board?"

They all nodded.

"I'm a bit iffy myself, I have to admit," Lauren said. "But I agree it's a big, weird world, and I've already eaten crow over the leucrota thing. So, sure, let's give it a whirl."

"All right," Calvin said, glancing at the clock. "We'd better start getting organized, then."

"What about, like, calling the police?" Lauren said. "If we really think this thing is at the warehouse, shouldn't we notify them and leave it up to the professionals?"

"We talked about this the other day."

"Yeah, but—"

"They're looking for a group of humans. If we lie and say the humans they're looking for are at the warehouse, they won't be prepared for what they find and we might have dead cops on our conscience. If we tell them the truth and explain what it is they're up against, they won't believe us and probably won't go at all. Besides, I want proof, confirmation that this is what we think it is. I want something for the Collection, preferably the actual specimen itself."

"Not alive, surely," Lauren said.

"No. We kill it. What else are we gonna do with it?"

Cynthia shook her head. "I don't know if I'm comfortable with that."

"Why? It's gonna wind up dead one way or another. Either we kill it or the cops eventually do."

"Yeah, but it's more the idea of *us* killing it that bothers me. I didn't sign on to this to become some sort of monster vigilante."

"I think this is just an atypical scenario. At least I hope it is. I for one don't really intend on making a habit of it."

"Besides, it's a monster, Cyn," said Donovan. "It wouldn't think twice about eating any of us."

"No, but see, that's the point. We're not monsters, so we *should* be thinking twice. Thrice, even. I mean, I kind of thought we'd try to photograph it, get some video of it, get some hair samples, scat samples, that sort of thing, then call the cops and tell them where it is and let *them* take care of it."

"We could, yes," Calvin said. "But like I said, the cops don't really know what they're dealing with and almost certainly wouldn't believe us if we told them. Since we know more about this thing and its habits than anyone else, we have a responsibility to do something."

"I suppose so. But I just want to be on record as not being very thrilled about it. And I think maybe this is something we should discuss more in the future."

"Agreed."

"My question is," said Lauren, "if we're going to try to take care of this thing ourselves, how do we do it? Shoot it?"

"I don't know," Calvin said. "Does anyone here own a gun?"

Everyone shook their heads.

"Isn't there stuff in the house?" said Donovan. "I mean, how did old Mr. May handle things like this? He must've had, like, rifles with telescopic sights and tranquilizer guns and things that shoot little tracking devices and shit like that. No?"

"He was an anomaly investigator, not James Bond," said Calvin.

"There're guns in the Collection," said Violet. "I saw some."

Calvin shook his head. "No. I'm not using anything from the Collection."

"But—"

"No." It was just one word, but he said it in such a flat and decisive tone that Violet snapped her mouth shut. Which was something just short of miraculous.

"Gun stores would probably still be open right now," Brandon said. "We could stop on the way and—"

"No," Cynthia said in a tone just as flat and decisive as Calvin's had been a moment ago. "If there're guns involved, I'm not going. I don't like guns."

"I'm not exactly a fan of the damn things myself," Calvin said, gesturing at the scar on his temple where Roger Grey had shot him five years earlier. "But they're the best option here. I mean, what else are we supposed to do? Stab it to death?"

"Mr. May never used guns, did he? We both read through all those files and he never once mentioned using guns."

"He used dynamite that one time. Are you saying that blowing something up with dynamite is somehow more morally objectionable than shooting it?"

Cynthia looked around the room. "Does anybody here even have any firearms training?"

Heads shook.

"That's what I thought," she said. "Giving guns to people who don't have any experience using them and then sending them into a scary and dangerous situation is a recipe for disaster."

"Maybe you're right," Calvin said. "But I can't think of a better alternative. Can you?"

"I agree with Cynthia," Tiffany said.

Calvin gaped at her, surprised. "What?"

She looked at him with a mix of guilt and stubbornness, as if she hated to stand against him but couldn't do otherwise. "I don't want any part of this mission if it involves guns. And if guns are to be a feature of this group, then I don't want a part of that either. I don't..." She lowered her eyes and her voice. "I don't like guns."

Calvin stared at her, remembering what her father had told him about the bad dreams she had had as a child after the alley incident. Tiffany had told him, too, but using less evocative language, no doubt in an attempt to downplay the trauma the nightmares had caused her.

She would wake up screaming in pure, primal terror from nightmares in which people were shooting her in the head, Andrew Fish had said. *Nearly every night for two years I sat with her for hours, trying to calm her down, to get her to stop crying and trembling like some beaten and traumatized animal.*

"All right," Calvin said gently. "No guns. We'll have to find alternatives."

Violet tsked and rolled her eyes.

Cynthia gave Tiffany a smile and a nod of thanks. Tiffany flashed a small smile in return. The moment Tiffany looked away, Cynthia's smile winked out, and she eyed Calvin with a cold, appraisive look. It wasn't lost on her that he had capitulated only when Tiffany entered the fray.

"So if we can't use guns, what're we gonna use?" Donovan asked.

"I don't know," Calvin said.

"I have a tire-iron in my van," Brandon said. "I'll take that. Those can be pretty nasty weapons. A good blow with that and it's good-night, doggie."

"Yeah, if you can get that blow in before it chomps your arm off," Lauren said. She looked at Calvin. "I have a can of Mace in my car. I can take that. We need longer-range stuff to help incapacitate it. Then someone else can swoop in and wham it with their tire-iron or whatever."

"Good idea," Calvin said.

"What about long-range weapons of a more lethal nature?" Lauren asked. "I don't suppose anyone has any bows and arrows? Crossbows?"

"Doesn't that just get us back to the problem of nervous, untrained people with projectile weapons?" Tiffany said.

"Dude, you've got a house full of shit," Brandon said to Calvin. "There's gotta be stuff in here we can use, even apart from the Collection."

Calvin nodded, then stood up. "All right. Let's take a very thorough tour of the house. But let's try to hurry it up. If my guess is correct, the leucrota lies low during the day and roams only at night, so I'd really like to get to that warehouse before it gets dark."

19

They started with the basement. There were four rooms down there. One of them, the wine cellar, contained nothing but decades-old, cobweb-festooned wine racks. Another contained only the furnace, the water heater, the fuse box, and a small stack of firewood. The last two were packed with a bewildering variety of junk, most of it stuff that Robert May had no longer had any use for (if he ever did) but for some reason was loath to throw away.

They found many interesting items in these latter two rooms—boxes full of old issues of *Mystery Magazine;* a paper grocery bag full of doll heads; a framed painting of a group of scantily clad shepherdesses lounging about a field at night while a gigantic full moon with a face on it leered down at them; an old battered sea chest with the words "Property of the Pirate's Club" stenciled on the side—but no weapons aside from an ancient sledgehammer whose splintered handle made it unusable.

They trooped back upstairs and hunted through the first floor. In a closet in the game room, tucked amid folding chairs and jumbo sketch pads and vintage jigsaw puzzles, they found a Louisville Slugger, its thick end scuffed and nicked but still quite solid and serviceable.

"I think I'll keep this for myself," Calvin said, hefting it with a smile. He liked the feel of it in his hands. It felt good and sturdy, able to bust skulls like cheap crockery.

In the kitchen they turned up cutting utensils galore. Calvin labeled some of them off-limits, since he used them and didn't want to have to restock his cutlery drawer with knives uncontaminated by leucrota blood; but everything else, he said, was fair game.

Grinning, Violet immediately snatched up the longest knife in the kitchen: a carving knife with a ten-inch blade and an antler handle.

"Hoo-rah!" she said, holding it up so the blade glinted in the light. "I'm ready for some big fuckin' game now."

Donovan pulled a butcher's knife from a drawer, and after some consideration, Cynthia took one, too.

"What about you?" Calvin asked Tiffany. "You're the only one without something at this point."

Tiffany shook her head. "None of this really feels right. I don't want a knife. I'd rather have something with a longer reach."

"Yeah," Cynthia said. "I'd prefer something longer range myself, actually."

"All right," Calvin said. "Let's keep looking."

The rest of the first floor yielded nothing better than what they already had, so they moved on to the second floor, which was also the last floor to search; the third floor's rooms contained only portions of the Collection, which was off-limits, and the room atop the tower contained no weapons or weaponizable materials.

Most of the second floor failed to yield anything either. In the bathroom Cynthia grabbed a spray can of vanilla-hazelnut air freshener off the toilet tank and asked Calvin, "Mind if I take this?"

"For what?" He figured she couldn't possibly mean for the leucrota hunt.

"Well, I was thinking it could work kind of like Mace. If the leucrota's like a dog, it probably relies very heavily on its sense of smell. And if we can screw that up enough, we might be able to disorient it and make it more vulnerable." She shrugged, looking a little self-conscious. "It's just an idea."

"It's not a bad idea," Tiffany said. "In theory, it's sound."

"I'll still have the knife, too."

"Well, all right," Calvin said, dubious. "You can take it if you want."

Calvin felt a bit uncomfortable letting everyone see his bedroom, though he wasn't entirely sure why. There wasn't anything embarrassing or revealing in it, especially since the bulk of its contents were still Mr. May's, and he didn't anticipate they'd be in there very long anyway. Just a quick once-over to check for weapons, then out.

As they entered, he kept his eye on Tiffany and was pleased and a little aroused to see that her gaze immediately sought out the four-poster bed. She regarded it with a small, thoughtful smile, no doubt remembering her and Calvin's all-too-brief interlude on the couch earlier. Then she glanced at Calvin. He smiled. Her own smile widened, and her cheeks suffused with blood.

"Whoa, check out the babe!" Brandon exclaimed, grinning at the painting on the wall opposite the door. The painting depicted a beautiful young auburn-haired woman reclining on a riverbank, her diaphanous white gown sheer enough to show her nipples (and probably her pubic hair, too, had one knee not been discreetly raised). It was so realistic it almost could have passed for a photograph.

"That's Anna May, Mr. May's aunt," Calvin said. "It was painted by Randolph Crow, Cynthia's great-uncle. Anna died in the big influenza epidemic of 1918, and Randolph, who was in love with her, shot himself right afterward."

Brandon stared at him blankly, then looked at the painting again.

"Dude," he said unhappily, "you sure know how to kill

a good woody."

They searched the room. The closet contained nothing but clothes, shoes, spare bedding. There was nothing under the bed except dust bunnies. A cabinet with lead-glass doors was full of books and assorted knickknacks.

"What about in here?" Cynthia asked, tapping her finger on a large trunk that was padlocked shut. "Did you ever find the key for this thing?"

"Yeah," Calvin said. "I did. The trunk's full of historical stuff. Old documents and ledgers and things, most of it relating to the May family."

"Ooh!" Lauren said, eyeing the trunk like a fat lady spotting an unclaimed box of bonbons. "Would it be too much to ask if I could perhaps take a peek inside someday?"

"Someday, sure. When we have more time."

"Who's this?" Brandon asked. He was peering into a cardboard box that sat on the seat of a rocking chair in the corner. The box contained some of Mr. May's items that Calvin had cleared off the bedside table and the dresser but had not yet decided what to do with. Brandon pulled out a small framed black-and-white photograph of a young woman with her hair in a bun and 1930s-style clothing. "She's kinda babelicious."

"Oh, that's Ethel," Calvin said. "Ethel Lewis."

"Mr. May's first love," Cynthia said.

"And File #1."

"What?" Lauren said. "She's a file?"

"Yeah. She was the anomaly." He glanced at the clock. "I don't have time to give you the full story, but I could give you the Reader's Digest version. Back in the summer of 1935, when Mr. May was a strapping young fellow of nineteen and was spending the summer home from college, a pretty young lady named Ethel Lewis showed up in town, claiming to be an anthropologist from Bard College who was here to research the Mima, the Indian tribe who used to occupy the area. She was particularly interested in the woods out back, since the area around Spirit Cave and Indian Hill was one of the Mima's holiest sites. Well, she wound up spending so much time around the woods that Mr. May's parents invited her to stay at the house rather than the crappy boarding house she was staying in downtown. Mr. May quickly grew enamored of Ms. Lewis, and she seemed quite fond of him, and soon he was accompanying her on most of her outings."

"Reading between the lines," Cynthia said, "I get the impression they were screwing each other all over the woods."

"Yeah," Calvin agreed. "Anyway, they were young and in love and everything was all wine and roses, at least for a while. As the summer wore on, she grew moodier and moodier, and sometimes Mr. May would find her crying alone in secluded corners of the house. She refused to explain why. Then one day they were up in the tower, just talking and looking out at the woods, and, um…" Calvin paused, swallowed.

"What, did she jump or something?" Lauren asked.

"If only," Cynthia said.

"No," Calvin said. "Totally out of the blue she gave him this sad smile and said, 'I'm sorry,' and then pulled out a straight razor and slashed her throat."

"Holy fuck!" Donovan said.

"Yeah," Cynthia said. "It sounded pretty awful. The file mentions that they were still finding old, dried bloodstains in odd corners up there a couple of decades later."

"What exactly was anomalous about it?" Tiffany asked.

She looked troubled by the tale, more so than anyone else, more than was warranted by a story about a long-dead stranger, however frightful her end. Calvin couldn't help wondering if Tiffany's psychological troubles had ever led her to contemplate suicide. "Just because no one knew the whys and wherefores?"

"That's not why," Calvin said. "The real mystery came afterward, when Mr. May tried to get in touch with her friends and her family and her college."

"Oh, I bet I know what's coming next," Brandon said.

Calvin nodded. "None of the names she gave checked out. None of the people she had named as relatives and friends even existed. Her college had never heard of her. Mr. May even sent photographs to the college, thinking maybe she had given him a fake name for some reason, but no one recognized her. He traveled to the towns she mentioned having lived in. No one there had ever heard of her or recognized her photo. Every single thing she had told him turned out to be a lie."

"Or a delusion," Cynthia said. "I can't help wondering if she wasn't seriously mentally ill. I mean, to kill yourself like that. Brr." She shuddered. "That takes a whole special level of...of something. It's horrible. I'm surprised Mr. May still went up into the tower after that. When we were up there with him that one time, he seemed totally okay with being there."

"Traumatic as it was, it had been nearly seventy-five years since it happened," Calvin said. "That kind of time span can soften even the worst pain."

"So you think. You're not even a third of the way through that span yourself yet."

"Didn't this Ethel girl have any ID on her?" Brandon asked.

"No," Calvin said. "That was another thing. On her body and in her luggage, there were no ID cards, no personal items, nothing. Just some clothes and toiletries, all of which looked pretty new. In the wake of the incident, Mr. May started researching other cases of mysterious people of unknown origin, like Kasper Hauser and Princess Caraboo. From there he branched out into other anomalous phenomena. And that's how the whole thing started. She became File #1, the first of thousands. He kept investigating the case on and off over the years, but when he died he knew no more about her than when he started."

The room was dead silent. Tiffany was clutching her elbows, her eyes downcast, her face the color of chalk. Seeing her like that, Calvin wished he hadn't brought the subject up.

Brandon set the portrait back in the box.

"Dude, you're such a downer today," he said.

"So old Mr. May had not one but two pictures of dead chicks in his bedroom," Violet said, gesturing at the painting of Anna May. While Calvin had been telling his story, she had sat down on the edge of the bed nearest the painting, seemingly oblivious to the annoyed glances he cast her. "That old geezer was kinda messed up when you think about it. Pining over lost girls and..." Her eyes narrowed. She leaned forward, the bedsprings creaking faintly, and peered at the painting. "What's that?"

"What's what?" Calvin asked.

Violet rose and took two steps forward, which brought her directly in front of the painting. She crouched a little, and it became clear she was looking not at the painting but at the bottom of its frame.

"What are you looking at?" Cynthia said.

"No, wait," Lauren said. "There's something there."

"What?" Calvin hurried over next to Violet and looked where she was looking.

On the underside of the painting's frame was a small protuberance about the size and shape of the eraser on a Number 2 pencil, painted the same gold color as the frame. At first Calvin thought it was a flaw in the frame or a weird bubble in the paint, but when Violet reached out and pressed it with her finger, the protuberance sank in with a faint click, and the whole painting, frame and all, swung away from the wall on unseen hinges like a door opening. Violet had to jerk her head back to avoid getting bopped on the nose by the frame's outer edge. The painting drifted to a stop when it was perpendicular to the wall. Behind it, in a recess in the wall, was a steel wall-safe one foot square. It had a gleaming silver handle on one side, and in the center was a large combination dial numbered from one to one hundred.

"Did you have any idea this was here?" Cynthia asked Calvin.

Calvin shook his head. He pulled the safe's handle, hoping that Mr. May had left it unlocked. He hadn't. The door didn't budge a millimeter.

"Have you seen anything that might be a combination?" said Tiffany. "It would probably be three numbers."

"No," Calvin said. "Not that I remember."

"But you can set your own code. He might have done that. What was his birth date? Do you know?"

"Uh…" Calvin thought hard for a moment, then tried 4-8-16 on the dial. The door still didn't budge.

"What about his name?" Tiffany said. "That's a three."

"It's three letters, not numbers," Donovan said.

"Just convert them into their number in the alphabet. A is one. B is two. And so on."

"So…" Calvin frowned, concentrating. "M would be…thirteen. Then one. Then twenty-five."

That didn't work either.

"You might have to pick it," Brandon said.

"Do you know how?" Calvin asked.

"No, not really. I mean, I've seen it done in movies, but…" He shrugged.

"I think you need a stethoscope or something," Donovan said.

"You could just blow it open," Violet said.

Calvin turned and stared at her, one eyebrow raised.

"What!" she said. "You can use that plastic explosive shit that looks like Sticky-Tac. They do it on TV all the time."

"Violet," said Lauren, her voice low and weary, as if she were sick of explaining very simple things to a child, "if you blow it up, you could end up blowing up whatever's inside."

"So just use a tiny bit of the stuff, a little blob like a wad of gum."

"No blowing it open," Calvin said. "The combination has to be around here somewhere. Mr. May was too careful and, well, I guess 'anal-retentive' wouldn't be entirely inaccurate, for him not to have kept the combination somewhere."

"What happened to Mr. May's wallet after he died?" asked Lauren.

Calvin stared at her, dumbfounded, thinking she was implying someone had robbed Mr. May's corpse, which was not only creepy but irrelevant to what they were talking about. Then he realized what she was getting at: Mr. May might have carried the combination in his wallet.

"It's over here." He strode over to the cardboard box

in which Brandon had found Ethel Lewis's portrait earlier.

Calvin rummaged through the box's contents, then pulled out a scuffed brown leather wallet. He sat down on the foot of the bed and started removing everything from the wallet. Everyone gathered around him and watched.

Out came credit cards, business cards, a driver's license that had been two years out of date when Mr. May passed away, a library card, a membership card for Bat Conservation International, a spare house key, a card on which Mr. May had written all of his personal information, a few pieces of paper with addresses and/or phone numbers written on them, a movie ticket stub, a list of books about ancient history with a few of the entries crossed off, a small reproduction of the photo of Ethel Lewis that now sat in the cardboard box, and a laminated card declaring that the bearer, Robert May, had been ordained a minister by the Universal Life Church.

Calvin opened the wallet's pockets as far as they'd go to make sure nothing was wedged in a corner. All he found were specks of lint and flakes of leather.

"That's it," Calvin said. He tossed the empty wallet onto the bed.

"The girl," Tiffany said, looking at the small photograph. "Her picture was important to him. Maybe the girl is the key. What was her middle name? Maybe her initials are the combination. Or what about her birth date?"

"Mr. May never learned her middle name or her birth date. Or if he did, he didn't write them down in the file."

He picked up the small photo and flipped it over to see if anything was written on the back. It was blank. He hurried over to the cardboard box, pulled out the framed photo, and slid off the backing. There was nothing written on the back of this one either, and nothing was inserted between the photo and the backing.

"Damn."

"He was a reverend?" Lauren asked, looking at the card of ministry.

"Apparently."

"I've heard of the Universal Life Church," Brandon said. "They'll ordain anyone. It's perfectly legal, too."

"He was a reverend like Squash," Tiffany said.

"Yeah, but Mr. May doesn't have skulls and secret tunnels in the basement," Cynthia said.

"No, the skulls are in the Collection. And the basement is a cluttered maze. Like the junkyard. Like the warehouse. A perfect hiding place for monsters."

"The Collection itself is a cluttered maze if you want to look at it that way," Calvin said. "And there are secret tunnels nearby; they're just sealed off behind the wall of rock at the back of Spirit Cave." He started to put the cards and papers back into Mr. May's wallet.

"*Chasing Amy?*" said Brandon, looking at the movie ticket stub. "I never met the old guy, but he doesn't strike me as the Kevin Smith type."

Calvin paused, staring at the stub and recalling his similar feelings about the movie poster in the office.

"No," he said. "He's not really the movie type at all."

He picked up the stub and looked at it more closely. The ticket had been purchased on December 15, 1996 at the May Cinema on Potts Road. Maybe the date was the combination. Maybe that was why Mr. May had kept the ticket stub. Calvin went to the safe and tried 12-15-96. It didn't work.

He shook his head and stuffed the stub back into the wallet. Maybe one of the other items in the wallet held some subtle clue to the safe's combination. Or maybe none did. Either way, they didn't have time to keep working at the problem right now.

Calvin got up, tossed the wallet back into the box, then turned and took a last look at the wall safe. Another new mystery to solve. They just kept piling up around here, didn't they? He swung the painting-door closed. It latched with a faint clack.

"All right, guys," he said. "It's getting late, and we still haven't found adequate weapons for everyone."

"There isn't anywhere left to search, is there?" Brandon said. "I thought this was the last searchable room in the house."

"The house itself, yeah. But there's still the garage and the shed out back. I think there are some gardening tools in there that might be useful if they're not too old and rusty. Let's go take a look."

20

Fifteen minutes later they were on the road to Kingwood. The search of the garage had yielded nothing useful, but the shed held a plethora of bladed implements. Tiffany came away with a sickle, and Violet supplemented her carving knife with a hatchet. Cynthia considered replacing her knife with a shovel or a hoe, but finally opted not to; they would require two hands to swing effectively, and she wanted to keep one hand free to use the air freshener, which she still felt sure would be anathema to a creature that counted scent as a primary sense, as many animals did. She just hoped the leucrota was in fact such a creature.

Before they set out Calvin insisted everyone equip themselves with a flashlight.

"We don't know if the power's still on in the building," he said. "And in any case, we don't know where the light switches are. We probably shouldn't turn the lights on anyway. Not unless we want to attract attention."

"Oh, I don't know," Lauren said with a small, nervous laugh. "A little police backup might not be a bad thing."

"It is if we want the leucrota for the Collection. And I do. But if you don't want to come, that's fine. I won't hold it against you. Or any of you," he added, looking around.

"No, no," Lauren said. "I'm game."

So was everyone else.

They soon hunted up enough flashlights for everyone, many of the flashlights coming from their cars' glove compartments. Then Calvin and Cynthia grabbed their investigator's kits, and everyone piled into Brandon's black van, which had been deemed the best vehicle for the job despite its decrepitude. A single vehicle was less likely to attract attention in the warehouse's otherwise empty parking lot, and Brandon's van was the only vehicle they owned big enough to fit all seven of them inside. It even had room for a dead leucrota, assuming the creature wasn't too much bigger than the bestiaries said. And a van, even an unmarked one, had a vaguely commercial air that would help it blend into a busy industrial area.

Brandon drove. Calvin sat in the passenger seat, the map book open in his lap. There were no seats in the back, forcing everyone else to sit on the carpeted floor.

They arrived at the Mad Hatter Novelty Company's Kingwood Distribution Facility at ten to nine. The sun was just about to set, leaving them nearly an hour before full dark.

Aside from the sign that bore the company's name and the top-hat-and-smile logo, the warehouse looked much the same as every other warehouse in the area. It was broad and deep and boxy, consisting of a single high-ceilinged storey constructed mainly of steel and concrete, its colors bland grays, browns, and creams.

After making sure no one else was around—fortunately all the nearby businesses had already closed for the night, and the only traffic in sight was a pair of cars passing through the Miller Road intersection a few blocks north—Brandon pulled into the lot and crossed row after row of empty yellow-edged parking spaces toward the building. A large sign that read "Closed No Trespassing" hung across the main entrance, and the doors were sealed tight with an industrial-strength lockbox.

"I just realized," said Brandon. "How're we gonna get in?"

"If the leucrota is using this place, it found a way in," Calvin said. "And if it can get in, we can too."

"I'm still not convinced it's here," Cynthia said.

"You might be right," Calvin said. He scanned the front of the building, but aside from the locked front door, he saw no other way inside. There weren't even any windows. To Brandon he said, "Drive around the building slowly."

Brandon did. The side of the building sported a single brown door halfway down. It too was secured with a lockbox.

"Keep going," Calvin said.

The back of the building was dominated by ten numbered loading docks with metal overhead doors, all of them locked tight. Halfway between the corner of the building and the nearest loading dock was a brown door that stood slightly ajar, the twisted wreck of a lockbox dangling from its handle.

"Oh, boy," Lauren muttered.

"There," Calvin said. "Park near that door."

Brandon did so, then shut off the van. With the growl of the engine no longer rebounding back at them off the building's outer wall, the ensuing silence seemed total and startling. Everyone stared at the slit of blackness visible through the cracked door. Nothing moved. Nothing made a sound.

Calvin slung his messenger bag over his shoulder, then twisted around in his seat and looked at everyone in the back of the van.

"Like I said before, if anyone wants to sit this out, I would totally understand."

"Fuck that," Violet said. "I'm ready to kick some monster ass. It'd be better if we had some guns, though."

"Yeah, and even though I feel like I'm practically hyperventilating here, I know I'd hate myself if I didn't go," Lauren said, her voice a little shaky. "So count me in."

Weapons and flashlights in hand, they climbed out of the van and crept toward the door. Calvin reached out and laid a hand on the knob. The broken lockbox gave a hollow rattle. He took a deep breath. Then he wrinkled his nose. Through the cracked door he could smell the faint but unmistakable stench of rotten meat.

"Do you smell that?" he whispered.

The others started sniffing too.

"Yeah," Cynthia whispered. "It smells like something died in there."

"Or some*one*," Tiffany said.

"I don't smell anything," Donovan said.

"That's probably because you smoke," Cynthia said.

Calvin pushed open the door and raised his baseball bat to clobber anything that might spring out. Nothing did. Inside, a yellow-walled, tile-floored hallway extended off into darkness. With the door open, the smell was much stronger, and underneath it a second, fainter odor was now noticeable, a rank animal stink that reminded everyone of zoos.

"Okay," Donovan said with a nod, his nose crinkling. "*Now* I smell something."

Calvin switched on his flashlight and shone it inside. The hallway ended after thirty feet in an unmarked gray door with a small square window in it. Two doors faced each other across the hallway halfway down. The tile floor was tracked with dirty footprints. In the corner to the right of the brown door were two empty bottles of Rolling Rock. Cigarette butts lay scattered about like spent shells in the aftermath of a shootout.

"Looks more like the bums've been hanging out here," Violet muttered.

Calvin stepped inside and advanced down the hallway, treading slowly and carefully to muffle his footfalls. The others followed, Tiffany first, then Cynthia, then Brandon, Lauren, Donovan, and Violet.

They paused at the two doors. A sign on the wall beside the door on the left read "Administration." A sign beside the other one read "Accounting." Scrawled in bright red spray paint on the Administration door was a big A in a circle.

"Anarchy, dude," Brandon whispered. "Rock on."

Calvin tried the Administration door's knob. It was locked.

The Accounting door, however, was not. Calvin didn't even need to try the knob to know that: The door had been forced open, leaving the knob askew and the metal around it dented. The latch plate lay on the hallway floor in front of the door.

With the tip of his baseball bat, Calvin gently pushed against the door. It opened halfway, then stopped with a muffled clunk, blocked by something inside. Thankfully, the blockage sounded like something hard and metallic, not something organic and prone to biting off faces.

Calvin shone his flashlight into the office. The place had been wrecked. File cabinets lay overturned, their drawers yanked out. Desks and chairs had been torn apart. Computers had been reduced to heaps of gray plastic shards and shattered green circuit boards. A couple of the light fixtures had been yanked partway out of the ceiling and dangled aslant on colored wires. The walls were covered with spray-painted slogans and symbols and crude drawings of faces and phalluses and women's torsos with gigantic breasts and gaping vaginas.

"Wow," said Lauren. "Somebody sure went medieval on this place."

"I bet it was those two graffitists," Brandon said.

"Pretty safe bet," Calvin said.

Tiffany walked slowly past Calvin and into the center of the room, her gaze roving over the graffiti as if she were searching for something. Calvin realized with a jolt of alarm that all these symbols and scribbles must remind her of the bizarre graffiti she had written during her breakdown. He fought off an urge to pull her out of here and move on to the rest of the warehouse. If he did that, she would probably realize he knew about the breakdown, and very likely get upset. Instead he watched her closely, ready to step in if she started reacting badly, though he wasn't entirely clear what it was he was afraid she might do.

Tiffany's eyes flicked past "Anarchy Rulez!" and "Debbie is a slut!" and "Wildboyz," then settled on another, odder piece of graffiti, which read, "You are being watched." It had been written in black magic marker in a small, careful hand. The writing and the sentiment expressed were different enough from the rest of the juvenile gibberish scrawled on the walls to give Calvin a chill. It was like a coherent message in the midst of white noise. A glance at Tiffany showed that she too found it disturbing; her eyes were narrow as she regarded it, her brows drawn down in a small frown, her lips pressed tightly together.

Then her attention was drawn to another part of the wall. There, between a water cooler and another piece of giant red graffiti that read "Whore's galore!" was another neatly black-markered message, too small and distant to read from here.

Tiffany strode over to it, Calvin following close behind. The graffito read, "A stranger, unafraid, in a world of sheep he slayed."

"Whoa," said Brandon, who had come up behind Calvin and was looking at the graffito over his shoulder. "That's kinda messed up."

"Yeah," Calvin said quietly. In his opinion "messed up" was something of an understatement. The graffito seemed like a reference to the leucrota, but if so, who wrote it? If it wasn't a reference to the leucrota, it was a hell of a coincidence. Then again, coincidences had been abounding ever since he met Tiffany. Or perhaps he was simply noticing them more.

"You ready to go on?" he asked Tiffany.

She didn't respond for a moment, just kept staring at the black words on the off-white wall. Just when Calvin was about to repeat the question, she tore her eyes from the graffito, looked at him, and nodded.

They returned to the hallway and crept toward the door at the far end. As they drew near, they saw that this door, too, had been forced open and stood slightly ajar.

Calvin tried to look through the small square window in the door, but the glass was too bleared with dust and grime and the interior of the warehouse too dark for him to see anything. He held still and listened but heard nothing except the nervous breaths and rustles of the others behind him, the sounds magnified in the narrow, confined space of the hallway.

He nudged the door open with his toe. The door swung about two-thirds open then stopped. The odor of rotten meat and zoos billowed over them, stronger than ever, the stink shoving rancid fingers up Calvin's nose and into his throat, making him gag. Behind him, he heard Lauren mutter, "Oh, that's bad," in a small, choked voice.

Gulping back his nausea, Calvin shone his flashlight through the doorway. Thirty feet ahead stood a steel shelving unit lined with red plastic bins that were filled with various objects too small to identify at this distance. The unit was about twenty-five feet high and fifty feet long and ended on either side in a wide aisle, across which another shelving unit laden with red bins stretched away beyond the reach of his flashlight. Behind these units were more units, one after another until they too faded into the darkness beyond his flashlight's beam. They probably extended all the way to the far end of the warehouse like rows of giant dominoes lined up and ready to fall.

He saw no monsters, or signs of monsters. The silence

from the warehouse was total yet also somehow worrying.

His heart pounding like a jungle drum, he took a deep breath, raised the baseball bat high above his head, and stepped out onto the warehouse floor, swiftly turning to his right with his back to the open door.

A huge, hulking figure loomed ten feet ahead and to his left, the flashlight's beam gleaming off what appeared to be two long, gray tusks. Calvin gasped and stumbled backward, bumping into the door and sending it swinging open another foot.

Then he realized the "monster" wasn't moving and was way too big to be a leucrota. And it had wheels.

No, not a monster, he saw now, but a forklift. The tusks were its forks, which had been left half raised.

"Are you okay?" Tiffany whispered from the corridor, her worried face dim and ghostly in the hazy backglow from her flashlight.

He nodded, not speaking, afraid his voice would waver in a horribly unmanly fashion if he did. He hadn't been prepared for how scary and stressful this would be. He almost wished he had brought a gun after all. Then again, he was so jumpy he probably would've just fired half a clip at the forklift and gotten struck by a ricocheting bullet.

Beyond the forklift the flashlight picked out stacks of cardboard boxes with the Mad Hatter logo on the sides and a cube-shaped gray plastic bin big enough to take a bath in.

More red graffiti on the wall to the right of the door caught his eye, and he started to turn to look at it. Then he realized he ought to check behind the door and make sure a monster with bear-trap teeth wasn't sneaking up on him.

Moving with what he had hoped would be fluid grace but felt more like pathetic galumphing, he spun around the edge of the open door and trained the flashlight beam on what lay beyond it...

Which turned out to be only the entrances to the men's and women's rooms, and a drinking fountain between them. Farther down along the wall, hazy and dark at the outer edge of the flashlight's range, were more big gray plastic bins, stacked one atop the other to a height of twenty feet like children's blocks.

The coast apparently clear (at least for the moment), Calvin stepped away from the doorway and waved for the others to follow.

They filed out of the corridor and looked around, their flashlight beams swinging this way and that like a light show at a rock concert.

"So, which way now?" Brandon whispered.

"I'm not sure yet," Calvin whispered back.

"We're gonna stick together, right?" Donovan said. "Safety in numbers and everything?"

"Yeah," Brandon agreed. "Because in the movies when they split up in situations like this they all get picked off one by one."

"Don't say that," Lauren said with a wince.

"Sorry, but it's true."

"I think we will have to split up, though," Calvin said. "I mean, look at the size of this place. If we don't split up, the leucrota could easily slip past us and out the building without our ever even being aware of it. Instead we should probably split into...uh..."

His voice trailed off. While he'd been talking, he had continued exploring the area with his flashlight and had finally directed the beam at the red graffiti he'd seen on the wall.

The problem was, the redness wasn't just spray paint.

Someone had sprayed "Wildbo" and then started to write another letter, no doubt a Y, the first line of which suddenly veered straight down and disappeared beneath crimson splashes that covered the lower half of the wall in great looping arcs.

The phrase *arterial spray* bobbed to the surface of Calvin's mind. He forced it back down. That wasn't something he wanted to think about too coherently. His nerves were strained enough as it was.

A puddle of dried blood several feet wide caked the floor below the aborted graffiti. A can of red spray-paint lay at the edge of the puddle, its label mostly obscured by blood. Long, curving lines cut through the puddle, showing where something had been dragged through the blood while it was still wet and had thinned the blood enough for the gray concrete floor to show through. Following these tracks with his flashlight, Calvin saw that as they exited the puddle an inversion occurred, whereby the tracks became lines of blood on bare concrete. The lines stretched off toward the interior of the warehouse, thinning as they went until they faded out altogether about fifteen feet away.

"Oh, man," Brandon said. His face was whiter than paper. "Oh, man. This is some serious shit."

"Yeah," said Cynthia. She looked at Calvin. "Are we sure we want to go through with this?"

Calvin nodded vaguely, only half aware of what she was saying. His attention had been arrested by Tiffany, who stood frozen, her mouth agape, her startled eyes and her flashlight pointed at something on the wall above the blood. Following her gaze, Calvin saw that she had discovered another black-marker graffito, this one to the left of "Wildbo." It read:

This is the house that Jack built
This is the dog that lives in the house that Jack built

"What the fuck?" Brandon murmured. "This is getting more and more messed up by the second."

"Look," Tiffany said in a voice so low it was almost inaudible. She pointed at the graffito's last few letters, which overlapped a splotch of blood. "This was written afterward. After the graffitist was killed. After the blood was dry."

"But..." Lauren swallowed. "But who would have..."

"Somebody very comfortable around blood," Calvin said. "And death. And monsters."

"Oh," Donovan said, pointing his flashlight at the bottom of the forklift. "Look. There's another one."

They looked. Peeking out from behind one of the forklift's wheels was a second can of red spray-paint.

"Poor dudes," Brandon said. "They came to leave a little street art and got chewed up by a monster instead."

"Street art, my ass," said Cynthia. "They totally trashed that office back there."

"Unless the guy with the black marker was the one who trashed it," Brandon said.

Cynthia glanced at the black writing on the wall.

"Maybe," she said. But she didn't really think so. The smallness and neatness of the writing, not to mention its accurate spelling and grammar, suggested someone calm and smart and calculating, not a juvenile rowdy who smashed stuff just for the kicks. Jesus, what kind of person would see and smell this kind of carnage then take the time to ink these spooky little missives?

What was it Calvin had just said? *Someone very comfortable around blood. And death. And monsters.*

Then again, they'd only just begun their exploration of the warehouse. Perhaps somewhere in here they would find the remains of a half-eaten corpse, a black Sharpie still grasped between its cold, stiff fingers.

But somehow she doubted it. Somehow she suspected that the leucrota would recognize and respect a fellow monster when it saw one.

She smiled grimly to herself. She was making an awful lot of assumptions and extrapolations from just a few silly scribbles. But when she glanced at the others, she could tell they felt exactly the same way.

"So do you still think we should split up?" she asked Calvin.

He hesitated, and she could see he was having second thoughts about not just his search plan but this whole monster-hunting safari.

"If we want to stop this thing, we'll have to," he said. "Like I said before, this building's so big it'll be able to slip past us and slink right out the door. As long as we stay in groups of two or three—"

"Being in a group of two didn't help these guys," she said, gesturing at the puddle of blood.

"No," he mused, staring at the blood. "No, it didn't, did it?"

"What about two larger groups?" Tiffany said. "Of three and four?"

Calvin glanced at the weapons they held, then at the puddle of blood again. He shook his head.

"We'd better not. We'd better just stick together."

He looked around. His gaze settled on the big gray plastic bin.

"Over here," he said, walking toward the bin. "Somebody help me with this thing."

The bin's sides were four feet square, and it was made of thick, dense plastic, making it far too heavy for one person to lift. The twin slots running through its base indicated it was meant to be moved with a forklift.

Calvin, Brandon, Donovan, and Violet got around the bin, one on each side, and while the others used their flashlights to guide them, they lifted the bin and carried it toward the door that led to the corridor they had just come down.

"Close the door," Calvin told Cynthia as they approached.

She did so, and they set the bin in front of the closed door.

"Now it can't get out," Calvin said.

"It might be able to push the bin out of the way," Lauren said.

"Maybe. But not without making a lot of noise. We'll hear it if it tries."

"So now what?" Cynthia asked. "Follow the tracks?" She gestured with her flashlight at the streaks of blood leading into the depths of the warehouse.

Calvin looked at the blackness that loomed beyond the flashlights' reach, then turned and shone his beam at the can of spray-paint under the forklift.

"Let's go this way," he said. "That can didn't get where it is from over here. I'm betting that one of the two teenagers died next to the door here, and the other one ran off that way. Let's see if we can figure out what happened to him after that. Besides, I'm thinking it would be best if we make a circuit of the warehouse and get a sense of the layout, then work our way inward."

With Calvin in the lead, they followed the wall north.

Twenty feet past the forklift the wall fell away on their right, dropping back sixty feet to the building's outer wall where the first five loading docks were located, their metal doors glinting in the flashlight beams. Here and there stood more stacks of cardboard boxes, along with a few stacks of wooden pallets. They also passed a stack of what at first glance looked like gray plastic pallets, but which a closer inspection revealed to be more of those big gray bins with their hinged sides uncoupled and folded inward.

A large office divided this group of loading docks from another farther down. The office sported a long window on the side that faced the interior of the warehouse, and a door on the side the group was approaching from. A sign beside the door read "Shipping/Receiving." The door was wide open.

Baseball bat raised high, Calvin led the others to the open doorway, then shone his flashlight inside.

Work stations. File cabinets. Bulletin boards. Computers nearly as outdated as Mr. May's. Overall it looked like any normal office, except...

A dark, humped shape like a long, low heap of filthy laundry lay against the far wall beneath a bulletin board that hung askew. The floor was stained dark red all around the shape. Four thin red lines that could only be the tracks of someone's fingers ran down the wall above the shape. The smell of rotten meat was nearly overpowering.

It was pretty much a no-brainer that the shape was one of the ill-fated graffitists, but Calvin felt compelled to make sure. Plus, there might be evidence in here that would provide some insight into the leucrota's behavior or biology and help them defeat it.

"You guys wait here," he said.

"Absolutely not a problem," Lauren said with a glance

at the shape on the floor.

"No way, man," Brandon said. "I'm coming, too. Strength in numbers and all that. Our little monster friend might be hiding in there somewhere, just waiting to strike."

"All right," Calvin said, secretly relieved not to go alone.

He and Brandon crossed the room toward the shape, constantly sweeping their flashlights back and forth to ensure nothing was slinking out from under a desk or behind a cabinet.

As they neared the shape, Calvin began to wonder why it still looked like a shapeless heap of dark clothes. If it was a body, shouldn't he be seeing hair by now? Skin? A face? Then he took a few more steps, and the truth became horribly clear.

The body lay supine, clad in what had once been a blue jacket with white piping, blue jeans, white Nikes, and a dark-blue Cleveland Indians cap. All of these articles of clothing had been saturated with so much blood they were almost completely the same dark-red color as the puddle around them. The body had no face, the entire front of the head from the ears forward having been sliced right off, leaving only a dark bowl full of a thick, mucky mass of decaying tissue. The front of the jacket had been torn away and the flesh underneath devoured, in some places right down to the spine. Plump, pale maggots squirmed across what remained of the corpse's rotting meat and organs.

"Oh, man," Brandon said. "That's...that's..." He turned, bent over, and threw up.

Calvin had been sure he wouldn't vomit. He was sickened by the remains on the floor before him, sickened as he had never been sickened in his life, and yes, his body *wanted* to vomit; a hot burning ball kept trying to force its way up his throat. But till now he had been able to swallow it back.

But when Brandon puked, Calvin lost the battle. It wasn't simply the fact that Brandon puked that did it, and it wasn't the sight of the puke, all tan and chunky. No, it was the *sound* the vomit made as it struck the tiled floor: a thick, heavy patter that swiftly grew wetter and splashier as the vomit piled up.

Calvin couldn't hold it back anymore. His throat seemed to both tighten and bulge simultaneously as the vomit geysered up his esophagus. He barely managed to turn his head in time to avoid throwing up on his own shoes. The stream of puke struck the side of a file cabinet, making a hollow drumming sound and dotting his pant legs with warm specks of backspray.

When he was done, he straightened up to find Brandon dabbing at his lower lip with the bottom edge of his shirt with almost dainty care.

"Ugh," Brandon groaned. "That's the last time *I* look at a half-eaten corpse." He tried to smile to show that the comment had been meant to be humorous, but the smile twisted into a grimace as he struggled to hold back a fresh wave of nausea.

"Let's get out of here," Calvin said.

"Awesome idea."

As they turned to go, Calvin caught a glimpse of neat, black writing on a large white marker-board on the wall. The board was dominated by the words, "Thanks for the 55 years!" in blue ink, and, below that, "Party at Neil's tonight! 7:30! BYOB!" in green ink. The black writing was in the lower right corner of the board, and it had been written in the same small, careful hand as the other black graffiti they had seen. It read:

It's a dog-eat-dog world
Bon appétit!

"Shit," Calvin muttered.

They rejoined the others outside the office.

"A body, right?" said Cynthia.

Calvin nodded. "A very well-eaten body." He hated how shaky his voice sounded.

Tiffany put a hand on his arm and gave him a sympathetic smile. He smiled back, suddenly achingly grateful that she was there, that he had found a girl as amazing as her. He felt an urge to sweep her into his arms and cover her face with kisses. Probably not a good idea under these precarious circumstances, though. And not with the stink of vomit on his breath.

Violet shook her head. "We shoulda brought guns."

"I told you," said Calvin. "We—"

There was a series of quick, faint clacks from somewhere in the warehouse. The way the sounds echoed in the huge space made it impossible to tell precisely where they had come from.

"Did you guys hear that?" Cynthia whispered.

"Yeah," Donovan said. "It's—"

"Help!" a woman's voice screamed from the darkness. "Help me! Oh, God, please help me!" The voice was shrill with panic.

Everyone aimed their flashlights in the direction they thought the voice had come from. All of the beams wound up pointing toward the interior of the warehouse, but otherwise no two quite matched up. Between them and the center of the warehouse dozens of those big gray plastic bins were scattered about like rubble from a toppled castle. Their flashlights picked out the sides of the bins in great, bright detail and sent the bins' shadows stretching long and black across the warehouse floor. At the farthest reaches of the flashlights' beams, they could just make out the hazy shapes of the foremost line of shelves and the red plastic bins thereon.

"Help me!" the woman's voice screamed again. "Please! Help!"

Cynthia stepped forward. "Maybe we should—"

Calvin extended his arm, blocking her.

"No," he said. "It's the leucrota. It has to be."

"But..." Cynthia shook her head and stared into the darkness. "How can we be sure?"

"So far this thing hasn't left anyone alive to cry for help. Not even close."

A moment later the voice said "help" again, only this time the word was low and half-formed, like someone absently mumbling under their breath. The leucrota must have realized they weren't going to fall for its usual trickery.

The clacks sounded again, louder this time, closer, though thanks to the way the noises echoed, it remained impossible to determine their exact point of origin. The steps grew louder and louder and faster and faster and soon blurred together into the unmistakable clatter of a galloping four-hoofed animal.

"Oh, shit," Lauren said, swinging her flashlight and her can of Mace back and forth, unsure where to point them. "Where is it?"

Everyone else's flashlights were likewise sweeping about. The clop of hooves rang out all around them now, resounding through the darkness.

And then the clatter abruptly stopped, and a tawny black-striped shape hurtled over one of the gray bins and landed twenty feet away, its hooves hitting the concrete floor with a sound as loud as a cymbal crash.

Slightly smaller than the lore books claimed—it was about as tall as Violet—the leucrota crouched there smiling its guillotine smile, its huge round eyes flashing yellow-green as seven flashlight beams converged on it. Flecks of dried blood caked its lips and ruff.

"Holy fucking shit!" Brandon said.

"Shoulda brought guns," the leucrota said in a perfect imitation of Violet's voice.

And then it bounded straight at Donovan, Violet, and Lauren, who stood apart from the others and farthest away from the office.

All three of them stood their ground, ready to fight. Lauren leveled the can of Mace, her finger on the trigger. Violet raised her hatchet. Donovan tightened his grip on his butcher's knife.

At the last moment the leucrota veered left toward Calvin and Brandon, both of whom had started moving forward to aid the others. Now they were caught completely by surprise.

"Yah, fuck!" Calvin screamed, jumping out of the monster's path. Brandon pirouetted away from the leucrota with surprising grace, swinging his tire-iron at it as he did so. The blow went wide, the iron whistling through empty air.

The leucrota proved defter. As it barreled past, borne along by momentum, it whipped its head at Brandon. There was a flash of bone and a loud clack, and when the leucrota skidded to a halt a few feet from the office door, it held a swatch of black leather between its mouth plates. Brandon glanced down. The bottom left corner of his leather jacket was gone.

The moment the leucrota stopped skidding, it was on the move again, spitting out the shred of leather and whirling around 180 degrees. This brought it face-to-face with Lauren, who had hurried after it, her can of Mace held high, ready to squirt the monster right in its ugly, grinning mug. Mouth open wide, the leucrota charged at her.

She yelped and stumbled backward, firing off a blast of Mace more from reflex than intent. Most of the spray passed harmlessly over the leucrota's head, but enough of the stinging mist drifted into its face to make it stumble to a clumsy halt, snarling and blinking and shaking its head like a waterlogged dog. Lauren's stumble, meanwhile, turned into a full-blown topple as she lost her balance and crashed to her ass on the concrete. The can of Mace dropped from her hand and rolled away across the floor. Donovan tried to track it with his flashlight but it whizzed off into the shadows too fast for him to follow.

While this had been going on, Calvin had snuck up behind the leucrota, and now he raised his Louisville Slugger, ready to deliver a mighty, battle-ending blow.

The leucrota stopped shaking its head and crouched. Calvin thought it must be getting ready to leap at Lauren, and he lunged forward to strike his blow before it could spring. But then he realized—an instant too late for him to do anything about it—that the leucrota was crouching with its front end lower than its rear, all its weight on its forelegs. It had sensed him behind it and was getting ready to kick backward like a mule.

He tried to whack it with the bat anyway, but before the bat could travel half a foot, the leucrota's rear hooves slammed into his thighs and sent him flying straight backward into Tiffany, who had come up behind him to help. The two of them crashed down in a tangle of limbs right in front of the office door, Tiffany's tailbone striking the concrete floor and Calvin's elbow ramming her in the solar plexus. Amid the pain and confusion, she lost hold of both her flashlight and her sickle. The flashlight rolled away in a swift, tight arc and thumped to a stop against the wall to the left of the doorframe, its cone of light picking out every pit and pebble on the concrete floor. The sickle skittered off in the other direction and joined Lauren's Mace in the darkness.

The leucrota spun around to face them, its hooves clocking on the concrete. Its eyes were watering from the Mace. Its nostrils flared and dripped. A low growl rumbled from its throat. It sounded pissed off yet pleased to finally have such easy prey before it.

Calvin's feet were just a snap from its lethal maw. But when he tried to swing his legs out of its reach, bolts of pain skewered his thighs, pain so bad it tore a scream from his throat. Oh, fuck! Had it broken his legs?

But the bat. He still had the bat. Throughout his fall, throughout his pain, he had somehow kept hold of it. Gripping its ash handle tight in one hand, he raised the bat above his head, ready to brain the leucrota the moment it got too close.

The leucrota's eyes flicked to the upraised bat, then back to Calvin's face.

"Well, well, well," it said in a voice that was slow and deep and sludgy and that resonated far more than any human voice ought to. It was the eeriest voice Calvin had ever heard. What made it even worse was that there was something mirthful in its tone, a mirth that was black and cold and cruel. "It's happening again, isn't it?"

What did that mean? What was happening again? And whose voice was that? Why did Calvin have the sneaking suspicion it was the same weirdo who had Sharpied the black graffiti all over the warehouse?

A growl replaced the eerie voice, and the leucrota dove straight at Calvin.

Calvin brought the bat down as hard as he could, and for one brief moment, as he watched the wide end of the bat blur toward the leucrota's head, he really thought that this was it, the end of the hunt, the successful resolution of their first real case, that in a fraction of a second he'd hear the leucrota's skull burst and feel the bat shiver with the impact...

And then at the last instant, the leucrota raised its head, caught the bat in its mouth, and bit down hard. The bat splintered with a noise like a rifle shot. Shards of ash clattered to the concrete. The handle twisted and fragmented in Calvin's grip, driving splinters into his palm. With a cry of mingled surprise and pain, he let go of the disintegrating bat.

"What's happening?" Tiffany cried. She was half-pinned under him, his head and shoulders blocking her view of the melee. "Calvin?"

Eyes fixed on Calvin, the leucrota spat out a mouthful of broken wood, then tensed, ready to spring again, this time to snap up something far tastier than old, dry wood. An arm, perhaps. Maybe a face.

And then Cynthia rushed in on Calvin's left, pumping blast after blast of vanilla-hazelnut air freshener at the leucrota.

The leucrota started to turn toward her, then caught a shot of air freshener square in the face. With a clipped yelp, it leaped five feet straight back, out of the spray's reach, and hunched there, hacking and snuffling.

Cynthia stepped in front of Calvin and Tiffany, her back to them, the can of air freshener and the butcher's knife pointed at the leucrota. Three shadowy figures were creeping up on the leucrota from behind, their flashlights pointed at the ground at their feet to dim the light and help hide their approach. Reflected light flashed milkily off a pair of lenses on the face of the foremost figure. Brandon. He was the only one who wore glasses. A fourth shadowy figure was hanging back, its flashlight likewise held low. Probably Lauren, who had lost her Mace.

"Get inside," Cynthia told Calvin and Tiffany over her shoulder. "Into the office."

He wanted to be manly and protest that he could still stand and fight. Except given how his legs felt, he wasn't sure he actually *could* stand anymore. And he no longer had a weapon anyway. Neither did Tiffany. Shit.

He rolled off Tiffany, who immediately let out a long, relieved groan. She started scooting backward into the office. Calvin crawled after her, his legs screaming. He could move them now, which he presumed meant they weren't broken, but every movement made him wince and suck air between his teeth. To make matters worse, his stupid messenger bag kept getting caught underneath him, its dead weight slowing him down. When Tiffany saw the trouble he was having, she yanked the strap off his shoulder and shoved the bag aside, then grabbed him under the armpits and dragged him into the office after her.

Its muzzle damp from the vanilla-hazelnut spritz, the leucrota glared at Cynthia with moist, runny eyes, its bone-smile gleaming in the light from her flashlight. Its eyes flicked from the can of air freshener to Cynthia's face, then to the knife in her other hand, then at her body. It was gauging its options with a lot more intelligence and calculation than Cynthia wanted to see.

"Don't even think about it, bitch," Cynthia said, her voice shaking. The sweat on her palms was making her grip on both the can and the knife slippery, unsteady. Her heart was racing. She suddenly wished she had chosen a more lethal weapon. A flamethrower, perhaps. Or a bazooka.

"Bitch," the leucrota echoed in Cynthia's own shaky voice.

Cynthia glanced at the quartet creeping up behind the monster. Brandon, now within striking distance of the beast, was raising his tire-iron. On either side of him Donovan and Violet were advancing toward the leucrota's flanks, knife and hatchet clutched tight. Lauren, though weaponless, was close behind the others, ready to shine her flashlight on the altercation once it started. Any moment now they would strike and—

The leucrota spun around, crying "Holy fucking shit!" in Brandon's voice, then lunged at Brandon.

With a startled cry, Brandon jumped out of the way, knocking shoulders with Donovan, who stumbled backward, arms outstretched for balance.

Seeing her chance, Cynthia dashed forward, both knife and spray can raised.

But the leucrota's lunge at Brandon had been a feint, and with barely a pause the leucrota spun around again to face Cynthia, only this time it didn't stop to stare at her; it streaked straight at her like a tawny missile.

Screaming, Cynthia blindly chucked the spray can at the leucrota. The can clonked off the leucrota's forehead, making the monster flinch and briefly stumble. By the time it recovered, Cynthia had whirled around and bolted for the office.

As she barreled through the open doorway, she heard a low, guttural snarl, and there was a brief, sharp tug at her right foot as it kicked out behind her. She didn't feel any pain, but she had heard that people who lose limbs in accidents or battles don't always realize anything has happened until they see the oozing stump where a chunk of their body had been a moment before, and she felt horribly certain that when she brought her leg forward, it would come without a foot, just a stump and a streamer of blood, and then, since she couldn't run on a stump, she'd crash to the floor and the leucrota would fall on her and tear out her throat before anyone could stop it.

But when her right leg swung into view, she felt a surge of relief to see the white blur of her sneaker at the end of it. Thank God. Thank...

No, wait. Something was wrong with it. When she put her weight on it, it slid a little and felt lumpy, uneven. And her heel! It felt cold, as if she had stepped in something wet. Oh, God.

She started to reach out to close the door behind her, but saw that Tiffany was already there, half-hidden behind the open door. As soon as Cynthia was clear, Tiffany slammed the door with all her might, right in the leucrota's snout. A pained yowl rang out on the other side of the metal door.

A moment later came an angry snarl, and the door shuddered as the leucrota flung itself against it. The latch held. They were safe in here unless the leucrota suddenly grew opposable thumbs. Or unless it decided to jump through the long window that faced the warehouse's interior.

Tiffany fell to her knees beside Calvin.

"Are you okay?" she said.

"I could be worse. Here"—he handed her his flash-light—"keep this on my hands."

She trained the light on his hands, then gasped when she saw the blood that covered them.

"I'll be fine," he assured her as he began to pluck the splinters from his palm. He noticed Cynthia examining the sole of her right shoe. "What about you?" he called to her. "Did it get you?"

Cynthia didn't answer right away. Had they been able to see her face they would have seen the color drain from her cheeks when she saw her foot.

The entire heel of her tennis shoe's rubber sole was gone, and the heel of the white sock underneath it was torn open. The topmost layer of skin on the rear half of her heel had been sliced away, exposing the rawer, redder skin beneath. The wound wasn't deep enough to bleed, and it didn't even hurt when she touched it. She had gotten lucky. Very, very lucky. Half an inch closer, and most of her heel would be gone and she'd probably be infected with the monster version of rabies or ebola or something.

"I'm okay," she said, her voice gusty with relief.

"So," Tiffany said. "What should we—"

The leucrota snarled somewhere on the other side of the door. Brandon cried, "Fuck!" Violet screamed in pain. Something heavy and metallic clanged to the floor. A moment later there was a loud thump and the sound of something hard and heavy skidding on the concrete. Donovan let out a quick, clipped cry. Then there was a confused jumble of sounds: running footsteps, clopping hooves, growls, thuds. The sounds quickly receded into the depths of the warehouse.

"Oh, no," Cynthia said, staring at the door with wide eyes. She looked at Calvin. "We have to do something."

Calvin had finished picking the splinters out of his palms and was now dabbing blood away with the bottom of his shirt. He looked up at Cynthia.

"I'm open to suggestions," he said.

It was only then that Cynthia realized how bad off they were: Among the three of them their stock of supplies had been reduced to a butcher's knife, a can of air freshener, two flashlights, and Cynthia's bare-bones investigator's kit; Calvin was too injured to be useful in a fight; and Cynthia herself was hobbling about on a damaged shoe.

"Um…"

Distant noises echoed through the warehouse. Clatters. Bangs. Urgent voices too far away to be understood.

Cynthia and Tiffany hurried over to the long window and looked out onto the warehouse floor. Wincing at the shrieks of pain from his hands and thighs, Calvin struggled to his feet and staggered after them like something out of *Night of the Living Dead*.

The interior of the warehouse was pitch-black except for the beams of three flashlights waving madly back and forth as their wielders raced down the aisles. One of the lights was on the far left side of the window and swiftly moving farther and farther away. The other two were speeding in the opposite direction, one flashlight a few feet ahead of the other, almost parallel with Calvin, Cynthia, and Tiffany's position and ten or twelve rows back. At first there were too many merchandise-laden shelves in the way to tell who was holding these latter flashlights. But then the pair of lights crossed one of the wide aisles that separated two rows of shelving units. As the rearmost light swept over the person in front, it revealed quick glimpses of a billowing black trench coat and a long brown ponytail.

"That's Donovan," said Cynthia, the relief in her voice palpable.

"And probably Violet right behind him," said Tiffany. "See how the light's lower down? She's the only one who's that short."

As if in confirmation, they heard Violet shout something, her voice faint and tinny through the glass. They couldn't make out much of what she was saying, but the word "fuck" was clearly audible. A moment later the duo entered an aisle in another row of shelves and mostly disappeared from sight again.

"Where's the fourth flashlight?" Calvin said. "Damn it, where's the fourth?"

"Maybe..." Cynthia swallowed. "Maybe somebody just dropped their flashlight."

"Great. That means someone's running around out there without being able to see where they're going. They'll probably run right into the leucrota. If they haven't already." Calvin felt himself on the verge of panic. This had been his idea, his mission-plan. If somebody got killed or maimed or...

He closed his eyes and took a deep breath, trying to rein in the sense of helplessness that formed the quivering, black core of his panic. He wasn't helpless, damn it. There were always options.

He turned and shone his flashlight on the floor just inside the doorway. As he had thought, one of the longer shards of his baseball bat had gotten dragged in here along with him when Tiffany pulled him to safety. It was long and sharp, similar to the stakes traditionally used to kill vampires.

No, he wasn't helpless at all.

He staggered toward the doorway.

21

When the office door slammed shut and propelled the leucrota backward out of the office, Brandon had been slinking up behind it again, tire-iron raised. Donovan and Violet had been close behind him, with weaponless Lauren nervously trailing last. They all tensed up, thinking the leucrota would notice them now and pounce.

Instead it shook its head, a few drops of blood flying from its nostrils, then snarled with rage and hurled itself against the door.

Seeing his chance, Brandon rushed forward and swung the tire-iron at the back of the monster's head.

But the leucrota must have heard him or, more likely, noticed the light of his flashlight swiftly brightening behind it and casting its shadow upon the office door, and at the last possible instant it leaped aside. Though it avoided a possibly fatal blow to the back of the head, it wasn't fast enough to avoid the blow entirely, and the tire-iron struck it hard on the right shoulder, throwing the leucrota off-balance and making it stumble.

Brandon raised the iron to hit it again, while Donovan, knife in hand, raced forward to join him. But the leucrota regained its balance a lot faster than they expected, and before either of them could strike a blow, it pounced at Brandon.

"Fuck!" Brandon cried. He threw himself out of the way and crashed to the floor, nearly losing his grip on the tire-iron in the process. Donovan slashed at the leucrota as it streaked past, but missed its sleek, striped haunch by a good five inches.

Violet had been right behind Brandon, and when he leaped aside, it put her directly in the leucrota's path. One moment she was looking at the dancing skeleton that Brandon had painted on the back of his black leather jacket, and the next the leucrota's grinning mouth and huge luminous eyes were hurtling toward her at a zillion miles an hour.

Violet turned her body like a door opening and leaned backward limbo-fashion in a desperate effort to get out of the leucrota's way. As it whizzed over her, she swung her hatchet at it, though the awkward angle didn't allow her to put much force behind the swing.

Both girl and monster landed blows, the hatchet slashing a shallow red line down the leucrota's right side, the leucrota's right front hoof slamming into Violet's right breast.

A bolt of pain shot through Violet's chest and right shoulder, and her right arm went half-numb. She staggered backward, screaming and clutching her tit. The hatchet slipped from her suddenly clumsy fingers and clanged to the concrete.

Thrown off by Violet's blow, the leucrota landed badly, its left foreleg buckling under it and sending it into a clumsy, twisting slide. It smashed into one of the big gray bins hard enough to make the bin skid two feet across the floor.

Donovan had chased after it the whole way, and now, before it could rally, he tried to stab it in the throat.

But once again the leucrota proved too quick. As the knife swished toward it, it lashed out and snapped its mouth closed on the stainless steel blade. The knife twisted painfully out of Donovan's grasp and went flipping away into the shadows, the front half of its blade now missing.

Donovan backed away from the leucrota, shaking his now-empty hand, which felt bruised and tingly as if he'd just high-fived The Hulk. The twin plates of the creature's murderous grin opened up and its tongue flicked out like a whip. The end of the blade flew off the tip of its tongue and rebounded off Donovan's coat, making him flinch.

He glanced behind him to call for help, then realized there was none to be had: Lauren, like him, was weaponless; Violet was still reeling from her injury; and Brandon was still picking himself up off the floor.

He looked back at the leucrota, and he could tell that it, too, recognized their sorry state of disarray. Its yellow-green eyes shone with terrible glee. Its evil grin seemed to grow wider.

"Oh, hell," Donovan muttered.

The leucrota charged.

Donovan turned and ran, grabbing Violet's wrist as he passed her and pulling her after him, their course leading them through the mini-maze of gray bins, then down one of the wide aisles that divided the rows of shelving units. Lauren started to run along with them, too, but in her haste her hip clipped the corner of a bin, and she crashed to the floor on her hands and knees. She was on her feet again a second later, but by then it was too late: The leucrota was bearing down on her, its maw open wide for the kill.

But during that same crucial second Brandon had also

regained his feet, and he sprang into the leucrota's path.

"Run!" he yelled at Lauren.

Lauren did, sprinting away after Donovan and Violet.

Brandon swung his tire-iron at the leucrota's head. The leucrota ducked the blow and lunged at his belly. He blocked the lunge with his flashlight. Growling, the leucrota caught the flashlight in its mouth and bit down hard, just as it had with Calvin's bat and Donovan's knife.

This time the trick didn't work so well. Unlike the bat and the knife, the flashlight contained two Energizer D batteries, both of which burst between the leucrota's bony plates, filing its mouth with battery acid. The leucrota howled with pain and outrage.

With the flashlight destroyed, its beam winked out, leaving Brandon literally in the dark. He instinctively took two panicked steps backward, away from the suddenly invisible monster. Then he stopped himself. Now wasn't the time to run; it was the time to strike, while the leucrota was disoriented.

He took a step forward again, then swung his tire-iron at the spot where he thought the leucrota was standing. The weapon swished through empty air.

The leucrota growled in the darkness, now sounding far more angry than pained.

Brandon swung the tire-iron again, aiming for the spot where he thought the sound had come from.

Swish. Strike two.

The leucrota growled again, louder, angrier. A hoof clopped as it began to move.

Fuck it. Brandon wasn't going to stick around for the strikeout.

He turned and ran, heading the same way the others had gone. Forty feet ahead of him Lauren was sprinting down the wide aisle, her body backlit by her flashlight whose beam swept back and forth, illuminating the bare gray floor and the ends of the metal shelving units in clear, bright detail. Farther down and to the right a pair of flashlights were receding down one of the narrow aisles that branched off the main aisle, the lights almost obscured behind rows of shelves and the merchandise they bore. Donovan and Violet. Damn, they ran fast.

Brandon heard the clop of hooves behind him and picked up his pace. Lauren must have heard the same thing, because she started running faster, too. After a few seconds, she veered down an aisle on the left and he nearly lost sight of her behind all the junk on the shelves.

Shit. What was she doing? Without a light of his own, Brandon needed to stick close to her. If he got lost in this darkness he'd be monster chow for sure.

He ran faster. When he reached the aisle Lauren had gone down, he was dismayed to find that she was already sixty feet away and booking like mad. Fleet genes must run in the O'Donohue family.

Brandon charged down the aisle after her, while behind him the clatter of hooves rang out louder and louder.

22

When Brandon hollered "Run," Lauren gladly obeyed and headed off in pursuit of Donovan and Violet, who, she saw with chagrin, looked like they were already halfway across the warehouse. Behind her she heard snarls and grunts, then the clang of something metallic hitting the ground. Glancing back, she saw nothing but darkness. Brandon's flashlight had gone out. Had the leucrota gotten him?

Sure enough, a cacophony of clips and clops rang out behind her, the horrible din growing louder by the moment.

She ran faster, but it was no use; the leucrota kept gaining on her. Much as she wanted to catch up with Donovan and Violet, she didn't dare remain on this straight, open course any longer. She had to start making turns in hopes of either shaking off the leucrota or slowing it down.

She swerved down the next aisle on the left. She was pretty sure that if she went a few rows in this direction and then made another left, she'd wind up near the door they'd entered through. From there, she wasn't entirely sure what she should do. She could try to flee outside and find a phone to call the cops. Or she could head back to the shipping office and reunite with Calvin and Cynthia and Tiffany (assuming they were still there). Or maybe she could find that can of Mace she had dropped and/or Violet's hatchet. Or, hell, maybe she could just find a damn light-switch. Something. Anything.

After a few seconds she heard quick clopping steps following her down the aisle.

"Shit," she hissed and ran faster.

23

As he galloped after his prey, the leucrota hacked and spat in an effort to cleanse his mouth of the bitter, stinging juice that had filled the shining metal club. Whatever this foul substance was, it burned worse than even the disgusting scent-markers the two females had squirted into his face. Not in many years had the leucrota had such difficulty killing its prey, not since men with metal shells and echoing voices had tried to kill him in the old forest where he dwelt. Then again, not in many years had anyone dared to attack him in his lair. Perhaps he had chosen his new lair badly. Perhaps this site was important to these creatures. No matter, though. He would kill them, eat them, shit them. He always did. Even the metal-shelled men. Under their shells there had been meat and blood, so tasty.

He slowed to a trot and looked down the aisle where the strongest male had just run, the one with glass panels in front of his eyes and the flappy black skin that tasted like dead kine. The tall brown-haired girl had run that way too. But the short brown-haired girl with the loud voice had run the opposite way. And that one was hurt. Not grievously, no. But hurt all the same, and for all her noise and vigor, she was the smallest of the intruders, both of which factors made her easier prey. And the long-haired male who had gone with her was thin and clumsy and clearly lacked battle skills. And he was now without a weapon, too. More easy prey.

And that was important, because the leucrota's injuries, though each one minor in itself, were slowing him down. It was wisest, then, to focus on easier prey.

He raced after Violet and Donovan.

24

When she realized she heard nothing following them, Violet stopped running.

"Hey," she shouted to Donovan. "I think it went somewhere else."

"Huh?" He stopped too and looked back at her. "Are you sure?"

"Yeah," She gently massaged her right breast with a wince. She had a feeling her whole tit was gonna be one big bruise tomorrow. At least her arm was feeling mostly normal again. Still a little tingly, but even that was clearing up. "Sure I'm sure. It must have gone after the others."

No sooner had she said this than they heard the clatter of hooves in the direction they had just come from. The sound was worryingly crisp and clear, as if there were no intervening objects between its source and their ears. They shone their flashlights down the aisle.

At first they saw nothing but darkness. Then there was a yellow-green glimmer at the farthest edge of the light. The glimmer grew larger and brighter and resolved itself into two round eyes with small black pupils at their centers.

"Fuck!" said Violet. She turned to run, but Donovan stood in her path, still gawping at the approaching leucrota.

"Move your ass!" she screamed, giving him a hard shove.

They resumed their mad dash toward the north end of the warehouse. As she ran, Violet reached out and swept the red plastic bins and their contents off the shelves and onto the floor behind her, hoping the jumbled debris would delay or even injure their grinning pursuer. Joy buzzers, jumping beans, fake ice-cubes with fake flies in them, battery-operated severed hands with fingers that wiggled when you pressed a button, fright wigs, X-Ray specs, wind-up teeth that started chattering the instant they hit the floor. The falling tricks and gags made a deafening racket as they fell. And then they made a more alarming racket several seconds later as the leucrota's hooves tramped them all to shards and dust.

"Shoulda brought guns!" Violet's voice cried out no more than fifty feet behind Violet.

"Stop ripping off my voice, you stupid fucking mutt!" Violet shouted.

They crossed one of the wide aisles, then plunged into the stacks on the opposite side. Here the shelves in each unit were fewer and spaced farther apart and bore larger items sans bins: ventriloquist's dolls, gray plastic tombstones with "RIP" on them, fake fire hydrants, life-sized cardboard figures of celebrities, garden gnomes with their pants around their ankles and big smiles on their ruddy, bearded faces as they flashed you the big white moon. Violet continued strewing this crap into the aisle behind her, and the leucrota's hooves continued pulverizing it like sledgehammers. The leucrota wasn't slowing down one bit, though it wasn't gaining on them either, which was good enough for now.

The end of the aisle appeared. Fifteen feet beyond it was the north wall of the building, against which stood stacks of wooden pallets.

When Donovan reached the end of the aisle he started to turn left. In the process, one of the pockets of his billowing trench coat snagged a large, angular screw-head on the corner of the shelving unit. The pocket tore free almost instantly, its stitches splitting down one side with a low, thick ripping sound, but the brief, hard tug was enough to throw him off-balance and send him crashing to the floor. He tumbled across the concrete, his torn coat flapping and twisting, his pockets' manifold contents spilling out and tumbling in a crazy cloud along with him. His flashlight slipped from his grasp, caromed off the floor, and went out. Somewhere amid the tumble, his right knee struck the concrete hard enough to make him scream. He finally came to a stop on his back, staring up into the darkness. The world seemed to tilt and swoop as if he were still tumbling. His knee throbbed with pain.

A flashlight beam cleaved the darkness above him, then swooped down and settled on him. Donovan held up one arm to shield his eyes from the glare. Violet's footsteps pounded toward him.

"What happened?" she cried. "What—"

With her flashlight fixed on Donovan instead of on the ground in front of her, Violet failed to notice the debris that had spilled from his pockets and was now strewn everywhere. She stepped right onto the tin of Altoids, which skidded under her weight with a shrill metallic screech, and her sprint turned into a slapstick headlong stumble, her legs flying every which way, her arms pinwheeling for balance. Before she could find that balance, she tripped over Donovan, her right foot clocking his injured knee. Donovan yelped in pain again, while Violet sailed over him, nearly horizontal.

She crashed down on the other side, her head hitting the floor with a sound like a pair of coconuts being knocked together, then tumbled away, limp. Her flashlight fell from her hand and rolled in a broad semicircle, coming to rest pointed right at Donovan and the clutter around him.

"Violet!" he called, sitting up. She didn't answer. In the dim, indirect glow of the flashlight, her body was a still, gray shape.

In a deafening clatter of hooves, the leucrota shot out of the aisle. It halted barely ten feet from Donovan and stared at him and Violet, its bony smile a broad, pale crescent.

"Look at the nice doggie," it said in the same sludgy, resonant voice it had used earlier.

Then it sprang.

25

"Where the hell are you going?" said Cynthia.

Calvin bent down, wincing at the pains in his thighs, and grabbed the long, stake-like splinter from the ruined bat.

"I'm going out there to help them."

"You can hardly walk! You're staggering about like a drunk on a merry-go-round."

"I can't just stand by and watch."

Tiffany brushed past Cynthia and joined Calvin.

"I'm coming with you," she said.

Cynthia rolled her eyes.

"Okay, fine," she said with a flap of her arms. "I'll come, too. If we're all gonna get eaten, we might as well do it together."

"We're a Three Musketeers bar," Tiffany agreed with a firm nod.

"Uh…" Cynthia had no idea what to say to that.

From the warehouse floor came a string of clatters and crashes. It sounded like merchandise falling off the shelves. A moment later a voice yelled something. The words were indistinct, but the tone was clearly Violet's.

"All right," Calvin said. "We'd better get out there."

He took a deep breath and flung open the door, raising the shard of his bat like a vampire hunter about to stab his prey. Judging by the cacophony in the distance, the leucrota wasn't anywhere near the office door, but it didn't hurt to be safe.

He shone his flashlight through the doorway. The beam revealed gray plastic bins, a butcher's knife with the tip broken off, a torn swatch of black leather, and a few small splatters of blood here and there on the concrete. Not great, but at least it didn't look as if anyone was dead or seriously injured. Yet.

Calvin leaned out and quickly shone his flashlight first to the left and then to the right to make sure nothing nasty was lurking on either side of the doorway. Tiffany's flashlight still lay on the floor against the outer wall of the office, its beam shining at nothing. There was no sign of the leucrota.

In the distance the crashes and clatters continued. A voice shouted something, the words obscured by the din. This time it sounded like Brandon.

Satisfied it was safe, Calvin looked back over his shoulder at Tiffany and Cynthia.

"Let's go," he said, and stepped out onto the warehouse floor.

26

As Brandon ran, he strained to listen over the sound of his boots clomping on the concrete floor and the chains on his jacket jingling and the faint thwack of Lauren's sneakers as she ran about thirty feet ahead of him. There was a distant, echoing racket in the direction Donovan and Violet had run, but beyond that, nothing. If the leucrota were following him he ought to be able to hear its hooves clip-clopping behind him. But he didn't.

He glanced over his shoulder, a risky move since it meant taking his eyes off Lauren's flashlight, his only guide in the darkness; without that dim but precious light, he could wind up going off-course in the narrow aisle and dashing his brains out against one of the shelving unit's steel posts.

He didn't see any big luminous eyes behind him. Which didn't mean much, of course; like a lot of animals' eyes, the leucrota's glowed only with reflected light, and Brandon doubted if the indirect light from Lauren's flashlight thirty-plus feet away was strong enough to make them light up at all.

More important than the lack of luminous eyes, though, was the fact that he could see the glows of Donovan and Violet's flashlights rapidly receding toward the far end of the warehouse. That, combined with the ungodly din coming from the same direction and the fact that the leucrota could be chasing only one of the two frantically fleeing duos, made Brandon screech to a halt.

He listened, body tense, suddenly afraid his conclusion

was wrong and that the leucrota had found a way to silence its hooves somehow, maybe with little booties or something, and that poor dumb Brandon was about to get his head ignominiously chomped off by a ridiculously implausible monster. But nothing happened except that the two distant flashlights and the din that accompanied them kept growing more and more distant, while on the opposite side of him Lauren's flashlight and her faint, rapid footfalls likewise kept growing more distant.

"Shit." He turned back around and hollered, "Lauren! Stop! It's not after us! It went the other way!"

27

Lauren had thought she was running for her life. With that swift, steady, somewhat hoof-like clop following her down the aisle, she envisioned the leucrota galloping after her with its Joker grin and its Gollum eyes. And so, when she heard Brandon shouting at her, she assumed it was the leucrota mimicking his voice in a clever attempt to lure her into its clutches, and she just kept on running.

Then she remembered that the leucrota could only mimic things it had already heard, and she couldn't recall Brandon having said anything like "It's not after us," and "It went the other way" during the whole time they'd been in the warehouse.

Then again, how smart was the leucrota supposed to be? Perhaps it had figured out how to string together bits and pieces from different utterances into coherent sentences.

"Lauren!" the Brandon-voice called again. "Where're you going?"

The tone of baffled frustration in that last sentence was something she was sure she hadn't heard in Brandon's voice tonight. The leucrota couldn't invent emotional tones, could it?

And then she realized two things: The voice had been farther behind her this time, and she no longer heard the heavy clop of steps.

Clopping steps! Like hooves! Of course. That meant it *couldn't* be Brandon behind her. This had to be a trick. It...

No, wait. Brandon had been wearing those big, hard-soled Docs, hadn't he? Crap. Maybe it *was* him.

She stopped and listened hard over the sound of her own gulping, wheezing breaths. She half expected to hear the clopping steps start up again, faster than ever, too fast for her to outrun. Instead she heard nothing. At least not nearby. There was a real ruckus coming from the far end of the warehouse.

"Lauren?" said the Brandon-voice again.

Lauren pointed the flashlight toward the voice. She saw nothing except the gewgaw-lined shelves stretching away into darkness. The speaker—whether Brandon or the leucrota—was beyond the reach of the flashlight's beam.

The steps began to advance toward her. Now that she listened closely, it did sound kind of like two feet rather than four, but with all the noise from across the warehouse, and with her fear muddling up her mind, it was hard to be sure. She backed away in synch with the figure's approach, maintaining a steady distance between them.

"How do I know it's you?" she said.

"Uh...because it is?"

Lauren gasped in frustration. "No, I mean, if you're really Brandon, say something you've never said before, something I know the leucrota couldn't be mimicking."

The steps stopped. After a brief pause Brandon's voice said, "The lavender marmalade quivered repugnantly when Ashlee Simpson's pet orangutan defenestrated the sixteen navel-gazing stevedores. How's that?"

"That's good."

The footsteps resumed their approach. This time Lauren walked forward to meet them. Soon Brandon emerged from the darkness. He was out of breath and sweaty from his run.

"I'm such a moron," Lauren said.

"What? Why?"

"I thought you were the leucrota. All I could hear were your boots clopping on the floor, and I thought they were hooves, and..." She shook her head. "And all this time it was going after Donovan and Violet."

"Yeah, well, it's an understandable mistake. I thought it was behind me, too, even though I didn't hear any hoof-clops at all. So if you're a moron, I'm an even bigger one."

"I won't argue with that. But if we don't get over there and help them, we'll both end up being the biggest morons ever."

"I hear ya."

Brandon stepped aside to let Lauren squeeze past; since she had the flashlight, she ought to be in the lead. She went, but she wasn't happy about it. Being in the lead meant she'd come to the leucrota first. And yet...

And yet despite her fear there was a part of her that was marveling at how utterly fucking fantastic this all was. Sure, she might get killed, sure all of them might get killed, but they were doing something momentous, something historic, something no one had ever done before. She had pulled her face out of the history books she'd always loved and found herself actually participating in something that might well one day be in history books itself. Caesar crossing the Rubicon. Columbus sighting America. And Lauren O'Donohue confronting the leucrota.

Lauren grinned. Sure, she was scared so bad her hands were shaking, and she really, really didn't want to be in the lead if and when they came upon the leucrota, but fuck it, if some future historian (like, say, Lauren O'Donohue) was going to write about this, she'd better act with dignity and bravery and grace lest unborn generations think she was an utter wuss.

Still grinning, flashlight showing the way, she started to run toward the distant din, Brandon's boots clip-clopping close behind.

28

Donovan started to roll away from the pouncing leucrota, but then realized it was too late. The leucrota was too close. If he tried to evade it now, all he would do was present it with his side or his back and make himself an easier and far more short-lived target.

Instead he remained on his back and tried to kick it in the belly as it landed atop him, its hooves crashing down on either side of his torso. All he got for his trouble was a glancing hoof-blow to the side of his already twice-injured knee, which made him cry out in pain yet again, his leg dropping back to the floor.

The leucrota lunged for his face, jaws wide. He raised his left forearm just in time, catching the leucrota across the neck and stopping its onrushing muzzle only inches from his face. Snarling, the leucrota pressed downward, trying to get at him, its bony plates gnashing and snapping, its throat muscles shifting and bulging against the side of his forearm. Its face was so close to his he could smell the Mace and the vanilla-hazelnut air freshener on its fur and the rancid stink of rotten meat on its breath, a combination of smells that made him gag.

It kept pressing forward, its hooves scrabbling and clacking on the concrete, and Donovan's forearm began to bend back under the monster's onslaught. He wasn't going to be able to hold it off for long.

"Help!" he shouted. "Help!"

"Help!" the leucrota cried in Donovan's own voice, its stenchy, humid breath washing over him like corpse-gas.

He heard no one coming to help. Where the hell was everybody? What happened to Brandon and Lauren? Shit. It looked like he was on his own. His arm sagged another inch, and the leucrota's razor-sharp teeth drew another inch closer to shearing his nose off.

He thought about trying to punch it or gouge out its eyes. But he had seen how fast this thing moved; if he brought his hand too close to its face the leucrota would probably just chomp it right off. He needed a weapon of some kind, one with some reach.

He looked around in desperation, hoping against hope that Violet's carving knife had landed nearby when she fell. All he saw were things that had spilled from his pockets. His Yoda action figure lay on its side a few inches away, its green, serenely smiling face fixed on his. Donovan grabbed it and chucked it at the leucrota. The figure bonked off the leucrota's muzzle, making the beast flinch with a startled grunt.

Emboldened by this tiny victory, Donovan groped around for another impromptu missile. His fingers fell on the red plastic squirt gun. He pointed it at the monster's leering face and squeezed the trigger. Nothing came out but a puff of air. Empty. Shit. He pegged it at the leucrota. It rebounded off the furry forehead with a hollow *pock*. The leucrota growled, droplets of saliva spattering Donovan's chin.

Donovan groped around some more, panicked, desperate. Every muscle in his forearm was screaming now, and under the leucrota's unrelenting pressure it was drooping like a tree branch under a heavy weight of snow.

Donovan found his address book and chucked it at the leucrota. This time the leucrota whipped its head around, caught the address book between its mouth plates, and in two quick bites reduced it to ribbons.

Snarling, angry, the leucrota renewed its assault, forcing back Donovan's arm farther than ever. Donovan frantically looked around for something else to throw, but he was out of ammo. Sure, there were still plenty of objects lying in view—a plastic packet of Kleenex, his earmuffs, the pen he had loaned Cyn the other day in the park—but all of them were well beyond the reach of his free arm.

No, wait: In his peripheral vision, he caught sight of something on the floor above his head. He groped wildly for it.

A cramp struck his left arm, and his arm folded back a fraction more, bringing the leucrota's gnashing jaws to within an inch of his face. Any second now it would start nipping bits off him.

His hand fell on the item above his head. It was soft

and lumpy and plastic-covered. In his panic, he couldn't imagine what it might be. Whatever it was, it wasn't anything very useful. Nothing that could stab or bludgeon. Still, anything that might buy him an extra second or two of life was a godsend right now.

He snatched up the object and flung it at the leucrota's face. It was his bag of pot. Like the address book, the leucrota caught it in its mouth and scissored its bony plates, shredding the plastic baggie. Marijuana spilled into the leucrota's mouth and rained down onto Donovan's face.

The leucrota didn't seem to like the taste. It drew back, Donovan forgotten, as it huffed and snorted and swirled its tongue around in an effort to sweep the pot from its mouth.

Seizing the opportunity, Donovan slugged the leucrota in the nose. Blood squirted from both nostrils like juice from a popped berry, and in its pain and surprise, the leucrota instinctively swallowed the mouthful of bud with an audible gulp.

Donovan punched it again. More blood splattered from its nose.

"Ha!" he shouted into its face. "Take that, Rin Tin Tin!"

Donovan cocked his fist to hit it again, but the leucrota recovered its wits and lunged at his face again. Donovan barely got his left arm up in time to block it.

Almost immediately pain lanced through his arm, and the arm began to buckle. This was it. He didn't have the strength to fend it off anymore. The leucrota's maw, now reeking of the thick, herby aroma of Mary Jane, drew inexorably closer.

The cone of light from Violet's dropped flashlight

wobbled, then rose four feet and fixed directly on the leucrota's face, lighting up every tawny hair in pinpoint detail and making the monster's pupils contract to dots. Growling, the leucrota broke off its assault and turned toward the newcomer.

Donovan felt a gush of relief, not only that the leucrota's attack had stopped but that someone had come, that he wasn't fighting this damn thing alone anymore.

"Hoo-rah, fuckface!" Violet hollered as she kicked the leucrota in the side of the neck. The leucrota emitted a harsh, choked cry and rolled off Donovan, who quickly scrambled to his feet. His relief increased when he heard the clatter of footsteps swiftly approaching. Flashlight beams speared through the darkness, growing brighter by the second as they converged on the battleground.

Back on its feet again and looking none the worse for Violet's kick, the leucrota glanced at the approaching lights, then glared at Donovan and Violet, who stood shoulder to shoulder in front of it. Its lips curled back from its bony plates, to which a few small wads of pot still clung.

"Look at you," it said in that sludgy, resonant voice. The sound made Donovan's arms break out in goose-bumps. It was the sort of voice death metal singers dreamed of having. "I have not seen the likes of you in all my long, long years upon this earth."

The leucrota crouched, muscles bunched, preparing to spring at Donovan and Violet. The duo tensed up, ready to fight as best they could.

And then the leucrota froze, blinked twice, and made a small, choked noise and a quick, full-body jerk that looked suspiciously like a hiccup.

Lauren and Brandon burst from a nearby aisle. Lauren

trained her flashlight on the leucrota and raised the Jart she had grabbed off a shelf on their way over here. Brandon gripped his tire-iron in both hands like a baseball bat.

A moment later Calvin, Cynthia, and Tiffany appeared, coming up the wide aisle that ran along the building's outer wall. Calvin was moving at a rapid hobble, his legs having improved a bit since the trio set out from the office. They added their flashlights to those already trained on the leucrota, which was now as brightly lit as if it were standing under a spotlight.

It barely seemed to notice. It just stood there, swaying slightly, its eyes unfocused. Every now and then it jerked with another hiccup.

"What happened?" Calvin asked. "Did somebody do something to it?"

"Uh..." Donovan licked his lips. "Kind of."

"What do you—"

"Fuckface!" the leucrota cried in Violet's voice. It craned its head forward until the cords in its neck were taut and straining, and then its sides began to bellows rapidly.

"Oh, shit, I think it's gonna—"

The leucrota vomited a stream of dark-green slush that bore an uncanny resemblance to cooked spinach. The puke splashed across the concrete, wet green gobs spraying everywhere. Everyone took a big step backward to avoid getting it on their shoes and pants.

"What's wrong with it?" Lauren asked.

At the sound of Lauren's voice the leucrota whipped its head around and stared at her, a string of green drool hanging from its lower lip. She shrank back and raised her Jart higher, afraid the leucrota was going to attack. Instead, after blinking stupidly at her a couple of times, it hiccupped again.

"Is it sick?" Cynthia said.

"Did it eat something?" Calvin said.

"Kind of," Donovan said again.

"Burn it down," the leucrota muttered in a man's voice none of them recognized. It staggered a few steps, its hooves clocking softly, then opened its mouth and retched.

"What do you mean 'kind of'?" Calvin asked.

"Well, um, I had a bag of pot that it sort of accidentally wound up eating."

"It ate a bag of marijuana?" Lauren said.

"Seven ounces."

"Oh, man," Violet said. "That was some good shit, too."

"I know," Donovan said sadly.

The leucrota staggered again, this time nearly falling, and then stood there wobbling unsteadily on its hooves for a couple of seconds. Then it raised its head to the unseen rafters high above in the darkness.

"Twelve thousand years!" it intoned in that now-familiar deep, sludgy voice. The words echoed and re-echoed through the warehouse: "Twelve...elve...ousan... years...ears...ears..."

Tiffany stiffened with a faint gasp that only Calvin heard. Calvin stiffened, too, recalling once again what her father had said about twelves being prominent in her psych-ward scribblings.

"Whose voice is that?" she muttered.

The leucrota stood there, still staring at the ceiling like a pointer scenting its prey amid the stars. Its body swayed drunkenly.

Then its head swung around in a broad, drooping arc,

its chin nearly grazing the floor at the arc's nadir, and came to a stop pointed straight at Calvin.

"I think things are about to get very interesting," the leucrota said in the sludgy voice, its tone thoughtful and darkly amused.

And then the leucrota hiccupped one last time and collapsed on its side with a meaty thud.

Everyone stared at the leucrota in silence. Its body, lit clear as day in the combined light of the five flashlights, lay perfectly still.

"Is it dead?" Brandon asked.

"It must be," Calvin said. "It's not breathing. Its chest isn't rising and falling."

"Was it breathing before, though?" Cynthia asked. "Did anyone actually check to see if it breathed?"

"It must have breathed," Calvin said. "In order to talk it must have been drawing air into its lungs and releasing it."

"Okay," said Cynthia, gesturing at the body. "If you're so sure, then by all means, please be the first to go over there and check for a pulse."

Calvin stared at the leucrota for a moment, then shrugged and said, "Okay." He strode forward.

Cynthia made a frustrated "uh" sound.

"I was kind of, you know, kidding," she said. "To make a point."

"I know," he said. "But I'm sure this thing's dead."

He stopped beside the body, his shoes less than a foot from its head, then crouched down, wincing at the pains in his thighs. He waved a hand above the leucrota's face, watching its eyes closely to see if they moved. They didn't. The leucrota's pupils had dilated to the size of silver dollars despite all the light shining on them.

Calvin pressed his fingers to its neck to feel for a pulse, its short fur coarse and bristly against his skin. He felt nothing, but he realized he wasn't sure where a quadruped's carotid artery would be situated.

"Does anybody here know anything about animal anatomy?" Calvin asked.

"Oh, sure," said Brandon. "I took a class on that: Doggie Doctor 101."

"I'll take that as a no."

He continued to feel around under the leucrota's jaw, moving with more assurance with each second the leucrota didn't stir. He didn't feel so much as a single flutter.

"Well?" Cynthia said.

Calvin grabbed the leucrota's right ear between his thumb and index finger and pinched it hard. No response. He looked at its eyes again, at those dilated pupils rimmed with yellow-green. He could dimly make out the reflection of his own face on the black pupils.

"It's dead," he said. "It's gotta be dead."

He started to stand up, but halfway there his aching quadriceps gave out. He wobbled for a second, then toppled backward with a clipped cry, sure that after having survived their brutal battle with the leucrota he was about to dash his brains out on the concrete in a display of grim cosmic irony. Instead, arms caught him under the armpits, and a pair of soft, warm breasts pillowed his back. He looked back over his shoulder. It was Tiffany.

"I've got you," she said quietly as she helped him up.

"Thanks," he said, smiling at her in a dreamy, contemplative way, the rest of the world suddenly far away, unimportant. He realized he was already in love with this girl.

She smiled back, her eyes telling much the same story.

"So, what, a bag of weed killed it?" Lauren said, unwittingly breaking the moment.

Calvin tore his gaze from Tiffany's.

"Um, yeah," he said. "It sure looks that way."

Lauren shook her head. "I'll leave it to someone else to make the 'Just Say No' joke."

"Death by Mary Jane," Brandon said with a chuckle. "That's fucking hilarious."

"It makes sense, though," Calvin said. "Whatever that anomaly in the woods really is, I think it's safe to say the leucrota wasn't native to our reality. So it stands to reason its body wouldn't be adapted to stuff we take for granted. Like how the Martians in *War of the Worlds* had no defense against the common cold."

"I don't think you even have to go that far," Cynthia said. "I mean, some normal terrestrial animals can be poisoned and killed by things humans eat every day. I think I read somewhere that tomatoes can kill cats."

"Yeah," said Lauren, "and chocolate is poison to cats, too." She frowned. "Or, wait, is it dogs that can't eat chocolate?"

"So who's up for helping me move this thing into the back of the van?" Calvin said, looking around at the others.

"I am not fucking touching that thing," Violet said. "No fucking way. I mean, you might say it's dead, but since when are you the expert on alien dogs? You couldn't even find its fucking pulse."

Lauren rolled her eyes. "Don't mind her. She's just a fulgurous perambulator. I'll help you move it."

"Fuck you, you skanky crackwhore!"

Calvin sighed, both relieved and dismayed that things were already returning to what passed for normal.

29

On their way to the final battle with the leucrota, Calvin, Tiffany, and Cynthia had passed a dozen metal dollies lined up against the warehouse's north wall. Now, Cynthia and Brandon went and retrieved one and parked it beside the leucrota's corpse. While they did that, Calvin and Tiffany went in search of something to wrap the leucrota's body in.

Their search took them toward the rear of the warehouse, where the zoo-like stink grew nauseatingly strong. In the southwest corner of the building they found a short corridor that led to a locked and chained side door. A big gray plastic bin lay on its side in the mouth of the corridor, its interior facing the warehouse. The bin was floored with a carpet of tattered rags and pieces of plastic and cardboard, all of them caked with filth and littered with black and tawny hairs. The floor nearby was covered with shit and piss, as well as some human remains that had been even more fully devoured than those in the shipping office. A scrap of a blood-soaked Megadeth T-shirt was visible amid the jumbled bones and wads of rotting flesh. This must be the other graffitist, the one who had been dragged out of the puddle of blood next to the entrance.

One hand cupping his nose and mouth to block out the stink, Calvin swiftly swung his light away from the gruesome find and fixed it on the overturned bin again.

"A doghouse," he said, his voice muffled behind his palm.

"What's that up there?" Tiffany said, peering at something on the wall above the bin.

Calvin raised the flashlight beam, revealing another black graffito. This one read:

If you got this far
You're a star, you're a star
Oh yes you are, a shining star—
A speck of light in the middle of endless darkness

Have a beautiful day!

"That voice," Tiffany muttered. She nodded at the writing. "It was him. I'd bet my life on it."

"It's probably just nonsense," Calvin said, trying to reassure himself as much as her. "It was probably just some nutty street person with a voice all shot to hell from too much cheap booze."

"Then why didn't he end up like *that?*" She nodded at the graffitist's remains.

Calvin didn't have an answer for that. Frankly, right now he didn't even want to think about it. Not here in the dark with the stench of death all around them.

"Come on," he said. "We still need to find something to wrap the leucrota in."

30

The leucrota's shroud wound up being a piece of merchandise called a Magician's Curtain, an eight-foot-tall, twelve-foot-wide piece of black linen adorned with glow-in-the-dark stars and moons and ringed planets. Judging by the photos on its box, it was meant to be a prop for amateur magicians to drape over their disappearing cabinets or ladies about to be sawn in half. Calvin guessed it sold equally well as a decoration for college Goths' dorm rooms.

Calvin draped the curtain over the dolly. Then, after snapping on latex gloves from his and Cynthia's investigator's kits, he, Cyn, Brandon, and Donovan hefted the leucrota's limp, heavy corpse onto the dolly and folded the ends of the curtain over it.

They spent a while wiping down any surfaces they may have gotten fingerprints on and picking up their litter—dropped flashlights, broken weapons, the swatch of Brandon's coat, the contents of Donovan's pockets—then made their way back to the rear entrance, Calvin pushing the dolly, which thumped and rumbled across the concrete floor. He walked stiffly, his thighs still sore, and he kept repositioning his splinter-jabbed palms on the dolly's metal handle to try to relieve their soreness. Cynthia was hobbling along on her damaged shoe. Donovan was limping from his thrice-injured knee. Violet alternated between massaging her bruised tit and rubbing the knot on her head she'd gotten when she tripped over Donovan. Brandon kept ruefully inspecting his damaged jacket.

"I certainly hope all our cases aren't going to take quite this big a toll," Lauren said, glancing about at the battered crew.

"*Our* cases?" Calvin said. "I take it you're fully on board, then?"

"Yeah. I'm in. Although at this rate we'll all be cripples before long."

"Hopefully this was the exception rather than the rule. But even if it's not, I don't plan to quit."

"Same here," Cynthia said.

Everyone else echoed the sentiment.

"Yeah," Lauren said with a sigh. "I guess I'd better start pricing wheelchairs."

It took a little effort to get the dolly through the rear exit, which was barely wide enough to admit it, but after a minute of grunting and straining and repositioning, they got the dolly outside and rolled it over to the van. Brandon unlocked the van's back doors, and the same four who had loaded the leucrota onto the dolly now hefted it into the back of the van.

While the others climbed into the van, Calvin rolled the dolly back inside the building and parked it next to the big bloodstain where the graffitists had been attacked.

He paused there a moment and shone his flashlight into the depths of the warehouse. The beam penetrated the blackness for only about forty feet, then faded out. He thought of the graffito they had found next to the leucrota's nest.

A speck of light in the middle of endless darkness, Calvin thought, then shivered. Being alone in here—alone with two rotting corpses, and a madman's scribbles, and the stink of blood and wild animals—was making him more and more uncomfortable with every passing second. The very atmosphere of the place felt tainted, irrevocably corrupted by what had happened here.

He started to turn to go but stopped at the sight of those looping bloodstains on the wall. He raised the light and "Wildbo" appeared, the unfinished Y dropping away in a long, descending line like a Black Tuesday earnings chart. Next to it was that creepy bit of doggerel carefully scribed with a black magic marker:

This is the house that Jack built
This is the dog that lives in the house that Jack built

"Not anymore," Calvin muttered, then left the building, firmly shutting the door behind him.

31

On the drive back to May they stopped at a payphone, which Calvin used to anonymously inform the police that there were a couple of bodies in the Mad Hatter warehouse.

"What if they still manage to trace stuff back to us?" Brandon asked as he pulled the van back onto Miller Road. He looked over his shoulder at the others, who, with the leucrota occupying the bulk of the floor space, were crowded against the walls in the back of the van. "I mean, there might be surveillance cameras that saw us coming or going, or we might've missed some fingerprints, or something."

"If anyone asks," Calvin said, "we'll tell them we went out there because our history-geek friend Lauren told us the tale of Gideon Squash, and we wanted to check out the key sites involved, especially since there was a rumor that some or all of them are haunted, and we're kind of interested in all that crazy paranormal stuff. And while we were looking around, we noticed the warehouse's door was open, so we foolishly decided to investigate, and the horrifying stuff we stumbled across was traumatizing enough to convince us never to trespass again. The end."

"Not bad," Violet said. "A nice convincing blend of fact and fiction. There's hope for you yet."

"Hey, breaking-and-entering isn't our only sin, you know," Cynthia said. "We stole that curtain thing, too. We're thieves now. We're racking up bad karma right out of the gate."

Calvin pshawed. "Once they see what's in the warehouse, I bet all the merchandise just gets burned. They'll probably strip that place right down to the I-beams."

"So you're just going to stick this thing in the Collection?" Lauren asked, motioning at the shrouded shape of the leucrota.

"Yep," Calvin said.

"But…shouldn't the world know about this? Shouldn't we, like, let some scientists study it?"

"No," he said simply. Seeing from her expression that she wasn't going to be satisfied with that, he elaborated: "It would be pointless. No one would believe it's what we say it is. Most would say it's just some genetic freak. A mutated hyena, or something."

"But we heard it mimicking us! We…" She trailed off, realizing the problem with that. "Oh."

"Yeah. They'll only have our word for that. It won't be mimicking anything else ever again."

"But it'll have unique vocal cords."

"More meaningless mutation. Look, if you hadn't seen it and heard it for yourself—if you only had a secondhand report to go on—would *you* believe it was an honest-to-God monster straight out of a credulous, scientifically slipshod bestiary?"

"Well, when you put it like that…"

"Simply put, no one's going to believe it. Even with proof right in front of them, they'll find ways to explain it away so that it fits with what's already known. Science is largely about averages. It's about aggregates of data and repeatability. This is a singularity. As such, it'll be seen as nothing more than a very peculiar outlier of established data sets."

"But what if more monsters start coming out of that thing in the woods? Shouldn't we let people know what they're up against?"

"If more stuff starts coming through, then yeah. That's why I'm going to preserve the leucrota in a way that'll keep all its organs intact: so if one day people are willing to accept it for what it is, it can be studied."

"What're you gonna do?" Cynthia asked. "Get it stuffed and mounted like some grotesque hunting trophy?"

He shook his head. "Taxidermy won't preserve it well enough. I think it involves cutting out a lot of the animal's insides to make room for the stuffing."

"If not taxidermy, then what?"

"Ever hear of Freez-a-Pet?"

32

A small white cinderblock building off Route 214 in Troy Township just east of Kingwood, Freez-a-Pet was open by appointment only. This was mainly because they didn't get a lot of business, "they" being owner and manager Nathan Gill and sometimes, when they were feeling helpful, his wife Esther and their teenage daughter Janice. But while business was scarce, it was nevertheless quite profitable, freeze-drying being a long and pricey process.

Despite the name, Freez-a-Pet prided themselves on the fact that they would freeze-dry any kind of animal—pets, livestock, game, anything. They'd handled jobs as small as mice and as big as horses. Last year they prepared a pair of baboons for an exhibit at the Kingwood Natural History Museum, a job that netted enough to finish paying off the Gills' mortgage. Still, most of their business consisted of cats and dogs that their owners—older women more often than not, though Nathan wasn't the type to wonder why—refused to relinquish to the cold liquefying darkness, opting instead to pay surprisingly hefty sums to preserve whole and lifelike and stiffly posed in some endearing posture like huge, furry Royal Doulton figurines.

Nathan's only scheduled client today had said he was bringing in something large and unusual but wouldn't specify what it was, which Nathan found very intriguing. His guess was that it might be an illegal animal from some rich fellow's private zoo. Nathan had handled a couple such jobs before, one a tiger, the other a boa constrictor. He didn't give a hoot if the animal was illegal as long as he got paid. Besides, the animals his clients brought him were dead, and as far as he knew it wasn't against the law to own a *dead* tiger.

When the black van pulled into the parking lot at the appointed time, Nathan hurried outside, eager to learn what the mystery animal was.

The van parked with its rear doors next to the entrance, and three people climbed out. Nathan was surprised by how young they were. And how well dressed. Unless they were on the job or at a funeral, most folks these days just slummed it in T-shirts and jeans, but the trio in front of him looked spiffy as hell. The blond fellow was wearing a black suit and tie, for crying out loud. The red-headed girl, who would've been a real cutie if she'd weighed about fifteen pounds more and had a pair of tits on her, and the van's driver, a fellow with glasses and slicked-back black hair, were a little more casually dressed—she in a nice white blouse and tan slacks, he in a gray jacket with patches on the elbows and black corduroy pants—but they still looked good. Too good. It likely meant this wasn't on the up-and-up after all. But as long as they paid, Nathan was willing to overlook all manner of down-and-down.

"Which one of you's Mr. Beckerman?" Nathan asked. He was reasonably sure it was the blond fellow, who had a certain air of leaderliness about him even apart from the suit, but Nathan figured he'd be polite and ask.

"That's me," the blond fellow said.

After a quick exchange of names and pleasantries, Mr. Beckerman led them to the van's back doors. He was limping a bit on both legs, his lips tightening in pain every now and again. Recent injuries, it looked like. Nathan wondered if they were somehow connected with the subject of today's business.

Mr. Beckerman opened the back doors. On the floor inside, a large, still figure lay shrouded by a paint-spattered tarp. Nathan's nose wrinkled at the odor that wafted out of the van. It kind of reminded him of an old dog-bed that hadn't been washed in years, except this odor wasn't from any dog. It wasn't from anything he was familiar with, and he was familiar with the smells of a wide range of animals. The unfamiliarity didn't bother him, though. On the contrary, it excited him. It meant a new species to add to the ever-growing list of those he'd handled. If it was something legal, he could even mention it on the website.

Mr. Beckerman put his hand on the tarp, then looked at Nathan. "Are you ready? I should tell you up front this isn't going to be the sort of thing you're used to."

Nathan chuckled. "Buddy, I've seen it all. I was a vet for ten years before I started doing this. I've seen all kinds of animals in all kinds of conditions. I doubt there's a thing you could show me that I haven't seen a hundred times before. Though I warn you, I can't fix a damaged animal. You need a taxidermist for that. I just freeze 'em."

"No, this isn't damaged at all."

Nathan waved a hand at the tarp. "Well, let's see what you've got."

Mr. Beckerman whisked the tarp away.

"Good lord!" Nathan cried, taking two big steps away from the van and its ghastly cargo. "What on God's green earth is that?"

"It's a mutant donkey," Mr. Beckerman said, "a member of a pack of severely inbred wild donkeys living in the Appalachians. We found it while we were doing some research on rural folk art in that area."

Nathan barely heard him. He couldn't take his eyes off the...mutant donkey, the kid said? That story stank worse than the odor still spilling from the van. This thing didn't look anything like a donkey, mutant or otherwise. For that matter, he doubted if it was a mutant at all. In his experience, mutants were sickly, short-lived things. This creature, despite its hideousness, looked like it had been frighteningly healthy when it died. Its coat was shiny. Its body looked robust and well-fed. Its teeth, or whatever you called those weird bony blades in its mouth, were whole and strong, with no sign of decay or damage. Its moon-like eyes seemed to glow with horrible luminance. Its nose…

Its nose was thick and black, just like…

"This looks more like a dog," Nathan muttered.

"We know it looks a little bit like that," Mr. Beckerman said. "But I can assure you, it's just an unusual by-product of the mutations."

"Mutations," Nathan repeated, not even trying to hide his disbelief.

Mr. Beckerman cocked an eyebrow. "Unless you're suggesting that a dog could have hooves."

"Uh…"

Nathan looked at the animal again. Yes, those were unquestionably cloven hooves and not, say, syndactylous paws that only resembled hooves.

"Well, no, of course I'm not suggesting that," he spluttered. "But…"

But what?

He didn't know.

In the face of his uncertainty his professional instincts came to the fore to guide him.

"Do you know how you want it positioned?" he asked.

"Can you put it in a sort of walking position?"

"Sure." Nathan glanced at the creature again, then licked his lips. "You know, a, uh…an animal this size, it'll cost quite a lot to freeze."

"That's fine. Money's not an issue."

"Ah." Part of Nathan had been hoping the high price would scare them away. Then again, it wasn't often he got a job this lucrative, and Janice would be starting college in the fall.

"It'll take about six months."

They all looked startled at that piece of information.

"That long?" said the redhead.

Nathan nodded, then took another glance at the thing sprawled in the back of the van. He imagined spending the next six months with that leering face.

"Then again," he added, "I might be able to get it done a bit quicker than that."

33

Shortly after midnight a week later, Calvin and Tiffany lay naked together in his bed, relaxing in post-coital bliss. They'd engaged in quite a lot of coition that day. They had been hungry to consummate their relationship all week, but given Calvin's injured legs they felt it best to wait. Now, though, the thunderhead-colored bruises of a week ago had faded to barely visible patches of watery yellow, and the soreness in his thighs was finally gone. Sort of. Actually, his thighs were sore right now, as was virtually every other muscle in his body, but it was a different, pleasanter kind of soreness.

When Tiffany had come over today and Calvin had announced that he felt well enough to finally do it, they lost no time at all, flinging off their clothes and screwing right there on the green leather couch. And then they did it again twenty minutes later on the parlor carpet. And half an hour after that in the library. And twenty minutes later on the spiral staircase, which had been interesting but rather uncomfortable. And so on. All told, they'd had sex fourteen times in seven different rooms in the last ten hours. Now that the dam of Tiffany's virginity had burst, her libido was pouring forth in an unquenchable torrent that was sweeping a surprised but wholly unresistant Calvin right along with it.

Now as they lay there in his rumpled bed, their naked, sweat-slick bodies snuggled tight, he shook his head with a smile.

"I think I've created a monster," he said.

Tiffany raised her head and looked at him, unsure of his meaning; in their line of work, after all, any reference to monsters could be literal. But when she grasped what he meant, she grinned and playfully nipped at his earlobe with a monster-like growl.

"Nope," she said. "I'm not from some workshop of filthy procreation. I'm a natural-born sex-fiend. Gosh, I can remember times when I masturbated ten, fifteen times in one day."

Calvin gawped at her.

She laughed, a little self-consciously.

"Those were just, you know, extreme cases," she said. "Usually it's just once or twice."

"Once or twice a *day?*"

"Yeah."

Calvin shook his head. "And here I thought *I* was oversexed, masturbating once or twice a week."

"Got you beat in the beating off department."

"Women don't 'beat off,' do they?"

"I don't know. Can you suggest a better euphemism?"

"They rub one out?"

She wrinkled her nose. "I'm not a Mafioso."

He pondered a moment, then said, "Oh, I know. I have a better term for it."

"What's that?"

"'That thing you're not gonna be doing anymore cuz

I'll be too busy banging your brains out.'"

"Ooh! I like that one!"

They lay in cozy silence for a time, then Tiffany said, "You could hire somebody to do it, you know."

He stared at her in shock. "What?"

She stared back, confused by his reaction. Then she understood and burst into laughter.

"I don't mean banging my brains out. I mean safe-cracking." She nodded at the painting of Anna May on the wall. "You could hire a locksmith to open it."

"Oh," he said, relieved. "Don't freak me out like that."

"I apologize for the non-sequitur. Although I have to say, your face is an adorable shade of red right now."

"No, I thought about hiring someone to open it, but I decided not to."

"Why?"

"Partly because there might be something in there I don't want anyone else to see, but more importantly be-cause...I don't know, I just feel like it's something I should do myself."

"A point of pride."

"Yeah, I guess. It's a challenge. And I'm certain Mr. May left a clue somewhere, if only to jog his own memory should it prove necessary. He was too careful a person not to."

She rested her cheek on his chest and began to idly play with one of his nipples, rubbing the tip of her index finger over it and watching it wobble back and forth.

"So where do you plan on putting Scooby-Doo once he's been well and duly popsicled?" she asked.

"I was thinking the south room on the third floor. That's where Mr. May put most of the freestanding items, and I figure I might as well continue that tradition."

"What, you're not going to put it in the parlor where visitors can see it? You're not going to give a place of honor to your first big success?"

"Definitely not. I don't want the cable guy or the meter reader seeing it. I want to keep what we do under the radar as much as possible."

"Why?"

"Because I don't want to wind up living in the middle of a media circus, which is what'll happen if what we do ever becomes public. We'll wind up with tabloids doing stories about 'The X-Files of May, Ohio,' and crowds of weirdoes in tinfoil hats camping out in the woods, and stuff like that."

"I respectfully disagree."

"What?" he said, surprised.

"Well, I'm sure it would happen a little bit, but I think it would be a flea circus instead of a three-ringer." She shook her head. "I just don't think you should be hiding your magic lantern under a bushel. I think if more people knew what you did, you'd wind up with an embarrassing wealth of strange phenomena to explore. You wouldn't have to keep digging through police blotters for things to investigate."

"We did okay," he said, a little defensively. "We got the leucrota in the end. And nobody got eaten."

"True," she said. "And at least now we know it's not me."

"What's not you?"

"The thing with the alley. It's clear now that my extreme reaction to what happened in the alley wasn't because I'm peculiarly hypersensitive to strange phenomena. Because if that were the case, I would've reacted equally badly to the leucrota. Which I didn't. Which suggests there was some specific quality to the alley incident that engendered my response."

Calvin nodded. "Whatever happened in the alley that night is something else we'll have to investigate. I still wonder if Mr. May learned of it somehow and it had something to do with why he added you to his will. In fact, just yesterday I started going through his file cabinets more thoroughly in search of anything that might explain the bequests he made. I haven't found anything yet, but there're still a lot more drawers to go through."

"Or maybe the answer's hidden in *there.*" She pointed at the painting of Anna May.

"Yeah. I'd better see what I can do about getting that thing open."

"Worry about it later." She snuggled closer and tongued his nipple. "You have something more important to open right now."

"Again?"

She raised an eyebrow. "You're not up for it?" Her hand glided down to his cock and started stroking it. It responded immediately, swelling and rising to fill her palm. "Feels to me like you're up for it."

He sighed. But it was a mock sigh. His body was already revving up for more sex.

"Okay," he said. "Once more and that's it, though."

Grinning, she straddled his waist and slid herself over him like a sheath.

He gasped, then added, "At least that's it for the next hour."

And so they made love once more, more slowly this time, making it last, savoring each other's bodies, the touch of their skin, the way they moved, the noises they made when they came. And when they were done, they just lay there in contented silence, two happy, healthy young lovers, the world magical and at peace and theirs for the asking.

www.ingramcontent.com/pod-product-compliance
Lightning Source LLC
Chambersburg PA
CBHW051949240626
47153CB00005B/1687